ROCKET'S RED GLARE

CY STEIN

Cover image designed by Cathy Helms, www.avalongraphics.org
Interior design and layout by Tamian Wood, www.BeyondDesignInternational.com

Paperback ISBN: 978-1-7341159-0-1
E-book ISBN: 978-1-7341159-1-8

For my children and grandchildren

CHAPTER 1

The late autumn can be cold and snowy in the West Bronx. On this cloudy, chilly mid-December day in 1940, the second year of the latest European war, the temperature was well below freezing at dawn and refused to budge during the morning hours. The forecast on the radio called for a continuance of the current cold snap for another week. For today, December 15, the weatherman proclaimed a fifty percent chance of snow, accumulating to several inches by the late afternoon rush hour.

As usual, the prediction was incorrect. A brisk snowfall had obliterated most visibility by the early afternoon. The wind, which blew in force down the avenues of the West Bronx and upper Manhattan, whipped up the small, dry flakes into tiny tornados, forcing anyone plying the streets to cover up their faces against the knifing chill. After several inches of light powder had accumulated, the administration cancelled all classes at City College's campus on Convent Avenue in upper Manhattan.

It was a short day for twenty-two-year-old Sid Peskin, one of City College's graduate students. Sid had arrived at his home at 20 Morris Avenue in the Bronx several hours previous, well before the mercury began its abrupt descent to a sub-arctic level. He was glad to be indoors and warm this evening and hoped his parents and ten-year-old brother, Benny, arrived soon. Better that no one should be exposed to the elements, which seemed to be worsening by the minute.

Sid's apartment building, grandly named the Wellington by the builder, had been constructed in 1917. A spacious lobby sported wall sconces and boasted the very latest in electric lights along with a tiled floor. Also present were long, lazy couches for visitors who could only be admitted to the building via a modern intercom system. For maximum efficiency, a dumbwaiter had been installed in the kitchen of every apartment for the rapid elimination of refuse. As advertised on radio and in the newspapers, all the best things were on offer there, and for a most reasonable monthly price, too!

Sitting at his desk in his bedroom on this cold, snowy afternoon, Sid was pouring over a set of physics problems his instructor had handed the class as homework, just before City College shut down for the day.

That stuff was complicated. What a bizarre way of describing reality, he thought, referring to a thorny question posed in an esoteric new branch of physics known as quantum mechanics. But who cared? No matter which way he looked at it, the stuff made no sense at all!

After three hours of work, Sid's brain was overheated from attempting to comprehend the mysteries of the physical universe as expressed in complex mathematical equations. Rather than continue, he shut his textbook, gathered his scribblings in a neat pile, and lay down his number two Ticonderoga-brand pencil.

He had to take a break, he thought, before his noggin spontaneously combusted. Maybe there was something interesting to listen to on the radio. WQXR, 1560 on the AM dial, his old reliable. They played good music. He hoped they'd be featuring something besides Christmas carols, though it was that time of the year again.

Sid stood and reached for the on-off knob on his boxy Zenith radio, vintage 1935, which had long occupied a shelf over his desk. The dial was already set at 1560 AM. But emerging from the speaker when Sid turned up the volume wasn't nice music, or a lilting Christmas carol. Rather, it was the voice of Charles A. Lindbergh, president-elect of the United States. He was presiding over a post-election rally of several hundred of his rabid supporters in the town of Alabaster, Alabama. It was broadcast to the American people through a nationwide radio hook-up and carried by WQXR.

"America is for Americans only!" Lindbergh proclaimed to the cheers of the good people of Alabaster. They devoured every word uttered by their hero. "I ask you, my friends," he continued, "has even one thing... one thing... improved for any of you since this Great Depression began all those years ago? I say to you that the Democrats have had their chance since 1932, and the only thing they've done with it is to betray the people! That's right—betrayal! Tell me, did Roosevelt's New Deal put even one more chicken in anyone's pot? Just one more chicken? Well, did it?"

How could this guy be the president-elect of the U.S. of A and still be talking as if he were still on a goddamn campaign? If only Franklin Roosevelt had lived. Sid sighed. But to Sid and his family and friends' regret, Franklin Roosevelt hadn't lived. His coronary arteries were occluded by the plaque produced from thirty years of smoking compounded by twenty years of inactivity because polio had put him in a wheelchair. FDR succumbed to a heart attack in the middle of only his second term.

While most of the nation mourned, a group of Republican Midwesterners—led by famous aviator Charles A. Lindbergh—saw Roosevelt's demise as their main chance. Wielding the message *America First!* like a weapon, the Lone Eagle and his friends traveled the nation preaching isolationism, nativism, and economic protectionism.

Sid could hear the Alabama crowd roaring, "No, no, no!" to Lindbergh's trashing of the Roosevelt administration, and imagined a broad smile plastered across his fair-skinned face as his short, blond hair blew about in the warm Dixie breeze.

"That's right," Lindbergh continued. "The Democrats have done nothing! Not a thing! Old man Depression is still knocking at our doors! He's crushing the farmer and burying the small businessman and everyone else who dares to have the grit and the gumption to try to make an honest living in this country by the sweat of their own brow and from the soil beneath the soles of their shoes. The Democrats and the late Mr. Roosevelt never did a thing for anyone, except to expand the government with their alphabet soup of federal programs and their endless lists of regulations to steal our freedoms and stifle our economic recovery!"

The airwaves filled with cheers of "Lindbergh! Lindbergh!"

"And my friends, my friends," he continued, trying to make himself heard above the noisy adulation. "My friends, you know that crippled Franklin"—he said the decedent's name with mild disgust—"I say, you all know that you were of little interest to our former president and his party, no matter what they claimed. I say to you that their words were empty. Empty! Why, he was a patrician, an elitist, the owner of a huge estate passed down to him generation after generation, one who believed that only the rich should rule. Now I know it is unkind to speak ill of the dead, but I am obliged to inform you that the man never worked an honest day in his life. Not one honest day! And what's more—"

A chorus of loud booing interrupted him. Sid felt sick to his stomach at the abuse heaped on a man he thought heroic.

He had to stop listening to that stuff. He'd heard Lindbergh's shtick many times before he became president and it had only gotten worse since. He couldn't believe anyone took this guy seriously. But he and many others were unable to look away, much as people can't bear to tear their eyes from a train wreck.

"Oh yes, oh yes, my friends, you can believe me," cried Lindbergh, carried away on a wave of his own rhetoric. "What's more is that Roosevelt came from the East Coast, no less! And even worse, from the State of New York, the home of all that is distasteful, abhorrent and offensive to our good Christian values! He came from the home of all that is crude, cruel, primitive, and un-American. And I'm not just referring to those greedy tycoons of Wall Street..."

The booing and hissing continued, relentless. Standing tall at the lectern, Lindbergh took a sip from his glass of water as he eyed the crowd.

"...Because even Wall Street, as despicable as its behavior has been, has its uses at times. I'm talking about that sink of un-Christian vice and political corruption in the city at the mouth of the Hudson River. Think Tammany Hall, folks. Think Tammany Hall, the Democratic political machine whose stench reaches all the way to the farthest corner of this land!

"I'm also talking about the Communists who make New York City their home and base, traitors who infiltrate and control the labor unions, using organized labor to spew forth their godless propaganda. And I'm also talking about all the immigrants to this country who aren't Americans and refuse to ever be Americans but who exert complete control over our banking, publishing, and movie industries! And mark my words, something needs to be done about this, my friends.

"Yes, something needs to be done! And I promise the hard working folks of this nation, something will be done! Look to Germany, folks. Look to Germany! Their Depression was equal to ours—yet behold their progress! Today, Germany is an orderly, economically stable country where everyone has a job, and everyone knows his place. And I guarantee that what has been accomplished in Germany can and will be accomplished in America! The way to do it is by always keeping America First!"

Lindbergh's followers understood precisely to whom the Lone Eagle referred. Sid Peskin could imagine the glow of rapture in their faces as the America First! crowd whistled, cheered, stomped its feet, and carried their hero off the platform. Here, at last, was a man who spoke honestly and plainly in the simple language of the people, not in the language of the professional politician. This was the man who identified the source of their problems, and who could provide them with solutions.

And Sid understood it all, too; those remarks were personal—the Lone Eagle, with every statement, and with every accusation, was referring to him.

Special to The New York Times—December 17, 1940
[Front page, above the crease]

LUFTWAFFE CHIEF GÖRING CALLS HALT TO BOMBING OF BRITISH CITIES

By Anders Rode Hansen

Hermann Göring, the Air Marshal of the German Reich, called a halt today to further air attacks on Britain's devastated cities. Göring, believed to be second in command to Adolf Hitler in the Nazi hierarchy, declared through a spokesman that "...England's [sic] Hurricanes and Spitfires were eliminated as a significant defensive force months ago, and our German invasion of the former United Kingdom, led by the brilliant strategic planning of the *Führer*, has proceeded far better than planned. We anticipate the termination of all meaningful resistance to our forces within a maximum of two weeks."

The German Reich and the United Kingdom have been at war since 1939, but there had been little shooting until 1940. Then, in rapid succession, the nations of Western Europe succumbed to the ferocious Nazi blitzkrieg. Winston Churchill, the British prime minister who has since fled to Canada with the Royal Family, had approached President Garner, Roosevelt's vice-presidential successor, for material aid during the conflict. However, his efforts were stymied in Congress by isolationists led by Lindbergh. Garner was unable to provide the ships, grain, or arms the British desperately needed. Instead, they were offered Ambassador Joseph P. Kennedy's advice that all was lost and there was little to do but surrender—a viewpoint earning him the permanent ill will of the British government and people, and his subsequent deportation to the U.S.

The British thought the English Channel an impenetrable barrier to invasion, but with the Royal Air Force all but eliminated, the Royal Navy was incapable of halting the Germans, despite the superhuman bravery of its crews. With little in the way of arms after Dunkirk, the British were slaughtered on the beaches and slaughtered in the fields. The Home Army fell back on London to make a last stand while the city suffered continuous Luftwaffe bombardment, and death and destruction daily. The Churchill government was replaced by a caretaker group of appeaser aristocrats centered around the former monarch's brother Edward VIII. The new King had long enjoyed a close, collegial relationship with the German *Führer*.

German armored columns have been seen as far north as Inverness, in Scotland. The remnants of the British fleet are reported to be sailing for North America to join the free British government. But in the south, the Union of British Fascists, previously suppressed by the Churchill government, has been authorized as the only political party in England—as the new province of the German Reich is to be known.

CHAPTER 2

The *Führer* of the Greater German Reich sat in his outsized chair at the black granite desk in his enormous office in Berlin's Reich Chancellery.

He swept back a lock of black hair from his forehead in a theatrical gesture automatic for him.

The despoiler of France and conqueror of England mulled over his many accomplishments. Who could have imagined that the nearly friendless boy from provincial Austria, the failed artist from the Viennese flop-houses, the runner between the trenches in the Great War at daily risk of death, could ever have risen to such heights. Indeed, to have become the greatest German of all time.

His thoughts focused on his father, Alois, a customs official in the old Austrian Hapsburg Empire.

That old bastard never thought he counted for much. He was little more than a troublemaker with a habit of making his thoughts known. *Ach, nein!* His father wouldn't tolerate that! At work, *mein Vater* took orders and resented it, but at home, he dished them out, expecting absolute, immediate obedience, and never tolerating questioning. *Mutti* Klara was a traditional *Hausfrau*, always most happy to oblige him. But his son, Adolf, never. And so began the beatings. *But, did he surrender his will? Never!* Hitler grinned.

Ha! And those politicians who consigned his movement and him, too, to the political ashcan—what did they understand? Nothing. Not how to pull on the heartstrings of the masses. Not how to control the will of a hundred thousand people as if it were a single individual. No, only he, the one who understood the people's fears and resentments—only he could succeed in seducing the masses in the very way they begged to be seduced.

The door swung open, followed by the sharp click of heels and the sight of a tall, uniformed figure, saluting. *"Mein Führer,"* an adjutant said, right arm raised, palm down. "Your distinguished guests, *Herr* Speer and *Reichsmarschall* Göring await the pleasure of your company outside."

"Thank you," said Hitler, motioning for the adjutant to usher the visitor into the holy of holies of the empire of the master race. He rose and pulled down on his brown jacket, which proudly displayed the Iron Cross First Class pinned on his chest. He'd earned the decoration in battle in northern France decades ago and wore no others.

No man should ever be able to proclaim he saw a rumpled *Führer*. He smiled to himself while again sweeping back that lock of hair.

Off in the distance of the cavernous office, the adjutant opened two vast bronze doors. Two of Hitler's paladins, the masters of the European continent, strode forward. One of the mighty ones was Hitler's personal architect Albert Speer, thirty-four years of age. Unlike many in the Nazi movement, Speer's origins were middle class. Not known to have engaged in as much as a street fight, Speer didn't dislike the Jews any more than he disliked a rainy day or a cold dinner served up by his wife. Albert Speer was far too civilized to stoop to Jew-hatred; that was for the Nazi primitives only, not for Albert Speer, *Architekt*. But like the entire German nation, Speer fell under Hitler's spell and soon conformed to his *Führer's* wishes.

He soon convinced himself that no document he ever signed, and no act he ever performed, was done so out of hate. Speer's professional life was lived for love—love for the *Führer*, love for what was right, proper and just, love for the German nation—and love for his own professional advancement.

The other man wore a military uniform of the purest white, replete with decorations that couldn't disguise his corpulent waistline. Unlike Albert Speer, Hermann Göring was a hater not only of Jews, but of anyone daring to get in his way. When Hitler launched his infamous Beer Hall Putsch against the state of Bavaria, Göring was there at his *Führer's* side. Wounded, he was given morphine for the pain and became an intractable addict. He also became the eventual head of the Luftwaffe, the dreaded German Air Force.

Reaching Hitler's desk at the same time, the two clicked their heels together, greeting their *Führer* with the ritual Nazi salute and a *Heil Hitler*. Hitler returned the salute with the same precision.

"Hermann," said Hitler, turning to the Reichsmarschall, "your boys did a spectacular job over England back in September and October. The British scum were wiped from the skies! Their Spitfires and Hurricanes were annihilated by your Messerschmitt fighters! Never had a chance! Not for a moment."

Hermann Göring bowed stiffly. "All my boys are fine lads. Good flyers, good Nazis, the best of the best! And an honorable mention goes to the American president, Lindbergh, for refusing aid to Britain and not getting the United States involved. He was wise not to do so—it was never America's fight. But only you could have seen the possibilities, *mein Führer*!"

"*Ja*, but I must tell you honestly, Hermann—my global strategy has been greatly simplified because Lindbergh is an amateur! He knows nothing whatsoever of politics or history. Nothing! I suppose he's competent to fly a plane in one direction, but to do little else. And his country is a mongrel nation filled with negroes *und Juden und* other unsavory elements. But to give the man his due, Lindbergh has demonstrated an understanding of the fundamental value of race in the world. Still, the current regime in Washington is both politically naïve and grossly incompetent. But we will be happy to use their incompetence to suit our purposes, won't we! The United States, *Herr* Göring, is like a weak woman waiting to be ravished by the most virile man in the room—us. Please sit, gentlemen. We have much to talk about today."

The two sat in leather armchairs in front of the desk. The recent string of German victories had happened so rapidly, with so few casualties against such powerful enemies, it caught everyone's breath. All Germans now believed Adolf Hitler was the messiah sent from heaven. He had led Germany from depression and destitution to dominance and would lead the nation to glory everlasting.

"Today, I want to discuss my further plans, my vision for our glorious empire. As we've told the great German people for decades: *Heute Deutschland, morgen die Welt!* Today Germany, tomorrow the world!" A fleck of frothy spittle clung to the corner of Hitler's mouth as he spoke.

The two men applauded. "Bravo, *mein Führer*," cried Speer.

"Yes, bravo indeed." Hitler grinned. "But there is still much to do so our enemies can never again hope to starve our people, like they did in 1916, and in '17, and again in '18. So they can never again humiliate the German nation and grind us into the dust with their filthy boots!" He paused. "The defeat of Great Britain is a good first step. The British Royal Navy has retreated to North America. They will be incapable of blockading our ports and choking off the import of foodstuffs to feed our people. *Und* so, we Germans will not starve during this war, like we did in the past one. The specter of starvation will be reserved for our enemies!"

Speer and Göring nodded. The man is the greatest military genius of all time, the nodding heads indicated. Speer dismissively recalled the admonitions of his father when told his son had joined the Nazi Party.

"Albert," cried the elder Speer, "why ever do you want to join up with that pack of ravenous, ill-bred wolves?"

"Because they promise to make Germany great again, *mein Vater*! And I believe they will."

"*Ja*, easy promises to make, Albert. We all want to make Germany great again, but what is the Nazi plan to do it? Through suppressing the press, banning the opposition, and beating up Jews, social democrats, and Communists in the streets? By subverting the duly elected and lawfully constituted government of Germany? By forcing idiotic racial theories down everyone's throat that you, Albert, know are lies? *Nein*, Albert! *Nein*! Your mother and I did not raise you to be a Nazi! And we have no doubt, my son, that if you join with this gang of thugs, it will be the worst mistake you'll ever make!"

Of course, Albert the younger did not listen to his father's words; in 1931, he became party member 474,481. And now he was sitting in the office of the Chancellor of the Third Reich, advising the *Führer* on matters that would shake the world!

Speer's thoughts focused on Hitler, as the *Führer* continued his ramble.

"Our greatest enemy in the east, the Soviet Union, won't recover from Stalin's self-inflicted wounds for years! *Nein*, decades! Imagine, gentlemen—imagine decimating your high command as Stalin did and expecting military performance! The General Secretary of the Communist Party of the Soviet Union is a madman! Totally insane!

"In the short term," continued Hitler, "the Soviet Union, rotten as it is, poses no problem for us. Their deliveries of oil, grain, and minerals—as per the terms of the Molotov-Ribbentrop Pact of 1939—have all been prompt and trouble-free. But this favorable situation will not last indefinitely, not with Stalin living in the Kremlin. Sooner or later, we'll need to put a stop to that wolf, too. *Und Deutschland* needs Lebensraum, living space, *meine Herren*. And, as we all know, the east is the cheapest place to get it.

"But the problem before us now is not the Russians. It is the United States of America."

Hermann Göring interrupted him. "But we have substantial support in America now. Great industrialists like Henry Ford, radio personalities like Gerald L. K. Smith, and even President Lindbergh are anti-Semites. They respect the vitality of National Socialism. The German-American Bund is faithful to you to the death, *mein Führer*. There are marches in our favor almost daily and—"

The *Führer* raised his hand. "Thank you, Hermann." He detested being interrupted. "Enough. I am well aware we have friends, many good friends, in North America. But the American media is controlled by a gang of stinking *Juden* and the racially ignorant fools who aid them! Just like things used to be here in Deutschland before I put a stop to it! *Jawohl*, and the irony is the Americans detest their own Jews. You know, they take polls about those sorts of things in that crazy country! But with Churchill in Canada giving daily radio addresses, and the *Juden* in control of the media and the banks, how long do you think it will be before the Americans take up arms against us again?

"*Und* what if they should ally with Stalin, who also attacks us? We'll have repeated the most terrible error of the previous German General Staff—fighting a two-front war!" Hitler pointed to his minions. "So, gentlemen. Are you interested in re-fighting the First War again?"

The Nazi paladins shook their heads, replying *nein!* in unison, Of course they weren't. No one was.

"Gut," Hitler said, leaning back in his chair. "I didn't think so."

"Then what is your plan, *mein Führer*?" asked Speer, leaning forward in his chair, his eyes shining. "Lead, and we follow!"

"*Ach,* Albert. It's simple. The American *Juden* have influence in their society. They must be silenced. But we are not in a position to do so at this time. The Americans must silence their *verdammte Juden* by themselves. They have the ability. What they need, *meine Herren,* is the will. At the moment, they do not have it! But what they lack, we will provide for them."

For as long as Sid Peskin could remember, he had a talent. That talent was a gift with numbers. Among his other feats, Sid could multiply multi-digit figures in his head with ease, always coming up with the correct answer.

"It's just a mental math trick I can do," he told amazed friends. But he could never see how his gift could help earn him a living. In the 1930s, when Sid was growing up, the most important thought on every adult's mind—the first on arising and the last before falling asleep—was employment. How was the man of the house going to support his family, feed them, clothe them, and pay the rent? He struggled with this problem every day but was no closer to a solution than he had been when he turned eighteen.

Sid loved his childhood neighborhood. It was a great place to grow up, if you ignored the congestion, the noise, and the dirt, and made enough money to live in it. Dozens of kids his age resided in the immediate area. Most were friendly. There was no better way to spend a Saturday than playing a pick-up game of stickball with his buddies Kurt, Bob, and Pete. Sid was never the best athlete in the West Bronx, but he was determined to make the most of the skills he had. So, over the years and with much practice, he became known as a fine hitter throughout the neighborhood.

Because all income had to be saved in case of a rainy day, Sid's horizons were limited to the Bronx. Except for outings to a distant cousin's place in Bloomfield, New Jersey, and yearly visits to the graves of his grandparents in uncongested Westchester County just to the north of the city, Sid had never left New York City. But his extensive love of reading—since he could get ahold of all the books he wanted from the West Bronx Branch of the NYC Public Library—allowed him to travel the entire world in his imagination.

From the ninth grade on, Sid saw less of his friends because he started at the prestigious Townshend Harris High School, a feeder school for City College. Finishing at Townshend Harris was a ticket to a tuition-free New York City public college. It was a schlep every day down to 137th Street and Amsterdam Avenue in Manhattan. But like with everything else in life, Sid got used to it and never had a better time in his life than when he was in high school.

The work could be difficult, but Sid always found time to hang out with his friends, playing stickball and arguing about which of the three professional New York baseball teams was the best. Sid was always partial to the Brooklyn Dodgers, not the mighty New York Yankees. And so, he found himself on the losing side of every argument. But no matter how many games they lost, Sid never lost faith in his Dodgers.

In school, math, of course, was always his best subject—he taught himself algebra and geometry, and he'd aced every test. Trigonometry was a breeze. Sid also did a lively business tutoring boys who struggled to grasp tangents and cosines.

But as time passed, Sid began to acquire a reputation as a smartass among the other kids, though he tried hard not to demonstrate the conceit he found so off-putting in some of the other smart boys he knew.

Part of Sid's resolve came from his intuition. He had an innate sense of what he didn't know. Another was that neither of his parents praised him to excess the way others did their children. The result was a confident young man who didn't require approbation from other people to support a fragile ego.

It was a good way to start out in life, which began for Sid in his last year at Townshend Harris. That was when Sid made two momentous discoveries: physics and women.

It wasn't as if Sid had been unaware of either before the age of seventeen. Both had long interested him, but their impact on him was relatively minimal. What stoked his interest in physics was a course he took during his senior year at Townshend Harris. In matters of the heart, it had been the brown-haired, brown-eyed Karen Klein, a Manhattan girl.

Karen Klein couldn't be described as alluring in a conventional way; her sallow and lightly-freckled face was often described as mousy. She dressed in a skirt hemmed well below the knee, teamed with a crisp white blouse that advertised her rather full development up top. But she refused to wear make-up, even the almost mandatory lipstick. Regardless, when Sid spotted her, in his eyes all those supposed deficits were assets—the young lady was very desirable.

Karen was an unconventional gal. Known as a "red diaper baby" because her parents were card-carrying Communists, Karen was brash, amusing, and formidably intelligent. She read just about everything—philosophy, history, and especially politics, all those subjects that either bored Sid or he tried to ignore. Sid's reputation intrigued Karen. She always had a soft spot for guys the crowd thought were eggheads.

The two hit it off immediately. They were both a little different, a little outside the mainstream. Karen had far more experience than Sid—lucky for him—in the art of love, the result of her red parents' disdain for "bourgeois morality." She'd also started early. He wasn't her first boyfriend, and she was very willing to instruct, teaching him necking and providing a brief introduction to the delights of petting. That was where she drew the line.

But alas, Karen was never a one-man girl. Within a few months, her curiosity and desire satisfied, she flitted away from Sid with a college man, an ardent fellow traveler who claimed he was soon off to Spain to fight for the Republican cause against the fascists in the Spanish Civil War. As Sid discovered later, Karen's new beau never did make it to Spain. Instead, he took a job with General Motors in Detroit.

By that time, Sid graduated from Townshend Harris and was on his way in the fall to City College to major in physics. He struggled to choose between physics and engineering. It was easier to find a job with a degree in the latter. But with encouragement from his father, Sid decided to follow his instincts, signing up for the City College physics program.

That's where he met Professor I. Bernard Strauss.

Sid had wonderful teachers in high school, but none so impressive or who could illuminate a complex subject with the same elegance and flair as Professor Strauss.

In 1935, when Sid matriculated at City College, Strauss was sixty years old. Born and raised in Capetown, South Africa, he had taken his degree in physics at McGill University in Montreal. There, he'd been a student of the well-known physicist Ernest Rutherford, a Nobel Prize winner who would later be known as the Father of Atomic Physics.

While working for his Ph.D. at McGill, Strauss played an important role in the discovery of the phenomenon of radioactive half-life. Moving on to America, he then took a job at City College where he rose over the years from assistant, to associate, to full professor. Of average height, thin and with pale skin, white hair, and a white Van Dyke he kept neatly trimmed, Strauss never lost his South African accent or his oratorical skills. The man was brilliant, and Sid was hooked.

During the next four undergraduate years, Sid took three courses taught by Strauss, culminating in his favorite, atomic physics, in his senior year. Only ten other young men also took that class, so Strauss came to know each of them well. Sid distinguished himself in this difficult and arcane subject, one that depended on a high order of mathematical skill.

Strauss didn't stint in his praise of Sid, proclaiming he simply must get a Ph.D. degree, and might even rise to the level of a physics professor someday. But Sid knew that was impossible. A Ph.D. would require four additional years of work, which would keep him out of the labor market for far too long. After a difficult conversation with his father, they reached a compromise: two years, enough time to attain a master's degree.

So, after he received the baccalaureate, Sid applied for and was accepted into the master's degree program at City College, beginning two additional years' study under Professor Strauss. Sid's friends were incredulous

"What, two more years with that old bastard? He's one tough sonuvabitch." "I hope you know what you're getting into." "Better you than me, Sid boy," were frequent comments. But an unshakeable bond had developed between student and teacher. It was based on a shared love of physics and math, a deep appreciation of the beauty and elegance of their description of nature, and an unquenchable desire for knowledge and scientific truth. The time Sid spent with Strauss was grueling, but were also some of the most intellectually stimulating times of his life.

CHAPTER 3

Unlike most New Yorkers, who disliked the chill of winter, Sid enjoyed the cold, crisp air of a late December day. The cloudless sky was a brilliant blue, and a soft onshore breeze dispersed the layer of fine black particulates and brown nitrogen oxides that often blanketed the great city.

Far better frost on the breath than the enervating humidity of midsummer—when the asphalt on the streets of the Bronx shimmered in the heat, and inhabitants of the stultifying tenements moved their mattresses out onto the fire escapes. There they bedded down, hoping to catch a few hours of sweaty sleep, waiting for the wisp of a cooling sea breeze driven up Manhattan Island from the ocean beyond.

Sid dressed in a comfortable black overcoat. He tightened his green scarf—knitted specially for him by his mother, Rosalie—around his neck, looked up and down Morris Avenue, and prepared to step off the sidewalk and into the street. Day-old newspapers and other detritus of the Bronx met his feet as a gust of wind blew between the five-story apartment buildings lining this residential street.

At this hour of the early morning, as the dull arc of the sun emerged from behind the grit-spewing chimneys of the West Bronx, only a rare auto progressed north up Morris Avenue from where it joined the greatest thoroughfare of the borough of the Bronx, the Grand Concourse.

From the north, coming down Morris Avenue towards the Concourse, the traffic was also scant. It consisted of a lone man wheeling a trash bucket and wielding a long stick with a sharp metal point at the end. He used it to spear old newspapers and whatever else the gutter had to offer.

As the street cleaner passed, Sid spotted a bright red automobile stopped in the distance on a cross street. When the streetlight changed, the vehicle turned right onto Morris Avenue and picked up speed in his direction, prompting him to step back onto the sidewalk. As it approached, he recognized its make and year.

It was a DeSoto. He could recognize that box on wheels from a mile away. It must have been an older model. No one made a car with a running board these days. And look at that front grillwork. It must be four feet tall! It had to be a model 1933.

The vehicle pulled up to where Sid stood. The driver leaned over and rolled down the right front seat window. "Well now," the driver exclaimed, poking up his head. "Where d'ya think yer goin'?"

Sid brightened. The man in the driver's seat had moved from their West Bronx neighborhood to Brooklyn five years ago, and they'd almost lost touch. It had been a rough and unfair parting as the two boys had grown up and attended school together. The goodbye was made no easier by Rosalie's references to Canarsie—Sid's friend's new home in Brooklyn—as the most remote place on the planet.

The truth was Canarsie in Brooklyn was no more than a long subway ride away from Morris Avenue in the Bronx—one train into Manhattan, then changing at 14th Street for the LL train to Canarsie. But Rosalie was either too busy or too tired to ever make the trip out. And as the boys became older, her presence was neither necessary nor desired.

"Joey!" Sid smiled. "Hey! Joey Falcone! It's been way too long!"

"Hey, waddaya mean? And whose fault is that, huh?" Joey's speech still bore a few of the characteristics of his early Bronx training. Sid's hand reached through the window to shake his old friend's paw.

"You're not afraid of shaking hands with a Jewish guy in public these days?" Sid asked. Joey recoiled without letting go.

"Ahhhh, shaddup!" said Joey. "Who are ya talkin' to?"

Sid shrugged.

"Besides, you know my mamma and the ole' man. No *fascisti* need apply with them. They saw enough of that before leavin' Sicily, when me and my sister were just *bambini*. Now get off that curb and in the car before you freeze to death out there."

"No can do, young man. I'm happy to see you, but I gotta go off to school. Some of us got learnin' to do, ya know?"

"You still doin' that stuff? Thought you'd graduated, since you're the same age as me."

"Still doin' it, Joey. Still doin' it. Another year and a half to go at City College for my master's degree, and I'm out. Into the wide world, with no possibility of a job. A Jew with a physics degree. Who wants one of those these days?"

Sid thought he heard Joey mutter, "Don't be too certain about that," under his breath, but he couldn't be sure.

"Hey, get in here anyway, Sid. The longer you stand out there, the colder I get. So, today's your lucky day. I'm givin' you a ride in my fine automobile."

"Swell of you, Joey. Real swell," Sid said as he opened the door and sat on the front seat, almost crushing his friend's hat. "Nice jalopy you got here."

"Nice enough to take us to 137th Street and Convent Avenue in Manhattan." The address of the College of the City of New York, the so-called "Harvard of the proletariat," where any boy—as women were educated at Hunter College in those days—smart enough could get a first-rate education regardless of ability to pay. Often, because of religious and racial prejudices, that boy had few other options.

"So, how'd you come by it?"

"How'd I buy what?"

"This device, this behemoth, with the seats and the radio and the grille work—it's beautiful. A work of art."

"Aah, I didn't buy it. I borrowed it from—well, from a friend, let's say. Yeah, a friend."

"Anyone I know?"

Joey turned and faced Sid. "Nah. No one you'd know."

Sid dropped the inquiry. "Know how to get to Convent Avenue?"

"Easy. South on the Concourse. Hang a right on East 161st Street and take it over the McCombs Dam Bridge into Manhattan. By that time, you're almost there. Remind me, when did you say you were graduatin' from that dump and gettin' a real job?"

"Another eighteen months. Why are you so interested?"

"Just watchin' out for you, kid, is all. Not tryin' to be nosey or nothin'. You know how things are."

Sid laughed. "OK, then I'll be the nosey one. How's your twin sister, Julia?"

"Who wants to know, huh?"

"Haven't seen her since she was about fifteen. Working?"

"Naah, finishin' up at Hunter College. Degree's in science education. Likes workin' with youngsters like all the dames do, God bless 'em. Just keep your hands off o' her 'cause I'm her older brother, and don't you forget it, Sid."

"And you might have to rub me out, right, Joey? That how it works in Brooklyn? Julia get any say in the matter?"

"Nope. Forget Brooklyn. Those are the rules of Messina, Sicilia, as clearly stated by the ole' man, *Signor* Falcone himself. And not 'cause you're Jewish, neither, just so you know. Guido is just an ole' fashion *padre della famiglia,* is all. Capish? Touch her, and he'll beat ya with a broom handle. Italian fathers and daughters, ya know how that goes."

Joey punched Sid on the point of his shoulder and smiled.

Sid had known Guido Falcone and his wife Maria for decades. They'd operated a small grocery store on Jerome Avenue underneath the elevated train, before relocating to Brooklyn so Guido could go into the butcher business with his brother, Favio. According to Rosalie Peskin, the Falcones never had a pot to piss in. It was an unkind thought, though true. But to Sid, no kinder or gentler souls existed. Especially Silvia, Mama Falcone.

"Would it be okay with Pops if I sent my regards to Julia?"

"I'll ask 'im next time I see 'im."

Sid knew his message would be delivered.

The red 1933 DeSoto, with its two inhabitants, its left and right running boards and its impressive front-end silver grille, reached W. 161st Street in the Bronx and entered onto the McCombs Dam Bridge. This steel structure spanned the Harlem River between the Bronx and Manhattan. (The Harlem, and its continuator the East River, weren't rivers, only extensions of the Hudson as it flowed around the island of Manhattan.)

A long viaduct over W. 155 Street in Manhattan connected that end of the bridge with Seventh Avenue. They were now riding along the Hamilton Heights, the high ground overlooking the Harlem flats to the south, where a large African-American community lived, often in poverty.

Joey Falcone made a left turn, drove south on Amsterdam Avenue, turned left on W. 135th Street, and pulled up to the traffic light on Convent Avenue. The gray and white stones of Shepard Hall—an impressive pile designed in the Gothic style and the main building on campus—came into view to the left.

"Ah, home sweet home, and all that," sighed Sid, about to pull on the latch to release the car door. "Just let me off here, will you, Joey? And thanks very much for the ride. It sure was great seeing you. We'll have to—"

Falcone reached over and grabbed a hold of Sid's wrist. "Wait," he said, gazing down Convent Avenue. "Don't get out. Look over there. Know any of those boys, Sid? Jus' keep your head low, and don't look at 'em."

Sid did as he was instructed, slinking down in his seat.

"Yeah, I know two of them," he said, after giving a glance at three young men, all wearing brown shirts and swastika armbands. Each carried a wooden club. They'd surrounded a young, thin, black student walking up the hill from Harlem to study.

"Tommy Ungard. He's their *Führer*. Another one's Bill Mundt. Fascist jerks. They hang around on Convent Avenue and call Jews names when we get out of class. We mostly ignore them, but looks like they've found themselves another victim this morning."

Tommy Ungard poked the black student with the end of his club. The student had no escape because every time he backed away, the other two fascists blocked his path. Then, with a rapid movement of his hand, the student swatted away the end of the club pointing at his face. That prompted Bill Mundt to slam his club down hard on the black man's wrist. Books tumbled to the pavement. Papers went flying and the wind scattered them in all directions.

Sid heard the man scream and saw him desperately trying to collect his papers. Ungard stepped on one and ground it into the dirt and asphalt of Convent Avenue.

Sid reached for the door handle, but Joey's meaty paw grabbed it and clutched at him, tightly.

"Falcone, we gotta do something before that guy gets killed!"

A blow to the gut from a club leveled the student to the pavement. Attempting to rise, he was bent double on the sidewalk and clutching at his belly.

"Jeez, Joey! Did you see that? The bastards are gonna work him over! Come on, let me outta here!"

"No."

"Whaddya mean, no, Joey? Can't you see what's going on over there? We gotta do somethin' or he's a dead man!"

"I said no."

"Joey, for Chrissakes..."

"I said no. No's no. We ain't doin' nothin'. At least you're not. I'm the one who's gonna take care of this problem. You just shuddup and keep your fuckin' head down. Got it?"

"Joey, what the hell are you gonna do? They got weapons and—"

"Shuddup and watch. You'll see."

Falcone exited the 1933 DeSoto, camel hair overcoat flapping in the breeze, and trotted over to where Mundt and his gang, armed with clubs, were about to beat the bejesus out of an unarmed African-American. Sid was caught between obeying his friend and feeling like a coward or joining him and risking a beating. But his hatred of the fascists overcame his reluctance, and he flew out of the car. Falcone was thirty paces ahead of him, leaving Sid astonished at how such a broad, stocky fellow could move so fast.

By the time Sid was halfway between the 1933 DeSoto and the prone black student, Joey had caught up with the leader of the fascist gang. Sid expected Joey to get brained. But instead of bashing in his head, the three fascists lowered their clubs, turned away, and scampered down the hill on Convent Avenue, heading toward the Harlem flats.

Joey helped the injured student up from the ground. He was in great pain and was cradling his right hand in his left.

"Smacked you real good, didn't they?" he said. "Should get that looked at, maybe get one of those X-ray things."

"Yeah, man, thanks." The student winced in agony.

"I'm Joey. Joey Falcone. Pleased to meet you."

"Thanks, Joey Falcone. Damn, thought those suckers were gonna kill me. Assholes!" He winced again. "Why don't they mind their own goddamn business? I wasn't bothering anyone. I was just—"

"Just let's get your papers together, okay?" said Sid. "No reason to make it worse than it is. What did you say your name was?"

"Never did. Name's Schuyler. I'd shake hands, but the damn thing hurts too much. And it's hurtin' more every minute."

"All right," said Joey. "That's 'nuf talkin'. Sid, put all his stuff in the front seat of my car. Schuyler, I'll bring it down here, and you get in the back. I'm takin' you to the hospital. That thing," he said, pointing to Schuyler's wrist, "is broken."

Joey and Sid gathered the books and papers, as many of them as they could, while the injured man looked on.

"Impressive!" said Sid to Joey as he bent down to retrieve some of Schuyler's scattered notes. "How the hell d'you do that?"

"How the hell did I do what?"

"Oh, come on. You know what I mean, Joey. One minute, those goons were about to beat the crap outta Schuyler, the next, they were running away like the cowards they are."

"Diplomacy, Sid. It's all about diplomacy. Sayin' the right things at the right time, y'know? You gotta know the right things to say, and when to say 'em. That's all."

"And you, Joey Falcone, know the right things to say?"

"Er... yup. I do."

"Because you, like, went to a school for diplomacy?"

"Yeah, a school for diplomacy. In a manner of speaking, yup, that's exactly what I did."

"Joey, honestly, what are you talking about?"

Joey stood up. "Sid, my friend. I know I don't have to tell ya, but it's a helluva bad world out there. Nothin' makes sense no more. Everythin' we learned from our folks about what's down and what's up, what's right and what's wrong, you can tie it up 'n' drop it in the Harlem River, capish?"

"Capish? Hell, of course you do! Now here's the good news, Sid. The folks who trained me want to train you, too. You should have a word with them. They might save your tuchus someday."

CHAPTER 4

At 7:30 in the morning, few students were present in the City College cafeteria in the basement of Shepard Hall. It wasn't due to the hour so much as to the inedible cafeteria food, in addition to the greasy, dirty ambiance of the place.

Except for the physics laboratory, the cafeteria was still one of Sid Peskin's favorite campus hangouts.

Along the sides of the cafeteria were twelve alcoves. Each contained low benches placed against the three alcove walls. A table stretched in front of the open side. A small window high on the back wall admitted as much feeble sunlight as it could on a day so near the winter solstice.

City College students gravitated to the alcoves based on their ethnicity and their politics. There was a Catholic alcove, an Orthodox Jewish alcove, and an African-American alcove, though there were few black students at City College. For Sid, who didn't have a spiritual bone in his body, Alcoves One and Two always caught his interest. These were where the leftist students congregated.

By late 1941, following more than ten years of economic depression, these young, passionate, idealistic, and often ill-informed young men had had just about enough of the capitalist system. In their view, failed American capitalism brought about too much misery to too many. Most of these students were Jewish, all were poor, and the vast majority were the children of immigrants to the United States. Not one could understand why—in this unashamedly rich country—some had so much while others had so little. They were determined to overturn the failed capitalist system in favor of the gleaming path toward the future: the guarantor of societal equality, Marxist socialism, as practiced in the worker's paradise of the Soviet Union.

Fortunately, never more than a few percent of all the students enrolled in City College were thrilled with the totalitarian police enterprise Josef Stalin had built on the wreckage of the Czarist state. These anti-Stalin leftists met in Alcove One and spent much of their time debating and denouncing the pro-Stalin leftists who took over Alcove Two. Otherwise, there wasn't much to do in either alcove, so visitors often spent the time before class playing chess.

Sid Peskin was an Alcove One man but not because he was a leftist. He had no desire to immerse himself in political-economic thought when there was so much to contemplate in the awesome physics of nature, from the very smallest subatomic particles to the thermonuclear processes of the largest stars. He could never be an Alcove Two man because everything he'd heard about Stalin—his starvation of the Ukrainians a decade earlier, his show trials and his purges, and his murderous prison camps in the arctic wastes of Siberia—repelled him.

Sid was an Alcove One man because the young anti-Stalinist leftists were the brightest, most stimulating conversationalists on the campus. In turn, they recognized Sid as a kind of intellectual equal who—though not political—possessed a body of arcane knowledge none of them had any hope of grasping. So most of the time, Sid found himself tolerated by the Alcove One crowd.

When he wasn't engaged in complex physics experiments, Sid loved to hear the leftists arguing the finer points of Marxist dialectics among themselves, especially when the Stalinists in Alcove Two spilled over into Alcove One, itching for a verbal altercation, a word fight.

But this morning, however, there was no fighting in Alcove One. There were only two students jitterbugging to a Benny Goodman swing tune scratched out on an old RCA Victor record player.

He sat at the bench placed across the Alcove One opening and slid along it until he found himself next to a young man of average height with bland features, except for his bottle-brush mustache. Next to him on the the bench was a dowdy woman with hair knotted at the back of her head in a tight bun. She had a flat, pallid face bearing a small mouth, with lips turned up at one end into a permanent sneer.

"Julius," said Sid to the young man on his right, offering his hand. "It's nice to see you again. But what are you doing here? I thought you'd graduated in '39?"

Julius shook Sid's hand. "You've a good memory, Sid. It was indeed last year, with a degree in electrical engineering."

"Ever get a job?"

Julius snorted. "Are you serious? I'm unemployed like everyone else. It's quite the fashion these days. Haven't you heard?"

The young woman opposite Julius figited nervously. "Who is this youngster, Julius?"

Julius turned to face her. "I'm sorry, my dear. Sid, this is my wife, Ethel. Don't know if you heard—we were married right after graduation."

Ethel Rosenberg gave Sid a quick smile and extended her hand for him to shake. Her grip was weak, her wrist limp, and her hand held with fingers pointed down. The physical contact was as brief as possible. It was as if the very act of shaking hands was distasteful.

"Pleased to meet you," said Ethel Rosenberg. Her body language indicated the opposite.

"Likewise," said Sid. "And congratulations, you two. I had no idea. Are both of you from the Lower East Side?" Sid referred to a district of Manhattan downtown, south of the street grid and northeast of the financial center, the home of about 250,000 of the children of Israel. It also housed large numbers of Italians and a sprinkling of others, most of whom were immigrants or their children.

"Alumni of Seward Park High, both of us. One of the finest high schools in the city, the incubator for the future leaders of the proletariat," said Julius with pride. "The heads of this nation's government when the revolution comes. You mark my words."

"Julius!" Ethel said, elbowing her husband in the ribs. "Don't talk like that. You don't know this person or who his friends are!"

"Oh, you always worry so much, my dear. But there's really no need to, Ethel. This is my old friend, Sid Peskin. He's not a spy for Hoover or the government... Though he's too bourgeois for my taste. Aren't you, Sid?"

"Well, good for you, Julius. But I have no idea who he is."

"I've trouble enough keeping track of myself, much less anyone else. Besides, I don't care about anyone's politics. Just trying to keep my head down and get my degree."

"And then what?" asked Ethel.

"Oh, I dunno. I haven't thought that far ahead yet."

"Sid," said Julius. "I've been out there over a year. There are no jobs. Hardly for anyone, and for sure not for people like us."

Sid nodded. Apart from the Rosenbergs' ideology, which he disdained, he knew Julius was telling the truth.

"Under the current system of government in this country, capitalist and nationalist, we don't believe there is much of a future for Jews in the United States—in the absence of a revolution. We need a revolution! A Communist revolution! Like when the workers and peasants overthrew the old order in Russia and embarked upon the creation of a workers' paradise. A revolution when the enemies of the people will be swept away like the creatures rejected from the ark by Noah before the great flood."

"Julius!" snarled Ethel. "For God's sake, keep your voice down. Hoover has spies everywhere."

"Oh. You mean those two boys jitterbugging? Naah," said Sid. "That's only Mike Fleischer and Norman Platoff. If Hoover is using either of those morons as spies, he has bigger problems than a small group of Communists. Believe me."

Edith held a hand up to her lips and tittered. "Yeah. Well, that may be. But you can't be too careful anymore. Not like back in the day, when we were open members of the Young Communist League and proud of it."

"Is that where you two met?" asked Sid.

The two gazed lovingly at each other. "Yes," Julius replied. "And what a grand day it was, wasn't it my love? Both for us, and for the revolution!" Their lips grazed in a brief, socialist smooch.

"I'm happy for you two lovebirds. Really, I am But as for the revolution and Communism—like that Hollywood guy said: include me out."

"You're making a big mistake, Sidney," said Ethel, sneering again. "The revolution will never forget either its friends—or its enemies. But you don't have to join the Party, Sid. Perhaps you could become one of our fellow travelers?"

"Not I. I'm not a hanger-on, and I'm too disobedient to make a good Communist. And besides, you Rosenbergs are too in love with Stalin to be taken seriously."

"You say that as an insult!" said Julius. "We wear our Stalinism as a badge of honor."

"Julius..." said Ethel, "keep quiet. There are spies."

"Frankly, I don't understand how you can still defend that man. He's murdered thousands, if not millions, of his own people."

"All lies, damned lies made up by the fake capitalist press in a blatant smear campaign to discredit him," scowled Ethel. "And besides, anyone killed in Stalin's Russia was either a shirker, a traitor, or just plain old pond scum. To this day, more than twenty years after the Communist takeover, there are many former people in the Soviet Union who retain their violent opposition to Communism, to the rule of the proletariat, and to Stalin's vision of the future, classless society: the workers' paradise.

"Like parasites, they bury down deeply into the fabric of the workers' state, undermining it from within, destroying the dreams of millions for their own selfish aims. Well, you are wrong, Sidney, very wrong! Such people deserve the sentence of death! They must be removed from society so the healthy elements can survive!"

Ethel slowly slid into her seat. Sid sighed. It was useless to argue with a true believer, but he gave it one last try.

"Regardless, Mrs. Rosenberg, I fail to see how you can defend the Nazi-Soviet Pact of '39. After beating on each other for years, the Nazis and the Communists have become best friends. I think your hero Stalin has betrayed you. He's ignored Hitler's conquest of the entire European continent except for the parts Stalin reserved as his own booty!"

Julius sniffed. "The party cadres cannot always grasp Stalin's strategic genius or his long-term plans. I view the pact as merely tactical, a way to buy additional time for the Soviet Union to prepare its own defenses."

"Which Stalin has accomplished by destroying his own officer corps?" asked Sid, referring to the purges that decimated the leadership of the Soviet military.

"You cannot fight a war with those at your back who'd betray you to your enemy," said Ethel. "When the Hitlerites come, as we know they will, the entire nation will be united behind Comrade Stalin against them. There will be no spies, saboteurs, or fifth columnists preventing our march to victory! If I were Stalin, I'd have done no less."

Sid glanced at his watch and noticed it was a few minutes to nine.

"It's been lovely arguing with you today, Mr. and Mrs. Rosenberg, but I must be off." He nodded to Julius and Ethel and shook hands with each. "A lecture on stellar nucleosynthesis, delivered by Professor Oppenheimer, is first on my must hear list. He's a genius. And he's here for one day, just to give us a talk. I wish you the very best in your Marxist evangelical work. Though I'm a capitalist, and you're both duty-bound to do away with me, it doesn't mean we can't still be friends."

"Of course not!" said Julius. "Let's stay friends—at least until the revolution. Then we'll send you and all your cronies to the Gulag. The camps will be set up in the outer Aleutian Islands. Sound exciting? It's wet and chilly there, even in the summer. Gulags are best in chilly places, I think. But why not avoid all the trouble coming your way and join with us now, Sid? The revolution needs good minds like yours. Since Hitler rules Europe, and things don't look so good here, what do you have to lose?"

"Call me when you come into your kingdom, Julius."

"Ha, you'll see it arising all around you before long."

Sid thought them tiresome, but with every moment that passed, it appeared more and more likely that Julius and Ethel Rosenberg had a point.

CHAPTER 5

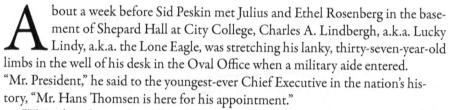

About a week before Sid Peskin met Julius and Ethel Rosenberg in the basement of Shepard Hall at City College, Charles A. Lindbergh, a.k.a. Lucky Lindy, a.k.a. the Lone Eagle, was stretching his lanky, thirty-seven-year-old limbs in the well of his desk in the Oval Office when a military aide entered. "Mr. President," he said to the youngest-ever Chief Executive in the nation's history, "Mr. Hans Thomsen is here for his appointment."

"Then show him in." Lindbergh smiled with an expansive sweep of his hand. He rose from his chair.

Within seconds, another door in the wall opened. In strode the ambassador from the Third Reich, the state that ruled most of the continent of Europe. In the year 1941, Hans Thomsen was a handsome, charming, forty-nine-year-old man who spoke and wrote flawless English. He was a lover of fine wine, a connoisseur of *haute* cuisine, a *bon vivant*, a skilled raconteur, and Nazified to the core of his bone marrow.

Lindbergh met him in front of the desk, hand outstretched, with a warm greeting. "Mr. Ambassador, good afternoon. I am always delighted to receive a call from you. De-e-e-lighted, as Theodore Roosevelt, one of my illustrious Republican predecessors, would say. Please, have a seat."

Lindbergh ushered Thomsen over to the sofa, while he himself sat on a nearby armchair. "I'm thrilled that your rank could be upgraded from *chargé d'affaires* to ambassador after my election. The late Mr. Franklin Roosevelt, my immediate predecessor, unwisely downgraded it in 1938 after that ugly business in Germany in the beginning of November—I believe it's now known as *Kristallnacht*, or something similar. Pardon me, German is not my first language."

"It is no cause for concern, Mr. President."

"What isn't, Mr. Ambassador?"

"Neither the fact that you do not know German like a native, nor *Kristallnacht*, of course."

"Of course. The first is no one's concern except mine. The second is of no one's concern except yours."

"The *Führer*—who sends his warmest greetings—agrees with you in all respects, Mr. President."

"And please return to him my best wishes and those of the entire American people."

"I will be certain to mention your kind thoughts in my report about this meeting to Berlin, sir. And I will also remember to mention your... ah, let's say, constructiveness in matters that are of great interest to the *Führer*. Especially those concerning die *Judenfrage*... excuse me, the Jewish Question."

Lindbergh squinted. "And is that the reason you wanted to speak with me today, Mr. Ambassador?"

"Not the only matter, Mr. President. There are some facts that my government would like to bring to the attention of your own, if I may be so bold?"

"Such as?"

"Such as the fact, Mr. President, that there are still newspapers in this country, the *New York Times* for example, that continue to write fake and scurrilous tales about my country and my government. The *Führer* has been greatly angered by such, such... libel, and demands it cease immediately!"

"Would you be kind enough to provide me with an example, Mr. Ambassador?"

"Yes, of course. Just yesterday, an article appeared on the front page above the crease. The correspondent claimed the Wehrmacht and the SS were committing atrocities in occupied Poland. We do not know who is spreading such a base and despicable rumor, but the *Führer* assures you on his sacred honor that no true German warrior would ever bring to harm any innocent civilian! And for what it is worth, you may have my personal word on it, too!"

Lindbergh took a deep breath. "Thank you, Mr. Ambassador. The news article of which you speak had already been brought to my attention and had caused my colleagues, and me personally, some distress. But I know you to be an honorable man and the product of a highly cultured society, one greatly respected by myself and by all Americans. The leader of such a nation must be taken at his word, especially when it has been given sincerely. So, I am much relieved that you tell me these rumors are unfounded."

Thomsen leaned back in the sofa, considering things. So far as he could tell, Lindbergh was little more than a Midwest yokel, an ignoramus knowing nothing of history or politics. A single flight over the Atlantic, and this ridiculous dolt believed himself fit to sit in the chair of Washington and Lincoln. Worse, his moronic countrymen were stupid enough to elect him! The *Führer* will crush this fool and this mongrel country as he has already crushed far more intelligent European states. "Quite unfounded, Mr. President. And I must also bring to your attention that the *New York Times*, and many other newspapers, in addition to most of your Hollywood film industry, are controlled by the Jews."

"I'm aware of that, of course, Mr. Ambassador. I don't like it, but I don't know what can be done to stop it. More than two million members of that race live in New York City alone, and millions more are scattered throughout the country. They have their friends, Mr. Ambassador, as Germany has hers."

"Of course, Mr. President. The *Führer* understands your problem and sympathizes. And here you also touch on the concept of race. The Third Reich is a society based on the centrality of the racial principle: that one race deserves to be the sole race dominating every aspect of politics, science, business, and culture on this planet. As the events of the past year have proven beyond doubt, this concept applies to we Germans as a nation. Other races were never designed for dominance and must support the functions, the goals, and aspirations of the master race. I am sure you agree."

"Of course," said Lindbergh. "Take the situation in my country. On the bottom are the negroes—an inferior population with no ability to progress in society above their current low level. Negroes must be treated with paternal neglect and never allowed to participate in governance. The Southern folks understand their negroes and handle them well. The Northerners also dislike their negroes, but hypocritically support them. On the top, then, are the white folks—born leaders and the drivers of business, culture, and science. That's the natural order of things. I would even say it's the way God designed it."

"Exactly, Mr. President. You've summed it up accurately."

"I've read *Mein Kampf*, ya know. Never was much for reading, but that sure was an impressive volume. Connected a lot of dots for me. Especially about the Jews."

"We think *Mein Kampf* is impressive also. I'm sure the *Führer* will be pleased you think so, too. Would you like an autographed copy?"

"Oh, I'd treasure it, Mr. Ambassador! There'll be a special place for it right here in the Oval Office!"

"But wouldn't that offend some of the Jews or their friends?"

Lindbergh huffed and rolled his eyes. "Then they will just have to get used to being offended. They've had their way for too long in this country! Almost think they own the place. Can you imagine? My problem is, Mr. Ambassador, that there isn't much I can do about them. And then there's that Constitution the Democrats are always babbling about. I'm not a lawyer, so I never read the whole thing, though everyone expects I should. But I get glassy-eyed from all that legal mumbo-jumbo.

And no matter what, some pissant shyster objects when I try to do the right thing for the country. They always do."

"I understand your dilemma, Mr. President, but only a man of strength and vision can do what must be done. Might I make a few suggestions?"

"Of course, Mr. Ambassador."

"For example, you could point out to your political opponents that the Reich is now the master of the Eastern half of the world and all its resources. We control Europe and have an unbreakable alliance with *Herr* Stalin and the Soviet Union, which provides us with all the grain and oil we need. We have approximately two million men under arms, and our submarines, while we speak, are patrolling the waters off your East Coast. And how large is your American army? 150,000 men, many still using wooden replicas for guns!"

"Yes, Mr. Ambassador. We are aware of those statistics. But we in the U.S. don't want war. We want to be good friends with your country and its great people!"

"Of course, Mr. President. We know that your intentions with respect to the Third Reich are always, ah... constructive. But the amity between us cannot extend to permitting those vituperative attacks against the Reich and our *Führer* made by your lying Jew-press. The *Führer* insists they be stopped, and the libelers held to account."

"Mr. Ambassador, I am as distressed by the smears the American press has leveled against your country and your *Führer* as you are. Their actions bring shame on our people. But don't believe for an instant that the people that slander you treat me with kindness. They don't. I despise their arrogance, their elitism, and their lies. Even as we speak, my lawyers in the Department of Justice are devising ways of procuring verdicts of libel against these tricksters. But because of our legal system, I have limited power in these matters."

"*Ja*, we understand your dilemma, Mr. President," Thomsen said in a Germanic monotone. "But now, you must understand ours. Perhaps it is undiplomatic to phrase the matter this way, but the *Führer* insists I inform you that he will no longer tolerate the disruption of our plans by the Jews. For years, they have been engaged in a conspiracy against him, and against Germany."

"Mr. Thomsen, I assure you I will do everything I can to assist the legitimate efforts of the German nation under the heroic leadership of your *Führer*, Adolf Hitler. But these matters take time. Some of what you ask may not be possible, but that won't be from any lack of effort on our part."

"Thank you, Mr. President. You are an honorable man. We trust you. The *Führer*, who is as great a diplomat as he is a military leader, anticipated your words. He has one further suggestion for you."

Lindbergh sighed. It was at moments like these when he wished he was back in his boyhood home of Little Falls, Minnesota, dusting crops for earth scratchers living barely above subsistence. But now it was his job to hear out the demands of Nazis who had little understanding of the problems he faced, even though he was sympathetic to their point of view. "Please, Mr. Ambassador. Tell me what Mr. Hitler has in mind."

"Ah, well, Mr. President, it's simple. Unlike Germany, America is a vast country. Your internal markets dwarf our own. Nevertheless, you should remember that exports still retain a certain importance to your economy, ja? But to export, you require export markets. The *Führer* points out that most of your export markets are now under the control of the Third Reich. Should the *Führer's* will not be heeded, the pressure on him from his followers to sanction those markets might well become... intolerable. Don't you think?"

A chill of cold fear ran down Lindbergh's spine as he rose, shook hands with Thomsen and watched him depart. He knew the threat came from Hitler himself. A drop in American exports was bad for business and bad for the moneymen who had levered him, Lucky Lindy, a provincial political novice, to the apex of political power.

What disturbed the Lone Eagle the most was that people, regular people like he was in his youth in Minnesota, would be thrown out of work if exports fell. The Great Depression, now eleven years in duration, would continue unabated, damaging his re-election chances. But the only other choice he had was to accede to Nazi blackmail.

It took Lindbergh little time to make his decision. He pushed a white button on his desk intercom.

"Anne," he said, speaking to his wife, the first lady, who was also acting as his private secretary. "Get Edgar over here now. Yes, I mean now. Right now!"

"Yes, Mr. President."

Lindbergh had only a few moments to ponder his dilemma before the elegant Anne Morrow Lindbergh stepped into the Oval Office.

"Well?"

"I'm so sorry, Charles. I spoke to Edgar's secretary. He's at a very important meeting and will do the best he can to come to the White House in about thirty minutes."

"Did you tell that fool it was the President calling?"

"Of course, Charles. But you know Edgar. He has a mind of his own and his own way of doing things. I'm certain he means no disrespect. Just has too much on his plate, is all."

In their long years of marriage, Anne had developed her own way of handling Charles Lindbergh. She understood his volcanic temper was thinly papered over by a mask of imperturbability. Unfortunately, the mask could often be rubbed away to reveal the seething cauldron underneath. Sensing this was one of those times, she remained buoyant to defuse his anger. Lindbergh caused the most trouble for himself whenever he shot his mouth off without thinking first. "While you're waiting for

Edgar, would you like a cup of coffee, dear? I know how trying these visits from the German ambassador can be for you."

Lindbergh slumped in his desk chair, a glum expression on his face. "The Germans. They're blackmailing me, Annie. Me! Can you believe it? The irony is, I agree with some of their ideas. Especially about the Jews of the world having too much power. And I thought Hitler and I had established a close relationship when I visited him in 1937. Now look how he's treating me."

Lindbergh rose from his chair and began to pace about the Oval Office. "You know what, Annie? You know what this tells me? That son of a bitch Göring has no influence anymore. Christ, when I was in Germany, I heaped endless praise on his baby, the Luftwaffe. He swore his eternal friendship, would you believe? What I'd like to know now is which part of eternal friendship is about... about... about, well, you know... blackmail!"

"It seems his boss has other ideas. One lump of sugar or two, dear?"

"Yes. I mean one, please. Now they're threatening that if I don't pick up the pace on the marginalization and exclusion of Jews from American society, they'll sanction our exports!"

"Oh, I think they're bluffing, Charles. Try to put it from your mind."

"I don't think so, dear. Hitler is very confident these days. And *Herr* Thomsen was definitive."

Anne sat on an Oval Office couch. "Oh, come, now. Germans always sound definitive. Something about their language, or their intonation, or whatever. It's a good starting position for a negotiation. But it's a bluff, I'm sure of it. And Hitler's the biggest bluffer that ever was. Problem is, no one has ever called him on his bluffs until it was too late."

Lindbergh sat on the couch next to his wife. "The history of the past five years according to Annie Lindbergh. Is that right, my dear? So, now I find you're not only a brilliant writer with an amazing intellect, but a historian, too? Y'know, I could use a person like you in my cabinet. What would you like your title to be?"

Anne sat back in her chair and laughed. "Oh, I think being first lady is about all I can handle right now. It can be tiresome enough to deal with those Washington society ladies—they chirrup and flutter about me like hungry little bird chicks waiting for a worm!"

"If you ever change your mind, please don't hesitate to apply for a cabinet position. Any position. Even one that's already filled. I'm skilled at convincing people to, ah... request early retirement. But now, dear, where the bloody hell is Edgar?"

Exactly a half-hour later, just as he'd promised, John Edgar Hoover—Edgar to his friends and colleagues—the Director of the FBI and the scourge of criminals in the U.S. of A, arrived at the White House and was ushered into the Oval Office. Anne Lindbergh had departed, leaving Hoover alone with the president.

His reputation preceded him. In 1941, J. Edgar Hoover was a popular man in America. He had spent the Depression years killing or incarcerating high-profile criminals and gangsters with a style that accrued maximum public accolades for the Bureau, and for himself. He was now a pudgy, balding forty-five-year-old man who collected dirt on anyone of importance in Washington.

Despite his position, he lived like a hermit with his mother and cultivated close relationships with his G-men, especially his Deputy Director, Clyde Tolson.

"I'm sorry it took me so long to get here, sir," said Hoover, breathless from the exertion.

"Have a seat, Edgar. Coffee, if you want it, too."

"Thank you, Mr. President, but it won't be necessary."

"Won't be necessary for you to call me 'Mr. President' either, Edgar. We've been friends for a long time, and you know how much I respect you and the work the Bureau does. Seems like every week, another criminal's being fitted for a black-and-white striped suit, or a coffin. One or the other. Who was the last one of 'em I heard so much about? Moses Mowshowitz? Bah, what a repulsive character. Even more than the usual. How many people did he finally admit to murdering? Twenty? Twenty-five? More? So, in honor of our long friendship, and for the work you do in keeping this country safe, Edgar, Charles will suit me fine."

"Thank you. What can I do for you today, Charles?"

Lindbergh briefed Hoover about his meeting with the German ambassador.

"Hmm. You're right. You have a problem. I don't think Mr. Hitler understands the Jewish question in the United States. It took him years to denationalize and destroy the German Jews. Why does he think it can be done any faster here? The U.S. has more than ten times the number of kikes Hitler had to deal with in Germany. For Chrissakes, there are more than two million of the Chosen People in New York City alone! The courts would never allow anything to happen to those bastards, and there's nothing we can do right now to change that."

"No, we can't, Edgar. But we must do something. A gesture perhaps, to start. Something that will satisfy the Germans for the time being. Perhaps the Mayor of New York can help?"

Hoover scowled, distaste curling his pudgy nose upward and almost into his beady eyes. "The Mayor of New York? Fred Trump? Bah! He's an insignificant real estate developer from one of the outer boroughs. Queens, I think. Don't know how he ever got elected. Somehow, he managed to convince the New York Hebes he wasn't their mortal enemy."

"Yes, sadly for them. They didn't know he's been a big financial supporter of the German-American Bund for years." Lindbergh was the favorite politician of the group, whose ideology embraced admiration for Hitler and all things Nazi underneath a thin patina of pseudo-patriotism.

"Of course I know, Charles. Trump also quietly posts bail for Bundists caught beating up Jews. That's not a bad idea when you think about it, but not everyone on the New York City Police force will just look away. Some haven't come over to our way of thinking yet."

"He may be helpful," the president continued. "Let's hear what he has to say."

CHAPTER 6

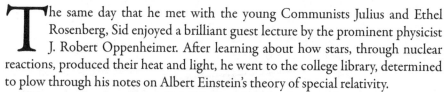

The same day that he met with the young Communists Julius and Ethel Rosenberg, Sid enjoyed a brilliant guest lecture by the prominent physicist J. Robert Oppenheimer. After learning about how stars, through nuclear reactions, produced their heat and light, he went to the college library, determined to plow through his notes on Albert Einstein's theory of special relativity.

Sid sat at a study carrel and read for most of the day. By late afternoon, he was pondering the practical significance of Einstein's famous equation $E = mc^2$, which the great physicist had derived more than thirty-five years previously.

Sid understood that Einstein's equation suggested even a very small amount of mass contained an enormous amount of energy locked up within it. This mass could be converted into energy in proportion to the speed of light squared, an inconceivably enormous number. The latent energy present in, say, a teacup, could liquefy the entire City of New York.

To satisfy his nagging intellectual curiosity about the relationship between energy and mass, Sid left his study carrel and walked over to the library stacks. These bookshelves held row upon row of scientific journals bound into hardcover volumes. By the light of a single, dull, incandescent bulb, he searched for a volume of the German physics journal *Naturwissenschaften* and for a specific article recommended by professor Strauss.

"1936, 1937, 1938," he said to himself, passing his index finger over the black spines bearing the journal name and year printed in white letters. "Ah, there it is, volume 27, 1939." His hand reached into the row of volumes. Gripping the black binding, he carried the book to his carrel, laid it down, and opened it to an article published by Professors Hahn and Strassman of the Kaiser Wilhelm Institute of Berlin.

Their paper appeared on page eleven. The two research scientists, in thick German writing, described a recent, simple experiment. But their conclusion was revolutionary! Atoms of uranium could be split to produce lighter-weight elements when irradiated by sub-atomic particles, called neutrons. This breaking apart of the uranium nucleus, the process of atomic fission, occurred with the emission of a tremendous amount of energy in the form of heat.

Sid, who could easily read scientific German, found the work remarkable. He was glad old man Strauss brought this to his attention, or he never would have heard of it.

He had also brought to Sid's attention two other research papers, both published in the prominent British journal *Nature*. Strauss claimed these papers confirmed and expanded the original Hahn-Strassman experiments. The first of these two papers had been authored by a man named Otto Frisch. Its companion was co-authored by Frisch together with Frisch's own aunt, the great physicist Lise Meitner. So, back into the dimly lit stacks Sid went, off in search of last year's issues of *Nature*.

The articles weren't hard to find, especially since the journal Nature was alphabetically located near *Naturwissenschaften*, near where he'd just been searching. Thumbing through the pages of Nature, Sid became so absorbed in reading that he didn't look up until he had almost returned to his carrel.

When he finally tore himself away from the pages, he was astonished to see an older gentleman sitting in his seat and rifling through his papers! Sid's jaw dropped.

The unwelcome intruder sported a chubby round face, a high forehead crowned with jet-black hair, a set of bushy eyebrows, and a pronounced jowl. He wore a black suit, white shirt, and blue polka-dot tie. Sid's heart skipped a beat as he dashed over to the carrel.

"Excuse me, sir," he said. "I don't mean to disturb you, but I can't help noticing you are sitting in my seat. Those are my papers you are looking through."

"Yes, I was perfectly aware of that," said the seated man without pausing for a moment in his examination of Sid's personal effects. "And I suppose you will be reading the Meitner and Frisch papers, too?" He pointed to the volume of Nature in Sid's right hand. The man spoke English fluently, though Sid couldn't recognize the accent. It wasn't one of the more common ones heard on the streets of the West Bronx in 1941.

Sid grit his teeth. "Listen, sir. Who are you, and what do you want? And kindly take your hands off my papers; they're no business of yours." He reached across the carrel and swept up his notes into his arms with no resistance from the intruder.

The man pushed back in his chair. "Very well. You're right, I suppose. I admit I've been ill-mannered today. Please forgive me. It's only that there is so much at stake..."

"First question: Are you with the U.S. government? If so, show me your badge. And second—do you have a name?"

The man laughed. "No and yes. No, I've nothing to do with the government. And yes, I have a name, though I shouldn't—I am... ah, I suppose it can't do any harm to say it. My name is Leo."

"And do you have a last name, Leo?"

"Of course. Doesn't everyone?"

Sid shook his head. This man was *meshuga.* "But you're not going to tell me what it is, I suppose?"

"That's right."

"And what are you doing here, Mr. *Meshuga*, ah... I mean, Mr. Leo? Are you a criminal? A book thief, maybe?"

"A book thief? Ha, my young man. No, I'm not a book thief. What I am is a very, very smart person—in fact, I could be a genius. I invent things. Things no one else has ever imagined! In some circles, I'm well known for my inventions. I see you don't believe me, but I'm probably the most famous person you've never heard of."

"Because of one of your inventions?"

"Yes. You could say that. Because of one of my inventions."

"Does one of your inventions have anything to do with atomic fission?"

Leo startled, and even in the dim light, Sid saw he had gone pale. "Who said anything about atomic fission?" he gasped. "And how do you know about it?"

"Oh, c'mon, it's obvious. The volume of *Naturwissenschaften* with the Hahn-Strassman experiment is sitting open on my carrel. You asked me if I was also interested in the Frisch-Meitner papers. And I learned about the term fission as I was skimming those papers after I retrieved the issues of Nature from 1939, right before I saw you. Now why don't you get up from my carrel and go away before I call security. You're too old to be a student, and I've never seen you before. So I doubt you're a professor, either."

Leo rose to his full height, about four inches shorter than Sid's five foot eight. "I don't want any trouble, Sid. Your name is Sid, correct? Sid Peskin? I do have the correct person?"

Leo wasn't *meshuga* after all. He was dangerous. Sid was alarmed.

"How did you know my name?"

"I can't tell you that. But I can tell you I know much more than that. About you, I mean. Also, that I'd like to call on you again sometime, Sid. May I do so, despite how, ah... obnoxiously unpleasant and awkward I've been?"

"Oh, I don't think so. I've no idea why you're here now, and I can't imagine why I'd want to see you again."

"I can understand your feelings, Sid. And I apologize. But please, until we meet again, do not share anything you learn about nuclear fission with anyone. No one! Promise me just this, will you?"

Sid made no promises. Instead, he stared open-mouthed as Leo turned and departed the library. But it was difficult for him to dismiss his odd interaction with that rude and queer little man. Something about Leo indicated he was serious—and very frightened.

Sid took a closer look at the Frisch and Meitner papers he'd just retrieved. Perhaps something in them was important, and not only to Leo (whoever he was). Perhaps whatever it might be was hiding in plain sight. He rubbed his eyes and wrote a few notes to himself.

After a long study of their contents, he stretched out and yawned. He hadn't found anything new. The papers in Nature reproduced Hahn and Strassmann's work in 1938, with some additional calculations. The experiments were believable, and their conclusions justified, but that was as far as it went. A clever research scientist with the right tools in the right lab could jury-rig an experiment to split an atom and obtain energy in the process—but this fission experiment was little more than a lab curiosity. And it was damned impractical, too! Sid suspected these experiments were probably the first and the last anyone would ever hear of nuclear fission. Except for that *meshuga*, Leo! And what was he doing in Shepard Hall, anyway? Weren't there a dozen other finer libraries in New York where he could bother the students?

Perplexed by the events of the day, Sid closed the journals and brought them over to a pile on the desk at the front of the library for re-shelving.

After glancing at his wristwatch, he groaned. "Jeez, it's five o'clock! Mom must be going bananas. I'd better get my tuchus out of here. She hates it when I'm out after dark."

It would take a train and a bus to get Sid from City College on 137th Street and Convent Avenue to Morris Avenue in the Bronx. Gathering his belongings, which consisted of the few papers Leo had examined plus the notes he'd made on the library articles, he donned his black coat, black gloves, and green scarf for the trek home.

A biting chill pinched him in the face the moment he stepped out of the library building. He approached the City College gate and crossed Convent Avenue, finding every breath almost painfully cold. A steep hill on 137th Street led down to Broadway, and to the welcome warmth of the subway train that ran beneath it. But after a few moments walking, so much buzzed through his mind he didn't notice the plummeting temperature.

Sid thought his encounter with Leo must have had something to do with Strauss. Or how else could this Leo have obtained his name and known where to find him? And at just the time he was researching nuclear fission, a subject of interest to Strauss, too! Or was his run-in with Leo a coincidence, having nothing to do with Sid at all? And what could be the reason for Leo's furtiveness when all he had to ask was a proper question, instead of rummaging through his stuff without permission? Damnation, this goddamn country was getting crazier by the day.

Sid shook his head. That was the instant when he thought he saw the same man—Leo—again. In the gloom, it was impossible to be certain. But the similarity in outline to Leo, even to the front brim of his fedora, snapped down to obscure his face, struck Sid. Someone was following him. But who?

Was it Leo? Sid couldn't be certain as he dropped down the stairs into the light and warmth of the underground station. It made no sense. Why would Leo want to follow him when they'd had a face-to-face conversation in the library only several hours ago? Why would anyone want to follow him for any reason? He had no knowledge that would be of any interest to an enemy agent—even if in Lindbergh's America, it had become ambiguous as to just who the enemy was.

The 137th Street stop, on the Number One, Broadway-Local Train that ran from the southern tip of Manhattan to the northern extremity of the West Bronx, was only forty years old, but was about as desiccated and decrepit as a human centenarian.

The station looked similar to most of the others on the IRT line. Its walls were encased in white tiles, which—outside of the NYC subways—were seen only in public washrooms. Black-coated electrical cables hung from black steel crossbeams that faded away into the station's painted black roof. The ambient lighting, as in City College's library, was weak and unsuitable for eyes that had trouble with the dark. At each end of the station, the cavernous openings of pitch-black tunnels, save for their red and green signaling lights, beckoned and repelled at the same time.

Though every NYC subway station had a Gothic look resembling the 1935 movie set of *The Bride of Frankenstein,* Sid loved them—the atavistic, unfinished rawness, the dark subterranean corners, the smell of grease and grime mixed with flecks of iron oxides sparking off the rails. But even Sid avoided the black circular spots on the platform, fossilized relics of discarded, chewed gum from ages past.

He also admired the architectural honesty of the stations' creators. When these tunnels had been constructed at the turn of the century, the goal of the entrepreneurs building the system was straightforward. They needed to solve the practical problem of moving large numbers of people around the city, from uptown to downtown in the morning, and back around the other way in the evening. In the 137th Street Station, no consideration but one was given to aesthetics. That was the pink mosaic depicting a classical three-headed lady. Symbolizing City College, and its motto *respice, adspice, prospice*—advice to its students to look to the past, the present, and the future—these three pink ladies could be observed at special sites where they had been incorporated into the uptown side wall.

The train Sid awaited grumbled and rumbled softly in the distance. Then, with a gale-force wind preceding it, the six boxy metal cars, their engineer sitting in the front right of the leading car, clack-clack-clacked and roared into the station. The vehicle's brakes forced it to a screeching stop. The doors opened, and Sid entered the third car along with a cluster of his fellow students. A brief glance to his right and left revealed nothing remarkable, and no additional sighting of the man in the creased fedora whose build resembled Leo's.

Sid loosened his scarf and removed his gloves in the warmth of the overcrowded car. He caught one of the last wicker seats available. Directly opposite him sat two elderly individuals, a man and a woman, possibly husband and wife. Both had short-cropped hair and wore ill-fitting ragged clothes. Their worn and shabby coats couldn't have provided much protection against a New York winter. Their attire was finished off with cheap gray socks and what were probably cast-off shoes. These were two of New York's urban proletariat, the species beloved by Julius and Ethel Rosenberg.

The Broadway-local train pushed forward relentlessly. After its stops at 145th and 157th Streets, it halted inside a huge barrel-vaulted, brick-ceilinged station at 168th Street. Its doors opened to allow passengers to catch the crossing A train and to receive new travelers. But on this evening, the doors of the Number One train remained open for longer than the New York crowd would tolerate. That led to the usual eye-rolling and grumbling.

Even the elderly couple sitting opposite Sid seemed to join in the general complaining, though their language was unfamiliar to him.

Sid listened to the music of their conversation. Wouldn't you know it? The wife sounded just like old Mrs. Farkas, from the third floor of his own building, when she spoke the language of whatever country she came from years ago.

He listened closely as the couple conversed with each other.

A thought occurred to him. When Mrs. Farkas spoke English, she sounded like that *meshuga*, Leo! That was an interesting coincidence! He might never learn much more about him, but Sid thought he should be able to figure out where he was from. He also needed to have a chat with Professor Strauss. Perhaps he could explain what the hell happened today.

The trip home usually took about an hour. But today, due to one delay after another, it took more than two and a half.

"Okay, your boy is here, Rosalie," hollered Sid's father—Sam—as Sid walked through the door of their fifth-floor apartment on Morris Ave in the West Bronx. "You can stop worrying now!"

Rosalie, in her apron, emerged from the kitchen just to the right of the doorway.

"Well, it's about time, don't you think?" Sid hung up his coat in a small closet set into the wall of the large foyer doubling both as a living room and a dining room.

"We were sick with fright over what could have happened to you! Don't ever do that to us again!"

Sid didn't take his mother seriously, but her concern for him was understandable. Unlike Sam, Rosalie hadn't been born in America. She remembered the terrifying world of rampaging Cossacks and government-instigated pogroms in her childhood home in western Ukraine.

"Nothing to worry about, Mom. Just a few long subway delays, that was all."

Rosalie jabbed a finger at him. "With what's going on in this world now, why shouldn't I be worried? Who knows? What if you'd had an accident? Or run into one of those Bundist gangs? I hear they're beating up Jews all over the city. How would we ever know what happened to you?"

"No problem, Mom. If you need to say *Kaddish* for me, I'll just send you a Western Union telegram to let you know. 'Dear Mom and Pop, stop. I am deceased, stop. Please say *Kaddish* for me... and please send money, stop. Yours, Sid.'"

"Now don't be fresh with your mother," warned Sam. "She only has your best interests at heart. Remember this, sonny boy! No one's ever going to love you more than your own mother."

"I sure don't think our president, Mr. Lindbergh, loves me much."

"Lindbergh! He's a real bastard, that one. An anti-Semite. A friend of Hitler— may his name be blotted out," Sam spat.

"Amen," said Sid and Rosalie.

"I still can't believe our countrymen were thoughtless enough to vote for that blockhead and his simple-minded foolishness," said Sam, raising a shaking index finger over his head. "Who knows what's going to be? No one... only the Almighty!"

"And he's not tellin'," Sid said with a sarcastic grin.

"Don't be disrespectful." Rosalie glared at him.

"The matriarch speaks," said Sam. "She has her rules, you know. And you'd better obey them while you're under this roof."

A boy no more than ten years of age emerged from a bedroom.

"Hi, Sid. You're late for dinner. Did they give you detention in college today?"

"Oh, hi, Benny," Sid said. "Yeah, as a matter of fact, they did. I tried to liquefy New York. Had to go sit in the library for a few hours."

Benny's eyes went huge and round. "Wow! Really? Like the Martians when they invaded New York? Remember? You and me, we heard it on the radio a few years ago! The Martians and that Orson Welles guy destroyed First Avenue with their spaceship's death ray! Zap! Pow! Pow! Take that, you coppers!"

"I think you have your radio shows mixed up, Benny."

"Nah," said Benny, as he returned to the room he shared with Sid. "I got it right!"

It was futile to argue. Benny knew radio programming better than Sid knew physics. Even though they teased each other without mercy, the two Peskin boys, despite being ten years apart, were always on the best of terms.

Sid wiped the sweat from his neck, the residue of his travel home.

Rosalie fussed. "*Oy,* Sid, you're all sweaty. If you're not careful, you'll come down with pneumonia."

"Or maybe cholera," said Sid. Sam returned to his newspaper and suppressed a laugh. The newspaper rustled, and Sam's leg swung as he rocked with mirth.

"I heard that, Sid! Stop talking with your father and sit down to eat already! Your dinner's getting cold! I don't spend all day in the kitchen just to see good food go cold and get thrown away."

Rosalie, born Rozalia forty-two years previous, ruled the home and brooked no opposition from anyone, especially not her husband or eldest son. On her menu this evening, a piece of boiled chicken breast and a small baked potato combined with steamed carrot slices. Though not a feast for the palate, Rosalie's kitchen provided a balanced meal and enough energy to keep Sid going. No one starved in the Peskin household.

Sid carved up the poultry, wolfed down the carrots, but declined the potato.

"What am I supposed to do with it now?" asked his mother. "C'mon, Sid. Be a good boy and eat it up. Make your *mammaleh* happy."

"Thanks, Mom, but I still think I'll pass."

"Sidney Allan Peskin. This is good, solid food. You should be more appreciative. There are children starving in Africa. You should be ashamed, turning down a good potato like that!"

"C'mon, Ma, we go through this at least once a week. I'm twenty-two years old, and those children have been starving for years. And before that, they were starving in Russia. So, how'd those children get from Africa to Russia if they were so hungry? Huh? Stop trying to make me feel guilty 'cause I don't want to eat a goddamn potato."

Sam put down his paper. "Is that what you learned in college, how to talk back to your mother and not feel guilty?"

"Yes. That and a whole lot more."

"Such as? Tell me what you learned. Better yet, tell me one thing you learned today. Just one thing."

Sid understood the game his father was playing with him. It was his old man's way of communicating.

"Nuclear fission."

"Oh? What's that?" asked Sam.

"I don't think you'd understand, Dad."

It was true Sam Peskin had only a high school education—at Washington Irving High in Manhattan, Class of 1914, to be precise—but he had a healthy respect for his own intelligence and disliked his son's occasional intellectual snobbery. "Try me," Sam replied. "You're a college man. Educated, right? Maybe a teacher yourself someday. So, go on—explain it to me, in a way I can understand."

Sid described the Hahn-Strassman experiments to his father, leaving out the details and omitting the subsequent confirmatory work by Frisch and Meitner.

"You're right, Sid. For a change. I didn't understand a word of it. And from what you say, this fission business isn't practical and probably never will be."

"Not that I can see."

"Hmm. I don't understand why anyone would work on something not practical. Didn't those two professors have better things to do? Like smoke cigars? Nothing's better than a good Cuban stogie, in my opinion. Can't live a decent life without a good Cuban and a game of pinochle. Which reminds me—when will you be done with this college business and finally get out to work? Things haven't been good in the cutting business in the Garment District for years, and we could use some more income around here. Just in case you haven't noticed, young man."

"No offense intended, Dad, but I didn't study physics to become a cloth cutter in the Garment District."

"No offense taken, son. Just don't underestimate the value of being a cutter. I never lost my job, even in the depths of the Depression back in '33. Okay, never made that much money, either, but somehow, we all survived."

"Yes, Dad, we did." He gazed at his father—the most important man in the world to him—with a mixture of great respect and with the deepest love for all the sacrifices he had made, and for everything he had done and given to him.

"Listen, Dad," Sid whispered. "I have to tell you something." He nodded his head in the direction of the kitchen.

Sam raised his eyebrows; he knew this wasn't for his wife's ears. He rose from his seat and walked into the large bedroom he shared with Rosalie, his son following. They both sat side by side on the single large bed.

"You didn't get one of those Hunter College co-eds pregnant, did you, Sid? 'Cause if you did..."

Sid chuckled. "No, it's nothing like that." He waved his hands and shook his head. "Not that I wouldn't mind..."

"The only thing you should mind is your manners, young man... although," Sam placed one hand against his mouth conspiratorially, "I suppose there's no harm in checking out the merchandise before you buy it. Girls are different now than when your mother and I were courting. Just do us all a favor..."

"And don't let Mom find out! Ugh. I think I'd rather die."

"Good. 'Cause if you do, and she does, you will. Now what's on your mind this evening, Sid?"

He briefed Sam about Leo and about his sense that he'd been tailed leaving City College.

Sam listened in silence. "Son, I can listen all I might. Still, even though I'm your father and all that, I'm not sure how to advise you. Your world isn't my world. I don't understand much about the things you do. But I want you to know I'm always here for you and always will be. I'm going to think about everything you've said. And please keep me informed."

The two shook hands firmly.

"Please don't tell anyone," said Sid. "Not Mom, not Benny, no one."

"Of course not. Your mother would want to go to the police. I think that would be a mistake on her part. We don't know if any organization connected with our mayor, *Herr* Trump, can be trusted. My guess is, none can. And be very careful, son, very careful. I don't have to tell you the world is a dangerous place and becoming more dangerous every day."

"I don't disagree, Pops. Thanks. I'll be careful. Oh, I forgot one thing."

"What's that?"

"Mrs. Farkas from the third floor. You know her, right?"

"That blabbermouth? Who doesn't know the woman, she talks so much."

"Where does she come from?"

"Her? Oh, from some godforsaken little shtetl somewhere in Eastern Europe. For some reason she told me once, though I really didn't wanna know. The name escapes me; it's a dot on the map, but the name of the place is so long, I can't remember it."

"Do you remember the country?"

"I'm not sure anymore. How important is it for you to know?"

"Very."

"Hmm. I'm afraid I can't help you, but maybe your mother can. Although this must be done without raising suspicions, so leave it to me. Hey, Rosalie!"

Rosalie soon appeared in the bedroom door, minus her apron; her chores for the day were finally finished. "No need to yell, Sam. These walls are so thin, what would the neighbors think? I heard you. Mrs. Farkas is a very nice lady. Very quiet, too. She's from Hungary, I think she said. Why?"

"Junior here wants to know. He says it's about something he heard on the train."

"Oh," said Rosalie as she departed, exhausted from a long day. "I don't think that's anything I need to know about."

Sid smirked. "Good work, Dad."

So, Leo was originally from Hungary—though knowing his country of origin did nothing to decrease the mystery surrounding him. To do that required additional research and a visit to Professor Strauss of City College's Department of Physics.

CHAPTER 7

S id had made a to-do list for himself. It consisted of three items: call Joey Falcone, stop in on Professor Strauss in his office, and study for midterm exams.

Joey had given Sid his phone number, but Sid couldn't place the call from home because the charge would show up on Sam Peskin's monthly phone bill. Phone charges were unacceptable to Sam, who considered all but emergency calls to be needless extravagances. Sid never could understand why—a quick phone conversation was more pleasant and time effective than writing and mailing a letter, and then waiting who knew how long for a reply.

So, after Sid accumulated some spare change from tutoring freshmen in basic physics, he dropped a dime on Joey from a phone booth near the City College gate.

"Sid! It's great to hear from you! To what do I owe the honor?"

"This one's a social call, Joey. Just wanted to thank you again for giving me a ride a few weeks ago. And to tell you how much I enjoyed the company, not that I want you to get a swelled head about it."

"Hey, my pleasure, Sid! We should do it again sometime soon."

"Joey, I can't ask you to come from Brooklyn so early in the morning just to—"

"Waddaya talkin' about, Sid? I was in your neighborhood anyway so, y'know, thought I'd swing by."

"And I'm glad you did, Joey. And that Negro kid, what was his name.... I'll bet he's happy, too. Yeah, if it weren't for you, Joey, he could've had his brains beat in. By the way, what did you say to those Bundists that convinced them to scatter? The cowards ran like roaches when a light's been turned on."

"Who me? Ahhh... nothin' much. Didn't have to. Just showed 'em my piece and said I knew how to use it."

"You carry a gun, Joey?"

"It's a tough world out there, Sid. Ya never know."

"Jeez. D'you ever take lessons?"

"Lessons? Nah. My uncle taught me. Good man. Known me since I was born. Yeah, Uncle Vince—now there's a man who understands how to take care of himself."

"So, just for my curiosity—what does Uncle Vince do for a living that he needs to pack heat?"

"Vince? Oh, he owns a candy store in Brownsville, corner of Saratoga and Livonia, smack in the middle of Brooklyn. Neighborhood ain't as good as it used to be. You always gotta be careful these days, says Uncle Vince."

Sid wondered what Joey's excuse was but thought it better not to ask.

"And Sid, I got a surprise for you. You're gonna get to meet Uncle Vince 'cause *Signor* and *Signora* Falcone are invitin' you and your folks over for Christmas Day! A real celebration with lotsa' Sicilian food! We figure you ain't doin' much anyway 'cause you're all Jewish."

"Oh, that's ridiculous, Joey. We're very busy! Every Jewish person I know goes to the movies on Christmas Day and then out to the local Chinese restaurant for dinner. Those are the only places open."

Joey laughed. "Hey, who you kiddin'? Everyone knows the Chinks ain't kosher for Christmas."

Sid chuckled at Joey's jumbled but good-natured statement. "Okay, Joey, I'll give it to you this time—you have a point. Just one question: Do my parents know anything about your party?"

"Not yet. But by the time you arrive home tonight, they will. Don't feel uncomfortable. The Peskins are all jus' like family to the Falcones, even though we live at opposite ends of the city. You just show up ready to have a good time! Capish?"

"I'll be there with my stomach empty and my mouth open. Take care, amico mio. I'm already looking forward to it, though it's still more than three weeks away!"

Sid hung up the phone. The first task on the list was complete. The second was to visit Professor Strauss, whose office sat on the third floor of Shepard Hall, several stories above the subterranean alcoves where he'd met up with Julius and Ethel Rosenberg.

Sid wondered what those two lovebirds were up to now. Would they ever accept that there wasn't going to be a Communist revolution in the good ole' U.S. of A? If Julius and Ethel thought about it, they'd realize that fears of Communists like them drove the naïve and uneducated into the arms of fascists, like Lyin' Lindbergh and his Wall Street and business cronies.

He climbed the stairs of Shepard Hall until he stood outside Professor Strauss' office. The door was closed. He knocked three times, but no one responded, which

Sid found odd. Strauss should have been there that time of day, just before mid-terms. But a nasty winter cold had been going around. Maybe Strauss caught it and decided to take the day off.

Sid returned to Strauss' office on Friday, but the results were the same. The office door was closed, and no one responded when he knocked. So, he decided to check in with Frieda, the departmental secretary, who sat in a small room two doors away.

"Hello, pretty boy," said Frieda, looking Sid up and down. Frieda was in her early thirties, blonde, intelligent, and well spoken, and loved flirting with the junior and senior college men. Her only problem was that she was five feet two and weighed over two hundred pounds. But the young men loved her for making the effort.

"Good morning, gorgeous," said Sid.

"It would be a better morning if you'd ask me out for the evening."

"I'd love to, sweetie. But you know I never date older women."

"Why, sugar? Too much for you to handle? Listen, handsome, you're at your peak, and I'm at mine. So why don't we just... peak together?"

Sid laughed. "Aw, Frieda, think of my reputation. Besides, you're far too much woman for me. No hard feelings, I hope."

"Never, my love. I've more than I can handle anyway. As always, it's your loss. Now, what else can I do for you today, darlin'? Hmm?"

"Not much. Looking for Professor Strauss. Well, I've been looking for the past three days. Seen him at all?"

"Can't say I have, kid Sid. Let's see if he's supposed to be on vacation this week." She fumbled through some papers on her desk. "No, he should be around. Hmm... I wonder where he is?"

Frieda arose from her desk, waddled out the door of her office and down the hall to Strauss' door. Sid followed. After several knocks failed to produce a response, she removed a key from inside a pocket in her dress.

"Always helps to have the master," she said, as she turned the doorknob and pushed open the heavy wooden door.

The inside of the office was darkened, as all the shades had been pulled down over the windows. A thin layer of dust covered the desk and everything on it, including a desiccated salami sandwich on toasted rye. Someone, presumably Professor Strauss, had taken a hefty bite out of it.

"From the look of that sandwich," said Frieda, "I'd say it's been sitting there for at least a week."

"Looks like Strauss departed in a hurry and then never came back for the rest of it. Y'know, I hope he's okay. He's no youngster."

"Yes, he's not married and doesn't have any children. If anything happened to him, we could be the first to know."

"Do you have a home phone number? He might appreciate a phone call. Maybe he's laid up with the flu or something and needs me to buy aspirin and cook him chicken soup."

The two returned to Frieda's small office.

"Here you go," she said, removing a small card from a file on the desk. "Wadsworth 7-0503."

"Wadsworth. I know that phone exchange. In Washington Heights, isn't it?"

"664 W. 161 St., Apt. 2A—though I'm not supposed to be giving out that information to students. Not far from where the Broadway-local meets the A train, a few minutes uptown from here. But before you go gallivanting, why don't you give him a call?"

"May I?"

Frieda picked up the receiver and dialed the operator.

"WA7-0503, please."

Sid could hear the ring tone at the other end of the line. Strauss didn't pick up.

"I'll try again later," he said. "But if I can't get an answer, I'll pay the professor a visit at his apartment. Christ, what's the worst that could've happened?"

Four days later, after having received no response to his repeated phone calls, Sid took the short subway ride from CCNY to Washington Heights to attempt to locate Strauss.

It was one of those rare, cloudless, blue sky days in which a cool breeze off the ocean had blown away the blanket of chemicals and dirt that hovered in the air above the city.

Sid exited the Broadway-local subway at the corner of 168th Street and Broadway, less than one block east of the Columbia-Presbyterian Medical Center. The hospital was one of the finest in the city, though it refused to grant staff privileges or to train doctors of Jewish descent. However, Jews were allowed to be sick at Presbyterian. It would have been difficult to refuse admission to the mostly middle-class people who lived in the hospital's immediate neighborhood.

Sid walked along Broadway until he came to W. 165th Street. A right turn down a short hill took him to Ft. Washington Avenue. From there, it was four short blocks of five story up-scale apartment buildings till he reached W. 161st Street.

664 West, Strauss' address, was in the middle of the block, toward fashionable Riverside Drive.

He enjoyed the walk. The weather was chilly, but not nearly as cold as it had been the past several days, and his coat, scarf, gloves, and cap kept him warm. He was also happy for the opportunity to exercise. It was a welcome change from sitting in a chair most of the day either listening to lectures or studying for exams.

When he arrived at the front door of 664 West, he found a stout old *babushka,* her much thinner daughter, and, sitting in her stroller, an adorable little girl about twelve months of age. The mother was maneuvering the stroller and baby through the door while the grandmother held it open, allowing Sid to slither through and onto the mosaic tiles of the first floor. Several yards in front, just to the left of a full-length floor-to-ceiling mirror, was the elevator.

Sid pushed a bronze button on the right side of the elevator door. With a rattle of machinery and a clattering clang, the cab descended. Sid pulled open the outer elevator door and entered it.

Apartment 2A wasn't hard to find as it was only two steps to the left of the elevator, around a corner. Sid pounded on Strauss' apartment door but failed to either hear Strauss' voice, or his footsteps coming to discover who was creating the racket. After waiting several minutes, he lost patience, and in a final attempt, gave the door-knob a quick turn. To his astonishment, the door opened in front of him.

"Professor Strauss!" he called out as he entered the darkened apartment. Like in his office in Shepard Hall, the window shades had all been pulled down, and the dark brown curtains drawn.

"Professor Strauss, I'm sorry for disturbing you..." he continued as he passed by the kitchen that contained a small dining table, and into a tidy parlor. But even in the gloom, Sid could see the pillows of the beige couch and matching chair were threadbare. At the other end of the living room was a door opening on a long hall that led to the bathroom and two large bedrooms.

"I'm sorry for disturbing you, but the door was unlocked, and we were worried something had happened. I mean, Frieda and me—I'm Sid Peskin—we were wondering where you've been and wanted to be sure you were all right."

But what Sid found when he entered the nearest bedroom, which also served as the Professor's study, was that the man was far from all right. I. Bernard Strauss was far beyond anyone's concerns. He lay sprawling in the swivel chair at his desk, a hole directly in the middle of his forehead. Sid reached out and touched his arm. He was stone cold dead.

"Oh my God," he blurted out, suppressing his urge to panic. Sid flung open the curtains, raised the blinds and looked around the room for Strauss' phone to call the police and a doctor.

Where the hell could it be? Shit! Why didn't this man keep his phone in his study like most normal folks? he thought, the instant before he decided to retrace his path through the apartment and check the living room. Bolting down the long hall that connected it with the death room, Sid stopped dead in his tracks by the person he saw sitting on the threadbare chair. The occupant of that chair had one leg crossed over the other in an attitude of nonchalance.

Sid's throat tightened with such fear, he could barely say the man's name.

"Julius Rosenberg," he croaked. "You... you...." Would Rosenberg now shoot him, too, so no one could finger him for Strauss' murder?

Rosenberg smiled. Sid recognized the insincere civility of the professional Communist behind the bottle-brush mustache.

"No, Sid." His voice was measured. "I know what you're thinking. But I didn't kill Strauss. Relax. I can see from here you're sweating from every pore in your body."

"I don't believe you. Stalinists—people like you—would murder their own mothers for the good of the cause."

Rosenburg's expression darkened. "I wouldn't believe all that bourgeois propaganda. Where did you get that tripe from? The Hearst newspapers? Run by a disturbed old lecher who creates fantasy castles in California? Listen! I was about half a block behind you. I saw the old grandmother and her offspring who graciously held the door open. I waited until someone else entered the building before I could sneak in. When I got up here, the door was ajar, and I heard you yelling for Strauss. So maybe it was you that walked in and killed him, huh?"

"That's ridiculous! I don't even have a weapon."

Sid needn't have been concerned. By the smell of death in the apartment, especially in Strauss' office, it was likely the man was murdered several days previously. "What are you doing here anyway, Rosenberg? You graduated with the class of '39."

"The professor and I go back a few years. We had several things to discuss today. Like you, I was having trouble contacting him and became concerned. Nothing wrong with that, is there? No Communist plot to overthrow society here, Sid."

Finding Rosenberg in the murdered man's apartment at the same time he was there disturbed Sid. But there was no use asking him more questions. "Okay, Julius. Have it your way. But right now, we have one dead Professor Strauss in the next room and no way of getting in touch with the authorities."

"Oh yes, we do. I'm sitting on it." He reached around behind his back, withdrew Strauss' phone, and laid it on the carpet. "Let's start making calls."

The next day, an article appeared above the crease in the *New York Times*:

CITY COLLEGE PROFESSOR SHOT DEAD AT HOME
POLICE SEEK COLD-BLOODED KILLER

By Anders Rode Hansen

I. Bernard Strauss, 65, Professor of Physics at City College, was shot to death at home and discovered by two of his own students. "We were worried because we hadn't seen him in some time," said Julius Rosenberg of Rivington St., on the Lower East Side of Manhattan, who graduated in '39.

"By coincidence, both Julius and I went to his apartment to see if he was ill. Instead, we found him dead," said Sidney Peskin of the Bronx, a current City College physics student.

Accolades for Dr. Strauss poured in from both the national and international physics community.

"It's a terrible day for physics and for humanity. Bernie Strauss was a first-rate scientist, a close collaborator, and a good personal friend," stated Professor J. Robert Oppenheimer of the University of California, Berkeley.

The august physicist Albert Einstein also provided his esteemed opinion of Strauss: "In these troubled times, he was a man who could always be counted on—a person of the deepest integrity, a man of great charm. I will miss him."

The president of City College, summing up, praised Strauss as a "teacher, friend, and role model, a man who believed in America and was a staunch anti-Communist. Professor Strauss always represented the best of our faculty and of our school. It is with a sense of great sadness that we say goodbye to him."

The authorities are looking for anyone with information related to this case and assure anyone who comes forward of confidential treatment.

Please contact Officer P. Reilly at the 33rd Police Precinct, 2700 Amsterdam Avenue, Manhattan.

Strauss, who taught physics to generations of young men, never married and leaves no immediate family. Funeral arrangements will be announced later.

There was another article in the *New York Times* that day. But Sid Peskin didn't see it as it was carried on page twenty-four. Who in their right mind would read page twenty-four articles?

PHYSICIST DISAPPEARS FROM TRAIN

By N. Annabel Lewis

Enrico Fermi, the prominent Italian physicist and expatriate who fled Mussolini, is missing. Fermi, 53, and his wife, were last seen boarding the Transcontinental Express train in Chicago after stopping off in the Windy City to consult with colleagues at the University of Chicago. Fermi, however, never arrived at his destination, the University of California at Berkeley.

Fermi was educated in Europe, and after immigrating to the U.S. with his wife, took a position at Columbia University in New York.

The FBI is investigating, and a spokesman said, "We are examining this matter and are eager to discover the whereabouts of Professor Fermi. We also want to assure the public there is no indication of foul play and that the Union Pacific Railroad has been fully cooperating with our efforts."

Perhaps Sid should have read page twenty-four of the *New York Times* that day. His life might have been much different if he had done so. But who knows?

CHAPTER 8

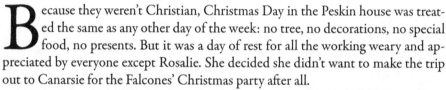

Because they weren't Christian, Christmas Day in the Peskin house was treated the same as any other day of the week: no tree, no decorations, no special food, no presents. But it was a day of rest for all the working weary and appreciated by everyone except Rosalie. She decided she didn't want to make the trip out to Canarsie for the Falcones' Christmas party after all.

"It's such a *schlep* to go out there," she complained when Sam woke her at 8:30 in the morning. "It'll take us two hours to get there on the train—and that's if it's running on time, since there's a holiday, an' all—and two hours to get back, Samele. And I just wanna sleep."

Sam bounced out of the bed. "Sorry, my queen, but we have to go, so let's get a move on. The Falcones are our good friends, and you wouldn't want to disappoint them! Look at it this way—you'll have the chance to be with me the entire day. Just don't bring them any of your *cholent*. One look at that brown goulash..."

Rosalie hit him over the head with her pillow. "Sammy! It's Wednesday today! What kind of a fool cooks *cholent* on a Wednesday! It's eaten only on *Shabbos*! *Shabbos*, Sammy! This is Christmas. Even the non-Jews don't eat *cholent* on a Wednesday! Didn't they teach you anything in Hebrew school when you were a boy?"

Sam knew the best way to get Rosalie up and active in the morning—criticize her cooking or anyone in her family, especially her mother.

Three quarters of an hour later, Sam, Rosalie, Sid, and Benny—the whole family—rode a nearly deserted express D train, picked up on the Grand Concourse in the Bronx. South, they went, to 14th Street in Manhattan, where they transferred to the LL line for the trip to its last stop—Canarsie, in farthest Brooklyn.

"Gee," said Benny as they arrived in Canarsie and departed the train. "Looks like the Bronx."

"That's because our neighborhood and this one were built at the same time, about fifteen years ago," Sid responded.

Benny tugged on Rosalie's sleeve. "Ma, are we almost there?"

"A few more blocks, Benjamin my boy. Why? Are you tired already? You've only walked three blocks," said Sam.

"I'm not tired. I just gotta pee. Real bad, too."

"The kid's ten years old, and already he has problems with his prostate," said Sam to Rosalie in Yiddish.

"I forgot to tell the boy to go to the bathroom before we left. Everything was such a rush! I was all mixed up this morning!" Rosalie replied in Yiddish to Sam.

"What does that mean?" asked Benny, who looked very uncomfortable.

"It means you have to hold it in, you little pisher."

"Be nice, Sam. Benny, keep your head up and try not to think about it. We're almost there."

The Peskins made a left turn onto Greene St.

"Over there," said Sid, pointing to number Twenty Five. "I can see the house number."

The dwelling of *Signor* and *Signora* Falcone was a two-family, two-story attached red and brown brick home typical of the area—very narrow but exceptionally deep. The family climbed the front steps and Sam knocked at the door, which quickly opened.

"Greetings! Welcome, Sam and Rosalie! Is-a cold outside! Please, come into my home," said Guido Falcone with a southern Italian inflection and the endearing tendency of speakers of the language to insert the ghost of a vowel at the end of many words.

"Mom! I gotta go!"

"Guido, I'm sorry," said Rosalie. "Benny's got a little problem. Is there a bathroom he could use?"

"Eh! No problem! No problem. *Bambino*, run upstairs and use the one there, caro mio. I just-a saw Joey go into the bathroom on-a 'dis floor."

Benny took off like lightning up a nearby staircase.

"Thanks," said Sam as he, followed by Sid, shook hands with Guido. The reunion called for a round of embraces, but Guido had learned that most Eastern European Jews refrained from such encounters, especially when between the sexes. Instead, he turned his head and shouted for his wife.

"Eh! Sil-vi-a! Come out of the kitchen and-a greet our-a guests!"

A very busy Silvia Falcone, a short woman of forty-five with black hair tied up into a ponytail which was then flipped and pinned to the back of her head, emerged from the rear of the house and into a great hug with Rosalie.

"Ah, it's so nice to see you again, my dear! I wish we never had to move away. But Guido must make a living. You know how it is," she sighed. "Sam, it's nice to see you again. And you, too, Sid."

Sam and Sid shook hands warmly with Silvia.

"Likewise, Silvia," said Sam. "It's been too long."

"Please. Let me take your coats. Freshen up and take whatever you like to eat and drink. I know you've had a long trip, all the way from the Bronx. And then allow me to introduce you to *la mia famiglia*. They all want to meet you!"

Sid left his parents talking to the Falcones and ventured into the house. Opposite the stairway was the living room, where Silvia had laid out an inviting spread. It was located just to the right of a decorated, illuminated Christmas tree spanning floor to ceiling. He recognized several of the culinary delights from previous dinners at the Falcones', but most of the Sicilian splendor that lay in front of him was unfamiliar.

A young woman's pleasant voice came from behind. "Any idea what you're looking at?"

"Oh," said Sid. "I've eaten your mother's delicious *saddi a beccafico* and *pasta 'ncaciata* before, and that's a fruit cake over there behind the *magnuli*. But as for the rest of it... oh, my... I'm sorry. You must be Julia! Joey's twin sister! We haven't seen each other in years! It's nice to see you again!"

It was nice for anyone, especially young men, to see Julia Falcone. Sid remembered her as a scrawny teenager, but during the intervening years, she had filled out spectacularly. Julia was taller than her mother and had long, jet-black hair, but had left two long locks at either side of her head, framing her face like parentheses. And what a dazzling face it was! Olive-complexioned with large, glorious eyes in the shape of almonds, thin lips hiding a set of perfect white teeth, a square, resolute jaw with exquisite definition at the angle of the mandible, her smile was utterly bewitching. And in addition to her feminine facial beauty, flawed only by a nose slightly too long to fit her face, was a lady with the shape of an hourglass undisguised by the dowdy green frock she wore. In the context of her face and form, the nose paled into insignificance.

"You're Sid, aren't you? Joey's friend."

"Yes. I'm glad you remember me."

"Ah," said Joey Falcone in person, having emerged from the ground-floor bathroom. "Hey! I was gonna introduce you two, but I see you've already met!"

"We have, Joey, my friend," said Sid, as his focus snapped back to Julia, *la bella donna*.

"Julia, what are you doing these days?" He wondered when that little girl had become such a sight. She must have men at her feet and at least half a dozen boyfriends.

"Oh, I'm finishing Hunter College with a degree in science education. I suppose I'll soon be out, looking for a job like everyone else," she sighed, resigned to the low likelihood she'd land one anytime soon.

"Interesting. I'll be graduating City College next spring in physics. I hope I get the chance to—"

Guido, who'd now brought with him his brother Favio, Favio's wife, and their clan of seven children, ranging in age from fifteen to four, interrupted their conversation. The smallest, a girl with a blue ribbon in her hair, hid behind her mother's skirts. One by one, Sid greeted them all while Joey and Julia watched.

Joey said, "Sid, before you go 'n stuff your face like a pig, there's someone else I'd like you to meet."

"Sure Joey, anyone. You have a beautiful family. And I don't just mean your sister."

Sid followed him to the very back of the house, into the kitchen. Sitting at a table was a tall, striking-looking brown-haired man. He appeared about fifty years of age, and had a high forehead, heavy lids, and lips that Sid thought could be described as cruel. As he and Joey approached, the man bit off the end of a cigar, lit it, and took a slow drag.

"Sid," said Joey, "I want you to meet my Uncle Vince, our *padre della famiglia*. Uncle Vince, Sid Peskin."

Uncle Vince took a few puffs on his cigar and looked Sid up and down. "So. Sid Peskin. Well, well. Nice t' meet ya, kid." He offered Sid his hand to shake. "Hoid a lot about ya. Nice t' finally see you in-a da flesh, so t' speak. Why don' you siddown, so we can have a talk? Please."

The please was not an invitation. It was a command. Vince Mangano exuded an aura of authority and seniority. Sid sat at the table in one of the empty chairs. Joey sat beside him.

Vince puffed on his cigar silently. He flicked the ashes into a nearby glass tray. "Joey tells me you study physics. Is what my nephew says correct, Sid?"

"Yes, sir. I'll be graduating from City College with a master's degree in physics in eighteen months."

"Good. Dat's nice. Very nice. Now let me ask ya another question. If you don't mind."

"I don't mind at all, sir." Padre Vince was endearing, in an old Italian gentleman fashion.

"So, you good at what you do? I mean, yer studies?"

The question surprised Sid, but he warmed to the older man's interest in him. Hardly anyone liked to talk physics.

"Yes, sir, I think so. I've done very well in physics. It's my favorite subject."

"Eh, Vincenzo," said Silvia, who'd migrated back to the kitchen. "How many times I gotta tell you—*non fumare!* And that's-a no smokin' in *la mia cucina!* You want all-a my food to stink-a like your cigar? Eh?"

"Scusi la mia sorella, signor," said Vince, rising from his chair. "C'mon, boys, lets the t'ree of us take a walk."

"Now, don't go far," Silvia yelled after them. "All the food will get-a cold!"

Joey and Sid followed Uncle Vince out of the house without their overcoats on this cold December day, heading into a detached garage at the side of the structure. Joey pulled up the garage door. They walked into a room that had been redone into an office space, with a desk, chairs, several lamps, and a good heater, which Joey turned on after he'd pulled down the door from the inside. The heating element soon glowed orange-red.

"So, kid. Tell me. Did you know 'dat *professore* who took da bullet? I t'ink his name was Strauss. Right?"

"Yes, I did. A terrible tragedy."

"I agree. A very unfortunate event. *Un disastro!* Ah, *la vita!* Life can-a be so fragile, eh? Well, too bad for 'im," said Vince, flashing a quick glance at Joey. "I mean, all-a da t'ings that go on in dis woild today!" He shook his head and extinguished his cigar in a bronze bowl that sat precariously on the edge of a small end table.

"Who can believe it? Not too long ago, 'dis was a great country for honest, hardworkin' folks. Now, sometimes I'm ashamed to be an American. Say, waddaya t'ink of dis Lindbergh guy that calls himself da president?"

"Frankly, sir, not much. And I disagree with pretty much everything he says and does. The man never should have been elected. I don't think he and his gang, including our mayor, Mr. Trump, are too fond of Catholics, either. But there are far more of you than there are of us Jews. So, you're tolerated, while we... we're defamed. Or worse."

"So, you're saying that other than dat, you're happy with Lindbergh in the White House," teased Joey.

Uncle Vince pulled another cigar out of his shirt pocket, bit the end off, and stuck it into the inferno of the heating element. In seconds, it also glowed orange-red, and Vince inhaled the calming smoke.

"Then let me tell ya da way my colleagues and me feel, kid." Vince reddened with frustration. "Lindbergh! *E' un figghiu de buttana!* And Trump... *e' un suo burattino.* Capish? Eh?

"He said Lindbergh is a son of a whore, and Trump is his puppet," whispered Joey.

"Couldn't have said it better myself," Sid said. "I can't even get myself to pronounce the words 'president' and 'Lindbergh' together in the same sentence. And after this nightmare is over, which I hope to God it will be in a few years, I never want to waste another thought on that man!"

"So, tell us how you really think!" laughed Joey. "Nah, I'm jus' yankin' your chain, Sid. Like you just heard, my family feels the same way. Even more strongly than you do."

"Impossible."

"Your friend here, he has da right ideas. Ya know, kid, I'm glad you came here today. Joey, I t'ink you have a good friend here. A man wid loyalty, a man wid *honore*. A real man, eh? Like-a da men used to be everywhere in dis country. Loyalty, honor, family! Ah! Where has it all gone? I ask you—where?"

"I don't know," said Joey, "but I think we'd better get back to our guests. You know how Silvia can be."

"Eh! *Mia sorella e ' pazza.*"

"He thinks his sister is crazy," whispered Joey.

Sid smiled. "A *Yiddishe mama* or *la mamma Italiana;* they're one and the same. But we sure love 'em anyway."

"Yer friend," said Uncle Vince. "He has da right idea. He's a good man! Now— we eat like Italians eat, eh!"

Five hours later, when most of the food was consumed, the satiated party-goers thanked the host and hostess for a wonderful time and prepared to depart. Benny, who'd amused himself with a new friend—a son of Favio's who was also about ten— was warned by Rosalie to make use of the bathroom. Or else.

Sid wanted to continue chatting with Julia.

"You've seen the outside," Joey had said as they returned to the house from the garage. "The packaging is beautiful... So, now try her brains."

Sid was even more enthralled than when they had first met. Julia was witty and intelligent, and seemed effortlessly confident without any of the irritating arrogance of so many other intelligent people he'd met. And what impressed Sid the most was the range and openness of her mind.

"I may be a science teacher someday, but I also have other interests in life. Even when I was a child, I was never satisfied with doing one thing at a time. I couldn't read just one book... I had to read two. Silly, I suppose, but I'm still much the same today."

"You read two books at once?" said Sid. He prompted himself to keep his eyes focused on her face and on nowhere else of her anatomy. It wasn't easy. "That's remarkable. How did you keep the words straight in your head?"

"Ha, now you're teasing, Mr. Peskin. That's not a nice thing to do to a girl. No, I gave up that trick once the books gave up their pictures. I'm a one-book girl now.

What I meant is there is so much I love to read about, not only science. There's art, and history, and there's music..."

"What's your favorite book?"

Julia blushed. "Oh, if you really want to know, I'll tell you. Though you may not think it suitable reading material for a woman."

"I'm not sure why what is suitable for a man to read would be unsuitable for a woman. My mother is a voracious reader. My father seems to be satisfied with the daily newspapers."

"I'm glad to hear you say that, Sid. I mean about women's intellectual abilities. In my family, your attitude wouldn't be popular, even among the women. The Falcones are very... ah, old world, traditional. Kitchen, children, church, and that's about it. It may be fine for other girls. But not for me. I want one of everything else... and two of whatever's left over!" She smiled wistfully, as if having what she truly wanted would be deeply forbidden.

Rosalie approached Sid, indicating the party was over. It was time to leave before the hosts threw them out.

"Julia, it was nice seeing you again. I had a wonderful time chatting this afternoon. You'll have to tell me about your favorite book at another time. And what movies you like. Do you get into the city much?"

"As often as I can. I love the museums and the restaurants."

"I hope we can visit them together sometime soon."

"I'd like that Sid," she said softly. "Please call me."

"Oh, I will, Julia. I promise. And soon."

"Okay, you two, time to break it up," interrupted Rosalie. Whatever other traits Sid's mother possessed, subtle sensitivity didn't rank among them.

"Julia, nice to see you again," Rosalie said. "But we have a long trip home."

"Good to see you, too." She departed for the kitchen to help her mother with the cleanup.

"Sid, do you have to use the bathroom? Make sure you go..."

He rolled his eyes with exasperation. "For Chrissakes, Mom! I'm almost twenty-three years old! Does it ever stop?"

Rosalie thought for a second and shook her head. "Young man, I'll be your mother till the day I die. So the answer is—no! It will always be the same." She beamed with a smile that threatened to swallow up her face. Every family, it seems, can be traditional in its own way.

The Peskins crowded into Joey's car for the short ride to the LL train. Today, Joey drove a late model Buick. No one breathed a word about the '33 DeSoto.

"Thanks for the ride, Joey," Sid said. After meeting Julia, he felt he must be the luckiest man in the world.

"No problem. Glad you could come out. Looks like you and my sister hit it off. Jus' remember. Lookin' is fine. Talkin' is fine. Touchin'," he waved his index finger back and forth, "is-a not so fine." He emphasized the Italian lilt, a reminder of all the men who'd come after Sid if his hands wandered.

"Eh! *Capisco.* I don't want to get on the wrong side of Uncle Vince."

"That's wise of you, Sid. Very wise. He likes you, ya know. But if anyone he doesn't approve of lays a finger on his niece, well..."

"Well, too bad for him, right?"

"Ri-i-ight," Joey answered.

Joey pulled the sedan up to the train station, one of the few at street grade in the entire NYC subway system. The Peskins said their goodbyes, paid five cents a head for the fare, and boarded a train about to depart for Manhattan. They were home in ninety minutes. Rosalie had little to *kvetch* about.

His head swimming with thoughts of the lovely Julia, Sid took in a magazine article to distract his thoughts. He lay in bed reading a James Thurber story in the latest *New Yorker* while daydreaming about Julia when Benny caught up with him.

"Hey, kid, what's up?" Sid said, tousling his brother's hair to Benny's great annoyance. "Isn't it past your bedtime?"

"No, not for a while yet, Sid. And don't mess with my hair! Gee, I saw you and that lady Julia making eyes at each other all day. I think she's sweet on you. She gonna be your girlfriend?"

"That, little man, is none of your little business. If she does, I promise you'll be the last to know."

"You better be careful there, big brother. That guy, Uncle Vince? He's creepy. And he was talking about you with some other creepy guy before you even came in. Not about Mom or Dad—only about you."

Sid swung his body so he was sitting on the bed. "Seriously, Benny? He was talking about me? Who was he talking to?"

"I don't know. Just some other weird looking guy I didn't see again. Funny thing was... that guy looked just like Uncle Vince."

"So, how come you overheard them, Benny?"

"Remember when we got there, and I had ta pee?"

"Yeah, Benny, I remember."

"Mr. Falcone sent me upstairs. I could hear those guys in the bedroom, but they couldn't see me. So, I went into the bathroom but left the door open a crack. I heard most of what they were saying."

"What did they talk about, Benny?"

"I couldn't understand everything. Most of it was in their language."

"Well, their language is a dialect of Italian!"

"I know that, Mr. Smartypants. So, I didn't get those parts. But sometimes, they spoke English, and that's when your name was mentioned. A lot. I also heard 'City College,' and 'Strauss,' and someone named 'Leo' and how he almost messed up the job. And, oh, the guy who looked like Uncle Vince—he told Uncle Vince to look you over real good, 'but be careful 'cause we don't know who he really is.' I heard him say it clear as a bell, so help me, Sid. Then I peed and got outta there."

Sid placed a hand on each of Benny's shoulders and looked into his eyes. "Benny, you're tellin' me the truth, now? You're not makin' up a story, like you do sometimes?"

"Honest, Sid, I'm not making up a story. That's what I heard."

"Do you swear it, Benny?"

"Oh, I swear it. I swear it."

"Double-dog swear it, triple-elephant swear it on your mother's honor."

"I double-dog and triple-elephant swear it on Mom's honor."

"Pinkie swear it?" The pinkie swear was the ultimate test of a man's fidelity.

"You bet, Sid. Put it there!" The two wrapped their pinkie fingers together to seal the solemn pledge.

"Benny, you've taken some mighty solemn oaths. Do you know what will happen if anything you have said is later found to be untrue?"

Benny trembled. The penalties for breaking the pinkie swear were unspeakable. "Sid, what's going on? I mean, those people give me the willies."

"Hey, me too, little man. Me, too. Let's sleep on it, you and me, like men. Things will be clearer in the morning. And Benny, remember. Don't breathe a word to anyone. Not to Mom, not to Dad. No one. Not one word. That's all part of the pinkie swear."

Benny gulped. "I promise, Sid. No one."

"Good. I know I can trust you." He saw Benny tremble as he ruffled his hair once more. But he didn't even try to stop him.

"You can trust me, Sid," said Benny, almost in a whisper. But who else, if anyone, Sid could trust was now an uncertain question.

On the same day that the Peskin family took their trip to Canarsie and Sid met the radiant Julia and the inglorious Uncle Vince, Ethel Rosenberg—born Greenglass—paced back and forth in the tiny apartment she shared with her husband, Julius, on Rivington Street on the Lower East Side of Manhattan. Ethel paced when she was worried. Today, she paced a lot.

"Your friend, Strauss, was a fool, Julius." She flung the angry words at her husband, implying he was no better. "You never should have trusted him."

Julius sat on the old, rickety wooden chair at a small, square kitchen table, his expression calm. The apartment housed a spartan kitchen and a bedroom just large enough to hold a double bed. A single toilet in the hallway sufficed for the needs of eight families. When that sole, critical porcelain vessel was stopped up, which was often, the calamity was unimaginable.

"You're overreacting, Ethel. As usual. No one knows what my business was with Strauss. Not a soul."

"What about that Peskin boy, Julius? The one who found the body. He'll never believe it was a coincidence you showed up on the same day he did."

"That's not what he told the cops, dear. We said we arrived together in the apartment. Who's to say anything different? There was no one else on the second floor who saw us. Frieda, the physics department secretary, corroborated Peskin's story. Others know Strauss and I were on the best of terms, that he was a mentor and an old friend. What motivation did I have for killing him? None. Not that I know who murdered him.. What I know is that I didn't."

Ethel slowed her pacing. "Yes, you've said that many times, Julius. But it relieves me every time I hear it. Oh, I'm so concerned about what's going to happen. I mean, with this goddamned administration. The latest I heard, through Earl Browder, the Party Secretary, is that Lindbergh has suborned J. Edgar Hoover, who is now reporting directly to the president and no longer to the attorney general. And our Congress lets Lindbergh get away with it! He's made no secret of what he'd like to do to us Communists, and of how the Constitution is no barrier to his ambitions. Browder feels it's only a matter of time before Lindbergh lets loose the Bundists. And when he does, you know Mayor Trump will instruct the local police to stand aside."

"As they did on *Kristallnacht* two years ago in Germany," said Julius. "Only in New York City, there's a great deal more glass to break."

"And after us Communists, it will be the Jews' turn. And then the blacks. And then whoever doesn't measure up to the new racial standards. New York will be a white man's paradise again."

"The irony, my dear, is that it never was."

"Tell that to the Bundists. Or to Trump. They don't read history books. It's... it's... disgusting."

"America has become a fascist state. But for us Communists, Ethel, there is no choice. Even if they come for us like the German rightists did for Comrades Rosa Luxemburg and Karl Liebknecht, whom they shot down like dogs back in '19, we must stay and resist and maintain our party discipline! We've buried down very deep, and our cadres are fanatically loyal to the cause. They'll never be intimidated by Lindbergh or Trump, or their myrmidons!"

"The Party of Lenin and Stalin, of Marx and Engels, will protect us. The shining star that points the way to the Communist future, when everyone will be equal, and where unearned capital will no longer exist! Oh, I long for the day when the U.S., rejecting fascism, embraces the Soviet Union as its model. It's a glorious thought, Julius. Ah, if I had to die for the cause to realize that vision, I'd be honored to do it."

"Your vision is the one that I live for, too, Ethel, every day of my life. And that's why we must stay here in New York, keep our heads down, and do everything we can to aid the only remaining democratic state on the planet, a true peoples' republic."

"Long live the Soviet Union!"

"And long live the Leader of its peoples, Comrade Josef Vissarionovich Stalin!"

Special to the New York Times, Sunday, January 26, 1941
[Above the crease.]

RIOT AT TEMPLE EMANUEL: BUNDISTS MARCH ON 5TH AVENUE TO 65TH ST. TWENTY INJURED.

By Wilson F. McPeters

Mayhem erupted Saturday afternoon when German-American Bundists, their *Führer* Fritz Kuhn in command, marched on Temple Emanuel, the epicenter of Reform Judaism in New York City. After the Sabbath service, worshippers were leaving the largest synagogue in the U.S. when they were pelted with rocks, bottles, and rotten food thrown by the Bundist gang. Though some women also joined in, the attackers were mostly young men 18 to 25 years of age, dressed in silver uniforms bearing swastika armbands. During the riot, the attackers chanted, "The Jews are our misfortune" and, "Jews out of America." The cry of "death to the Jews" was also heard. The victims fled back into the sanctuary and barricaded the door. The police arrived on the scene after the rioters had dispersed. The injured were taken to either New York Hospital or Lenox Hill Hospital.

Temple Emanuel, ironically founded by German Jews in 1845, boasts one of the largest and wealthiest congregations in New York City and has become the religious home to numerous Wall Street financiers and newspaper magnates. Tensions between the New York Jewish community and the German-American Bund have run especially high after the recent election of Charles Lindbergh as president.

When asked for comment, Rabbi Nathan Krass said, "Those who try to break our bodies may succeed, but they will never break our spirit. America is as much our country and New York our city as it is theirs. We will not be bullied by street thugs! Our intention now is to seek

```
justice for our members, and the punishment of these miscreants by the
fullest extent of the law. In the meantime, we pray for the recovery
of everyone in hospital, and wish them a refuah shelemah, a speedy
recovery."
```

The Hearst papers buried the story on p. 18. It was noted in Bundist circles that the Jewish Ochs family owned the *New York Times*.

CHAPTER 9

On January 27, 1941, Frederick Trump, Mayor of the City of New York, sat at his capacious desk in City Hall in lower Manhattan. Resting on the top was a bottle of Jack Daniels that Trump hid in a cabinet at the bottom left of his desk. He poured some of the golden-brown liquid into a glass and, with one motion, threw his head back and downed it.

"Ah-h-h…" he said as he looked to his guest, Patrick F.X. O'Sullivan, New York City Police Commissioner, as the hot liquid poured down his throat. "That's a good way to start the morning. So Patrick, ya dumb mick, did ya see the *New York Times* today?"

The commissioner was a Trump appointee who had replaced the tough, incorruptible Louis Valentine, police commissioner under the late Fiorello LaGuardia. O'Sullivan, on the other hand, had a different set of mores.

"I certainly did, m'lad. Now would you mind sharin' some o' the wealth? I think it's about time to collect what's due me."

"As you say." Trump poured out a glass of Jack Daniels for his commissioner.

"Bah, niggers and kikes, niggers and kikes," he whined, as O'Sullivan imbibed the offering. "This city's lousy with 'em. I'll tell you this Paddie—" Trump began to slur his words. "I'll never rent anything to a nigger in any of my buildings. Or to a Hebe, either!" Before becoming mayor, Trump had been a real estate developer in Queens, one of the City's outer boroughs. "But I ain't worried about the niggers 'cause they can't afford my rates. The kikes, on the other hand…"

As he dispensed another fifty cubic centimeters of his trove, an alcoholic buzz settled over his thoughts.

"The kikes, on the other hand, sometimes, I gotta give 'em credit. They know what they want, and they know how to get it. Smart little bastards, too. Like cockroaches.

No matter how many of 'em you squash, they keep coming back. Yep, the kikes know how to win. Not like Fritz Kuhn and his Bundist boys, who I've supported in one way or another for years. Y'see, Paddy, killin's an art. Now, I don't mean walkin' up to someone and whackin' 'im with a bat. I mean—slowly killin' him—real slow like, so he doesn't even know he's bein' killed. That's a true art. And the Hebes, I must admit, are masters of it."

"Now Freddy, don't go soft on me in your old age. It sounds like you got some feelins' for the Chosen People. Those would be seriously misplaced, me boy."

The Jack Daniels flowed first into one glass, and then the other, and then down both gullets at the same time.

"Naah. Hate 'em. Every one of 'em, from their white-bearded rabbis to their newborn baby boys about to get their manhood sliced. And you know why I hate 'em so much?"

"'Cause they're Christ killers?" asked the commissioner, now almost blottoed.

"Naah." Trump waved a hand in the air, his gesture of dismissiveness. "It ain't that. I hate the Hebes because I know that under no circumstances will any of 'em listen to a goddamn thing I have to say." O'Sullivan's woozy brain registered bafflement. Wasn't everyone in this grimy corrupt village obliged to listen to their mayor? Wasn't it his job, too—to obey and protect those in authority? O'Sullivan had early on learned the rules of heirarchy from his father's right hand and his God-given church, and the swift punishment meted out to those who defied it.

"Hey, Fred, we better cut it out before we get well and truly sozzled. Where I'm sittin', it's still only nine o'clock in the mornin'. How 'bout you?"

"Yes, we should. Ya know, Patrick, this job is killin' me. I hate being mayor and livin' up on 91st Street in Gracie Mansion. Me and my wife, Mary—well, we'd be happier back in our home in Queens."

"Well, Freddy boy, no one forced you to take the job. You volunteered for it, I seem to remember."

"No, I didn't! That's the thing—I didn't! That sonuvabitch Lindbergh made me do it! Now he thinks he owns me. An' you know what, Paddy?"

"Oh, I do know what, Freddy. Yer full o' malarkey, that's what I know. Ya always wanted a high-ranking political job. Charlie L. offered, and you jumped like a hurdy-gurdy monkey."

"Yesh, you're right there, Paddy. On my best days, I'm full o' malarkey. But at least I'm honest about it, which is more than I can say for most. Charlie L. has me by the balls an' jus' keeps on squeezin'. His buddy J. Edgar's got the dirt on everyone from here to Canarsie. Not like I dishagree too much with the big man in the White House. I jus' don' like the idea that, if I ever get outta line, one tug on the leash..."

"And you'll be back singin' his tune."

"Yeah, and with a high-pitched voice, too. Makes me look weak, ya know. And I can't stand lookin' weak—like I'm a loser or somethin'. Fred Trump is a winner, Paddy! Fred Trump always hash been and will alwaysh be a winner! Fred Trump built up hish real estate business from nothin', and now he's Mayor of New York! That's winnin'! But not to Charlie L., Paddy, not to Charlie L. He wants me dancin' to hish tune." Trump reached for the Jack Daniels, but this time mustered enough self-control to refrain.

"And by the way, you drunken Irishman, good thinkin' not allowin' your boys to get involved when the Bundists raided Temple Emanuel the other day. Charlie L. will be very pleased."

"Ah, say nothing more, Freddy, say nothin' more. 'Twas the least I could do for the cause. The Hebes have been earnin' their comeuppance in New York for a long time. And I'm delighted to see them finally get it."

"You're a good man, Paddy, even though—like most shantytown Irishmen—you can't hold your liquor. Or your women."

The police commissioner laughed. "Hail Trump, full of self-pity! I believe that for reasons of national pride, I should be very insulted—especially for your comment about us Irish being unable to hold our liquor. But for some reason, I really don't care what you say." Within seconds, the head of the Commissioner of the Police of the City of New York tipped over, and P.F.X. O'Sullivan, mouth wide open, fell into a deep, stertorous sleep.

Fred Trump thought the man was an idiot. But a useful one. Loyal, too. That's why he appointed him. The fool would do anything for a box of old bones and a rubber ball. He wondered how often O'Sullivan got drunk before breakfast. But it was none of Trump's business. He could sleep it off here in the office for the rest of the day, for all Trump cared. As long as he didn't interfere with any Jew ass-kickings by the Bundist boys. Trump almost pitied those damned Hebes. If he didn't dislike them so much!

CHAPTER 10

The White House
January 27, 1941

I'm sorry, sir, but I don't think this will look right. I shouldn't be talking to you about these matters."

The president sat back in his chair. Charles Lindbergh was a master at not revealing his true feelings, but far from being the master of events, as he believed himself to be, events were beginning to master Charles Lindbergh. He could not, for example, grasp the idea that appeasing Hitler did nothing to satiate the dictator's cravings. Neither for power nor for human sacrifice on the altar of his racialist theories. Just the opposite—the more Hitler got what he wanted, the more he craved. And what he wanted from the American president was a pattern of national repression that spiraled in a great un-American crescendo, leaving no one with any doubt who was in control. Nevertheless, Lindbergh still clung to the fatuous hope that just one more gift, one more concession, would transform the Nazi monster into a *gemütlichen* teddy bear.

"I'm telling you, Edgar. For at least the, oh, five hundredth time by now. I know the news from occupied Poland is not good. But Hitler is no threat to us. It's the Russkies he'll be turning on next. You'll see. All the smart money is on the Germans going east. They hate the Bolshies, you know."

"Yes, I'm aware of what our State Department has been saying for many years about Bolshevik, and now Stalinist Russia. How it's not the Germans, but the Slavs, and especially the Russians, the *untermenschen* of the East, who are the big threat to Europe—subhuman hordes who'll flood into Deutschland at the first opportunity to ravish those pure-blood German maidens."

"I've no doubt they're correct, Edgar."

"I agree, sir. There's more than a grain of truth to their views. But Communists, regardless of nationality, are an insidious threat to us not only in Europe, but here in the U.S., too. Their cadres persist in attempting to undermine our government and our way of life. They want it replaced by the 'dictatorship of the proletariat'. That's what they claim, though I think their propaganda masks a lust for personal power. And as far as I'm concerned, there are far too many pinkos and fellow travelers among the well educated pseudo-intellectuals in this country who support them. No coincidence most of those people are Jews."

"None at all. Starting with that print icon of the Communists and others of their ilk, the *New York Times*. You know what to do, Edgar. You've done it before. That's why I admire you and the Bureau—not only for your work, but for your loyalty."

Hoover rose from his chair. "Thank you, Mr. President. You can be assured that we at the Bureau will always have your back."

"No, my thanks to you, Edgar. And, oh, before I forget—why don't we take the leash off Fritz Kuhn and his Bundist lads. Let's ramp up the pressure. Time to cry havoc, and let slip the dogs of war, don't you think? Our financial backers and German friends will be pleased."

"Yes, sir. And—just between the two of us—nothing would give me greater personal pleasure."

The New York Times, Tuesday, January 28, 1941
[Front page, above the crease.]

NEW YORK TIMES FIRE DAMAGES PRESS
DAILY PRINT RUN DELAYED & REDUCED

By Clement P. Hoskins

Early morning January 27, 1941, a fire broke out at the *New York Times* offices and printing presses at 229 W. 43 St., just east of 8th Avenue in Manhattan, destroying an office and severely damaging one of the presses which had to be shut down. This led to a delay in the production of the January 6 issue and curtailed the number of newspapers printed.

"It could have been a great deal worse," said Arthur Hays Sulzberger, the *Times'* publisher, "were it not for the quick thinking of the night staff, who rapidly doused the flames, at no small risk to themselves. Fortunately, the only injuries were some mild instances of smoke inhalation by a few of our courageous firefighters."

An investigation is proceeding, but a forensic team from the City's Fire Department has already determined arson as the most likely cause of the blaze.

"We don't know who committed such a heinous action," said Sulzberger. "But whoever did so attempted to strike a blow against the press freedom guaranteed by the First Amendment to the Constitution. We were caught off-guard last evening. That will never happen again."

On Friday, January 10, in the early evening, Sid Peskin was at home in the West Bronx studying the fundamentals of quantum mechanics. At the same time, Benny struggled with the higher concepts of elementary school arithmetic. Sam, as usual, read the daily newspaper. The *Times* had resumed printing its usual number of copies, ensuring the senior Mr. Peskin his evening's relaxation. Rosalie sat in a chair, concentrating on knitting a sweater for Benny, who had every intention of thanking his mother for the gift, and then stuffing the offending item into a drawer and wearing it as little as possible.

Things were so tranquil in the Peskin household that when the phone rang, everyone jumped as if a mortar shell had struck.

"I'll get it," said Sam, while the entire household perked up their ears to hear whom the call was for. "Oh, yes, he's here. I'll get him. Sid! Phone!"

Sid bolted out of bed, and for the moment forgot about wave functions and energy eigenvalues, the language of a new physics incomprehensible to all but the initiated. "Coming!" he said, wondering who it could be. Rushing to the phone, he picked up the receiver. "Hello?"

"Sid," said a man's voice on the other end of the line. It seemed familiar, though he couldn't place it.

"Who would you like to speak to?"

"Sid. This is Julius. Julius... Rosenberg. I'd like to speak with you. In person."

Rosenberg sounded nervous. Sid covered the receiver with his hand. "Rosenberg," he mouthed to his father, emphasizing the words like a mime artist.

"I wonder why he's calling?" Sam folded his newspaper back into its original shape and placed it on the side table.

Benny appeared from the room he shared with his big brother. "Is it for me?" he asked.

"No! It's for me. Didn't you hear? And isn't it past your bedtime?"

"No, it's not past my bedtime, Mr. Smartypants." Benny stuck his tongue out in Sid's direction.

"Sidney Allan Peskin!" Rosalie roared, placing her knitting in her lap. "Be nice to your brother!"

"Rosenberg!" Sid said into the receiver. "Why are you calling me? For Chrissakes, it's 7:30 in the evening! Can't this wait until sometime tomorrow?"

"Hear me out, Sid. Please."

Sid covered the receiver again. "My Communist acquaintance, Rosenberg. I wouldn't call him a friend, but he wants to have a chat. I'm not inclined to talk with him. What do you think, Dad?"

Sam sighed. "During ordinary times, hardcore Stalinists should be avoided. All that justifying the unjustifiable and toeing the party line makes honest folks into liars and everyone else into robots. But unfortunately, we don't live in ordinary times. So, I'm afraid it's your call."

Sid thought for a moment. "Okay, Rosenberg. I'm listening."

"I'm at a phone booth on the corner of Morris Ave and the Grand Concourse."

"What? You came all the way up here to the Bronx just to talk to me?"

"Yes."

"But how did you know..."

"Let's just say I played a hunch. I know you and your curiosity. I doubted you'd pass this up. So, will you meet with me? I promise I'm alone and unarmed. Just as you found me in Professor Strauss' apartment."

"Because it was such a *schlep*, five minutes, Julius. The lobby of 25 Morris Avenue. I'll let you in. You'd better be alone."

"I'm there in five minutes, Sid. Alone." The receiver clicked dead.

"I'll be back in about a half hour," Sid announced. "I'm meeting Rosenberg downstairs."

"Put on a warm coat," Rosalie admonished him. "The outside door opens and closes so often it gets cold in that lobby."

"I won't be cold, Mom, I promise."

"*Oy*, Sid. No matter what I say, you want to do the opposite. Who raised you? Oh, I know—it must have been your father."

Sid laughed, shut the door behind him, and walked over to the elevator. In a few minutes, he was in the lobby.

Five minutes later, Rosenberg appeared. Sid cracked open the lobby door, allowing just enough room for Rosenberg to slide in.

"Hello, Sid."

"Hello, Julius. If you're here to sell me your peculiar brand of Stalinism, I'm not buyin' it."

"Sid, listen. Hey, you're an intelligent guy. Why do you trust the words of the same capitalist plutocrats that produced monsters like Lindbergh and Trump? Think about it! Come over to the light, Sid, and help us build a new world founded on decency, sharing and equality!"

"Is that why you want to speak with me, Julius? To convert me to your new religion by reciting Soviet propaganda?"

Rosenberg was indignant. "The CPUSA, the Communist Party of the United States of America, is independent of the Soviet Union. We are completely self-funded!"

Sid rolled his eyes. "Somehow, I doubt that, Julius. I don't think there's enough cash in all the Communists of America combined to fund your activities. But I'm not going to argue with you. Tell me what you want." Sid looked at his watch. "I'll give you sixty seconds. Then I'm gone."

Rosenberg thought for a moment. "Okay, Sid. I'll do it your way. This is what we want."

"Who's the we, Julius?"

"The we, Sid, is Earl Browder. You know who he is?"

"Yeah, the Secretary of the CPUSA, the guy who takes his orders from Stalin directly. It's all very hierarchical, like the Catholic Church."

"Something like that, I suppose. And what we're proposing is that you ally with us."

"Me? Ally with you? Why me? I'm not a party, or an organization, or even a well-known person. I'm just a humble schlepper trying to finish my Master's thesis and land a job. Nothing more!"

"Don't sell yourself short, Sidney. For one, you're a highly trained physicist. There aren't many in this country. You have information in your head almost no one else has. You also have the ability to analyze data that has impressed all your teachers, including the late Professor Strauss."

"May he rest in peace," said Sid, intoning the ritual phrase in memory of the dead. "But I have no plans of ever turning Communist. And I can't think of a single good reason to be associated with a Stalinist party. Your policies are wrong-headed from start to finish."

"Everyone will respect your political decisions, Sid. We Communists know how to work effectively with members of many other parties."

"Oh! Did Joe Stalin give you permission? 'Cause as far as I know, you've never worked with any other party without trying to destroy it. Or has the CPUSA gone soft?"

"Neither, Sid. The Republican Party has turned fascist. Lindbergh used to represent the isolationist America First crowd. Now as president, he's looking for support from the European dictators because he shares their personalities and views."

"He thinks Hitler is his friend. He doesn't understand what everyone figured out a long time ago: *Herr* Hitler is nothing but a psychopathic killer who divides the world into those being exploited, and those to be exploited in the future."

"Correct, Sid. But with the fall of the Western democracies, like it or not, the Soviet Union is the only show in town."

"Ha! But the Soviet Union is also supporting the Nazis! And has been since late '39 when they made a deal to carve up Poland and the Baltic States between them!"

Rosenberg sniffed. "Stalin only did what any Russian leader would have done, Sid. His actions were a tactical arrangement to buy time and territory. Hitler's number one target is Russia. Always has been. *Lebensraum*, living space for the master race. Agricultural expansion is his real goal, so that Germany will never starve again as it did during the First War. Hitler's talked about it for decades. The real show will be in Eastern Europe. War is coming there soon, Sid, you'll see. And it will be the most terrible struggle in the history of humanity."

Sid thought for a moment. "Okay, Julius. Everything you said is plausible. But there's nothing I can do to affect the outcome of such a titanic struggle one way or the other."

"You can't Sid, and neither can I. But each of us, in our own small way, must do as much as possible."

"And what role does the CPUSA plan for me?"

"Oh, at the start, only the sharing of information. We have intelligence you may want. In return, we would expect you to keep us informed on matters of interest to us that come your way. I think you'll find we're really on the same side, Sid. Lindbergh and his minions are set on destroying any independent sources of power in this country; they view them as a threat to their own. Communists and Jews are the first targets because we're not popular anyway. After us, who knows? Follow the Nazi playbook on how to set up a totalitarian, racialist state. God knows, Lindbergh sure is.

"Listen Sid—we've burrowed very deeply into many layers of society. We have friends at every level. You wouldn't believe the number of prominent people quietly working with us, people who can and will help us. People who could also help you."

"For example?" Sam Peskin had taught him never to trust the Communists. Perhaps everything Rosenberg said was propaganda designed to suck him in as a fellow traveler.

"For example, I'm sure you'd still like to know who, on an evening months ago, followed you down the hill on 137th Street to the subway after you left City College for the evening."

"I would. Well, then, I suppose it's obvious. The only way you could ask me that question is because it was you."

"Not me, Sid. One of our operatives."

"For Chrissakes, for what reason?"

"For the reason that friends of Leo have had an unfortunate tendency to wake up dead lately, my friend. I. Bernard Strauss, to name just one. We don't want the same to happen to you."

Sid gulped. "I never sensed any danger.".

"One often doesn't, until the fatal blow strikes."

"Do you believe I'm still in danger?"

"No. We don't. In fact, we no longer believe you were ever in any physical danger at all, unlike Enrico Fermi. I suppose you've heard of him?"

"He's one of the greatest atomic physicists on the planet. Strauss once told me that Fermi had the clearest mind of anyone he'd ever met. That says a great deal about Fermi, and about Strauss, too."

"Unfriendly forces were getting too close to him. The result of certain, ah... indiscretions, let us say. We had to pull him out. But you, on the other hand—no offense intended—you're not Fermi."

"No offense taken, Julius. But if my mother ever found out about this, she'd tie me to a bedpost. I'd be flogged worse by her than by anyone else who might catch me."

"Then she's a good woman, your mother. I'm sure she loves you very much."

"She does. I think I'll keep her."

"Now, will you enter into a gentleman's agreement with us?"

Sid paused. The thought of trusting a Communist, and Rosenberg no less, tied his stomach in knots. He hoped the feeling didn't show on his face. But if there were important information to be gained, it might be worth the risk. "Just one other thing, Julius. You mentioned Leo. Give me the low down."

"I'm sorry, Sid. But that's classified. Besides, for the moment it's better you don't know. What I can say is that you will find out everything you need to know in good time."

"That's not very satisfying, Julius."

"I understand, Sid. But right now, that's all I can do."

"Then tell me what you want."

"Any information you may hear on who killed Professor Strauss and why he was killed. And if you hear anyone else talking about Leo, please also keep us in the know. For now, that's all. So, can we enter into a gentleman's agreement?" Julius extended his arm for a deal-sealing handshake.

"Sorry, my friend. But I'll have to think this one over."

"What's the problem?"

"Oh, nothing that can't be worked out. I'll just need an iron-clad guarantee you won't get me killed working with you. My mother would want it as part of any deal."

"Sid my boy, in these days and in this world, that's not a guarantee I'd care to give to anybody."

By the time Sid returned to the family nest on the fifth floor, he was more mystified than ever. Finished with his quantum mechanics for the evening, he tried to make sense of the events of the past several weeks.

So. It was that fellow Leo who visited him in the City College Library a few weeks back. He was the one who started everything. Leo was knowledgeable about nuclear fission, or why would he be so interested in the scientific articles Sid was reading? He was also terrified about their conversation being discovered. Jesus, Rosenberg said that Leo's friends were being killed, so he had a damn good reason to be terrified! Professor Strauss must have been a friend of Leo's, or how would he have known to meet Sid in the library? Or was that meeting a coincidence, and was Leo was looking for someone else? Or for no one else? And if Sid's meeting with Leo wasn't a coincidence, why on earth was Leo looking for him?

In addition to Strauss' murder, Enrico Fermi, an internationally acclaimed physicist, went missing from his train on the way to visit J. Robert Oppenheimer at Berkeley. That was the same Oppenheimer, also an atomic physicist, who recently lectured at City College at Strauss' behest. But what connection did that have with Fermi's disappearance, if any?

Rosenberg knew far more about Leo than he let on. He probably also knew what happened to Fermi, but that piece of intelligence seemed to be a Party secret. And why on God's green earth were the Communists approaching him now? Sid had nothing to offer them. Too many questions, and not enough data to provide any answers.

Sid's brain ached. As a physicist, it was easy to view daily life as a series of math problems to be solved; everything was potentially soluble, wasn't it? But sometimes, the data had holes. Big holes. Dark holes.

Sid had invested a nickel in a Baby Ruth candy bar and waited until after dinner to devour it at his leisure. After momma Rosalie's off-white, tasteless, boiled chicken, the chocolate, nuts, and caramel were a sweet treat for the taste buds. Consuming that Baby Ruth bar was a guilty pleasure Sid hid from his mother, who didn't like him wasting precious money on candy. The glucose spike fueled his remembrance of Christmas past, and his encounter with Julia Falcone.

Benny might only be ten, but he was a bright kid with no reason to make up a story. Especially one about him. Why two Mafia goons, Vince and his look-alike, wanted to look him over, was beyond his understanding. Whatever the reason, it couldn't be related to nuclear fission. They lacked the education to comprehend advanced physical concepts. So what in heaven's name was it all about?

Sid dropped the uneaten end of the Baby Ruth into his mouth.

Mmmmm, he thought. *I don't have a clue.*

On Saturday in the morning, the Orthodox Jews living in Sid's neighborhood trooped to the local synagogue to pray. At the same time, the folks at Temple Emanuel on East 65th St. and 5th Avenue in Manhattan returned to their synagogue en masse, a demonstration of their indomitable spirit in the face of Bundist threats of violence. A hired security force of seven men, each bearing a Mannlicher rifle, discouraged Bundist violence as much as anyone's indomitable spirit.

However, on this morning, thoughts of prayers penned in medieval times and muttered in incomprehensible languages were among the farthest things from Sid's mind.

"Sid," said Rosalie. "It wouldn't hurt you to pray in the synagogue every now and then. God favors those who pray to him."

"Thanks for the advice, Mom. Why don't you go to the synagogue and tell God you'll be praying for both of us?"

"*Oy,* Sidney, who raised you to be such a heathen?"

"That would be me," said Sam, hand waving high over his head.

"Oh, you! Ha! For you, Yom Kippur should be two days long, you have so many sins to atone for."

"That's why your parents never liked me, dear."

"That's why I don't like you, either, Sammy Peskin, my handsome young man."

"I think I'll just leave you two lovebirds to yourselves." Sid laughed. "I'll be meeting the lovely Julia today at noon and have to get going."

"Dating a *shiksa,* Sid? God in heaven, Sammy, he really is a heathen!"

"For Godssakes Mom, I'm not marrying the woman!"

"Not yet, anyway. *Oy,* Sam, your son's gonna break my heart with the *shiksa.* I just know it. And then, when I'm dead and buried, maybe he'll appreciate me."

"Okay, Mom, you can put a cork in it. Julia and I are just friends. We barely know each other. And her relatives are some of the creepiest people alive! Especially Uncle Vince!"

"All mobbed up," said Sam. "The entire older generation of that family. Be careful what you say to that girl, Sid. Don't compromise yourself. You never know what can get back to the wrong people."

"We're on the same page, Sammy. Don't worry. See you all later." Sid threw on his coat, scarf, cap, and gloves and headed out.

"Sammy?" said his father, with a shrug of his shoulders. "Not Dad?"

"I have no idea," Rosalie said. "Must be something else you taught him."

For an early February day in New York City, the weather was marvelous. A sky with only a few white cloud puffs allowed the bleak sun of the winter season to provide warmth after a prolonged period of frigid overcast. The sun's radiance, combined with a light onshore breeze, pushed the mercury to slightly over forty degrees Fahrenheit, perfect weather for what Sid had planned.

For convenience, the two young folks decided to meet at noon on the platform of the westbound LL train, as it arrived from Canarsie at 14th Street and 7th Avenue in

Manhattan. From there, they would catch the the Broadway-local downtown. Not wanting Julia to wait alone in the Stygian depths of a subway line built around the turn of the century, Sid timed his own travel for an 11:30 a.m. arrival. As each train rumbled through the station on its way to its western terminus at 8th Avenue, Sid anxiously paced the platform, hoping to catch a glimpse of Julia. Finally, at about fifteen minutes past noon, she arrived.

"Ah, I thought I was never going to make it here!" said Julia.

"Turbulence?"

"Ha, turbulence! On a train? No, silly. Traffic. We stopped in the tunnels for what seemed like a half hour. I hope you weren't waiting long."

"Only about a quarter of an hour," Sid fibbed.

"Oh, so if I'd arrived early, I'd have been all alone in this gloomy place, eh? At the mercy of the subway ghouls and who knows what else, eh? Is that what you're saying?"

Sid enjoyed Julia's sense of humor. It reminded him of his mother's, absent the whining self-pity. Where many men his age, and older, might be threatened by female assertiveness, Sid admired the intellect of anyone who could crack a good joke. And in Julia's case, it was also impossible not to admire her beauty; her face was as glowing as Sid remembered on Christmas Day. But a complete picture of this young woman was obscured today by her long brown coat, knitted wool cap, and a set of elegant, expensive-looking black leather gloves that she removed and held in her right hand.

"So, where are we going now, Sid? I've been looking forward to being surprised. But wherever we're going, I hope it's not expensive. I know how dear money is these days."

"Thanks, Julia. That's considerate of you. Not all girls would be that way."

"To tell you the truth, I think the only people worse than men who refuse to recognize that women are intellectually capable are the women who enable the stereotypes men have of us. Silly clucking hens, so many of 'em! Women who'll never read a newspaper, much less a book. And they have little in their pretty little heads besides the latest fashion, or the most scandalous Hollywood gossip, or whose husband is sleeping with whose wife in the neighborhood. Ah, I know women are creatures of their biology more than men, and I deeply respect those who believe the highest calling in life is to be a devoted wife and mother, but..."

"But that's not you, Julia. I remember. You made your feelings very clear on Christmas Day."

"I'm sorry, Sid. Many people, especially my father, tell me I talk too much."

Sid smiled and touched her shoulder reassuringly. "You can feel free to talk as much as you want, Julia. I enjoy hearing what you have to say. And I agree with all of it."

He took her arm gently, and they ambled off through the white tile-covered subterranean passages and toward the southbound Broadway local. Within minutes, they arrived on the platform, just in time. The train had announced its presence with a gust of subway tunnel air and the screech of its brakes.

Sid motioned for Julia to step aboard the train, its doors wide open for a short time. She hopped on and he followed. They stood alongside each other, Julia holding onto an overhead strap to offset the swaying of the train.

"I should try to chatter less. In case I give away all my secrets."

"Your secrets are safe with me, Julia. Funny, I've had many of the same thoughts myself. Once or twice, I've thought the words in my head and heard them coming from your mouth. Have you always been this way?"

"What way? Loquacious?"

She mulled over the comment. "Oh, you mean different? Yup, ever since I was a kid. I never wanted to play with the other little girls; I thought they were, well, silly. I always hung out with the boys. I think my parents thought I was weird, and I guess to them, I was. Then as I got older, I became interested in science. And developed a whole different kind of interest in boys."

The Broadway local clack-clacked, clack-clacked through the tunnel underneath Greenwich Village, on the way to its last stop at Battery Park at the southern tip of Manhattan. The ruckus it produced was so deafening that talking was futile.

After stops at several stations, Sid and Julia arrived at the terminus and emerged from underground at Battery Park.

"It's a short walk from here to the Staten Island Ferry. I thought it would be nice to take a boat ride around Upper New York Bay. And when we get to Staten Island, we can turn right around and come back to Manhattan on the next boat. I hope you like my idea, Julia."

"I think I like it very much, Sid. It's warm enough today to sit on the boat's upper deck and get some sun after this cold winter we've been having."

Straight ahead stood a solitary pushcart whose owner cried out his items for sale.. "Get ya pretzels heeeere, nice hot pretzels, get 'em while they're hot, get ya pretzels heeeere! Hot chestnuts, hot chestnuts, get 'em while they're hot! Cracker Jacks, Cracker Jacks!"

"Lunch?" asked Sid.

Julia nodded.

"What'll it be, folks?" asked the pretzel vendor as they approached.

"A plain pretzel for me," said Julia

"And I'll have a salted one," replied Sid, inhaling the warm, pungent, odors that enveloped the pushcart.

The pretzels were handed over with a request for twenty cents, which Sid paid.

"Nothing better than a hot New York pretzel," Sid said after taking a large, salty bite.

"Delicious. On par with a freshly-baked onion bagel, right from the oven. But look, Sid, there's a ferryboat in the terminal now. How often does it run on Saturdays?"

"Not as often as they do on business days, so we should hurry. But just for my curiosity, how did you become a connoisseur of onion bagels?"

"Experience. I always love to learn new things. Especially about bagels."

Within moments, they entered the ferry terminal building and Sid forked over five cents each (such a deal!) for the ride. They scurried onto the boat just before the large, metal bow bridge connecting it to the terminal was drawn, and the massive ropes undone that restrained the boat while docked. The captain rang the bell, powerful engines roared, and the boat, juddering out of the slip, was on its way to Staten Island, the least populated borough of the City of New York.

Clutching the remains of their pretzel lunches, Sid and Julia climbed the steep, narrow staircase to the upper deck and found a pair of empty seats along the starboard side.

The boat chugged along over the smooth surface of the bay as the occasional seagull swooped down and over the side rails.

"Look behind you, Julia!" Sid turned his body and motioned with his hand. "What a terrific view of the skyscrapers of downtown New York with the Empire State Building right in the middle of the island overtopping all of them, as if it were receiving their homage!"

"You can see all the way to the George Washington Bridge. That's at 179th Street in Manhattan, I think."

In moments, the ferry passed two more iconic sites. First, on the starboard side, near the New Jersey shoreline, was the now little-used Ellis Island. A short hop to its south, the enormous bronze mass, now oxidized green, of the Statue of Liberty, her mighty torch held high over the radiate crown gracing her resolute gaze, guarded the harbor.

"Majestic," whispered Julia.

"Which one? The Statue or Ellis Island?"

"Both, I think. My parents came through Ellis Island when they were little. My father told me a story about how, before they got off the boat from Italy, they heard one explosion after another and were very frightened. Turns out it was the 4th of July."

Sid laughed. "My grandparents came through Ellis Island, too. As did many others. But no longer. The Johnson-Reed Act of '24 prevented most people like ours from coming here."

"I heard on the radio that Lindbergh has instructed the poem about the 'tired, poor, and huddled masses yearning to breathe free' be removed from the Statue's base. The people described in the poem are not the right kind of people for him."

"Is there anything that man says that doesn't offend someone? He has no common sense, no empathy, and no ability to be diplomatic! Your people are fine with me, Julia. Even Uncle Vince, though he does seem, ah... distorted."

"Distorted! Ha, ha, ha! That's a diplomatic way of referring to Uncle Vince. Yeah, he's as you say—distorted. But don't ever let him hear you say it. Oh, he's really okay, I suppose, once you get to know him. My uncle Phil, his brother, is even more twisted. And secretive. He sneaks in and out of the house at all hours without anyone hearing. No one ever knows what he's up to."

Sid realized that Uncle Phil must have been the man Benny overheard talking to Vince on Christmas Day.

The remainder of the boat ride to Staten Island was not as interesting as its first several minutes. Sid and Julia spent it discussing the relative merits of Disney's vs. Warner Bros.' cartoons. They concluded that Warner's animated shorts were far superior to anything Mickey Mouse offered. They also concurred that Disney's *Fantasia,* premiered just last year, was a masterpiece, a work of genius both artistic and comedic. Julia spoke passionately of her love for the great music featured in the film, so Sid grasped her ungloved hands and belted out *che gelida manina,* the only words he knew from Rodolfo's aria from *La Bohème.* After the time she'd spent on the top deck of the Staten Island Ferry, cruising New York Bay without her gloves on, Julia's hands were in fact painfully cold.

The two young adults also conversed in some depth about several cultural icons of the recent past. One subject of discussion was 'Minnie the Moocher,' a jazz piece written and performed by Cab Calloway.

"The fella's a hoot," said Sid. "I never saw another human being move the way he does. Must have extra sets of joints."

"Extra joints of all kinds, I'm sure. My parents would never let me listen to that Moocher song when it was played on the radio. They said it was vulgar."

"Well, it is about sex, drugs, and dreams. Two of the three, not sayin' which, are most unsuitable for young ladies."

"Ha! Despite my parents, not too vulgar for Hollywood, even after the censor started his work in '34. Groucho Marx gave Minnie a mention in one of his recent movies. I think it was *A Night at the Opera,* in '36. For seventy-five cents, he said he could get you a picture postcard of Minnie..."

"And for a dollar twenty-five, he could get Minnie herself. With a leer that said, 'if you know what I mean.'"

"And who didn't know exactly what he meant?"

The Statue of Liberty and Ellis Island now appeared to port as the ferry headed back to its Manhattan slip.

"You see a lot of movies?" asked Sid.

"Some. I'll save you the trouble of asking me for my favorite. It's *The Wizard of Oz*. The color! The music! The acting! I saw the picture three times when it came out a year and a half ago."

"Hmmm... not *Gone with the Wind*? I'm surprised. I thought that was every woman's favorite."

"Oh, you're trying hard not to get on my good side, Mr. Peskin. I am certainly not every woman, as I pointed out earlier. *The Wizard of Oz* is number one for me, but *Gone with the Wind* is a close second. I adore historical fiction, especially in a movie, because that's the only way of seeing how it really was... how things looked to people living at that time. And because I always learn something new! It's like science. There's always something new, something fascinating to learn, and I never intend to stop!"

"What would you like to learn about in science, Julia?"

"Oh, about everything!" She waved to Lady Liberty as the ferry slid by. "I'm intrigued by Einstein's Theory of Relativity. How mass expands as speed increases: the consequences of the speed of light being the absolute limit of velocity. Why 'E' happens to just equal 'm-c' squared. We young ladies weren't taught these things at the Hunter College for Women."

"And I'd be happy help you. You're describing what's called special relativity. If you understand high school algebra, which I'm sure you do, you'll easily grasp it. General relativity is much more difficult. And after you master Einstein, Julia, anything else physical, er, I mean, in physics I can help you with?"

Julia ignored his pun. "Ah, I don't want to presume on your time, Sid. But several Professor Peskin lessons for the novice on basic quantum mechanics would also interest me."

"Of course. I'll make a note of it. Anytime, Julia."

"And the work of Dr. Oppenheimer on how stars generate new atoms in their interiors."

Sid startled. Once again, he'd crossed paths, in a manner of speaking, with the famous Berkeley physicist.

"And, ah, whatever you can tell me about the subject of nuclear fission..."

Sid's jaw dropped. Why was this girl asking him to tell her what he knew about that damned subject? Was that the reason she wanted to go out with him today? Was she working with Leo, whoever he was? Or against him? Or for someone else? Or, hard as it was to believe, could it be that Julia's request was just a coincidence? Oh, for god's sake, Strauss was dead. Was that also a coincidence?

Sid was quiet for some time, wondering how much he could or should say to her.

The boat pulled into the slipway they'd departed from several hours ago.

"Julia, for my curiosity—how did you hear about nuclear fission? And why the interest in that subject? Every serious physicist I know thinks it's only a laboratory phenomenon with no practical use."

"Oh. Professor Strauss, God rest him, told me all about it. It's—I don't know— interesting, I suppose."

"Professor Strauss? He was at City College, and you're at Hunter. They're miles apart across the City. How'd you meet him?"

"Oh, you're a nosey one, aren't you? There's a seminar series that brings City College professors to Hunter College every few weeks to give a lecture. I heard him speak about eight months ago. He gave a wonderful talk. It's terrible what happened to him, poor soul."

Sid heaved a sigh of relief. Everything Julia said was plausible.

With a dull thud, the Staten Island Ferry docked in Manhattan.

"Time to go." Sid offered his arm to help Julia up.

The two walked quietly to the subway at the Battery. The pretzel seller and his pushcart were long gone. They were lucky to catch a departing train just as the doors were closing. At 14th St., Sid walked Julia to the LL train heading for Canarsie. She had refused his offer to escort her home, informing him in no uncertain terms that she would be fine, that she didn't want him spending his time on the subway. And also that she had such a lovely day out she didn't want it ruined by Sid not taking no for an answer.

It was long after the winter sun had set that Julia returned to her parents' home at 25 Greene Street in Canarsie. All the occupants were out, and no lights had been left on. She turned the key in the front door lock and stepped into the outer foyer.

But before she could locate the light switch, a man growled to her from the depths of the darkened interior. "So, my child, you're finally home."

Julia screamed, dropped her purse, and in a panic reached for the switch to turn on the overhead lights. "Uncle Vince!" She gasped, clutching her chest. "What are you doing here! Jesus Christ, you frightened me! And I'm not your child."

"You are whatever I say you are, and when I say it. Don't ever forget where you come from, my child. So. Tell me. Is this Sid Peskin everyt'ing we tink he is? Or have we been deceived?"

Julia paused for a moment. "Oh, he is, Uncle Vince. He is. Everything." And a whole lot more, she thought. A whole lot more. Tears of anger and shame welled up within her.

"But I'm very tired after a long day. Please do me the courtesy of going home. And Uncle Vince, one thing before you go. That debt you said I owed you? You remember it?"

"How could I not, my child?"

"Good. Consider it fully discharged."

CHAPTER 11

The White House
February 10, 1941

Charles Augustus Lindbergh paced the rug-covered parquet floor of the Oval Office. Despite the unrelenting attacks of his critics, he knew the correct path, the one he had to follow. Regardless of verbal assaults from Communists, Jews, the press, and other traitors, he, the American president, remained steadfast. It was his political enemies, the ignorant, the misguided, who failed to understand the fundamental rule of history imposed by nature: Empires were built by the genius and ethic of their founding stocks. And in America, the founders were northern Europeans. All other ethnic and racial groups were permitted to participate in the benefits of the Empire by the consent of the founding stock. This consent could be removed without notice, depending on political and economic exigencies. It was incomprehensible that so many people failed to grasp this basic concept.

This was the reason why he, Charles Augustus Lindbergh, founder of the America First movement, was elected: To ensure the lesser peoples who now inhabited the United States were taught the hard rules of political and racial logic. When last year he'd stood on the Capitol steps and taken the oath of office to uphold the Constitution, he'd also sworn a silent oath to always keep faith with his voters. Come hell or high water, their president was going to do what he promised them he would do.

This morning, he had much to ponder. Ambassador Thomsen of the Third Reich had already come and gone, bearing a new bucketload of 'suggestions for furthering German-American relations.' The president wasn't displeased that these suggestions incorporated clever methods of marginalizing American ethnic and racial minorities. The German ambassador also pointed out that, in the opinion of the *Führer*, the

Lindbergh government had been insufficiently active in both promoting racial separation and in cracking down on Communist anti-German propaganda. Lindbergh countered by referring to the recent upswing in Bundist attacks on anti-German elements, and to the arson attempt on the Jewish-owned *New York Times*. That blessed event was thwarted only by providence and sheer luck. Ambassador Thomsen said, "Luck is something in which the *Führer* does not believe."

Lindbergh also bemoaned his difficulties with the Congress. But the *Führer's* ambassador wondered how that could be, since both the House and Senate were in Republican hands. The meeting ended with a friendly handshake, but the lad from rural Minnesota detected frost in the ambassador's smile.

Face-to-face meetings with J. Edgar Hoover were no longer possible because of the risk of discovery and disclosure by the 'lying press'. Instead, the FBI chief and Lindbergh agreed to maintain contact through a liaison. The man they selected as their go-between was a 23-year-old naval attaché and a recent Harvard graduate. He was the second son of a wealthy, well-known anti-Semite and America Firster whom Lindbergh had known and trusted for years—and on whom Hoover had collected dirt, heaps and heaps of dirt, for more than a decade.

Anne Lindbergh knocked on the outer door of the Oval Office. "Mr. President, a Lieutenant Kennedy is here to see you."

"Send him in, Anne. We have a great deal to talk about."

Lieutenant Kennedy, a painfully thin young man with a gaunt Irish face but a winning smile, stepped into the room and smartly saluted.

"John F. Kennedy at your service, sir!"

"Nice to see you, John. I believe we've met before."

"Sir, that's correct, sir. Please, if you don't mind, sir, call me Jack," he said in his Boston accent that dropped the "r" whenever possible. "Everyone else does, including my *faathaah*."

Lindbergh retreated to his desk and sat in his chair. "At ease, Jack. Take a seat, please. You're among friends. I've known your father, Joe, for at least ten years. He's a wonderful man, a great man. And I hear you're a chip off the old block."

Kennedy smiled. "Dad got it right about the Brits, didn't he? He always said they didn't stand a chance against the Germans."

"He's always had it right about the Jews, too."

Kennedy didn't reply.

"So now that you're here, Jack, what does my friend Edgar have to say?"

This is a handsome man, thought Lindbergh. He could see the quality, the flair he has for leadership. He also probably has a girl in every port—he'd been reported to be as oversexed as a satyr; people say he hops from bed to bed like a rabbit in heat. Lindbergh made a mental note to remind Edgar to create a file on Jack Kennedy's sex life. At least his family was above reproach—that was a good recommendation. But could Jack Kennedy be trusted?

"On what subject, sir? You know Edgar. He has a great deal to say on many things, when he wants to."

"I know, Jack, I know. Though most often he's more silent than the Sphinx. By the way, would you like a cigar? I have some of the best of the Cubans—*Romeo y Juliettas.*"

"Thank you, sir," said Kennedy, as he reached to receive the cigar offered by the president. It came from a row of half a dozen placed in a bowl on his desk. Next to the bowl was a silver lighter. With a flick of Lindbergh's fingers, the lighter's lid mysteriously popped open, and a small flame emerged.

The two lit up. "There's just no substitute for Cuban tobacco. *Viva Cuba!*" said the young naval lieutenant, as he flicked the ash off the end of the cigar into a glass bowl.

Lindbergh also enjoyed a relaxing smoke, "So, young man. What does Edgar have for me today? And where the hell is this Fermi character and why hasn't Edgar found him yet?"

Thomsen had made it clear that he wanted Fermi, minus his Jewish wife, deported back to Europe. But first, Hoover had to find the sonuvabitch.

"Listen, lieutenant, everyone in Washington is talking non-stop about this Fermi business, and it's making me look bad. This is terribly unfair to me, Kennedy, oh, just terribly unfair. No president has ever been treated this poorly! Tell Edgar it's got to stop! He should be making me look good, but he's not!"

"Yes, sir. Do you mind if I write all this down?"

"Yes, I would mind, Mr. Kennedy! First rule in politics: Never write anything down; it'll come back to hurt you later. You got that, lieutenant?"

"Yes, sir, I got it. Never write anything down."

"Now, you tell Edgar I also want everything he's got about this fellow I. Bernard Strauss, the physics professor from City College in New York who was shot a few weeks ago. Since they're both physicists, does he think Strauss' death is in any way related to Fermi's disappearance? And tell him he needs to figure this one out and soon, or the Democrats in Congress may start asking questions. Not that I can't handle them. You got all that, Kennedy?"

"Yes, sir. Fermi and Strauss—are the situations related. Yes, I'll ask him."

"That's right, Kennedy, be direct," said Lindbergh archly.

Kennedy squirmed in his chair. "Yes, sir. I'm sure Mr. Hoover would like to discuss these matters with you in person..."

"But he can't, so you're here."

"I always do the best I can, sir."

"I'm sure you do, kid. I'm sure you do. So, let's get down to business. What's the latest that Edgar has about Fermi?"

"Ah... Mr. Hoover would like me to inform you the Bureau has still not been able locate the professor. Something about finding a needle in a haystack, sir."

"Hmmm... that's some needle, Kennedy. One of the most brilliant minds in the world, and we've lost him like a misplaced penny? And what about the Strauss murder? What's the status with that investigation?"

"Hoover has no evidence that Fermi's disappearance and Strauss' murder are connected, sir. But like you, he's concerned that they are not unrelated events."

"Any indictments pending on the Strauss murder?"

"No, sir. Not yet. But there are suspects. Mr. Hoover is focusing on the Communist connection. A well-known card-carrying Communist agitator named Julius Rosenberg was one of the so-called students that found the body. He's been a Party man for years. And both the New York City cops and our forensic experts believe Strauss was murdered by someone he knew."

"Rosenberg, perhaps?"

"Mr. Hoover doesn't think so, sir. He says that Rosenberg's alibi checks out. The other person that found Strauss, a current City College student, is squeaky clean, and vouches for Rosenberg."

"I think the Bureau needs to question the witnesses again. Maybe they saw or heard something useful they don't remember. Mr. Hoover has ways to help people recover from memory losses."

"Yes, sir. I'll relay this to him along with the other items we've discussed."

"Thank you, lieutenant. That will be all. Oh, and please go straight to Mr. Hoover. No shilly-shallying, as you Irish say."

Kennedy frowned. "Pardon me, Mr. President. But that's not an Irish expression I've ever heard."

"Never mind, Mr. Kennedy, never mind. Just do as you're told. Remember: straight to Hoover and without delay. Whatever lady is sharing your bed this week can wait until the evening."

New York Times, April 5, 1941

REDS BATTLE BROWN SHIRTS IN CHELSEACOMMUNIST AND BUNDIST CONFRONTATION AT PARTY HEADQUARTERS

By William Gunn

At least one thousand Nazi-inspired Bundists and an equal number of members of the Communist Party U.S.A. and its allies faced off in a violent clash yesterday that left five dead and at least one hundred injured.

The Bundists had mounted a torchlight parade scheduled to stop at the national headquarters of the Communist Party when they were intercepted on 8th Avenue and W. 23rd St. by a large contingent of Reds crying "No to fascism!" and "Nazis go to Germany!"

A melee erupted with the Bundists striking out with brass knuckles and steel-tipped jack-boots, countered by the Communists flinging rocks, glass bottles, and trash. However, the dead, all Communists, were mostly the victims of daggers employed by the Bundists to deadly effect.

After dispersing the Communists, the mob took out its anger on Party Headquarters. The building was broken into and ransacked. Furniture, followed by books and documents, was thrown into the street and set on fire.

The Red forces charged the Bundists, most of whom had scattered. With fists flying, the Communists drove the Nazis away from Party Headquarters. Enraged Bundists threatened to return soon with "ten times the power."

Earl Browder, the Chief of the CPUSA, said: "Communism is true Americanism. Fascism has no place in this country, despite the ignorance and brutality of the Nazis of New York and of those in the White House who aid them and give them comfort and a place at the table. We have never, in the entire history of this land, seen an administration whose policies and actions are so inimical to the welfare of the vast majority of the people of this great nation, who also suffer under the weight of oppression by capitalists and plutocrats. The death of five of our members only inspires us to greater efforts! They will be avenged!"

Earlier that day, before the Bundist march.

"Oh, no you're not, Sammy!" cried Rosalie. "There's going to be trouble! A lot of trouble! You know it, too! What are you doing, marching with Communists? For Chrissakes, you've never had a good word to say about any of them! So why help them now? Explain it to me, Sam, if you can!"

It was true. Sam Peskin might have described himself as a socialist, but he didn't care for the Communists. "Watching them at a meeting," he used to say, "is like watching a field of wheat in a breeze. The heads always point in the same direction."

Sam also suspected that the CPUSA was directly funded by the Soviet Union—worse still, that it was a mouthpiece for Josef Stalin, whom he considered a murderous tyrant.

But this evening, despite the pleadings of his wife, when the phone message came from his union local, Sam answered the call of duty. The working man, the average lunch-pail Joe, Jews and non-Jews, blacks, whites, and anyone else who was a decent, thinking human being, Communist or not, had to stand up against Bundist bigotry, even at the risk of life and limb. And Sam, as he'd been for two decades, was proud of being a dues-paying, card-carrying union man.

"Don't worry about him," said Sid, as if anything he could say would make a difference to his mother when it came to the welfare of her family. "Dad, I'm going with you. Mom, I'll watch out for the two of us."

Rosalie had exhausted herself arguing with Sam.

"Another *meshuga* heard from. Between the two of you, there's as much common sense as in a hole in a bagel." She shook her head, resigning herself to an evening of anxiety over their fates.

"Mom sure has strong opinions," said Sid as father and son grabbed their coats and headed to the apartment door.

"That's what I like about her. The woman speaks her mind. No beating around the bush with Rosalie. You always know what she's thinking. You're too young, yet, Sid. Wait a bit. You'll learn."

And at that moment, how could Sid not think of Julia, also a woman who spoke her mind? But that personality trait was where any similarity between the two women ended.

Later that day, after the Bundist march.

"That's a nasty bump on your head, Julius. When you're home, you might want to ice it."

"Hurts like the devil," said Rosenberg, who was wobbly after his skull had been whacked by a wooden Bundist club. "A small sacrifice to make. My comrades marching under the hammer and sickle were victorious. That's all that matters."

Sid sighed. With victories like this one... He'd hoped not to meet up with Rosenberg this evening, but when he saw him staggering about bleeding from an inch-long wound in his scalp, he'd felt compelled to help.

"C'mon, kid Commie." He grabbed Rosenberg by the shoulder. "Let's find you a seat."

Rosenberg shrugged. "No, I'm really all right. Many of my comrades in the vanguard against the fascists were far more bloodied than me, yet they kept up the attack! In a moment, when everything stops spinning..."

"Suit yourself, Comrade Vanguard." Rosenberg almost swooned into his arms. "But until you can vanquish the enemies of the working man, how's about a tactical retreat to the top of this fireplug?" The device was the double-headed variety that provided a flat top the size of an average pair of buttocks for anyone in need of a temporary rest.

Within seconds, a middle-aged Hispanic man came running over.

"*Señor* Rosenberg! *Señor* Rosenberg!" The man was panting and sweating from his exertions. "*Ai, dios mio, Señor* Rosenberg. I'm happy I foun' you!" he gasped.

"Sid, let me make an introduction. My friend is comrade Luis Lopez Vargas. He's a good man, and one of us."

"Ah, Jewish then?"

"Don't be obnoxious, Peskin. Señor Vargas is from Puerto Rico."

Sid stuck out his hand. "Nice to meet you, sir. Remarkable. You don't look Jewish." Vargas appeared confused.

"Don't mind him, Luis," Rosenberg said, pointing to Sid. "He's *loco* in the *cabeza*. Also, a tool of the capitalists, and an enemy of the people. But I'm trying to convince him to be a fellow traveler. *Comprende?*"

Vargas laughed. "*Sí, Señor. Comprendo bien. Buenos tardes, el señor loco.*" The two shook hands.

"I prefer pinko, Julius. It's so much more colorful. Forgive my poor Spanish, Vargas. You know, I think we have much in common. Julius makes us both miserable."

Vargas unleashed a flood of rapid-fire Puerto Rican Spanish no one could understand.

Rosenberg said, "Señor Vargas is a fellow traveler who often comes to CPUSA meetings. That's how we met. He's also the superintendent of a residential building in upper Manhattan. Fixes leaky faucets, mops the floors, makes sure the trash makes it to the curb for pick-up, those sorts of things. Lives in the building, too. *Señor* Vargas is also a very observant man."

Sid had a sense where this conversation was heading, but nothing could have prepared him for what he heard next.

"I suppose you've already surmised the address of *Señor* Vargas' building, haven't you, Sid?"

Sid cleared his throat. "I'll take a wild guess. 664 West 161st Street. Where Strauss was murdered."

"The same. 664 West 161st Street. Incidentally, owned by our mayor Fred Trump, who has been attempting to break into the Manhattan real estate market. Señor Vargas was distraught over what had happened to his friend Professor Strauss. And in his own building, too! Of course, he wasn't interested in chatting with the local men in blue. To people like Vargas, and myself, New York's finest are the enforcers of a system that represses the working man. But when he heard through the CPUSA that there was interest in Strauss' murder, one thing led to another, words were spoken, introductions were made, and here we are."

"With you making Señor Vargas miserable."

"Only because he was looking for me and knew I was wounded. I told you he's a good man. The CPUSA is doing its best to be helpful to you, Peskin."

Sid's interest peaked. "What did you tell Julius, Señor Vargas? Professor Strauss was an excellent teacher and a wonderful man. Everyone wants to know who could have done this to him."

Vargas glanced at Rosenberg.

"It's okay to tell him, Luis."

"Eenglish... my Eenglish no so good. *Sí,* but my eyes, ah, my eyes, they are very good." Vargas tapped his temple. "Every day, I watch. Every day. Many time, I see car. Big car... bright red car, drive roun' and roun'... you know? An' I know... he lookin' to park. An' I see driver, too, with my own eyes."

"I'll help you out, Luis. It was a big, bright red car. Luis saw it often, sometimes once a week, sometimes more. He didn't think anything of it at the time. He's also certain he didn't see it on the day of the murder."

"This is all correct?" asked Sid.

"*Sí, es verdad.* Everyt'ing."

"What was the make of the car?"

"Luis used to work as an attendant in a parking lot in the Theater District downtown. He knows his cars. It was a bright red 1933 DeSoto. The front-end grille work is the giveaway, Luis says. There's no doubt about it."

"Did he get a license plate?"

"No. He had no reason to. But he did get a good look at the driver. It was a young woman. And a very good looking one, too."

CHAPTER 12

April 15 was tax-day in 1941, as it was every year. It was also the date of the reopening of the great New York World's Fair of 1939 for its third consecutive season, held over from the planned two seasons by the demands of an appreciative public. The federal administration provided funding, believing it better to keep the proletariat diverted by bread and circuses, rather than thinking deeply about serious national problems.

The great extravaganza, an expression of the pride of the world's nations in their products, their science, and their technology, was held in Flushing Meadow Park in the New York City borough of Queens. A majestic 610-foot tall white spire called the Trylon and a 180-feet in diameter white Perisphere—containing a diorama known as the Democracity, which detailed the urban landscape of the future—had been erected to symbolize the event and to leave visitors so awestruck, they'd never forget it.

But while the fair of 1939, the last year of peace in Europe, was optimistic in its outlook, this year's version was shorn of most of the first season's playfulness. The British exhibit had folded along with the British nation. Both were dearly missed by many New Yorkers. The formerly British pavilion was now occupied by an Aryan art exhibition consisting of statues of heroic, blond warriors and their submissive female helpers. The exhibit was the property of the Greater German Reich, which now controlled most of the European continent.

The French exhibit, which in 1939 had demonstrated Parisian *haute couture* to the women who could afford it, and to the curious who couldn't, was pallid by comparison. Many of the best Parisian couturiers had sailed for North America; those who remained were happy to collaborate with their grim new overlords.

The Canadian pavilion, which many had expected would be a beacon of hope, was disappointing, little more than a stuffed mélange of the mammals of the North. It was rumored that the Canadian government, under the influence of their British guests, would be producing an artistic testament to the indomitability of the Anglo-Saxon and French spirit. Mr. Churchill and the Free French leader Charles de Gaulle would deliver video addresses to buoy the spirits of the fair-goers.

But that idea foundered after the Third Reich complained about the Canadian plans to the president, who placed the pressure of the pocket book on the fair organizers. The appearances of Churchill and DeGaulle, along with much of the planned exhibit, were quashed.

After their first date, when Julia and Sid spent most of the day cruising Upper New York Bay courtesy of the Staten Island Ferry, they'd arranged several more.

"It's astonishing," Julia told Sid, "how easy it is to take all of New York City's wonders for granted. I have the Statue of Liberty literally in my backyard, but I've always been too busy to pay her a visit."

Sid was much the same way. Outings of the Peskin family were mostly confined to the homes of relatives. So, in the few short months during the spring of 1941, the two compensated by visiting as many of the inexpensive attractions of the city as possible.

One memorable Saturday found them on the observation deck of the Empire State Building, eighty-one stories above 5th Avenue and 34th Street. A cool breeze whipped about the structure's points, forcing Julia to keep one hand on her broad-brimmed hat as she peered over the giant edifice's edge.

"A penny for your thoughts, Julia," said Sid, coming up behind her.

"Ha! I'm thinking that if I dropped your penny over the side, Sid... Oh, I suppose you know the rest of the question."

"No, it wouldn't harm anyone on the street below. Air resistance. But I hope..." He wrapped his arms around her waist, "...I hope you won't resist."

She turned in his arms, indifferent to the half-dozen others also taking in the view of the city, locking her fingers together behind Sid's neck, kissing him deeply but briefly

"Hey, you two, get a room!" snarled one offended middle-aged observer with a thick Brooklyn accent as he passed by on his way to the elevators.

"Jealous!" whispered Sid as they kissed again. "Who wouldn't be?"

"You better not tell your mother about what we just did. She'd have a conniption. And you'd be, I don't know, excommunicated, or whatever happens when a Jewish guy kisses outside the faith."

"With my mother, it would be more like an exorcism. What she doesn't know can't hurt me. But you have to promise to keep quiet about, you know, us, to Uncle Vince. I think he'd regard what I, ah... we did as constituting touching."

Sid felt an involuntary twitch of her hand, accompanied by a small gasp. "Oh, I know how to keep a secret, Sid." Using her first two fingers, she made a motion of a key turning within a lock across the center of her lips. "I'm Sicilian, remember? Took the oath of *omertà,* the vow of silence, at birth. And we Sicilians take our oaths very seriously! Even Sicilian babies must be silent! Crying is not permitted! Ha, you think I'm kidding? I didn't cry until I was thirteen. And then I really let loose."

"Silently, I suppose."

"Of course."

"You're a big tease, Julia."

"Only because you allow me to be, Sid. I appreciate that. It's one of the things I like about you."

"How about we take the elevator to the very top? The 102nd floor."

She ran her fingers through his hair. "Only if you kiss me again, sweetie."

Sid and Julia had shared those kisses at the top of the Empire State Building earlier in the spring. Later during that same spring, they planned a visit to the World's Fair, which neither had visited during its first two years.

It was a long ride on the World's Fair Train, built to move crowds from 42nd Street out to Flushing Meadow Park and the World of Tomorrow, the Dawn of a New Day, in Queens. This Saturday, the train was packed with fair-goers coming to see the some of the marvels that would soon be in everyone's home. Wonders like nylon, which could be woven into the sheerest stockings, and fluorescent lights, which could glow almost forever. On display at the AT&T exhibit was a device producing a mechanized synthetic voice, while the IBM pavilion showcased electric typewriters and a calculating machine that employed punch cards. In the Government Zone were the pavilions of the nations. Italy, with its 200-foot-high waterfall; the USSR, boasting the industrial products of Communism; exotic Japan; and an offering from almost all the South American nations.

In the Communications and Business Zones, the exhibits of numerous companies that surrounded the Trylon and Perisphere represented the industrial might of the United States: AT&T, U.S. Steel, Swift & Co., RCA, Borden and General Electric all proudly proclaimed the superiority of their products and of the American way of life.

Sid and Julia took in all these wonders, reassured by some, skeptical of others, but mostly just bemused. But Julia was sensitive enough to notice from his conversation that Sid was troubled. She'd given him no cause to be offended—she was certain about that. So she decided that until he wanted to talk about what was troubling him, she'd enjoy the day and let him work matters out by himself.

The Transportation Zone, reached by a bridge on the Street of Wheels that spanned the Grand Central Parkway, contained by popular opinion the most magnificent display the fair had to offer. Located here was the exhibit of the wealthiest and most productive firm of corporate America, the General Motors Pavilion. It was the single biggest draw of the entire fair.

After entering the pavilion, Sid and Julia were transported in moving seats over an enormous diorama representing the U.S. of the future. It featured a futuristic car-based city, complete with miniature highways, half a million individual homes, and upward of 50,000 miniature vehicles, all made by GM. A million trees of various species filled the empty spaces representing the countryside. All the elements grew wondrously in size as visitors moved through the exhibit, becoming life-sized at its conclusion.

Julia was entranced. Sid, however, was silent and looked unhappy. For the moment, she ignored him.

"That was astonishing, Sid," she exclaimed. "I've never seen anything like it. The artistry, the detail, the craftsmanship..."

"Yeah." Sid's voice was leaden. "The propaganda..."

Julia paused for a moment. "Ah, listen, Sid. I can't help noticing that you haven't exactly been yourself today."

He managed a weak smile. "How so, Julia?"

They passed by the Ford Pavilion, found an unoccupied bench, and sat.

"You didn't tell me one decent joke or make a single word pun all day. That's not the Sid I know. And you seem very unhappy. So, tell me—what's wrong?"

What should he say? What could he say? Who was this woman? A special, unique creature? An intelligent, beautiful person inside and out whom he believed he understood? Or, true to her birth family and upbringing, a ruthless manipulator with a stone heart who took after Uncle Vince?

What was the worse alternative? Running the risk of ending their relationship after a truthful discussion, or continuing on, not knowing, always having suspicions? Sid knew what his mother would say—just dump the *shiksa,* already!

He turned to face her on the bench. "Julia, you are the most amazing woman I've ever known."

"Oh... bu-u-ut...?"

"There is no but. I have the deepest regard for you. I really do."

Julia thought for a moment. "Sid, are you trying to break up with me? Because if you are..."

Sid waved his hands frantically. "No, no! That's the last thing I want to do."

"Then why don't you tell me what's on your mind. Spending an entire day with a person as morose as you've been isn't exactly a girl's idea of a good time, ya know."

Sid took a deep breath. "Okay, Julia. Let's get this all out in the open before I explode. It's about Strauss..."

"Strauss? I don't understand, Sid. He's dead! What can he possibly have to do with...?"

"I'll tell you what! I'll tell you the truth. Then you have to tell me the truth! That's how I work. Understand?"

Julia slumped back on the bench. "Understood."

"The building where Strauss lived. 664 W. 161st Street."

"Yes, I remember it."

"There's a superintendent. His name is Vargas. He knows cars. He saw a red 1933 DeSoto near that address many times recently. He said the driver was a good-looking young woman. I think that woman was you."

Julia paled. "Sid, I..."

"He got a partial license plate." That was a lie, but she couldn't know.

Tears moistened her eyes. "No, Sid, no. I know how this looks, but no, I didn't kill him. I could never kill Bernie Strauss. Or anyone. Besides, I wasn't there that horrible day. And if this Vargas, whoever he is, says I was there, he's a terrible liar and I curse him with a terrible Sicilian curse." She reached into her purse for tissues to absorb her tears.

"Even so, you went to visit Strauss at his apartment many times, Vargas says. Was that all about physics lessons, or is that none of my business?"

"Oh, it really is none of your business. But I'm going to tell you the truth. Because you've come to mean so much to me, Sid, and I don't want to lose you. And if I don't tell you the truth, you'd never believe me."

"You met Strauss at Hunter College when he gave a seminar, as I remember."

"Yes," she said, blowing her nose. Her eyes were bloodshot with tears. "Professor Strauss was very persuasive. Both as a teacher and... and as a man."

"And he persuaded you to meet him at his apartment for more... ah, study?"

She nodded. "And one thing led to another, and in between the lessons, well... Before long, we became lovers. So why would I ever want to hurt him?"

"Did you love him? He was old enough to be your grandfather."

"Did I love him? Yes, I suppose I did, in my own way. But why does it matter how old he was? If two people truly love each other..."

"Yes, I suppose it doesn't. It's just, I don't know, unusual."

"You thought you knew Bernie, and you did, but only in part. You knew 'work' Bernie. I knew private Bernie. He was smart, and so funny. And also very kind. In many ways he was much like you, Sid."

"Thanks, Julia." Sid exhaled. "I hope I don't end up like him." Bernie Strauss may have been kind, but he took what was available and vulnerable without a second thought.

"I'd do anything to find out who did that horrible thing to him, Sid. Anything!"

"Did you tell the police what you know?"

"In my family, telling the police anything is just not done."

Likewise having an affair with a much older man and her parents discovering it, Sid thought. And if they ever did find out, Julia might never be allowed out of the house again. Perhaps even shipped off to a convent for all he knew, a death sentence for one of Julia's temperament.

He remembered the conversation he'd had with Benny—after his younger brother overheard Julia's Uncle Vince talking with her Uncle Phil during last year's Christmas party at the Falcones'. About how he, Sid, was to be 'looked over'. Was that Julia's job? One she was forced to take because Uncle Vince had discovered his niece had strayed? Or perhaps there was something even uglier beneath the patina of Julia's charm and elegance.

But the larger question of why he was of any importance to a Mafioso he'd never met, never done business with, and never owed any money to, remained unanswered. And why would Julia continue the relationship with him if she were only out on a job for her family?

But if it wasn't Julia who murdered Strauss, and it wasn't entirely out of the question that it was her, then who did? And why did he, or she, do it? Sid was almost certain he knew the answer to both. But he was soon to discover he was dead wrong.

At the same time Sid and Julia were absorbed in the World's Fair and in each other, Fred Trump, the City's Mayor, was meeting with the president and a group of anti-Semites, white supremacists, and authoritarian types—his closest friends and confidants.

Let us go around the Oval Office to greet the collection of powerful men that composed Lindbergh's cabinet. Seated there, in addition to Trump and the president, were Joseph P. Kennedy, stock market speculator, former Head of the Securities and Exchange Commission, and currently Secretary of the Treasury; Gerald L.K. Smith, rabid anti-Semite of the radio dial, now White House Communications Director; Henry Ford—the industrialist whose racialist newspaper, *The Dearborn Independent,* was fulsomely praised by Adolf Hitler himself—now Secretary of Labor; Herbert Hoover, former president, on whose watch the Great Depression had mushroomed from a problem into a catastrophe, now Secretary of Commerce; and the youngest, the 27-year-old, all-star University of Michigan line-backer and center, and prominent America Firster, Gerald R. Ford of Michigan, as current Secretary of

War. In fairness to young Ford, though free of any credentials for his job title, he was also free of racial prejudice. There was no evidence Gerry had any desire to become familiar with either.

Trump experienced a jolting frisson at being in such august company, especially the Detroit oligarch Henry Ford. This was a man he'd admired from afar for decades as having reached the apogee of American wealth accumulation. Before the president entered, he tried to strike up a conversation with the venerable old man, now seventy-six years of age.

"Mr. Ford, I'm thrilled to make your acquaintance."

Ford looked at him with rheumy eyes.

"Pardon me. But who did you say you were?"

"Fred Trump, sir, Mayor of New York."

"Hmmm... well, hello, Mr. Trump. Sorry. I'd not heard of you before. Mayor of where, you say?"

Trump was astonished. He'd thought anyone of importance had heard of him.

"New York, Mr. Ford. New York, the most mongrelized city in the entire U.S. of A. We're bursting at the seams with the lower forms, as I'm sure you know. Your *Dearborn Independent* was spot-on in describing the sources of the troubles I face every day as mayor, especially with the Jews. But I haven't seen the paper for some time. Are you still publishing?"

Ford looked Trump over.

"No, I don't publish the *Dearborn Independent* anymore. Haven't for some time now, young man. Not since back in '27."

"Oh. I'd no idea, Mr. Ford. Hmm. I got hold of a German version in '37, but I didn't realize it was a reprint. Your paper was a bright beacon of anti-Semitism in the darkness of naïve, un-American tolerance, sir. A timeless clarion call for action. Why did you cease publication?"

Ford growled. "Lawsuits, and plenty of 'em. Those Hebrew lawyers were slicker than mine, son. Had to apologize to the Hebes, too. Well, I suppose they did have a point..." Ford's voice trailed off.

Trump was perplexed. He hadn't expected an admission like this from such a famous anti-Semite. Oligarch or not, the old fool had no business being at this party! Couldn't he see the way the political winds were blowing?

The invited guests all rose when the president entered the Oval Office through a doorway that led from his private office space. Lindbergh had his hair cut in a striking, new, masculine fashion—cropped close to the scalp from his mid-temples down, the barbaric style favored by the leader of the German SS, Heinrich Himmler.

He motioned with his hands. "Sit down, gentlemen. Please sit down."

Lindbergh sat at his desk.

"Thank you all for coming to Washington at such short notice. The reason I've asked you here is to solicit your collective help solving a difficult problem that's come up. My administration, despite our best efforts to keep our beloved country out of another European war, is slowly but surely being dragged in that direction. Joe, I think you may have a few words to say about this."

Lindbergh glanced at Joe Kennedy.

"That's correct, Mr. President. My agents, and those of the European neutrals, have been reporting that Hitler and his closest advisors are considering a military strike on the North American mainland. This will be accompanied by a propaganda barrage against the political and economic influence of Communists and Jews here in the U.S."

"I've been telling you this would happen for years," interrupted Gerald L. K. Smith. "But has anyone ever done anything? No! There are too many Jew-Communists and cowards in this country, and it's all a result of race mixing."

"Oh, calm down, Gerald!" snapped Herbert Hoover, who by courtesy was still called Mr. President. "You're not making sense now and you never did. Not all Jews are Communists, and not all Communists are Jews. I'll admit both are better than the negroes..."

"With all due respect, Mr. President," interrupted Fred Trump. "You're from Iowa. There are no Jews or negroes in Iowa."

Hoover snarled. "Mr. Trump, I was the president of this country for four years. I've known Jews, Communists, and negroes. I know what I'm talking about!"

"The lower orders mind their manners differently when they visit the White House than when they visit the streets and shops of Boston, Mr. President," countered Joe Kennedy, sitting on the arm of one of the couches. "I shouldn't like to associate with any of 'em. So I shan't." Hoover thought Kennedy's long Boston 'a' the affectation of a parvenu.

Ford the motor mogul piped up in a soft, wheezy voice. "And what does my namesake, young Mr. Ford, from my own home state of Michigan, think? I hesitate to give my own opinion, for fear that one of you lawyers here might bring suit against me."

Ford and the older men in the room chuckled.

"Wha...?" exclaimed Gerald Ford, waking from his reverie in response to Henry Ford's question. "Oh... uh, I've known a few of each, I think. Fine people. Fine people. You can learn a lot from everyone."

One could have heard a pin drop in the Oval Office.

Trump thought this fella'd taken one too many on the noggin. Henry Ford whispered to Gerald Ford that Communists were not fine people, and that Jews and negroes were not often referred to in such a manner among the Republican elite.

"Joe," commanded the president. "Finish what you were saying."

Kennedy cleared his voice. The assembled guests stopped chattering.

"Thank you, Mr. President. We are facing some pressure from our German friends. But despite the loose talk, we're not about to be attacked. Just the opposite. The Germans don't have any way of transporting the men they would need for such an enterprise across the vastness of the ocean, and they have no landing craft to off-load their troops when they arrived here. Isn't that right, Mr. Secretary of War?"

"Yup, that's true." Gerald Ford always made it a point to be agreeable.

"And there's no evidence of the marshaling of an invasion force in western French ports. Therefore, there'll be no invasion. Not now, and as the president and I believe, not ever. The Germans are bluffing, and they know we know it."

"Though the American people don't," said Gerry Ford, who realized where Kennedy and Lindbergh were going.

"True," said Lindbergh. "But Hitler has given us exactly what we want—the cover with the American people to do what we need to do in order to keep him happy. Nothin' wrong with keepin' folks happy where I come from. Don't forget, there are lots of fine people, very fine people, in Germany, in the German government, and in their security services."

"Ah, except when those fine people are tryin' to light your house and barn on fire so they can make off with your wife and daughter. Jesus, Charles! I'm from Iowa. Last time I looked, that's not so far from Minnesota. We Iowans are more circumspect about who we appease."

Herbert Hoover hadn't been so outraged since the banks had failed back in '32, knowing that would cost him another term as president. "And frankly, I don't much care for where this discussion is heading."

Lindbergh ignored him. Kennedy wanted to throttle the querulous ex-president.

"Oh, for God's sake, tell it straight, Joe. You're not a lawyer." Hoover's Midwestern twang grated on Trump's ears. "It seems to me the real question you're asking is how we can maximize our usefulness to the Germans before they attack us, like they did the French, Dutch, Danes, Norwegians, Belgians, Czechs, Poles, and British. Am I missing anyone, Gerry?"

"Nope, don't think so, Mr. President. But I promise I'll get back to you on it."

"You do that, Gerry. Well, I'm not a lawyer either, and I'm not running for anything. I'm just a simple fisherman from Iowa, so I can tell it straight. At this point, appeasement's a chicken-shit policy, Charles. It hasn't worked with the Nazis and it never will. That fellow Chamberlain tried appeasement a few years ago and lost his entire dang country and the British Empire, too. Shit, you know me, Charles. Everyone in this room knows me. I've been a loyal Republican my entire life, and I'll be one till I die. I opposed Roosevelt because I always opposed big government. But I've learned my lesson. The French are gone and the Brits are gone, too. I advise you not to make nice with dictators and Nazis. You need to crush 'em like the cockroaches they are."

Hoover smacked his fist into his wrist. Kennedy gnashed his teeth. In his long career as a Wall Street financier and Hollywood mogul, he'd seen off, finessed, and bullied specimens far more hard-boiled than Hoover. Only over Joe Kennedy's dead body would a failed ex-president be allowed to convince this ignorant president to mobilize the youth of America to fight in Europe—never mind in support of the ancient Hibernian enemy, the British. He and Rosemary had three sons—Joe, Jr., Jack, and Bobby—who would be at risk should there be another war. And Joe Kennedy had plans, great plans, for his sons, especially for the eldest, Joe Jr. Herbie Hoover had two sons too old to be drafted. What family members did he have to lose?

Fred Trump wanted to speak. The Mayor of New York, the greatest city in the U.S., had been quiet. But he'd formulated a plan that would suit the administration's needs and could be applied to all forty-eight states.

Lindbergh recognized Trump. "Sir, what does the mayor of our great northeastern Sodom and Gomorrah have on his mind today? Speak up! Don't be afraid! We're all Republicans here."

Fred Trump had a tendency to speak too quickly and to fire off phrases without thinking, as if there were no filter between his brains and his voice box. Today, in the presence of presidents, their advisors, and fabulously wealthy oligarchs, Trump had been uncharacteristically quiet. But as soon as Lindbergh gave him permission, he reverted to his usual talkativeness.

"Martial law, Mr. President," he proclaimed. "Declare martial law! Think about it for a moment. You'd bypass Congress. The power of the president would be almost unlimited. I believe even the courts can't restrain the chief executive once martial law is declared."

"Interesting thought," said Kennedy, stroking his chin. "We'd be able to muzzle the press, which would be a tremendous help."

Gerald Smith was right behind Kennedy. "The Communists and Jews, too. And you can put 'em all on boats back to Europe. The least seaworthy craft that can be found, too."

"I can see the advantages," said Henry Ford. "But I'm concerned that martial law might be bad for business."

Trump rose from his seat on the couch. "With all due respect, Mr. Ford, I must disagree with you. Look at what's going in my city. We have Jews and Communists fighting Bundists in the streets almost every day. Street traffic and public transportation have been disrupted. The constant brawling has physically damaged many solid businesses and has had a negative impact on economic development. I have a stream of Wall Street financiers flowing through my office every few hours—to a man, they're complaining that the investment climate in New York is turning sour again because of the street violence. You've probably heard from them, too, Mr. President. These are not men who can be taken lightly or simply ignored."

Trump took his seat. He was pleased by his own eloquence.

"I've heard a significant number of lives have been lost on both sides in the violence," interrupted the Secretary of War. "But there are persistent rumors that the New York City cops stand by passively when Bundists beat up Jews or negroes."

"C'mon, Gerry," Trump snarled. "Where'd you hear that crap? In the pages of the *New York Times*? Whaddya' expect? The rag is owned and operated by Jews."

Trump neglected to mention that he and the *Times'* owner and publisher, Arthur Hays Sulzberger, were bitter political enemies. It all began early in his real estate days, when the newspaper carried stories about Trump's exclusion of blacks from his buildings.

"Trump's got a point," Gerald L. K. Smith said. "You can't deny it. No one will ever get a fair deal from the Jews. Stick to the Hearst papers if you insist on reading anything. I get all my news off the dial, and for my nickel, the more people the Bundists beat up, the happier I am."

"And we're all concerned with your happiness, Gerald," said Joe Kennedy. "But as a practical matter, Mayor Trump raises an important point. We have similar problems in all major American cities. In my own hometown of Boston, and also in Chicago, Philadelphia, Baltimore, Buffalo, Detroit, St. Louis, you name it—almost all the major American cities have been affected by ethnic rioting."

Kennedy faced Lindbergh. "Mr. President, in my opinion, Mr. Trump's idea, an excuse for a declaration of martial law, is brilliant. And it might just fly with the public."

"The public be damned," said Gerald L. K. Smith. "I like it! Oh... but I hope no one will be will be muzzling me, too."

The Oval Office burst out in a chorus of laughs.

"No," said Kennedy. "That would be impossible, Gerald. No one can muzzle you. The crackdown will be selective, targeted to those elements that are uncooperative or unsupportive. I don't think you fit either of those categories."

Lindbergh was anxious to proceed. "I believe it's time to take a vote, gentlemen. This will be open ballot, one man, one vote. The majority rules. And after you declare, you must state the reason for your position. Mr. Kennedy?"

"I say yes. We can accomplish a great deal of the president's America First agenda absent a carping press and a dilatory Congress."

"Mr. Trump?"

"Yes, of course. The Bundists may object as they'll no longer be able to attack Jews and Communists at will on the streets. But in time, they'll learn to appreciate the benefits of this action."

"Mr. Smith?"

"Yes, and yes again. I want to see the day the lying press gets what it deserves.

"Mr. Ford of Ford Motors?"

The elderly industrialist shook his head. "Ah, well. It's a sad day when, at my age, I have to come to Washington to be asked to give my support to a such a measure. What about the Constitution, gentlemen? What about the Constitution? Does it no longer count for anything? Our form of government, our democracy, has been perpetuated for 150 years. And now a small group of conspirators sitting in this room wants to eviscerate the glorious document that patriots have spilled their blood to defend."

Several members of the GOP coughed.

"Wonderful speech, Mr. Ford," said Kennedy. "May I presume you vote against?"

The motor mogul lifted his right arm and balled his hand into a fist. In the blink of an eye, his thumb pointed down.

"Duly noted as a vote against," said Kennedy. "And you, Mr. Secretary of War? Please try to remember who appointed you, and who your constituency voted for in the last election."

"Is he old enough to vote?" The wisecrack came from Gerald L. K. Smith.

Gerald Ford ignored the jibe. "I may not be schooled in the ways of Washington. But I know right from wrong."

"Ah, the two Fords from Michigan stick together," said Kennedy.

"I never did like Washington much, anyway," replied the younger Ford.

"The feeling is mutual, I'm sure. And with your attitude, don't expect to have much success in this town, either." Not if I can help it, Kennedy thought. "And you, Mr. Hoover?"

The ex-president rose and headed for the door of the Oval Office.

"I swore an oath, once. Back in '28 when I stood on the Capitol steps with the chief justice and a Bible. I don't remember anyone cancelling my oath. Gentlemen, this meeting, and your plan, is a sham. It's an illegal power grab, pure and simple. And I will have no part of it."

Hoover opened the door of the Oval Office and turned back to face the gaggle of schemers.

"I lived here for four years when I was president. So please, don't bother. I can show myself out." He closed the door behind himself and disappeared.

Kennedy exhaled. "Ah, well, that's our Herbie Hoover. You can never count on him when you need him."

Lindbergh spoke last. "By my tally, that's three for and three against. The deciding vote, therefore, is mine."

CHAPTER 13

The New York Herald Tribune,
Wednesday, April 17, 1941

LINDBERGH DECLARES MARTIAL LAW

By Vartanig G. Vartan

In defiance of jeers and catcalls from Congressional Democrats and some members of his own party in both Houses of Congress, President Charles A. Lindbergh today declared martial law, covering all forty-eight of the United States. The White House released this statement: "Because of the unacceptable increase in violence that has recently consumed our communities, both large and small, and to prevent further chaos and loss of life, I, Charles A. Lindbergh, President of the United States, employing the power of my office as described in the Constitution, hereby proclaim martial law in the United States of America and all its territories and dependencies. The right of habeas corpus is hereby suspended. The extent of the maintenance of other specific civil laws and civil rights will be decided at a later time."

Reaction from legal scholars and other authorities has been swift and unfavorable. Louis D. Brandeis, recently retired Associate Justice of the U.S. Supreme Court opined, "Lindberg's blatant act of executive overreach is nothing more than a naked attempt to impose his will and the program of fringe elements of his party on the entire nation. As such, the proclamation is clearly unconstitutional and, I am confident, will soon be overturned in court."

However, Homer Capehart (R-IN) was more positively inclined toward the president's proclamation, seeing in the imposition of martial law "...the strong medicine necessary to cure the ills of Communism and cosmopolitanism that so severely afflict this great nation. It is a noble action of a great president."

The extent to which martial law will intrude on the daily business of the nation is unclear. When pressed for additional information, a spokesman for the White House responded, "I'll let you know when I know." When asked when that might be, the spokesman shrugged his shoulders and said, "Ask the president."

According to unnamed sources, Mr. Lindbergh has received extensive advice on the imposition of martial law from Joseph P. Kennedy, secretary of the treasury and former ambassador to Great Britain in the Roosevelt administration. The same sources confirmed former President Herbert Hoover was so opposed to Lindbergh and Kennedy's action that he departed a recent meeting with the two and others in disgust. Spokesmen for both Hoover and Kennedy declined additional comment.

That same day, two federal marshals sporting black overcoats and black fedoras escorted Arthur Hays Sulzberger, the publisher and editor of the *New York Times*, from his office at 229 W. 43 Street. Sulzberger refused to leave even after he was shown the federal warrant for his arrest. To the dismay of his associates, he was then handcuffed, manhandled out of his chair and down the stairs, placed in a police van, and driven off. After booking, Sulzberger was then taken downtown to the Manhattan House of Detention, known better as 'The Tombs,' where he awaited arraignment and trial in federal court on a charge of federal income tax evasion and sedition.

About a half hour after Sulzberger's removal, large numbers of Treasury and FBI agents and New York City policemen, the latter commanded by Patrick F. X. O'Sullivan, Police Commissioner, converged on 229. W. 43rd. Bearing rifles and bullhorns, the officers went from floor to floor, announcing that pursuant to the declaration of martial law by the president, the *New York Times* was hereby shut down. All employees had five minutes to vacate the premises or they, too, would be arrested.

Most panicked and fled, but a hardy few refused, claiming their rights under the First Amendment. Predictably, their heroism faded when confronted with the level barrel of a loaded shotgun. After the building had been emptied, men in blue wrapped heavy chains across the building's entrances and padlocked them shut. Later that evening, after checking in by phone with his police commissioner to ensure everyone on their list had been detained, Fred Trump returned to his wife, Mary, to the borough of Queens, and to his two-story Dutch colonial dwelling. And what a happy man he was! For not only had his ideas gained the backing of the best and brightest—in his opinion—of the land, but the program he'd proposed had been enacted by the highest authorities. But what really tickled his fancy was that he was free, for a spell, from the chronic carping and complaining of a press that refused to give him the credit to which he felt he was entitled. And now, his enemy the *New York Times* was shuttered, its presses cold and silent.

Yes, they'd hit him, but he'd hit them back twice, ten times as hard. That was the law of life. Americans had had it too good for too long and had become too weak, too effeminate to understand the struggle for survival the Germans and their allies intuitively grasped. But they would learn. And Lindbergh and Kennedy and Trump would be their willing tutors.

No one noticed the twinkle in his eye or saw the swing in his step, but with every breath he took, Frederick Trump finally knew, deep in his soul, that after thirty-five years on earth he was, in every possible way, one of life's greatest winners.

As Sid Peskin grew to know Julius Rosenberg, he began to separate Rosenberg the person from Rosenberg the political activist.

"He's really not a bad guy," said Sid to his father one Sunday afternoon as they relaxed at home before the start of another workweek. "Just a little paranoid—OK, a lot paranoid. And also very misguided. About Stalin, I mean. About everything else, he holds his cards so close to his chest you never know what he's really thinking."

"And now he'd better hold them even closer," said Sam, who was attempting to dial in some of the big band music he adored on their Zenith radio.

"Leave him alone while he's fiddling," snapped Rosalie. "Your father gets cranky if he can't hear Benny Goodman on demand. Sammy, the radio stations don't program their music with you in mind."

Sam ignored her and continued to play with the dial, stopping only by the sound of a cool jazz trumpet.

"Louie Armstrong. Like I always say, if at first you can't have Benny Goodman, Louie Armstrong is an excellent substitute."

"Yeah, but maybe in a week or two Lindbergh will take Armstrong off the airwaves because he's black. Nothing that sonuvabitch does would surprise me anymore."

"Sid, watch your language!" admonished Rosalie.

"Under the circumstances, I would have used far harsher words, dear. What I can't believe is that our supine Congress is letting him get away with it. I'm no lawyer, but it seems to me that proclaiming martial law on the basis of a pretext, and in the absence of a clear threat to national security, is an insult to the Constitution.

"I'm sure the real lawyers will have their say in good time. Lindbergh can't silence them all. No doubt they'll argue the merits of our beloved president's proclamation all the way to the Supreme Court. But at the moment, martial law is the law of the land, and we all have to live with it."

"Even me?" asked Benny, who'd popped his head out of the bedroom he shared with his brother.

Rosalie smiled affectionately. "A comedian, this kid! Yes, *bubbeleh*, even you! You think you're living in some other country, ya little pisher?"

"He doesn't really understand yet. Give him a year or two." Sam winked at his youngest son.

"You think we'll have to put up with martial law for that long, Dad?" Sid asked.

"Ah, hard to tell. Perhaps if Congress grows a pair… but it's not likely. There are too many ignorant people in this country, and they elect ignorant people to represent them."

The phone rang. No one moved to answer it but Sid.

"Hello?" he said as he picked up the receiver. Hearing the voice at the other end, he covered the mouthpiece and softly said, "Rosenberg. Again."

None of the Peskins responded. Rosenberg had called Sid so many times he'd ceased to be a matter of interest to anyone but Sid.

"Where are you, Julius? Are you in any trouble?"

"Not yet," Rosenberg lowered his voice to a whisper. "But they've taken Browder. I'm too much of a small fry to be bothered with, that's my guess. So, I'm holed up in our apartment on Rivington Street with Ethel."

"How's she doing? I know how edgy she can be."

"Oh, Ethel? She's the strong one. Sometimes I think I could go to pieces, but she always keeps the faith. Says things have to hit rock bottom before the people will open their eyes."

"What can I do for you today, Julius?"

"Nothing for me, Sid. I'm calling you to preserve my sanity in these insane times. And to let you know everything is swirling, swirling around… So much is happening. Lindbergh's proclamation of martial law has catalyzed political activity among the masses he never dreamed of. He'll never be able to control it, no matter what he and his bosom buddy Joe Kennedy think. I'm now certain Lindbergh will be out of office within a year, eighteen months at most."

Rosenburg was a dreamer. There was no way Lindbergh would be ousted. Not with the mood in this country and the congressmen who supported him.

"Julius, hold on for just a moment." Sid covered the mouthpiece of the phone receiver.

"Hey, Dad. Has martial law 'catalyzed political activity among the masses'?"

Sam Peskin put down his ever-present newspaper. "Hmmm... no, not that I've noticed."

"Thanks, Dad. Sorry for the interruption, Julius. Go ahead."

"Oh, no problem, Sid. I just wanted to let you know to keep your head down. We still don't think you're in any danger, but you never know. Somehow, you've gotten yourself into the middle of things like you're the eye of the hurricane. Everything circulates around you, destroying everything it touches. But you calmly drift through. I'm not sure how you do it."

"Any news on Fermi, Julius?"

"None I can tell you, Sid. But you will know something soon. I guarantee it. Just be patient a little longer. Lindbergh and Kennedy think they have trouble now? They have no idea what trouble means."

The Treasury Building, Washington, D.C.
May 1, 1941

Memo to Files: Meeting between President Charles A. Lindbergh and John F. Kennedy, Lieutenant, USN.
Author: J. Edgar Hoover, Director, FBI.

Lieutenant Kennedy met with the president earlier today, who was again irate about the lack of the ability of the Bureau to locate Fermi or his wife. Kennedy informed the president there were now two additional highly prominent scientists missing, along with several others somewhat less known.

The two at the highest level are J. Robert Oppenheimer of Berkeley and John von Neumann, a genius mathematician revered by colleagues, some of whom refer to him as 'the smartest man of the 20th century.' Oppenheimer is a physicist who has, among other subjects, studied nuclear reactions in stars.

Other well-known scientists that have vanished include Robert Sorber, a physicist at Columbia University; Hans Bethe, a German immigrant, and an astrophysicist at Cornell University; and Edward Teller, a Hungarian immigrant, and a physicist at George Washington University.

On my request, Kennedy also mentioned that all these scientists are Jewish. Other highly visible atomic scientists who are not Jewish, such as Ernest Lawrence and Glenn Seaborg, both of the University of California at Berkeley, have continued with their daily work.

When questioned, they insisted they knew nothing about the disappearance of their colleagues, though they remained concerned for their welfare. However, we do not yet know if the above-mentioned scientists vanished because they are Jewish, or if that is merely a coincidence.

Kennedy also stressed that, unlike Fermi, all of the above-named individuals disappeared with their wives and families from their homes. At the Sorbers' home, we know their last meal was lying half-eaten on their kitchen table, indicating they departed in great haste when the summons came.

After so informing Lindbergh, Kennedy reported that subsequently Lindbergh lost his composure, and paced about the Oval Office shrieking, "Give me Fermi, damn you, Kennedy! Give me Fermi!" and making threats against his 'enemies' in the press, in Congress, and even in the Bureau. He (Lindbergh) accused the director of 'dragging his heels' in the investigation, and of being in league with "that dirty Roosevelt clique who 'wants to sabotage [my] administration.'"

At times, Kennedy said he doubted Lindbergh's sanity, stating for the record, "I think that, since he proclaimed martial law, he's going to pieces because of the stress."

Note for potential future use: The rumors about Jack Kennedy's satyriasis appear to be true. He was observed and photographed by Bureau agents having sexual intercourse on at least five occasions with one Inga Arvad, 27, a Danish journalist who was Hitler's personal guest at the 1936 Olympics in Berlin.

Arvad seemed to have been a particular favorite of Hitler, who referred to her as "a classical Nordic beauty," and introduced her to the Nazi hierarchy. She may or may not have had a relationship with Hermann Göring, Commander of the Luftwaffe, and it is not clear if she still maintains contact with him or with anyone in the German intelligence services.

The *Führer* of the *Grossdeutsches Reich* relaxed in a large stuffed chair in his mountain eyrie at Berchtesgaden in the German Alps, close to the old border with Austria. It was a border that he, more than any other, had helped to obliterate in '38, when Austria and Germany were merged. An enormous glass picture window in front of him provided a stunning view of mountain meadows filled with golden wildflowers, rushing crystal clear streams. In the distance were the magnificent Alps that, by mid-May, had finally lost the wintry covering of snow at their peaks.

Hitler loved retreating to his chalet, far from the frenzy of Berlin, the capital of the *Grossdeutsches Reich*, for a spell of rest and relaxation. He also loved to get away, if for only a few days, from his ever-squabbling paladins.

On this trip south, only a few members of his staff accompanied the *Führer*. One, army adjutant Gerhard Engel, poured tea for Hitler and his visitor, a man referred to in the West as Hitler's favorite architect, the thirty-five-year-old Albert Speer, when Hitler stood and waved his arms as words spilled from him.

"So, Albert, when will you begin designing my new capital city you've promised me? And don't tell me again that such and such is not possible or that the ground is too marshy or some other imbecilic excuse! I demand a domed hall that will seat at least a hundred thousand people. My Great People's Hall must be at least ten times larger than St. Peter's in Rome. It shall sit at the intersection of two perpendicular boulevards, each a minimum of ten car lanes wide. And don't forget a triumphal arch, Speer. We must have a big, huge triumphal arch. Our arch should be stupendous, awe inspiring! Greater than a hundred meters in height! The Arc de Triomphe in Paris will fit into the opening of our arch, with room to spare. And after all our plans have been completed, I shall christen our beautiful re-designed Berlin...Germania."

Adolf Hitler became so frenzied by his own verbiage that he broke wind with a force that surprised even him, and startled Speer. Ever since he had adopted a vegetarian diet years ago, he'd had gastrointestinal problems unrelieved by his personal physician, Dr. Theo Morrell. Despite all serious medical opinion, Hitler swore by Morell's treatments, and was especially fond of a drug named Pervitin, a.k.a. methamphetamine. Morell supplied it when his *Führer's* energy level was low. He also attempted to relieve Hitler's chronic hypochondriasis, plying him with medical reports about the superlative state of his health. It was, he informed Hitler, the best state of health he'd ever seen in a man of similar age.

Given Hitler's rantings, Speer presumed Hitler's last Pervitin dose must have been only about an hour ago. He had no choice but to sit and listen until the drug wore off and Hitler calmed down.

"Jawohl, mein Führer. It will be done exactly as you say. The designs will be completed within a month. You can be assured of it!"

"Do it, Speer. Do it now, you understand? I want Germania completed as soon as possible. It will be part of my legacy to the German people! With our upcoming conquest of the Soviet Union, which should take no more than three or four months, Germany will need a capital city worthy of the master race."

Speer wasn't surprised that Hitler's next target would be the Soviet Union.

"I applaud your grand vision, *mein Führer.* Not only architecturally, but politically, too. Not only have you rescued Germany from Communism and led our nation to victory in the West, but under your leadership, Germany will also fulfill its glorious destiny. I thank God he has given us a leader like you, *mein Führer*, and for the blessings he has granted me in being allowed to work with you."

Hitler smiled. "It's true, Speer, very true. Divine providence has been my guide and helper for all these long years. Who would have thought I could possibly have survived for the four long years of the Great War? Or that I, a voice crying in the wilderness, could have rallied the entire German people to my program, against the lies of the Jewish press and the machinations of so many idiotic politicians? I'll tell you, Albert. No one. No one at all. They laughed at me, Albert. At me. Can you believe it? But who is laughing now, eh? Who is laughing now?"

Hitler and Speer doubled over in hysterics. A young, shapely, sandy-haired woman with a round, pleasantly Germanic face entered the room and handed Hitler a card, on which was handwritten a message.

Speer thought she must be Eva Braun. He'd heard of the woman rumored to be Hitler's mistress, but the two had never met.

The *Führer* frowned. "Excuse me, Speer, but it's urgent business. I'll return momentarily. We must continue our conversation. It's wonderful to be able express one's thoughts to someone as knowledgeable and honest as you."

"Thank you, *mein Führer*," replied Speer. "I'll wait as long as necessary. Please don't hurry back on my account."

Two hours later, Speer still sat in the same stuffed chair, sipping his tenth cup of tea, and growing more and more restless. When Hitler finally returned twenty minutes later, his mood had turned sour.

"Idiots, idiots, and more idiots!" Hitler ranted. "I'm surrounded by them."

"Mein Führer?"

"My generals, Speer, my generals. Every Prussian one of them... a pack of worthless idiots. I know more about their business than the lot of them put together."

"May I ask, *mein Führer*, what the problem is?"

"The problem, Speer? The problem? The problem is those amateurs won't be ready to begin Operation Barbarossa, the conquest of Russia, until the third week in June!"

Hitler's rant left Speer astonished. The German General Staff contained within it some of the most brilliant military minds in the world. "Perhaps they are concerned that prolonged operations will expose our troops to the Russian winter and—"

"Fools!" cried Hitler. "Fools and knaves. And so is anyone that agrees with them. So Speer, which one are you? A fool or a knave? Come on, out with it, man."

"I think n-n-neither. I was merely trying to suggest..."

"Oh, you were merely trying to suggest, were you *Herr* Speer! How helpful. Like that simpleton *Herr* General von Klegner, who dared to tell me he was concerned with the reaction to Barbarossa by the Americans. Now why should I give a *pfennig* about what that squalid nation has to say? America was born of miscegenation among negroes, Gypsies, and Jews, and long ago committed racial suicide. I can tell you about the Americans, Speer."

Speer bit his tongue. He knew their economic and military contributed to the loss of the Great War, recollecting how close the Germans had come to victory, only to be defeated when the Americans poured men and materials into Europe. In the current struggle among nations, he fervently hoped the *Führer* preferred to fight only one war at a time.

But Hitler was dreaming of global conquest.

"Give me three good months, Speer, just three good months. That's all I ask. And our armies will shake the rotten tree of Jewish Bolshevism, and its foul spawn the Soviet Union, to the earth! Then, while the Americans dither under the feckless leadership of their ignorant president, Mr. Lindbergh, we Germans will become a continental nation like they are. We will play the Americans for fools, my friend, and they will fall right into our trap every time. None of the half-wits around Lindbergh have the will to power that we do, Speer, not a single one of them! Except for that Irishman, Kennedy.

"Now there," Hitler proclaimed, eyes incandescent while spittle accumulated at the corners of his mouth as he jabbed his right index finger in the air. "There's a clever operator, that Kennedy. Too bad his son Jack is such a wastrel. He must have received a bad genetic inheritance from his mother. But one can't have everything, of course."

"*Mein Führer*, the Americans will also make easy targets for our armed forces. With your strategic brilliance, they are doomed."

Sweating and breathing heavily, Hitler sat down in his stuffed chair and swept that lock of invading hair away from his face. "*Ja,* Speer. *Ja,* I agree. They are doomed. Along with all their kikes and niggers, along with all the other sub-humans that live in that country. But... there is one thing that concerns me. Shall I tell you about it, Albert?"

"Please, *mein Führer*. I shall always observe the strictest silence in this matter, as with everything you say."

"Fermi," said Hitler. "Enrico Fermi. I must have him."

"The Italian physicist? I don't understand. Why?"

"*Ja,* Speer, the Italian physicist, who stupidly married a Jewess bitch. And even more stupidly, was allowed to emigrate to America by my friend Mussolini.

"You look confused, *Herr* Architect," said Hitler, noting his guest's frown

"At the moment, I cannot tell you everything, Speer. But the physicist Heisenberg claims that, without Fermi's knowledge and intellect, he cannot progress with the tasks we have assigned him. I assure you that what Heisenberg and his group of scientists is doing of vital import to the security of the *Heimat,* our homeland. So I have put pressure on the Americans to find the man and send him back to us immediately. They can keep the wife, of course."

"Ah, so this is why Lindbergh declared martial law not long ago."

"A wholly inadequate action on his part. But I suppose it was the best that well-intentioned ignoramus Lindbergh could do. I smell the Irishman's hand in things, Speer. He's the only man with a true racial consciousness in Lindbergh's circle. Tsk, tsk, a rare gem of an individual, wasting his God-given talents in such a swamp. But don't ever think that because Kennedy favors us, he doesn't favor himself more. That's America! No deep roots in the soil, no proper recognition of the value of race, no understanding of high culture."

"What can I do to help, *mein Führer*? I beg you, ask anything of me."

The *Führer* motioned Speer to rise, and placed a hand on each of his shoulders, drawing the two men face to face. "If you want to be my true friend, Albert," he said, so close to the architect, their foreheads touched, and Speer could smell Hitler's last vegetarian meal on his stale breath, "for the sake of the Divine Providence that has always protected me in the past, and always will protect me in the future, for God's sake, Speer, go—and get me Enrico Fermi."

By the middle of May, the academic year at City College was almost finished for its undergraduates. But for Masters and Doctorate-level students, one academic year ended the day before the next one began.

Sid spent much of his time at the end of this term as he had at the end of last term, studying for his final exams. His last year at CCNY was supposed to be devoted to an experimental research project. But with the death of his mentor, Professor Strauss, Sid had to choose another thesis advisor. This time, a little older and wiser, he made his decision based on more objective criteria than when he'd glommed onto Strauss.

It came down to a choice between Professors Devers and Cronin. Both men were long-term members of the professoriate, but Devers had the stronger interest in atomic physics. He suggested Sid purchase a textbook that, not coincidentally, he had written. The work described the properties of sub-atomic particles; electrons, protons, and neutrons, tiny critters that constituted the atom and its nucleus, and was available from Devers directly for the sum of $3.50. Sid hesitated to ask his father for the money until he realized he had no other way of affording it. He'd neglected his tutoring business in favor of moping about the apartment. Rosalie was the first one to notice.

"Sid," she barked as she entered the room he and Benny shared. Benny was on an overnight sleepover at the American Museum of Natural History with his class.

"Put a smile on your face, *bubbeleh*," she said, squeezing one of his cheeks. "I can't stand to look at you anymore! And you used to be such a happy little boy!

What's wrong with my little boy? Is it the *shiksa*? I'll tear her throat out if she's giving you trouble, I'm warning her."

Sid sighed. "Thanks for the concern, Mom. But I'm not a little boy anymore."

"That's what you think, Sid. To me, you'll always be a little boy. Understand?"

"I suppose I have no choice."

"Sid! This is your mother. You're not talking to Yente the Matchmaker! So, tell your mother... is it the *shiksa*?"

He took a deep breath. "Okay, you win, Ma. Damn, you always make me give it up, don't ya? Yeah, it's the *shiksa*. Y'know, the *shiksa* has a name. It's Julia. I think you should call her by her correct name."

"Well, Mr. Formal, if you feel so strongly about it, I'll call the *shiksa* by her right name. Julia. Y'know, that's a nice name for a *shiksa*."

"Ah, hell, Ma, you really can be obnoxious." Sid put his hands over his ears and tried to take cover underneath his pillow before Rosalie snatched it away and hit him over the head with it.

"You've known Julia for years! Ever since she was a little girl!"

"She was Julia when she was a little girl. Now that she's dating you, she's a *shiksa*."

Sid closed Devers' book and sat up in his bed. "Okay, okay, I give up. You're not going to leave me alone until I spill the beans, are you?"

"It's a blessing to have a child that understands his own mother. So now, if you know what's good for you..."

"Okay, you win Mom, you win. I surrender. I admit that... er, I have been, ah... thinking a great deal about the ah, *shiksa,* er, I mean Julia."

"I think you can't get her out of your mind. True, Sid?"

He remained silent.

"Okay, now that we've established that you're smitten with the lady, that she appears to you every night in your dreams..."

"You're overdoing it, Mom. I don't see her in any of my dreams."

"Ah! That's great! Dr. Freud was right after all! I always knew it!"

"Mom—what are you talking about?"

"Sigmund Freud—you know him, right? The Viennese guy. That Dr. Freud. The one who said that if you don't see someone in your dreams, it means you're getting over her. Right? So, you, my Sid, are getting over this girl. See, it's all just science, and as you always tell me, science is never wrong."

Sid burst out laughing. "I may have said something like that on occasion, but your use of my statement is, well... unique! But I feel better after having spoken to you than I have in weeks."

"And that, Sid, my boy," smiled Rosalie, "is what I'm here for."

Later that evening, violating Sam's injunction about making unnecessary phone calls, Sid rang the *shiksa*. Lucky for him, Sam had turned in early for the night.

Julia picked up on the fourth ring. The two hadn't spoken in several weeks. The last time they did, the conversation was perfunctory, though Sid promised to call again at an unspecified time in the future. In the interim, he'd given their relationship much thought, undecided if Julia was only playing a role. But somehow, the conversation with his mother helped him focus his mind and overcome his doubts.

"Hello."

"Julia... it's Sid."

A long pause. "Sid... I, ah, I didn't expect to hear from you."

So far, so good, he thought—she didn't hang up. Nothing was so final as that 'click' in midsentence. Sid could feel his heart racing. He hoped hers skipped a beat too.

"It's been a while, I know. May I ask you a question, Julia?"

"Hmmm... yes, I suppose so. Though depending on the question, I can't promise an answer."

"Fair enough, Julia. Fair enough. My question is—are you taken yet? I mean, like by another guy. Because if you are, this may be a short conversation and I a very unhappy Sid."

Julia laughed. Sid pictured her in his mind; dark hair tossing about, back arched, head thrown back, lips parted revealing her dazzling, brilliantly white teeth. "And if I did have a new boyfriend, would you be jealous, Sid Peskin? Ha! Now you're being silly. What makes you think I'd allow you to just walk away? I'm not the kind of gal that gives in without a fight. I'll never give in. Except, in matters of good taste and common sense, of course, as I believe Mr. Churchill once said. I knew you needed time, and I'm not so needy to deny it to you. So, my question for you is—what changed? Why tonight?"

"Oh, just something that occurred to me—in the middle of examining some mighty hairy, highfalutin' concepts in atomic physics for about the twenty-fifth time. Jeez, I thought I understood mathematics until I met this stuff. It's wild."

"So. You buried your head in horrendous equations, and that's when you first thought of me! How romantic. You really know how to sweep a girl off her feet, don't you?"

"Okay. Have it your way. I saw a vision of the girl of my dreams brushing her black lustrous hair, her dark eyes and ruby red lips so willing, so inviting. How's that?"

"Oh, for God's sake, Sid. It's just awful. Now tell me the truth, young man."

"Okay, okay. My mother told me to poop or get off the pot. So here we are."

"Yeah, that one has the ring of truth to it."

"So whaddya say? This Saturday at noon at our favorite spot?"

"The 14th Street westbound platform of the LL train it is. I'm looking forward to another pass through of that station. And then where to, good sir?"

"Oh, I was thinking uptown this time."

"We're going slumming in Harlem?"

"Hmm... no. More like slumming at the Museum of Natural History on West 79th Street. Benny says the place is fabulous. Especially the dinosaurs! And I'm told the gemstone exhibit can simply blow your socks off. Rumor has it they've a topaz that weighs a metric ton! But I haven't been there in so many years, I barely remember it."

"And I can't think of a better way to spend an afternoon," said Julia, even though she'd been there more times than she could count and had long ago lost interest in the place. "I'll see you then, Sid."

"G'bye, Julia."

The phone receiver went click. Sid glanced at the clock hung on the wall of the living room. The hands told him it was nine and he had at least three hours of work to do. And then he was up at five tomorrow morning.

But no matter how much effort he made to keep his head in his books, Sid couldn't keep his thoughts off Julia. Finally, knowing it was hopeless, he gave up on studying for the evening, intending to make up the work on successive days.

Benny was fast asleep when Sid crawled into his own bed in their shared room. As he often did, before falling asleep, he allowed his mind to wander, sometimes re-thinking the events of the day, sometimes pondering the mysteries of the physical universe as revealed in the language of mathematics.

But tonight, after his conversation with Julia, he was too exhilarated for his thoughts to focus on any of the technical terms of physics or math. Tonight, his wandering consciousness produced visions of glowing, white stars emitting broad beams of light, and of earthly fireworks exploding one after another, generating dozens if not hundreds of brilliant points of light that faded ever so slowly. These things he saw, and much more, before a deep sleep at last overcame him.

Next thing he knew, the alarm clock was jangling him awake at 5:30 a.m., well before sunrise. He sprang out of bed, refreshed and clear-headed. Rosalie was still sound asleep. Sam was already in the kitchen, drinking his morning cup of coffee.

Benny said, "C'mon, Sid! Turn that thing off already, will ya?"

Sid flicked the lever that turned off the alarm bell ringer, and quickly dressed. "See ya later, kid." Benny didn't reply.

Those few words Sid spoke to Benny were enough for him to know that something was different this morning—that during his sleep, he'd somehow achieved a transcendence to a higher plane of mental acuity. Overnight, he had grasped an essential aspect of the physical universe that only he, and perhaps no one else in the history of humanity, had ever grasped. It was an ecstatic yet quiet feeling he'd never known existed. Perhaps this new plane of existence was akin to the nirvana that Buddhist acolytes could attain after years of meditation—a sense of being at peace with himself and at one with the universe, and with every being in it.

"Dad," he said to Sam as he stepped into the kitchen to join his father. "I think a hell of an interesting idea came to me last night."

CHAPTER 14

O ver the next few days, Sid's exalted feelings dissipated, but he became increasingly convinced his idea was correct. To investigate further, he returned to the City College Library in Shepard Hall and spent the next few days, from the moment the library opened in the morning until it closed in the early evening, tracking down potential leads in the physics journals. He looked at his hypothesis from all possible angles, attempting in the way of a serious scientist to prove that he must be wrong.

Sid learned a great deal about physics through his efforts, but nothing he discovered indicated he was off base, speculative, or violating any previously known physical law. In fact, all the data he examined pointed to the exact opposite. He was also certain that what he'd come up with was novel, meaning that while someone may have thought of his idea previously, it had never been published.

That was a relief to Sid not only because he was concerned about being scooped. Rather, he recognized that the consequences of his thought, if correct, could also be unspeakably horrendous for huge numbers of people.

Because of the gravity of the matter, and in light the fate of I. Bernard Strauss, Sid decided not to speak of his hypothesis to any of the other City College physics professors. Instead, he turned to the only person on earth who he was certain could grasp the difficult issues involved. Fortunately, this recent immigrant to America lived only fifty miles away from New York, in Princeton, New Jersey. His name: Albert Einstein.

In 1941, Albert Einstein, the gray eminence of the physics world and a Nobel laureate, was sixty-one years old. Though even he would admit he was well past his scientific prime, he remained the most respected scientist in the world for his colossal findings of thirty years in the past. These included the theories of special and general relativity—both of which had been experimentally verified. By 1933, at the Nazi accession to power, Einstein was the Director of the Kaiser Wilhelm Institute for Physics and a professor at the Humboldt University of Berlin.

But Einstein's long years of service and critical contributions mattered not a whit to Hitler's Brownshirts. They managed to conflate the relativity of physics with relativity in the social sciences. That was anathema to the notion of Aryan racial superiority. So, Einstein and the theory of relativity were both ejected from Germany.

"Jewish intellectualism is dead," proclaimed Josef Goebbels. Einstein himself was "an enemy not yet hanged." In the following year, his works were publicly burned by university students. Fortunately, by then, Einstein was safe in the U.S. where he thought he was free from people who, in his words, "more than anything else in the world, fear the influence of...intellectual independence."

That was before the advent of the Lindbergh right-wing political and social phenomenon. As a member of a marginalized group in society in Germany, Einstein felt he lived on sufferance in his adopted country. So, he carefully cultivated the persona of an affable, mild-mannered, slightly eccentric egghead, in stark contrast to the wild hellion he'd really been in his younger days.

To further his benign image, Einstein grew his salt and pepper mane unfashionably long and dropped any formal attire from his wardrobe, giving him a persistently informal, unkempt look. The effect was that, in a conversation with Einstein, all anyone would see and hear was Einstein's mask. But the press loved his carefully-crafted image, and so did the public. As a senior citizen, he was a beloved figure in the United States and had long since become a household name.

Sid didn't allow his idea to moulder away in his head for long. He gave up any additional studying for his final exams, hoping he retained enough information to squeak by with a passing grade. Instead, he scribbled on dozens of fresh, crisp sheets of white paper, filling them top to bottom with formulas and numbers. He was aided by his ancient wooden slide rule, a calculating gizmo that doubled as a chewing stick before Sid realized he'd chewed off some of the numbers.

If only he could get his hands one of those manual metal calculating machines about now. But some of these calculations were so difficult, he doubted it was worth working for the decades it would take to figure things out.

The mathematical complexity alone was another good reason for Sid to approach Einstein. But he had no idea how to get in touch with such an eminent person and keep his idea confidential at the same time.

Aside from his contributions to physics, all Sid knew about the greatest physicist of the 20th century was that his current employer was the Institute for Advanced

Studies in Princeton. Would the great Einstein take a cold call from a lowly Masters degree student unknown to him? And even if he would, given the nationwide manhunt underway for Enrico Fermi, would Einstein be concerned his phones were tapped? Were letters to him opened and read, too? It was impossible for Sid to know.

So Sid decided to go to the only person he believed he could trust in such weighty matters: Frieda, the deeply zany secretary of the City College of NY physics department. He found her inspecting files in her tiny office on an upper floor of Shepard Hall.

"You want what?"

"Oh, c'mon Frieda. You heard me. I need to speak with Einstein. Albert Einstein. You know who he is, right?"

Frieda gazed at him from over the tops of her glasses.

"I heard you the first time, young man. But what I want to know is why you're coming to me? Do I look like the phone operator? Or is this another college prank like the time you guys made me call Manitoba just so you could ask about the weather? The administration deducted that one from my paycheck."

"No prank, Frieda my dear. No prank, I promise."

"Hmm… you fooled me once, Sid Peskin." She batted her lashes. "How do I know you're not foolin' me again? Huh?"

"How do I know if you have Einstein's real phone number? Huh, Frieda dear?"

They stared at each other, at a standoff.

"I got bad news for ya, Sid. The cops confiscated all the late Professor Strauss' stuff. Including his Roladex, which contained contact info he accumulated over a lifetime. I told 'em it was my card file, but they didn't believe me."

"Thanks, anyway, Frieda." He slowly backed out through her door. But when he was about a yard or two away, she called after him.

"Sid. C'mon back in here."

"Okay, Frieda. Whaddaya want now?"

"Siddown."

Picking up the phone receiver from its cradle, she dialed, "O."

"Princeton, New Jersey," she said when the operator came on the line. "Hello? Hello, operator? Please get me 52-5-16." She covered the receiver and smiled at Sid. "Just wait. You're gonna owe me big for this one, Sid. Payback will be at my discretion. This better be important."

Suddenly, she brightened and bolted upright.

"Albert! Albert *liebschen,* how are you? It's me, Frieda! That's right, from *le Trocadero en Paris* and… oh, yes… that's right, Albert, from many, many other places, too. Oh, I remember it all so well, the days… and the nights, Albert, the nights, when we'd gaze at the stars and at each other. It's been so long. Fate has been cruel, but now we're not far apart again."

There was a long pause while Frieda listened, laughed, and nodded. "Yes, my love, I'd be delighted to. But right at the moment, I have a young man in my office who says he must speak with you about some, er... something."

"It's a mathematical problem of physical interest," Sid said.

Frieda repeated it into the receiver. Another pause. "He's a very nice young man, Albert." She covered the receiver with her hand again. "He wants to know if you're a Bundist or a Lindberghite."

Sid vigorously shook his head.

"I think he's insulted you should ask, Albert. Good. Good, and thank you, Albert. I'll tell him. And I promise to call back soon. *Auf wiedersehen, mein Kätzchen!* Kisses and bye-bye!"

Frieda hung up the phone. "This Saturday, 112 Mercer Street, Princeton, New Jersey at 10:00 a.m. That's the best I can do. And remember. You owe me."

Sid's eyes widened. "I'm astounded! Wow! Just who the hell are you? I don't know how you came to know Einstein, but someday, you'll have to enlighten me! Fantastic... if I'm not being pranked!"

Sid thought he heard her mumble "fat chance" under her breath. "You'll have to be at 112 Mercer Street, Princeton, this coming Saturday at 10 o'clock sharp to find out, Sid."

"But isn't the professor worried his phone might be tapped? I mean..."

Frieda rolled her eyes. "Listen, buster. He's Albert Einstein—the man who discovered the basic laws and principles of the known universe. I think he can handle an FBI phone tap."

Sid planted a big, wet kiss on her cheek. "Your country is in your debt," he said, rushing out of the room.

"Oh, yeah? Then tell my country to pay up already. I need the money."

In his exuberance about his upcoming meeting with Einstein, Sid had neglected one issue: transportation to Princeton. With the advent of martial law and the national search for Enrico Fermi, train and bus traffic coming in and going out of New York was being monitored. The last thing Sid needed was to encounter any Bundists, or Mayor Fred Trump's cops.

But this wasn't Sid's only problem.

He cursed inwardly when he remembered that this Saturday was also his date with the enchanting Julia Falcone. But it didn't matter. Compared to his meeting with Albert Einstein, the American Museum of Natural History and its dinosaur skeletons, blue whales, elephants, and other long dead, stuffed big game, and even its one-ton topaz and rare gemstones, was of secondary priority.

And Julia? Would she accept his explanation for the postponement? Or would she feel Sid was just putting her off, toying with her affections? Under similar circumstances, that's what the shallower young ladies he'd once dated might have thought. And Julia could consider his behavior rude.

But was there really a choice? This visit with Albert Einstein was on a matter of potential significance for the security of the United States. And if Julia was the woman he thought she was, both feminine and scientifically minded, she would encourage him to do what he thought was right.

Perhaps Sid could have his cake and eat it, too. Arriving home later in the afternoon, he dropped a pile of Liberty Head dimes into his pocket. He then went outside into the breezy, warm air and placed a call in the phone booth on the corner of Morris Avenue and the Concourse.

Plunk-ching, plunk-ching! The dimes fell in their slots on the payphone, crediting Sid twenty cents. It was enough for a short phone call to Canarsie, Brooklyn.

Julia picked up after several rings. After a minute's worth of pleasantries, Sid provided her with an abstracted form of his latest work, leaving out the technical details. He pledged her to secrecy for evermore.

"Now here's my problem, Julia, my dear. Albert Einstein wants to see me about it."

She gasped. "Oh my god, Sid! Albert Einstein? The Albert Einstein? That's... that's... oh, I don't even know what to say! Oh, my God, what an honor! So, what's the problem?"

"He wants to see me this Saturday. It was the only day he was available."

"Oh, Sid, you're being silly again. I'm so happy for you no matter what day you're visiting Einstein. Whatever you've come up with, it must be really something to have impressed him. Wow! A visit with Einstein! You just have to do this! Don't give a second thought about me. The museum's been there for years. It can wait a little longer for our visit."

"Julia, thanks. Thanks for your understanding and encouragement. I didn't want to take them for granted, but I thought that's what you would say. It's the kind of woman you are—a one-of-a-kind kind."

"Compliment accepted, sir. But I just thought of something. How do you plan to go to Princeton, New Jersey? It's much farther than Canarsie."

Sid explained his reservations about traveling by train or bus.

"Oh, I get it. I get it. Y'know, I have a thought. Let me ask Joey if I can borrow the car for half a day on Saturday. It shouldn't take longer than that, should it?"

"I doubt it. Unless *Herr* Professor is more talkative than I anticipate. He'll probably hear me out and throw me out. I'm sure he's very busy."

"My brother's around somewhere. Let me see what I can do. Call you back soon."

"Julia, you're a doll. I hope we'll at least get to spend some time together on Saturday."

"On one condition, Sid. You don't get off so easy."

"Name it, Julia."

"I get to meet Einstein, too. I wanna turn the science girls at Hunter College green. Just green! What a hoot it'll be when I tell 'em all how I spent my weekend!"

On Saturday, driving a grey 1938 Ford, Julia picked Sid up at the corner of W. 179th Street and Broadway in upper Manhattan, at the eastern terminus of the George Washington Bridge. As traffic was light, and the military presence non-intrusive, they sped across the massive bridge, its six-lane span suspended by huge steel rope cables 250 feet above the grey-brown waters of the Hudson River.

The view from the passenger's seat was spectacular, ranging from the forest of sky-scrapers in lower Manhattan's Financial District far off in the distance to the south, to the leafy suburban, bedroom communities of Westchester County in the north.

The two fell to chatting about everything and nothing, each pleased to be back in the other's good graces. Both were thrilled about the upcoming meeting with Einstein.

The road from the bridge led through the low-lying meadowlands and skirted the industrial areas of northern New Jersey. At the town of Elizabeth, not far from Newark, they passed the gigantic Standard Oil refinery. This mass of steel towers, gasoline storage tanks, and miles of exposed metal piping belched a perpetual stream of foul-smelling effluents that coated the landscape. Soil and air were defiled in the pursuit of maximum corporate profit, regardless of the damage done to the environment or the people that lived nearby. Neither, of course, was of much interest to members of the Lindbergh administration.

Once past these horrors of the industrial age, northern Jersey morphed into a delightful region of rolling hills and verdant farmland, interspersed with copses of pine and oak. Within an hour of crossing the bridge, Julia drove into the town of Princeton, and with the help of a friendly gas station attendant, managed to locate Mercer Street.

112 Mercer Street was a pleasant two-story colonial dwelling with three windows on the upper story and two, plus a left-sided door, on the lower. Traffic was light, and only a few cars were parked nearby.

At 10 a.m. sharp, Sid and Julia exited the 1938 Ford and, as per their agreement, made their way to Einstein's door. Sid, with butterflies in his stomach, rang the doorbell. Einstein's housekeeper answered and asked them to remain outside.

"The professor will be with you in just a moment."

With Germanic precision, Albert Einstein appeared, his salt-and-pepper hair uncombed and wild, his blue shirt and gray slacks both rumpled. But he seemed as genial and avuncular as the press portrayed him.

"Professor Einstein." Sid offered his hand. "It's a great honor to meet you."

"Ze pleasure ist mine, I assure you," replied Einstein, grasping Sid's hand in return. "I presume you are Zidney Peskin."

Sid nodded.

"Ach, sehr gut. Ja, you are ze young man my dear friend Frieda zent. *Und* who, may I ask, is zis charming *frau?* Frieda didn't mention a zing about you, my dear."

Sid thought he detected a slight leer in Einstein's eye.

"This is Julia Falcone, Professor. My, uh... dear friend."

Einstein laughed. "Zo. As I suspected. It's a great pleasure to meet you, too, Mizz Falcone. Tell me—are you also interested in physics?"

"Very much so, Professor. And like Sid, I'm also very pleased to meet you."

"Wonderful. But now I'm afraid we must get down to business. Zid, you and I must take a walk. Zis is now how I must live in ze free country of America, because someone has put listening devices—you call zem 'bugs,' I zink—in my house. Zey bugged my phones, too, but a few of the boys at ze Institute of Advanced Study and I... well, it's best you don't know precisely what we did.

"Mizz Falcone, please do not be offended, but ze conversation between Zid and myself zimply must be private. I know it is rude of me, but if you wish, you are free to rest from your journey here in my house. Please..."

With a sweeping motion of his hand, Einstein indicated that Julia should enter. She complied graciously.

"We will not be gone long, I promise. I'm quite busy, as you can imagine. But a recommendation from Frieda must be taken most zeriously."

Julia disappeared into the dwelling. Einstein and Sid walked along Mercer Street without talking and then turned right at the first corner. The older man looked back over his shoulder, taking care that no one was following.

"Zo, *Herr* Peskin, I also have a question for you. Zat girl, Mizz Falcone—she's what zey call a real looker. Is she intelligent, too?"

"Extremely."

"Ja, zat's always an important quality in a woman. *Und* what of her temperament? Is she stable? Does she allow you to work, or does she disturb you with her troubles? Does she—what ist ze word—*ach, ja.* Does she 'cluck about,' talking much nonsense?"

"Oh. No! She's wonderful, Professor. I think we respect each other very much."

"Zen you're a lucky man, Zidney. My first wife, Mileva, she was a very intelligent woman. Brilliant, even. But terribly unstable. Too many problems she wanted me to zolve for her. A great pity. You know, I can zolve problems of a mathematical and physical nature. But women's matters, *ja...* are too complex. Zey lose me, you know."

Sid didn't respond.

Einstein shrugged. "Well, zat's the way zings go. Now, let's discuss your 'mathematical problem zat relates to physics,' as Frieda mentioned in our phone conversation."

Sid described his work in the elegant language of mathematics, and showed Einstein several of the equations he'd derived, which he'd jotted down in a small notebook. Einstein, again looking up and down the street, perused the book with interest, nodding his head in agreement at some points, furrowing his brow at others, but retained his interest and serious expression throughout.

"*Herr Gott!*" he exclaimed as he reached the final page. "Peskin, I believe I'm correct zat you are still a graduate student at City College? Zen I must ask: How did you arrive at zese ideas? *Und* before you answer, ze first zing I must tell you is—never, ever utter a word about what's in zis notebook to anyone! Anyone! *Gott sei dank* you came to me first and to no one else! It is correct zat you are a graduate student, Peskin?"

"Yes, sir."

Einstein snapped the notebook shut. "Do you have a copy of zis book?"

"No. I mean, yes, I have my notes. The rest is all in my head."

"Und did anyone help place zis work in your head? Like ze late Professor Strauss, for example?"

Sid didn't like what Einstein implied. "No, sir. None of this work was Strauss'. I believe I'm the first person to discover what I've presented to you today."

Einstein reopened the small notebook. "Peskin, if everything you zay here is verified, zen you may be as far ahead of ze physics community now as I was back in 1905 when I discovered relativity. This work is truly brilliant. And from zuch a youth, too! *Ach,* well, I was a young man too, a long time ago. But, I must tell you, and please don't be disappointed. You're not ze first person to recognize ze concept of a chain reaction resulting from nuclear fission *und* neutron emission. Zat honor belongs to someone else."

Despite Einstein's kind words, Sid knew that in the world of science, the first horse out of the gate collected most of the kudos. But he took it in stride and didn't let his feelings show.

"May I know who first proposed the concept of the chain reaction? I'm not aware anything has been published on it."

"Zat's true, Peskin. *Und* before your work, it was a highly theoretical concept. But after examining your notes, I'm convinced a chain reaction can really happen, under ze correct circumstances. I will certainly speak to ze inventor, my good friend Leo, later today."

Sid froze. "Leo the Hungarian?"

Einstein laughed. "I'm not sure he'd like to be thought of that way. But yes, Leo iz, or waz, Hungarian. His name is Leo Szilard. It's a good Hungarian name, though

Leo is Jewish. While it's true zat he originally postulated ze idea of a chain reaction, you, *Herr* Peskin, are years ahead of anyone with respect to its practical development. And zough you've not mentioned it, I believe you are also aware of what zat could lead to."

"Yes. The possibility would exist of making a weapon of enormous power—one such as mankind has never seen before. The ultimate terror-weapon. A monstrosity that could consume an entire city and reduce perhaps all of civilization to ashes. Nothing less than an atomic bomb." The eyes of the older scientist and his young acolyte met in full knowledge of the existential horror of what each, in his own way, helped to conjure up.

Sid and Einstein agreed that under no circumstances could these secrets ever be allowed to fall into the hands of the Nazis or their American admirers.

"And you know, perhaps Leo Szilard knows what has happened to Fermi and ze other scientists who have disappeared of late. I zertainly don't know where zey went. But zis I can tell you, young man. Should anyone discover that you are now one of ze foremost minds in atomic physics in zis or any other country, you may be in extreme danger. Extreme!

"In a very real zense, Mr. Peskin, I have no desire to have the knowledge that you do. And, for your sake, I wish you did not have it, either. I have tried during my life to live as a pacifist. Yet my greatest discoveries may now be turned into horrible weapons of war. Zis is a difficult burden for one man to bear, but for me, zere is no choice. I hope it will not be your lot in life, too.

"But for ze moment, we, you *und* I, must have a plan. I will call Leo Szilard today. I will be discreet, I promise—your secrets are safe with me. You zay everything you've done has been memorized. *Gut.* Then destroy your notebook *und* all your notes until zere is nothing left. Nothing! Zey cannot be allowed fall into ze wrong hands. Zen wait until I call you."

Sid scribbled his home phone number on a scrap of paper and handed it to Einstein. The two walked in silence back to Einstein's residence at 112 Mercer Street where Sid retrieved Julia. She'd spent the time sitting in Einstein's living room, making polite conversation with his housekeeper.

"Thank you, Professor. I hope to hear from you soon."

The two shook hands. "You will, Mr. Peskin. I promise."

Sid and Julia returned to her car and drove off.

"My God, Sid. You and Einstein spoke for over a half an hour! What on earth did he say to you?"

"Oh, nothing much, Julia. We just discussed some technical details bearing on my work. You know, fancy mathematics and other boring stuff. Nothing anyone else would be interested in, believe me. I'm sure he thought I was a complete waste of his time."

Sid scheduled the next day, Sunday, for study and rest. The thrill of meeting Einstein, coupled with the wonderful half-day spent with Julia, still clung to him like the fragrance of newly blossoming flowers.

Sid thought, if it weren't for that jerk in the White House, he'd be a content young man right about now. But for his own good, he knew he had to let his political feelings go. Einstein's valuation of him as a physicist were far more important than the babblings of a presidential impostor.

He was astonished by some of Einstein's thoughts. From whom did Einstein believe he was in danger? From Lindbergh at the federal level, or closer to home, from Fred Trump and the NYC police who understood little but fashionable brutality? And how was Leo Szilard, a good friend of Einstein's, a part of the events of the past six months? Was he, as unlikely as it seemed, in some way also a threat? Without a doubt, Einstein was on the side of the angels, one of the few people in Sid's life whose ethics were beyond reproach. Thus Leo, too, should also be above suspicion. But how well did the two physicists really know each other—and was Leo as trustworthy as Einstein believed him to be? Every man had his price.

Sid grimaced at the thought. These threads were more tangled than the equations of quantum mechanics! Unfortunately, the good night's sleep he got on Saturday night did nothing to help resolve his dilemmas.

At 9 a.m., Sam and Rosalie were still snoozing, and Benny was frantically fiddling with the radio dial to hear re-runs of one of his favorite programs. The half-hour drama was called *Sky King* and was about a pilot living in Alaska who owned a two-seat airplane. With his niece Penny riding shotgun, the two crime stoppers dropped in from the skies to catch bad guys *in flagrante*. It was great adventure stuff for a young boy. Benny stepped back from the radio after picking out the *Sky King* theme song. He began to hum and sing along.

The phone rang. Sid picked it up immediately.

"Sid, this is Leo. The Hungarian. The professor asked me to call. I can't talk now, and don't try to talk with me. Meet me at the phone booth on the corner of Morris and the Concourse in fifteen minutes. Yes or no?"

"Yes," said Sid. The receiver went dead.

Sid dressed quickly.

"Hey, Sid," Benny said, seeing his older brother make for the front door. "Where ya goin'?"

"I'm takin' a hike, Benny Boy," he said, grabbing the light jacket that held his secret notebook.

"Ooooh! I've told you a thousand times. Don't call me Benny Boy. Or I'll call you Kid Sid. You used to hate that. Remember?"

"Okay, okay, I remember, little man." Sid laughed as he stopped at the doorway. "I promise. Don't be so angry."

Benny glowered at him.

"Listen, Benny. I have an idea. Let's you and me restart the morning. Good morning, Brother Benjamin. How are you this morning?"

"I'm fine, Sid. Where ya goin' today?" said Benny with one ear on Sid and the other on *Sky King*.

"I'm takin' a hike, if that's okay with you, dear Brother Benjamin?"

"Yeah, it's okay, I guess. But before you go, can you tell me what this music is? I hear it every week. I like it, kinda."

"I really don't know, Brother Benjamin. It's called classical music, but I've no idea what piece it is. I'll ask Julia. She knows all about that stuff."

"Okay, see ya later, Sid, ya weirdo."

"And we were doing so well!" Sid laughed. "Be back in a few minutes, Brother Benjamin."

Sid walked out the door and closed it gently. He didn't know it at the time, of course, but the two brothers were not to see each other again for a far longer time than a few minutes.

Gabbing with Brother Benjamin had cost Sid precious minutes. To ensure he'd arrive at the phone booth at the agreed time, he dashed down the staircase and burst out of the building to the astonishment of an elderly couple returning from an early morning's walk.

Once outside in the warm, humid air of an early day in May in New York City, Sid stopped and looked first to his left, to the north, then to his right. From where he stood, the phone booth at the end of Morris Avenue, where it intersected the Grand Concourse, was visible, but at this moment, empty.

Strange, he thought, looking at his wristwatch, which showed it was now the exact time Leo and he were supposed to meet.

Perhaps Leo went down to Jerome Avenue—a short block west of the Concourse—to pick up a newspaper or have a cup of coffee. If I wait on the corner, I should see him climbing back up the hill.

Sid walked a short distance down Morris Avenue, lost in thought about the many questions he needed Leo Szilard to answer, starting from their encounter in the City College library last November to his relationship with the late Professor Strauss. Sid presumed Leo must now have information relayed from Albert Einstein.

Unfortunately, as he had both eyes on the phone booth and his head in the clouds, he neglected to look backward. If he had done so, he might have seen a black four-door Chevrolet puttering down Morris Avenue, dramatically picking up speed when the driver observed him.

Sid was about fifty feet from the intersection of Morris and the Concourse when the vehicle passed by, braked abruptly with a loud screeching of its tires, and hung a sharp right turn onto the sidewalk, where it stopped perpendicular to the street and directly in front of him.

Stunned by nearly being run over, Sid froze in place as three large men, all in their twenties and thirties, piled out of the automobile and surrounded him. Each wore a heavy black overcoat inappropriate for the season. Underneath, each man wore a white shirt and a black tie fastened at the neck by a Windsor knot. All heads were covered by black fedoras, hands by black gloves, and feet by brown, expensive leather shoes. Unsurprisingly, each had broken out into a profuse sweat, which Sid guessed wouldn't improve their dispositions much.

He wondered who'd sent this troupe of grim-faced goons. There were so many possibilities, he couldn't be certain. But any doubt was removed when their leader, stepping out of the car last and standing and scowling at the open door, commanded,

"Peskin. Inta' da car." His clipped accent indicated his first language was Sicilian as taught to him as a toddler in Brooklyn by his immigrant mamma.

Sid considered making a run for it down Morris Avenue but thought better of it when the man who'd circled behind him pulled out a .357 Smith and Wesson revolver and stuck it in his back. Resigned, he raised his hands and followed the leader into the car's back seat, wedged between two large masses of overdressed, sweating Sicilian man-flesh. Within seconds, Sid was blindfolded and his wrists tied together in front of him.

Sid thought it a lousy way to die. First, he'd be tortured with a lead pipe and have all his bones broken. Then, God knew what. The police would find his body in the lake in Flushing Meadow Park or maybe stuffed into the Trylon at the World's Fair. And all because he kissed a Mafia princess. Okay, maybe a little more than kissed. But it was her idea.

He laughed at his imagined fate, though his heart was bursting inside his ribcage.

"Hey! What's so fuckin' funny?" asked one of the Mafiosi, lighting up a cigarette in the closed car.

"Nothin'," said Sid.

"Den keep ya dirty mout' shut! Capish?"

Sid didn't reply. Instead, he coughed from the acrid smoke, while resisting the urge to waft his hand or wind a window down.

Someone hard-smacked the side of his head. Sid saw stars.

"Shaddup," barked the Mafioso, inhaling his cigarette. "Or you'll get much woise dan a little pat on da head."

"All right, quiet down," ordered the capo. "Da Boss said t' bring 'im in, not ta' kill 'im. Cut 'im some slack, won't ya?"

Sid was relieved for the moment. A watery grave or another visit to the Trylon at the World's Fair wasn't imminent.

For the next hour, the car drove through New York City in what seemed to Sid a random pattern. Thankfully, no one laid another hand on him. After what felt like half a day but was no more than three quarters of an hour, they came to a halt.

"Last stop. Everyone out," ordered the capo. Sid was pulled out of the car by pairs of hairy hands and manhandled onto the sidewalk. In front of him, he heard the creak and then the chimes of a door opening, and after a few steps, smelled something sweet in the air. He was in a candy shop, and had a vague recollection of Joey Falcone mentioning that his Uncle Vince worked out of a candy store in Brownsville, Brooklyn.

Once inside, Sid was pushed along until he reached a staircase. Placing one foot carefully in front of another, he descended the steep flight one step at a time. At the bottom, he was shoved to the side and ordered to sit in a hard chair. His sore wrists were freed and the blindfold yanked off.

In front of him, in an unfinished cellar cut out of the natural rock, glowed a naked, low-wattage, incandescent bulb, hanging on a shabby, long cord. In the shadows, Sid could make out a large number of wooden barrels and boxes scattered about in the gloom. To the left of the lightbulb, standing and smoking a cigarette, stood Uncle Vince, kitted out in the same uniform as his goons—though his color was a light tan, as opposed to the kidnappers' black. To Uncle Vince's right stood a man who might have been his double, but with far less hair through the middle of his scalp and a wilder look in his eyes. He assumed, from Benny's description, this was Julia's Uncle Phil.

To the right of the two Sicilian mobsters was another individual who was also sitting in a wooden chair but with one leg crossed over the other in a calm, relaxed pose. He had a pleasant, thin face that tapered to a jutting chin, a soft, almost rosebud mouth underneath a slightly bulbous nose, and a receding brown hairline. He looked to be in his mid-forties. Sid guessed he was of average height, or possibly a bit below. Whoever this person was, he had little of the facial features and nothing of the body habitus of a Sicilian; if he had to guess, the man was Jewish. But it was the eyes that described him best—the glint of gray steel, the gaze of a focused, deadly predator who would size up his prey, stealthily move in for the kill, strike the fatal blow, then steal away for another deadly ambush. A convulsive shiver tore through Sid's body.

A fourth man, who'd lingered in the darkness behind the Mangano brothers, unseen to Sid, stepped forward. Though he was still in shadow, Sid recognized him as the person he'd come to meet at the phone booth earlier in the day: Leo Szilard.

His first instinct was to rip the man's throat out until he remembered that Einstein spoke well of him and that Leo and he possessed secrets that could alter the future of humanity. But Sid's fear was overwhelming his ability to think rationally.

"Good afternoon, Mr. Peskin," said Uncle Vince. His tone reminded Sid of a prosecuting attorney. "You've, uh... caused us a bit o' trouble dese last few mont's. Whadaya have to say for y'self. Eh?"

Sid could barely breathe from terror. All he could think of were Julia's warnings about her family's old-world attitudes.

"Jeez, Uncle Vince," he gasped between breaths. "I'm sorry. I'm real sorry. I... I know I shouldn't have touched her. But... but I think she's the most beautiful girl I've ever seen and..."

"An' dat you ain't never gonna see her again. Right, ya little shit?"

Sid ached to tell Vince a lie—that he'd renounce Julia and swear to never see or speak to her again. But perhaps the lack of physical restraint suggested to Sid it might be safe to speak the truth.

"No, Vince," he said, shaking his head vigorously. "I'm gonna see her again, and no one will stand between us. I'll see her again as much as I can 'cause... I love Julia. And some day, if she agrees, I think I'll marry her."

Vince and Phil laughed uproariously, and even the dour predator on Sid's right cracked a smile. Leo's expression remained unchanged.

"So, Lepke," said Vince. "So! Whaddya t'ink o' ma boy here? Told ya he's da right man for da job! He may be a little shit, but he's loyal little shit! Ain't ya, Peskin!" Sid was hopelessly confused. Especially when Vince clapped him on the back.

"Yes, sir," Sid said, beginning to believe he wasn't ending the day as fish food, after all. "But I thought—"

"You t'ought I wuz gonna 'cap you for messin' aroun' wit' my niece?" Vince said, referring to a mob custom of breaking the knees—or kneecapping—those who got on their bad side.

"Sid... Ah, Sid... dat's ole' woild. Dis is America. It's a whole new woild out dere. Julia... hey, she's an adult. She does what she wants. And who am I, or anyone, ta interfere? Eh, Sid?

"So, listen now an' listen good. We're all friends here, Sid, ain't dat right? All on da same side, right? Ri-i-ight! So, I t'ink a round o' introductions is in order. Ya know me already. Vince Mangano." The mobster pronounced his last name with the accent on the first syllable.

Sid nodded in recognition, a weak smile on his lips. This had to be the most depressing 'welcome to the family' a man could ever have.

"And I'm his brother, Phil," said the junior Mangano, leering with the glinty eyes of a hungry crocodile. He took Sid's hand and pumped it up and down. Because the cellar remained cool, even during the warmest part of the day, neither of the well-dressed Mangano brothers had broken into a sweat.

"And I'm Leo Szilard, Sid," said the physicist, leaning forward and offering Sid his hand. "Sorry about today. But we felt we did what was necessary. By the end of the day, I'm sure you'll understand. And by the way, our mutual friend speaks extremely highly of you. He says there are aspects to your work that will cut years off our joint... er, little project."

Sid took Leo's hand with reluctance. "I think there's a great deal we need to discuss, Dr. Szilard," he said angrily. "My first question is—if I may ask—just where the hell am I? In the cellar of a candy store on the corner of Saratoga and Livonia in Brownsville, Brooklyn?"

The Mangano brothers shook their heads in unison.

Phil spoke first. "Naaah. We don' go dere no more. Da place is lousy wit' feds. Ya know, Hoover's boys."

"You're in Queens, Sid," said Leo. "In Kew Gardens. Nice place, so enjoy it while you're here. Close to the F train."

"Yeah," Vince interrupted. "Nice place. Right under Trump's fuckin' nose, too. But the sonuvabitch'll never find us. Never! Know why, Sid my boy?"

"No, Vince. But I could take an educated guess."

"Naah, don' bother. Patrick F. X. O'Sullivan, his Police Commissioner, is on our payroll, too—when we think to pay 'im, which ain't often dese days. Dat fuckin' mick also wants ta' muscle into our territory. We keep throwin' 'im out. Gets 'im pissed off. Like he has some rights to our business. But don' worry. We'll take care o' the little prick in good time," squealed Phil Mangano, who received an icy stare from his brother for breaching the prime Mafia rule of *omertà*—silence. But due to this day's critical business, no one was about to demand the imposition of the mandated punishment—death.

The gray-eyed predator stood and faced Vince. "Okay, boys, let's get on widdit," he said in words even more clipped than the Sicilians'. "No more chit-chat."

"Yes, sir," said Sid, seeing that the Mangano brothers deferred to the predator's authority. "We've never met. I'm Sid Peskin."

Gray eyes gazed at Sid through narrow slits. "Louie, kid. My friends call me Lepke. Lepke Buchalter. I'm a local businessman. Mattresses. Nice to meet you."

Buchalter removed a pack of Camel cigarettes from his coat pocket, took one, and placed its tip between his lips. With the flick of his Zippo lighter, Lepke drew the nicotine-laden smoke long and deep into his lungs.

Sid's eyes widened with fear as he felt his stomach tie itself in a knot. Thank God they'd never met earlier. He'd read about this local 'businessman' for years in the papers. Mr. Buchalter's 'business' was murder for hire.

Over the years, it was reported, Lepke had become so proficient at his occupation, that after murdering his way through Brooklyn, he rose to command a substantial 'corporation' staffed by other experts in the trade. The papers' crime writers dubbed the business Murder, Inc., and during a five-year rampage, the organization was responsible for dozens of deaths in Brooklyn alone.

"Cigarette, kid?" asked Lepke, offering the pack to Sid.

"No thanks. I... I don't smoke."

Lepke shrugged. "Suit yourself. It's really a disgusting habit, anyway."

Leo spoke up. "I want to explain the reasons you were brought here. You deserve nothing less. Especially after everything we've put you through for the last several months. So, hear me out, Sid. Please. You're a very intelligent boy. Once I put the pieces together, you'll understand."

Sid thought for a moment. Leo was a brilliant physicist at the top of his game and a friend and confidant of Einstein. Buchalter was also a master of his own despicable occupation. And the Mangano brothers had risen from deepest obscurity to control numerous illicit activities, especially narcotics trafficking, throughout New York, raking in millions of dollars a year even in these tough times. These were smart, confident, successful men.

"Okay, Leo," Sid said, "I'll give you a chance. I'm listening. So spill 'em. I mean all the beans. And make it nothin' but the whole truth, so help you God."

"Good. Nothing but the truth, Sid. I promise."

Sid nodded. "Then please proceed. You'll have my rapt attention."

Leo pulled over an empty chair and sat next to Sid. "Thank you," he said. "First, I want to reassure you that we—you, me, the Mangano brothers, and Mr. Buchalter, in addition to many others you've never met, and in all likelihood never will, are all on the same side. The people you have before you today, Sid Peskin, represent the heart of a deeply hidden organization dedicated to the removal, by legal means, of the cold hand of Lindbergh and his cronies in government and the extirpation of all racist and Nazi influence in our society. The Congress is impotent. The courts have failed us. We act on our own.

"Winston Churchill, the last British prime minister, our leader in spirit, vowed to never give in. And we, American patriots all, will also never give in. We oppose Lindbergh and his minions. We are the Resistance. And we want you to be part of our team."

Were it not for Sid's experiences of the past half-year, Leo's tale would have sounded wildly implausible. He coughed again from the smoke of Lepke's cigarette. "Why did you have to kidnap me? I was just beginning to think we were on the same side."

Leo pursed his lips. "There are many things you don't understand, Sid. Complex forces are at work. You will be enlightened soon, I promise. But what we did, what we had to do, was in everyone's best interest, including yours. Suffice it to say that you were in great peril, mortal peril."

Sid sat upright in his chair and looked into the faces of the Mafia dons, one after another. These men were hardened criminals, murderous psychopaths who thought nothing of committing the vilest acts whenever it suited them. But these vicious gangsters were energized by Leo's remarks—even the nervous, nicotine-addicted Mangano brothers had refrained from filling the cellar with cigarette smoke.

"The Resistance, huh?" said Sid. "Well, well. Ya know, I've been waiting for the last six months for an invitation to join up!" In a war, one couldn't always be choosy about one's allies. The enemy of Sid's enemy could also be his friend.

CHAPTER 15

The afterglow of his meeting with Lindbergh carried Fred Trump through the next several weeks, his mind a simmering stew of new ideas and projects and ways to make wads of cash.

For example, defense industry stocks had been kicking up as rumors of an impending German assault on the Soviet Union gained strength. But Fred Trump had the inside edge from his meetings with Lindbergh. The market was overbought because the president had no intention of getting the U.S. involved in a European war. So, he did what any American with inside information would do: As he was certain defense stocks would be falling, he short sold them on the open market.

Trump speculated in gold, platinum, wheat futures, pork bellies, and orange juice, always trading on insider information, squeezing out the last drop of useful knowledge from his informants, whom he soon discarded. But for the access he provided to Lindbergh, many were happy to oblige him. Within a very short time, his personal net worth increased considerably. Trump was a happy man—some of the time.

The dough was nice. Money meant security, a down-payment on a nice house, a lovely mink coat for Mary, and the ability to raise and educate two—maybe three— children. Fred Trump loved little children. Watching toddlers dance and stumble on the grass, or run after soap bubbles or butterflies, never catching one, always brought a big, broad smile to his face. Even if the child was a negro or a Jew, to Fred, all the little folk were delightful.

But as they grew, their cuteness waned. Fred believed all children over the age of eight had to learn the hard lessons of life. Life was cold. Life was hard. If you appeared weak, you'd be taken out with the trash. Some learned as they grew. They were successful. Others didn't learn. They were failures. He, Fred Trump, was a success. He had no time for failures.

Now was the time to make his move, to fulfill the dream of a lifetime: not only to break into Manhattan real estate, but to do it in such a way that no one, no matter how wealthy, or socially upper-crusted, would ever exclude him again. He'd force the Central Park West and Park Avenue tuxedo-wrapped fat cats to accept that a boy from Queens could make it big on their own turf. He'd compel them to welcome him and his descendants to their fancy city and country clubs. There, in society's upper echelons, every weekend consisted of a round of alcohol-saturated parties in the evening, golf in the daytime, and love affairs whenever and as frequently as possible. That was the grand life Fred Trump envisioned for himself.

To accomplish all this, Trump would build not small apartment buildings like he'd done in the outer boroughs, but structures for the millennium, for the ages. Massive, limestone-clad skyscrapers, the greatest in New York, taller even than the iconic 1,250-foot Empire State Building! As mayor, Trump had almost everything he needed. He knew the heads of all the major construction companies and could obtain permits at the snap of his fingers. There was but one item he lacked—cold, hard cash and plenty of it, the kind of cash no bank would ever lend him.

But oh, happy Trump! Not only was he the smartest man on earth, he may also have been the luckiest! Because of the prominence he'd attained in the Lindbergh administration, it was only a matter of time before the German ambassador, Hans Thomsen, invited him to a reception, to be held in the German Embassy on elegant, up-scale Massachusetts Avenue in Washington, D.C.

Trump accepted the invitation with alacrity. After purchasing a tuxedo for himself and a new gown for Mary—no one could ever accuse Fred Trump of not being uxorious or Mary of having simple tastes—the couple took the train from Penn Station in New York to Union Station in D.C., checked into the elegant Mayfair Hotel, and called for a cab to take them to the German Embassy. This outpost of the Third Reich was housed in a large, luxurious, recently purchased private mansion.

After depositing Mary with a gaggle of wives of Midwestern congressmen and other Lindbergh supporters, Trump scanned the crowd like the pilot of a great ship upon the seas, his eyes roving in search of the German ambassador. He found Thomsen chatting with his counterpart from Vichy France, a Nazi puppet state consisting of the rump of pre-war France south of the Loire River the Germans didn't occupy. Thomsen's companion was a tall British gentleman with pallid skin, a narrow face, and thin lips. He was balding almost to the vertex of his skull and possessed the cold blue eyes of a patrician, which he was. Trump soon discovered this was Lord Halifax, an arch-appeaser in the Chamberlain government before the Nazi conquest, and now Hitler's choice as Head of the British Legation to the United States.

"Mr. Trump! I am delighted you could come to our little party this evening."

Trump smiled and gave a slight bow. "The pleasure is all mine, I assure you, *Herr* Ambassador."

The Frenchman, who sported an old-fashioned mustache that was waxed and curled at each end, looked down the end of his haughty Gallic nose at the arriviste. But observing the diplomatic niceties in front of his German master, he turned to Trump and said, "Pardon, *Monsieur*. I do not believe we 'av ever 'ad ze opportunity to meet."

"Oh, but I have been rude, *Monsieur* Henri. Please accept my apologies. Mr. Trump, please meet the representative of Vichy France."

Since France was no longer an independent country, she had neither an ambassador nor an embassy any longer. But the Nazis maintained the fiction of independence by allowing their puppet state to send a "representative," a stooge under their control, to neutral countries like the United States.

The two shook hands, but Trump had no interest in the preening little Frenchman. In his mind, a moment spent dealing with this loser—who represented a whole country of losers—was a moment of time and money wasted. The French had battled it out with the Germans in a fair fight and lost. As a nation, they were weak, decadent, and effeminate compared to the muscular, vital, manly Germans. Trump shed no tears for Paris. The stronger nation had emerged victorious. The immutable laws of nature were proven once again: One either ate, or was eaten.

Trump hid his revulsion and smiled pleasantly at M. Henri.

"And, oh, pardon, this is Lord Halifax, the representative of England. Lord Halifax, Mr. Trump, the Mayor of New York."

Trump noticed that the island nation which had, until recently, controlled an empire on which the sun never set was no longer referred to as Great Britain. It was now simply England. The Nazis had carved up Great Britain into three smaller principalities based on their ancient ethnicities. Scotland and Wales were now officially independent countries but remained under the German jackboot. England had been plundered of its industrial wealth, which was loaded on railway trains, then on barges for the cross-Channel voyage, and then re-loaded on trains for transshipment to the Reich. The country was slowly being transformed into the pastoral nation it had been before the Industrial Revolution, to the immense enrichment of the Nazi state.

Oswald Moseley, the head of the British Union of Fascists, the so-called Black Shirts, was installed by the Germans as the prime minister of the monarch-less English government. Moseley then named the oleaginous Halifax as the English representative to the U.S.

Halifax smiled and extended his hand to Trump. Another loser from another country not worth saving, in Trump's estimation. This was one of the aspects of

Lindbergh's campaign Trump found most attractive. Unlike Joe Kennedy, Trump had no sons to protect from going off to yet another European war. Nevertheless, as a successful businessman, he resented paying his hard-earned taxes to assist an effete British government ruled by a stuttering king and his blustering prime minister, Mr. Churchill. Even before this latest war began, wasn't it obvious the sun was setting on the British Empire—and that the rising sun in Europe was the Third Reich? And that anything lent or leased to the former Great Britain would never be returned? That was a bad deal for the U.S! Trump, like his leader, Lindbergh, was fed up with his beloved country making bad deals and with the politicians who made them.

"Good evening, Lord Halifax," he said, hoping to spend as little time as possible with the English representative.

Halifax' diplomatic antennae twitched at Trump's greeting. He'd known Franklin Roosevelt well—the two patricians took to each other on sight, and Halifax genuinely grieved when he died. But in contrast to Roosevelt, whose statesman-like qualities he recognized and appreciated, he sized up Trump as a typical American conman, risen to high political office through the vagaries of the American electoral system. "Very pleased to meet you, Mr. Trump. Are you here in an official capacity tonight?"

"At my invitation," said Thomsen.

"Ah, wonderful," said Halifax, who no more wanted to chat with Trump than Trump did with him. "Wonderful." And that was where the conversation ended. By this time, M. Henri had drifted off, his eye on a supremely attractive Italian actress entertaining a wolf pack of Teutonic admirers.

"And will we have the opportunity to meet your lovely wife, Mr. Trump?" asked Thomsen unctuously, his silken words attempting to show that not all Germans were as savage as the conquerors of Poland.

"Oh, Mary? She's around somewhere, I suppose," said Trump, looking around but not locating her by eye. "But if you don't mind, *Herr* Ambassador, I'd like to have a private word for a moment. If I may."

Trump's request was undiplomatic. But Halifax said, "Oh, it's quite all right, *Herr* Thomsen. We can continue our discussions later. Mr. Trump has traveled some distance. I'm sure he has important business to discuss with you." Then, turning to Trump, "Very nice to have met you, Mr. Trump. Kindly give my regards to your wife." All was standard diplomatic bonhomie.

Trump gave the British representative a half-smile as Halifax departed in favor of a tray of canapés offered by a stiff-backed, unsmiling German waiter. Trump had achieved his purpose; gaining time alone with the German ambassador. He would make the most of it, because he, Fred Trump, knew how to make deals—and the deals he made were the best deals possible, the greatest deals the human mind could conceive.

The ambassador, irritated by his rudeness, was drawn by Trump to the corner of the large central room. Thomsen found himself behind a substantial floor-to-ceiling marble pillar, which seemed to support the overhead promenade on the second floor but was merely decorative. "So, Mr. Trump, what is so *verdammt* important that I must be separated from my guests this evening?"

"I apologize deeply, Mr. Ambassador. I meant no harm, sir, but I have information that may be useful to members of your government. I felt obliged to inform you of it as soon as possible."

Thomsen's expression changed from anger to inquisitiveness. "Oh. Then perhaps we should find a more private space. Come, follow me."

He led Trump through a door in the wall and into a comfortable office that held a desk and two chairs. A framed picture of the *Führer* addressing adoring crowds of his enthusiastic supporters hung on the wall opposite a desk cluttered with papers.

"Please, Mr. Trump, have a seat. But touch nothing." Trump did as he was instructed. Thomsen took the other seat, behind the desk. "Proceed," he ordered.

"Yes, sir." Trump sat in a leather covered chair at the side of the desk. "What I want you to know, *Herr* Thomsen, is at this very moment, a syndicate is being assembled in New York."

Thomsen's eyes narrowed. "Syndicate? A syndicate consisting of whom, Mr. Trump? What is their purpose?"

Good, thought Trump. The mark senses the bait. Now I hook the sucker and reel him in. Simple!

"Their purpose, *Herr* Thomsen... their purpose is nothing more than to build a skyscraper in New York City."

Thomsen lay back in his seat and yawned. "*Herr* Trump, please. There is nothing that could interest my government in a new skyscraper going up in New York. It's like meeting a new bureaucrat in Berlin. There are so many, you can't avoid them, and another one is not so interesting."

Trump was not about to be put off. "But this one will be different, *Herr* Thomsen. I will build the tallest, most recognizable structure in New York. It will be a landmark. People will come to see it from all over the country. I shall call it Trump Tower, and whenever Americans think of New York City, the image of Trump Tower will come first to their minds. And now, I am giving your government the incredible opportunity to get in on the ground floor of this amazing project! Think of the benefits for your country to have that picture of your *Führer*, Adolf Hitler," he pointed to the wall picture, "hanging there! Right there, in the most famous and highly visited building in America! Imagine the possibilities, *Herr* Ambassador! Imagine what it would mean!"

For some time, Thomsen neither moved in his seat nor uttered a word. Trump could hear the pounding of his heart as sweat accumulated in his palms. *"Ja,* I am… imagining. *Und* just how much will this great opportunity cost the Reich?"

Trump looked deeply into the blue-gray eyes of the ambassador, calculating his answer. Any perception on his part of a lack of confidence, and Trump knew the deal would fail. So, he pronounced every word precisely, taking care each and every syllable could be understood. "A mere thirty million dollars, *Herr* Ambassador. A hundred and twenty million Reichsmarks. A great bargain at the price, I think. And there are many asking after this space, so I do not know how long—"

There was no further change in the flat expression on Thomsen's face. *"Und* you would like me to pass this on to the appropriate financial people in my government?"

"Yes, sir. I would. Very much."

The ambassador sighed. "Trump, I have a question. You are a German? Am I correct?"

"I'm an American, sir."

"Ja, ja, I know, I know that! Of course, you are. But your ancestors, they are all German, are they not?"

"Yes, sir. Some Swedes, too."

"No Juden?"

"Why do you ask, sir?"

"Because you are a lying, swindling type of businessman, like they are. So. I will pass on your request for a thirty-million-dollar loan so you can begin the construction of Trump Tower. And I will also add the following suggestion. It is well known to our intelligence services that you have the ear of the American president. If you would provide us with some insight on his thinking *und* perhaps relay some of our thoughts to him, I'm sure that would—how do you Americans say it—'grease the wheels.' I suggest this course to avoid any misunderstandings between our countries, *und* to keep the peace, you understand. The war in Europe is over, *Herr* Trump, *und* we are the victors. We now want nothing more than to enjoy the fruits of our victory in peace."

"Of course, *Herr* Ambassador. Nothing is more important than keeping the peace. It's a noble goal. If we work together, I'm certain it can be done. I accept your terms as a basis on which to move forward."

The two men shook hands and agreed their underlings would arrange the details at a later date. Thus, Fred Trump became a witting agent of the Nazi regime, which by mid-1941 had murdered tens of thousands of its political enemies, ghettoized and enslaved its Jewish population, and terrorized the remaining peoples of its vast, racial empire. Just how much of this Trump knew was a matter of debate. Most likely, he was unaware of the details, though everyone with a flicker of intelligence could grasp the big picture.

Trump was an intelligent man, especially in his own estimation. He was neither mad, nor psychotic, nor demented, nor afflicted with any mental illnesses known or unknown to psychiatric practice. The problem with Fred Trump wasn't that his reasoning was flawed; the problem was that he reasoned from premises that most people found abhorrent. He would do nothing disinterested, nothing that reeked—in his opinion—of selflessness, nothing that failed to burnish his reputation, his purse, or his glory. Concepts of the greater good and the public benefit never entered his thinking. And he didn't give a good goddamn who noticed, or who he harmed in the process.

CHAPTER 16

The New York Herald Tribune, June 23, 1941
[Above the crease.]

HITLER INVADES THE SOVIET UNION

By David Gunn

In the early morning hours, more than 3.5 million men, supported by thousands of tanks and hundreds of aircraft, on a front extending over a thousand miles from Lithuania to the Black Sea, burst through the border defenses of the USSR and drove toward Leningrad to the north and Kiev to the east.

By the early evening yesterday, the German spearheads, and soldiers from their Hungarian, Romanian, and Italian allies, had penetrated more than thirty miles from their initial jumping-off point.

Official reaction from the Soviets was muted, and there has been no direct word at all from the Kremlin. Unconfirmed rumors have alleged that Josef Stalin, the Soviet Communist dictator, has been confined to his summer retreat at Kuntsevo outside Moscow since the invasion began, in a state of mental and physical collapse brought on by the betrayal of his erstwhile ally, Adolf Hitler.

In contrast, German sources have painted a glowing account of the performance of their troops.

"In the first several hours alone," stated a spokesman for Herman Göring, "our Luftwaffe has destroyed hundreds of Soviet aircraft in addition to numerous stores of aviation fuel. Red Army troops are in rapid retreat on all fronts. Towns near the border welcome the troops of the Wehrmacht and our allies as liberators from the Jewish-Bolshevik terrorists ruling in the Kremlin. In the Ukraine, the locals are bringing us bread and salt, the traditional greeting of welcome and peace. The strategic genius of our *Führer*, Adolf Hitler, has once again emerged triumphant over the barbaric enemies of civilization!"

In a statement, Hans Thomsen, ambassador of the Greater German Reich to the United States, claimed that "with respect to German interests, the behavior of Stalin and his henchmen has long been provocative. This, plus the Kremlin's longstanding suppression of legitimate popular grievances—in favor of a Jewish-Marxist ideology incompatible with common European values—required defensive intervention by our armed forces. Our aims are the destruction of the entire rotten edifice of the Communist state and the liberation of its many imprisoned peoples."

Wall Street responded to the news with a broad sell-off in stocks. A White House spokesman appealed for calm, stating that President Lindbergh has offered to mediate any differences between the dictators and has sent messages to both Hitler and Stalin, expressing his lasting hope for the attainment of a negotiated settlement.

So far, no response from either party to the conflict has been received.

The White House
June 22, 1941

Charles Lindbergh sat at his desk in the Oval Office. A report from J. Edgar Hoover lay in front of him. Without opening the report, he knew its contents. It related how, despite a nationwide search by the FBI, Enrico Fermi—and also now Robert Oppenheimer, both top-ranked physicists—had vanished and could not be located. The mathematician John von Neumann was also missing, and there were still no suspects in the murder of the lesser-known physics professor, I. Bernard Strauss.

And now, as if things couldn't get any worse, there was war in Eastern Europe. Lindbergh buried his head in his hands. He hadn't seen it coming. The Soviets had been delivering grain, iron, and non-ferrous metals to the Reich until the very moment the war broke out. The Soviets' behavior wasn't at all provocative—in fact, it was supine. Stalin had gone out of his way to avoid antagonizing Hitler. The Mountain Eagle knew better than anyone just how militarily weak the Soviet Union was because so much of that weakness was his fault! The purges he'd organized over the past half-decade had claimed the lives of hundreds of military commanders and senior officers and sent others, who were desperately needed to rally the troops at the front, to rot or freeze in the Gulag.

No wonder the Red Army was on the run. Lindbergh was certain it wouldn't stop running until it either was destroyed by the Germans, or reached the Volga or perhaps even the Ural Mountains. Either way, the Soviet Union's fate was sealed. It was doomed, and with it, the International Communist Movement. At least there was a silver lining to all of this bloodletting. It would also cast a warm light on his sagacity in keeping America out of the war. But for the moment, the Russo-German conflict would have to take care of itself.

"Anne," he called out via the intercom. "Please get me Fred Trump in New York."

The president was quickly patched through by telephone to Gracie Mansion on the Upper East Side of Manhattan, the traditional home of the Mayors of New York. Trump wasn't in residence, so the operator put Lindbergh through to his personal home in Queens.

Trump picked up the phone. "Hello."

"Fred, this is the president."

"Good morning, Mr. President. To what do I owe the honor of this call?" It always thrilled Fred Trump to speak with the Chief Executive Officer of the United States. Unfortunately, Lindbergh didn't know he was speaking not only to Trump but also to Wilhelm Canaris, Commander of the Abwehr, German intelligence.

"This isn't a social call, Fred, so we can skip the pleasantries. I want to know if your boys picked up Peskin. I presume they did. I'd also like to know where you've taken him."

A long silence over the phone line followed before Trump spoke. "Ah, Mr. President... I'm sorry to say we, ah... we don't have him."

"Trump! This is a serious business. Stop making frivolous comments. I don't have the time. Where is Peskin?"

Trump sighed. "I'm sorry, sir. But it seems, that, ah... he's also disappeared."

If Anne Lindbergh had come into the Oval Office at that moment, she would have seen a vessel in her husband's left temple pulsate and his cheeks flush deep red with anger. "Trump!" Lindbergh said, clenching his teeth. "Are you telling me you can't find Peskin, either?"

"Ah... yes, sir. Can't find him. But we're investigating—"

"Trump!" snapped Lindbergh. "What are you talking about, man? How did Peskin slip through your fingers? I can't understand. Is it true what people say about you, Trump? That you're a moron? Shit, I forgot a word—that you're an effin' moron? Jesus H. Christ, man! Hoover's been watching Albert Einstein for months, and guess who shows up? Guess who, Fred?"

The tongue-lashing from a man he considered a mere aviator made Trump grit his teeth. But if he valued his job and the German money he hoped to bag, he had to remain courteous and respectful to the president. "Sid Peskin, sir."

Trump put some distance between his ear and the phone receiver as Lindbergh's self-control dissolved. "That's right, Fred," he yelled into the receiver. Trump winced.

Lindbergh wasn't finished with him. "When Strauss was killed, who showed up to find the body? Sid Peskin. We surveil Einstein to catch Fermi, and who shows up for a chat? Sid Peskin! And now he's disappeared, too? Trump, if I didn't know better, I'd say either the little Jew boy knows how to choose his coincidences, or he's the mastermind behind everything that's happened with our physicists and God knows what else! You and the Police Department of the City of New York are hopelessly incompetent."

Poor Fred! One moment on top of the world, the next under the bus! It was fortunate for him that Lindbergh slammed down the receiver. It gave Trump a chance to calm down. He figured Lindbergh would cool off, too, in a day or so, which gave him time to work out the problem.

Lindbergh jammed the desktop intercom with his index finger, almost dislocating it. "Anne!" he barked. "Get Edgar on the phone. Now, please!"

Anne Lindbergh didn't answer. Instead, she appeared in the Oval Office. "Charles," she said softly, "Jack Kennedy is waiting for you. He's been waiting for over an hour."

"Ahhhhh, why should I give a damn about a mere lieutenant?" Lindbergh snarled. He ran both his hands through his hair.

Anne recoiled. "Charles!" she said in wide-eyed surprise. "I'm astonished at your behavior. I've never seen you like this. You are the president. At the very least, you should treat the office with the decorum it deserves. Why don't you take a few deep breaths and have a cup of tea, hmmm? I'm sure you'll feel much better after you do. Now, what shall I say to young Lieutenant Kennedy? He's lots of fun to talk with, but I suspect he has better things to do than cool his heels with me."

Lindbergh had to act quickly or run the risk his wife might become a member of Jack Kennedy's harem. He'd known for some time Anne Lindbergh had a roving eye. "Please ask Lieutenant Kennedy to call on me at this time tomorrow. If I'm not busy. If I am, I'll kick out whomever I'm busy with. I really do want to have a chat with him."

Anne smiled. "Very well, Mr. President."

"And don't forget to call Edgar, Anne. Right after Kennedy leaves."

Five minutes later, Lindbergh heard J. Edgar Hoover's familiar voice on the other end of his phone line.

"Edgar, how are you today?"

"Very well, for an old war horse, I can't complain."

"Good. I want you around for many years to come, Edgar. You're a real asset to this administration. I thank my predecessors in this job every day for picking you to head the Bureau. Please give me an update on the progress of 'Operation Snowflake.' I have the checklist in front of me." 'Operation Snowflake' referred to a special group of agents set up in the Bureau at his order. They were authorized to remove from society, by means legal or extralegal, any members of the group identified as 'Murder Inc.'

"Harry Maione and Frank Abbandando, dead," said Hoover. "My G-men caught 'em in an ambush in Brooklyn. They tried to surrender. Fools! Harry Strauss and Martin Goldstein, likewise. Strauss accidentally fell down an elevator shaft. I wonder who left the door open. And Goldstein... well, he had a, uh... problem with his car."

"What kind of problem?"

"It exploded. They scraped swatches of him off the pavement."

"Excellent. Jake 'The Jerk' Golub and Phil Cohen are still in prison?"

"Serving a dime each, but we'll figure a way to never let them out."

"So far, so good, Edgar. What about the big shots? Albert Anastasia, the so-called 'Lord High Executioner,' Vince Mangano's underboss?"

"On the lam. Running as fast as he can. We're closing in."

"The Manganos, Vince and Phil?"

"Technically, they're not 'Murder, Inc.,' Mr. President. The brothers have gone to ground. We haven't been able to locate either one."

"There seems to be a great deal of that going around these days," Lindbergh snorted.

Hoover ignored him. "Same with Meyer Lansky, Bugsy Siegel, and the 'Chairman of the Board,' the one called Lepke Buchalter. If you recall, sir, Lepke ordered the hit on Abe 'Kid Twist' Reles, a strangler who became a stool pigeon for us. Reles got thrown out a hotel window in Coney Island the night before he was to testify against Lepke. Ha, ha, ha! Yeah. Reles was surrounded in his hotel room by New York's Finest, too. 'The canary who could sing but couldn't fly,' the press called him. The mob despises traitors, Mr. President."

"And I don't much care what they like or don't like, Edgar. These men are the scum of the earth. I made a promise to my supporters to get rid of them, and that's exactly what I'm going to do! The farmers in Iowa don't care about Jews or foreigners, and if a few Italian or Jewish gangsters in New York get rubbed out, to use their colorful language, so much the better. No one will miss them. Besides, Edgar, once 'Murder Inc.' disappears, their turf is ours, and we can put their assets to far better use than they ever could! We can no longer permit any independent powers to flourish in this country, especially not in its largest city! And not when that power is controlled by a vile collection of misfit Italian and Jewish proletarians!"

"I'm all over it, Mr. President. I'm your man, faithful forever. I also want to see those arrogant bastards humbled. I want to see them beggin' for mercy before my G-men riddle them with bullets and leave their mouths eating dust."

"It's a lovely thought, Edgar. Make it happen. What about Fermi and the other scientists? Any news? The Germans are becoming more and more autocratic and demanding." Lindbergh sighed. "I suppose that's what happens to a nation when it conquers half the world and feels invincible. But their economic threats are very real, Edgar. Sooner or later, we need to come up with those scientists, or a reasonable facsimile of 'em, or we'll pay a very heavy price."

"Mr. President, I believe I've come up with the answer to our problem."

Lindbergh brightened. "Sounds like good news for a change, Edgar. Go on."

"Sir, I put in a call to a former agent, a G-man who retired only a few years ago. He had an outstanding record with the Bureau. Was in on most of our successful operations in the early '30s. I've coaxed him out of retirement and put him in charge of tracking down the scientists and that little pest, Peskin. You may have heard of him. His name is Melvin Purvis."

It would be difficult to find a person alive in Lindbergh's 1941 America who hadn't heard of Melvin Purvis. The legendary giant G-man—though he was but 5'3" tall—was director of the forces that had tracked down some of the most notorious desperados and public enemies of the early 1930s. The notches on the stock of his gun included Baby Face Nelson, Pretty Boy Floyd, and the notorious John Dillinger, whom he personally nailed outside a Chicago theater. Purvis was tough, ruthless, and wasn't averse to inflicting grievous bodily harm on any of his victims he thought deserved it.

Hoover was fibbing; Purvis required no coaxing to return to work at the Bureau. He never had any intention of retiring in his mid '30s. Hoover pushed him out because Purvis attracted more favorable publicity than he did.

"Purvis? Back to the Bureau? That's excellent, Edgar! Just the man for the job! The scientists are as good as captured! And the crooks will be shaking in their shoes when they hear who's on their trail. Cry havoc and let slip the dogs of war, Edgar!"

"Mr. President?"

"It's Shakespeare, Edgar. Anne reads the Bard of Avon to me every night before we go to sleep."

"Shakespeare. Yeah. Ya mean like *Romeo and Juliet?*"

"No, like *Julius Caesar.*"

Hoover furrowed his brow. "Mr. President, I fail to see what Julius Caesar's dogs have to do with—"

"Never mind, Edgar. Just do your job. I'll see to everything else."

"Yes, sir. And before I forget, sir. I believe Lieutenant Kennedy would be an excellent assistant for Purvis. Give the young man some real-world experience. He's wasting his talents sitting behind a desk, though I know he's not afraid of exposing himself to physical harm. Joe Kennedy's son's a good man, and he's loyal. I know how you prize loyalty, sir."

Lindbergh thought that, like Purvis, Kennedy must be developing an independent fan base. Washington society, especially its matrons, was gaga over him. Hoover wouldn't like that. The Bureau head kept his friends close—especially Clyde Tolson, the G-man with whom he shared all his time, both on and off the job. He thought those two surely were sinning against the word of God. But such unspeakable things must be overlooked for the greater good, so long as both men remained discreet. Jack Kennedy, on the other hand, was constitutionally indiscreet. He brought his exile from the Bureau's inner circle upon himself.

"Loyalty above all else, Edgar," said Lindbergh. "Loyalty is the bedrock of everything we do, the glue that holds us together. Think about it. Enemies surround us! Foolish, delusional people who, in a heartbeat, would destroy all we've worked for these many years."

"Yes, sir, Mr. President. As always, you've hit the nail right on the head. As you've said many times, our enemies are bad people!"

"They're mean and spiteful, too. Ya know, as we've been chatting, I've been thinking about your idea, Edgar. I like it. I like it a lot. Jack Kennedy's a loyal man and very intelligent. A team combining Purvis' brawn with Kennedy's brain would be invincible. Yes, Edgar, I like it very much. Oh, won't 'Murder, Inc.' pee its pants when they hear who's back and coming after them? And I want them all, Edgar, every one of 'em—be they alive, or be they dead!"

CHAPTER 17

The cellar of a candy store, Kew Gardens, Queens, NY

One after another, the mobsters climbed the stairs to the ground floor of the candy store, leaving Sid alone with Leo Szilard. "I still don't understand why you kidnapped me, Leo," said Sid, who was able to relax in the absence of the gangsters.

"Mind if I light up?" Leo opened a silver cigarette case.

"I do, actually. Lepke's smokes damn near killed me. Sorry, Leo, but the smoke makes me choke."

He replaced the silver case in his coat pocket. "I understand."

"Thanks. Now please explain to me what happened today. And then I want to go home. By now, my mother will be frantic."

"Sid, I'm sorry. You can't go home. Not now and probably not for a long time. Not that the gentlemen upstairs will let you. They won't, of course. But they have good reasons to keep you here. It may surprise you, but they have expended a great deal of time and effort choosing just the right person for a very special job. You are that person. Trust me, Sid. You are probably the only person on the planet who can succeed under conditions where failure is not an option.

"But of equal importance, you cannot go home because Lindbergh would probably kill you and your family. Matters have reached a breaking point in this country. The 'powers that be' are insecure and fearful, and more irrational and reckless than ever. We know for a fact you are on a list of individuals the regime will sweep up within the next twenty-four hours. We could not allow the information you possess in your head and notebook to fall into the hands of Lindbergh and his cronies. That would be an unmitigated disaster! This administration leaks at high levels, with the information finding its way to the *Abwehr*. We're not sure who the leaker is, but one way or another, we will find out."

Sid wanted to scream for the nightmare of this day to end, but he knew it would be useless. What about his parents? Would they ever know what became of him? Would they believe him dead and recite the *Kaddish* while he was alive and well in Queens? Where would he live? With Leo Szilard, a man twice his age—watched over by a merciless gang of killers, day and night? Would Benny grow up without his older brother, his instructor in the nuances of stickball? Absent any communication from Sid for weeks, months even—would Sid's lovely Julia also grow weary and abandon him? Of all the losses he could suffer, hers would hurt the most.

Sid fell back in his chair, staggered by the thought of losing everyone and everything he loved. "Leo, you son of a bitch! Why did you do this to me?" Tears formed in his eyes. "I never asked for this... this... insanity! Yeah, maybe that's what this is. Insanity. You're a crazy man, Leo. Nothing you say is the truth. I'm gonna walk up those stairs and right outta here and go straight to the nearest police station and file kidnapping charges."

"Sid, I understand you're angry. I would be, too. But if you tried to do something so stupid like try to go to the police, you would be dead before your foot hit the curb. Buchalter and the Mangano brothers are nasty, dangerous men. They are also fearful men, and they mean business.

"I, on the other hand, am not a nasty man, though I also mean business. I know the lean and hungry look of the professional Nazi. I saw it in Germany, which I fled in '33."

"Lean and hungry look," Sid repeated. "Shakespeare. *Julius Caesar.* 'Yond Cassius has a lean and hungry look.'"

"Yes. The look of a predator, grasping for power. The same look I see in the fanatical eye of the Bundist and of the Joe Kennedys and Fred Trumps of this country. I never supposed I'd see here what I saw in Germany. That vision still gives me nightmares." Leo shivered. For an instant, he relived in his mind the image of Nazis beating up Jews on the broad boulevards of Berlin and the indifference of passers-by.

"Ah, well, I could never have survived under the Nazis. So, I fled to Britain soon after Hitler took over. That's where I conceived the idea of the chain reaction after atomic fission—in Bloomsbury, London, in 1934, standing at a traffic light, no less. It came as an epiphany, as if I were on the road to Damascus! My life has not been the same since. Lise Meitner had a similar notion as I did, though several years later. I've been told Flyorov, too, in the Soviet Union. So, I regret to inform you, Comrade Peskin, that you are somewhat late to the party."

"So Einstein told me. I was foolish to imagine I was the one and only."

"There is no shame in being one step behind Meitner or Flyorov, my friend. Nonetheless, if your work is correct, you have overleaped all of these giants of atomic physics and into the lead. And I must say it again: A person with your talent and knowledge must work for the Resistance, not for Lindbergh and the *Abwehr*."

"You gave the order to kidnap me. Correct, Leo?"

"Yes."

"Are you the head of the Resistance?"

Leo laughed. "No, certainly not. I admit I joined early, even before the last presidential election. But I am not the head. In our circles, he's referred to as the Boss, or the Omega. I'm sure you understand the reference."

"Of course. Omega is the Greek letter symbolizing electrical resistance. Have you ever met the Omega?"

"If I had, I wouldn't admit it."

"But you must have met people who know him. Or else the Omega is the man behind the curtain in the *Wizard of Oz*."

"I'm sorry, Sid. But at the moment, I can tell you no more about him. He's mysterious because he must be to survive."

Sid pursed his lips. This was more blather. He wanted answers. "Why did you involve the mob in the Resistance?" he asked. "They're nothing more than stone-cold killers."

"That's an easy question. We need stone cold killers, and they need us. The Resistance began as a group of scientists who understood the way the political winds were blowing and the threat to humanity posed by allowing certain critical information to fall into the hands of the Nazis. But we aren't men or women skilled in countering the violence of our enemies. We needed physical protection. The mob stepped up. They also despise Lindbergh. He's been very bad for their business—and for the health and safety of several of their made men. That's a challenge to their power that must be answered. Like Lindbergh, the mob dreads the appearance of weakness."

"Do you know you're riding on the back of a crocodile? And does this mean Lepke is the Omega?"

The question provoked a full-throated laugh from Leo. "Oh, heavens, no! I couldn't even imagine that! What an utter catastrophe that would be, for everyone. No, Lepke is not the Omega. Like all of us, he's accepted the role of good soldier and obeys the Omega's orders. For the moment. But we now live from moment to moment."

"Knowing Lepke's reputation, I find it hard to believe he'd obey anyone's orders."

Leo gave him a sly look. "Well, you're here, aren't you?"

Sid paused, deep in thought. "So, the Resistance is under the protection of the

Commission," he said, referring to the council of the five Mafia families who controlled organized crime throughout the country. "It's clever of you to have arranged this *mésalliance*. Tell me, how did you make the connection? I mean between the Resistance, mostly scientists, and the mob, mostly murderers. One can't just call the telephone operator with a request to put you through to the Chairman of the Board of 'Murder, Inc.'"

"Sid, you're pitching me another softball, as you Americans say. Is that the correct phrase?"

"Could be. Depends on your answer."

"Fair enough. You may recall Lindbergh and his gang are bitter enemies of the Communists."

"Yeah. It's a battle to the death between the forces of evil. They hate Communists more than negroes, Jews, and foreigners combined."

"That's an accurate description of the America First mentality. But many scientists, who are also Resistors, see no moral equivalence between the Reds and the Rightists, since they, the Resistors, are Communists in spirit."

"Fellow travelers. I know all about them."

"Only a few Resistors are card-carrying party members. But the real strength of the CPUSA is in the labor unions, especially in those representing the garment and needle-trade workers. The Ladies Pocketbook Maker's Union is a good example. All of its officers are Communists, passionate believers in Stalin and the Revolution. But for the time being, they choose to behave within the rules. So, they devote their energies to negotiating with factory owners for fair wages and good working conditions for their members. But the owners hire muscle, supplied by Lepke, to disrupt union meetings and activities. The union then hires its own muscle, also supplied by Lepke, as protection against the goons hired by the owners. Lepke collects double, and everyone suffers."

"So, the alliance between the mob and the Resistance was mediated through the CPUSA."

"Yes, it was."

Sid thought of Julius Rosenberg and his comment about how Enrico Fermi had been removed from a transcontinental LL train. His whereabouts were still unknown. "Is Fermi one of yours?"

Leo absent-mindedly pulled out his cigarette case but remembered his guest's smoke aversion as he began to remove a cigarette. "Pardon me," he said, replacing the case in his inside coat pocket. "I've lost my train of thought. Now, where was I?"

"Enrico Fermi, Leo. I asked if he was one of yours."

"Yes, of course. One of our earliest members, like me. A mind as clear as his couldn't stomach the current stupidity."

"Why was he removed from his train?"

"Because we found out Hoover's men were going to meet him in San Francisco, where Professor Fermi would have been arrested. Soon after, he would have been on a plane to the Third Reich."

"And Oppenheimer, the Berkeley professor?"

Leo nodded. "Ours, too. Along with John von Neumann the mathematician, and many others. But not Einstein, for the moment. The choice was ours, not his. Someone had to remain our antenna above ground. Because of his popularity and the cachet of his name, Einstein is virtually untouchable. But that may change, too."

"Are they all safe and well?"

"Yes, of course."

"Do you know where they are?"

"Oh, yes. I do."

"And will you tell me where they are?"

"No. But very soon, Sid, I'll let you see them for yourself."

20 Morris Ave, Bronx, NY
The evening of June 25, 1941

Rosalie paced anxiously around the apartment, unable to sit still. "When is she going to get here already?" she asked Sam. The quiver in her voice reflected the fear she'd felt since Sid's disappearance.

"Rosie, don't worry," said Sam, trying to calm his agitated wife. "It takes time. She's not coming from around the corner. And then she has to park the car, too. So give her a chance."

"Sammy, I just can't stand it anymore. If he was okay, I know he would have contacted us by now. This is not like our son, Sammy. I'm his mother, and I'm telling you something terrible has happened to him!"

"I've checked all the local hospitals, Rosie. Morrisania, Lebanon, St. Barnabas. Even went up to Montefiore Hospital on E. 210th Street. Nice place but it needs some serious work."

"I don't care how nice it is or it isn't, Sam Peskin. All I want is my... our son!"

"And none of the hospitals in the Bronx have him, Rosie. I can't check every hospital in the entire City of New York!"

"And why not?"

"Because there may be over a hundred of them. Big ones that are household names, small ones no one's ever heard of..."

"So? Isn't our son worth the effort?"

"Of course, he is, Rosie, of course he is. When you put it like that... sure."

"Then what's stopping you? The phone is on the side table next to your chair, on top of your newspapers."

Sam had an idea. "Hey, Benny!" he called to his younger son, who'd retreated to his room. "Come out here!"

The door to Sid and Benny's bedroom creaked open. "Whaddaya want, Dad? You guys find Sid yet?" His bottom lip quivered.

"No. How'd ya like to help me find him?"

Benny's eyes brightened. "Really?"

"Yup. All you have to do is call the operator and ask her for the phone numbers of the hospitals on my list."

Benny pouted. "Aw, that's no fun!"

"It is for me," said Sam.

"C'mon, Dad. I thought we were gonna do something really interesting! Like Batman does, swooping in to rescue people at the last second!"

"Benjamin," said Rosalie sternly. "Go help your father. Go on, be a good boy."

"Does helping Dad mean I can get outta goin' to synagogue Saturday morning?"

"No. You both help your father and you go to services."

"But Mom..." Rosalie always had a deaf ear for Benny's whining. "There's a team from Walton Avenue coming here to play us Saturday morning. It's like the preliminaries for the World Series of stickball! I can't miss it. My team will kill me."

"Then you'd better consider what the Lord thy God will do to you if you don't show him the proper respect on the Sabbath. That'll be far worse than what your team will do."

"Who made you into an Old Testament preacher?" asked Sam.

"Never mind who. Just start dialing, you two."

The phone marathon was soon interrupted by a loud knock at the door. Rosalie hurried to open it. "Oh! Julia! Thank the good Lord; I thought you'd never get here," said Rosalie as the two embraced. "We had the cops up here last night. They thought he might have run away on his own. I said that was impossible. Not my Sid. And I know he'd never run away from you, Julia. Never. He thinks the world of you. Then they asked me a whole bunch of questions, muttered a few words, and then left. We haven't heard from them since."

"Rosalie, I know how hard this is for you. I came as soon as I got your call. And I know what you're thinking, I really do. But I also know he's still alive. I just know it!"

"You're... you're so young and optimistic, Julia. And that's wonderful, but sometimes... But oh, for God's sake! What's wrong with me? I shouldn't allow you to stand in the hall like this. Please, please come in. Sam! Move your newspapers aside and make sure Miss Falcone has a place to sit down!"

Julia stepped into the apartment. "Thank you, Rosalie. Hello, Sam. Tell me. Did Sid say anything at all about where he might have been going? Any word at all?"

"No, not a word," said Rosalie. Sam nodded his agreement.

"It's just—there's been a rash of top scientists who've disappeared recently," Julia pointed out.

"Honey, Sid's no top scientist! He's just a little pisher of a graduate student who hasn't published a thing! Anyone who thinks different is *meshuga* in my book."

"I may be *meshuga*, Rosalie. "But your own information's out of date."

"According to who, exactly?"

"According to Albert Einstein, Nobel Prize winner and physicist extraordinaire. We visited him recently. You may not have been told."

"No!" Rosalie exclaimed, her eyes as round as saucers. Her mouth gaped. "Tell me again, Julia… You and Sid? You visited Albert Einstein? The real one? And he spoke with you?"

"Not so much with me. Mostly with Sid, about an idea Sid came up with. It was something or other to do with nuclear physics. Einstein said it was revolutionary. I didn't understand very much, even when Sid sort of explained it."

"And you expect me to understand it?"

"The point, my dear Rosalie, is that I think it's possible Sid has disappeared precisely because of his scientific work." Julia was always pleasant, even as she marveled at how Sid could live with this character.

"Mom!" called Benny, who was fiddling with the tuning dial on their half-moon-shaped Zenith radio.

"Quiet, Benny. We're having a serious adult talk about your brother."

"Then you better come quick, 'cause Sid's on the radio! I mean, it's the police talkin' about Sid!"

Rosalie, Julia and Sam dashed to the radio, straining to hear the transmission.

"Repeat," said the announcer. "The authorities are hunting for Sid Peskin, 23, who was kidnapped in broad daylight outside his apartment building at 20 Morris Avenue in the West Bronx. A neighborhood couple going for their Sunday morning walk reported that a man, probably Peskin, was alone on Morris Avenue when a red auto with a large front grille, possibly a '33 DeSoto, sped in front of him, jumped the curb, and mounted the sidewalk. Three burly individuals wearing black overcoats jumped out of the automobile and hustled Peskin into the car and drove off. The couple was too far away from the incident to provide further information. The New York City police are appealing to anyone with knowledge of this event to contact Patrick F. X. O'Sullivan at the Office of the Police Commissioner, 240 Center St., New York, NY. The identities of all callers will be held in the strictest confidence."

Rosalie wept. "I just want my Sid back home safe with us!"

Sam hugged his wife. "He's alive! Somewhere out there, I know he's alive."

"From your lips to God's ears, Sam. We have to be strong and live in hope."

"I will never lose hope," said Julia. She felt a finger tugging at her skirt. It was Benny.

"Say, are you really Julia? The girl my brother is sweet on?"

"Yes, young man." she smiled. "I'm Julia. You met me last Christmas at our house in Brooklyn."

"Wow! You're even prettier than I remember!"

"Benny, mind your manners," scolded Rosalie. "Oh, how can I be angry with you, my *boychik?* Thank you for letting us know about the announcement on the radio."

Rosalie hugged Benny and planted a slobbering kiss he didn't appreciate on his forehead, leaving a shiny wet mark. "Eeeeeuuuuw, Mom!" he yelled, wiping his wet cheek on his sleeve. "If I'd known you'd do that to me, I'd 'ave turned the radio off!" Benny ran away to the bathroom to ensure all contamination was removed before any of his stickball friends could notice.

"Has there been a ransom note? Julia asked.

"The cops asked us that question last night," said Sam. "No, nothing."

"Didn't think so." She paused in thought. "I don't know who took Sid or why. But he's out there. And I swear to you, Sam and Rosalie, I'm going to find your son. No matter if it takes me the rest of my life to do it!"

Julia was too angry to wait for the elevator. Instead, she tore down the stairs and out the front door, into the warm, humid evening air. She didn't know if Sid was alive or dead. But the manner of his disappearance, as described by the elderly couple that witnessed it, was typical of a mob action.

"God damn everything!" she said, gritting her teeth. Carefully placing Morris Avenue under surveillance to prevent happening to her what had happened to Sid, she walked toward her car. It was only about two blocks away. Looking about but seeing no one, she slid the key into the driver's side lock, and turned it. The lock popped open. She eased herself inside and onto the seat and closed the door.

But as her right hand prepared to insert the key into the ignition, her shoulder was wrenched and held so tightly it was fixed, immobile. She screamed from fear and pain, twisting around in her seat to better see her assailant. His face remained obscured in the gloom, but Julia caught a glance of a Patek Philippe wristwatch reflecting the dull orange glow of a New York City street light. She'd seen that watch before.

"Let go of me, *figghiu de buttana,*" she yelled, using her free left hand in a vain attempt to dislodge the fingers digging at her shoulder.

"Don't be so angry, child." She recognized her attacker. Uncle Vince—Vince Mangano. "You're only going to get yourself hurt."

"*Vafanculo, stronzo!* I'll be as angry as I want until you give me back my man! Christ, Vince, you have the most god-awful way of announcing your presence!"

Mangano let go of her shoulder. She turned in the car seat to face him, desperately wanting to spit in his face. "That's nasty language for a little girl. 'Specially since I ain't had nuttin' to do wid' whatever happened to him."

Julia's lip curled. "Hey, Vincenzo," she spat, reverting to the Brooklyn accent she'd long ago purged from her speech. "Who the fuck ya kiddin'? I've been observin' you and your operation since I was a kid. Three wiseguys with black overcoats in the West Bronx? C'mon, I know who their workin' for! So why don't you jus' tell me what's goin' on? So, like we can all be a family again?"

Mangano cackled. "I wanna give you a word of advice as to how the world woiks, child. We, my brother Phil and I, and our colleagues, we used to be men of honor. We had our code o' conduct, and no one, on pain of deat', would dream of violatin' it. We honored families, and no matter what was done against us, we held da wives and families of our enemies sacred! Well, sweetheart, dem old values is gone! And it's because Lindboigh, Hoover, and their stooge Trump made it real tough for all of us ta survive. It's become each man for himself, even widdin da families. So, don't think dat 'cause you're my niece it automatically, it like—makes ya safe. 'Cause it don't.

"Now, ya listen to me, little girl," he said, placing his mouth next to her ear and whispering into it, a serpentine hiss. His breath stank from a pack-a-day cigarette habit. "Don' go askin' no questions. Don' get involved—ever again. You don' wanna know nuttin'. It's not healt'y. Ya go home and forget all about dis guy Peskin. Find ya some nice Sicilian boy, get-a married, and have a couple o' nice *bambini*. Have a good life an' make yer folks proud! Peskin's dead to you now, child. And if you ask any more questions, den I'm-a warning ya, child—yer on yer own. Don't be countin' on my protection, such as it is!"

Mangano flipped up the inside door handle, got out of the back seat of the car, and closed the car door behind him.

In the front seat, a trembling Julia wondered what Vince had meant when he referred to Sid as 'dead' to her now. There were so many questions for which she desperately needed answers. Why was he the victim of a Mafia kidnapping, when the only connection he'd had with the mob was through her? Perhaps his disappearance in some way was related to his scientific work. But that didn't make any sense; mobsters didn't understand science. But that meant Sid's kidnapping didn't originate with Vince Mangano; it must have been contracted to him. So, who was desperate enough to do the contracting, and why did they do it? Perhaps it was Fred Trump, but Mangano and Trump never did any business together, as far as she knew; the hatred between them was too visceral. Lindbergh was as unlikely a candidate as Trump, for the same reason.

Was her uncle hired to do the unthinkable—to have Sid murdered, as if the ties of family meant nothing to him? Could Vince Mangano be that cruel? She didn't allow herself to consider an answer to that question. Perhaps Sid was still alive but held incommunicado, and in that way 'dead' to her.

Nothing made sense, she thought. Nothing! But there was one person still in New York who, so far as she knew, had not yet disappeared. If anyone could lead her to Sid, it was him. And in the morning, she would be on his trail like a bloodhound, grim, determined, and focused—and if necessary, at the risk of her own life.

CHAPTER 18

Julia's first stop was at 137th Street and Convent Avenue in Manhattan. Her Hunter College ID got her past City College security in a heartbeat, and she ran up the staircase to the library in Shepard Hall. Breathless, she almost collided with the librarian, an older black woman, at the library door.

"Hey, honey," the woman said, recovering from the near accident, "whatever it is you want, you're still gonna need my help."

"I'm so sorry!" Julia said. "I do... I need help desperately, and I'm just in a terrible rush today!"

"Hmm. That seems obvious. If the help you need's about a man, let me tell ya somethin': they ain't worth it. Not a one of 'em."

Julia didn't have time for this woman's woes.

"Can you kindly direct me to the librarian?" she asked.

The older woman raised an eyebrow. "Hmm... you just about ran her over."

"Oh! Please. I mean, I'm sorry. But I... I need a picture. Of a man named Leo. Leo Szilard. Ever hear of him?"

"Who, Leo Szilard the physics guy?"

"Yes! That's him! You have a recent photo?"

The librarian thought for a moment. "Does Leo hang with that fella Einstein?" she asked.

"I know the two are good friends. Why?"

"Hmmm... come with me for a moment," she said, motioning with her index finger.

The librarian led Julia to a small dusty room behind the main desk. Against a wall of the room stood two wooden file cabinets. The librarian opened the top drawer of one of the cabinets and removed a thick folder.

"Here... 'bout five years ago," she said. "We had us a celebration of Einstein and his theories. Interesting stuff, if you've ever read 'em. Now I've been workin' here almost thirty years, so I remember the day like it was yesterday. I also seem to remember that fella Leo Szilard was here, too. Here are the pictures. Maybe one of 'em will help you."

Julia took the folder and thanked the librarian profusely. Both women left the room, the librarian retreating behind the main library desk while Julia sat at a carrel and opened the folder. It contained reams of photos, probably more than a hundred in total. Almost every one featured Einstein and people who Julia presumed were City College staff and students. She smiled at seeing a photo that caught a glimpse of a younger, shyer, Sid Peskin, hiding in the background.

None of the black and white photos were useful. She could easily recognize Einstein—in those days, who couldn't? But people she'd never met before always surrounded him. There was nothing in any photo that identified anyone—until she had searched through almost eighty camera shots. The last one was a formal picture that included, in addition to Einstein, the president of the City University of New York, the dean of City College, and all the other scientists and luminaries that attended the Einstein celebration. The participants were lined up in neat rows, with Einstein at the front and center. And thank God, at the bottom of the photo was a printed legend. Starting from the left of the second row and counting toward the right were the names of six people who were unknown to Julia. The seventh name was Leo Szilard's. He was standing behind Einstein, but his face was clearly visible.

"Bingo!" she exclaimed, like a tiger catching sight of her quarry. "I've got you cornered now!"

The instant that Julia set Leo's features to memory was the moment she also realized she had no idea where to find him. But she remembered Sid had said he was Hungarian. As an immigrant who might desire to remember the sounds and smells of his former homeland, she thought Leo might often dine at the most prominent Hungarian restaurant in New York. By consensus, this was the Café Budapest, located in Yorkville on the Upper East Side of Manhattan, at 86th between 2nd and 3rd Avenues.

Julia had rarely, if ever, been to that neighborhood, which stretched from about 59th to 96th Streets, and from York Avenue on the East River all the way over to Lexington, west of 3rd Avenue. Its inhabitants were lower middle class central and eastern Europeans—Czechs and Slovaks, but mostly Hungarians, along with a sprinkling of Jews, an ethnic pool vastly different from what she'd experienced growing up in the Italian section of Canarsie. But she loved the different character of the neighborhood, familiar yet also exotic—especially the wide variety of different foods on display in the shops. She made a mental note to return there to shop after Sid was found and they were together again.

Julia reached the Café Budapest at 4:30 in the afternoon, via the subway that ran underneath Lexington Avenue, one block west of Third. She bought a local Czech newspaper and positioned herself several yards away from the entrance in front of a store selling paprika and other Hungarian spices, hoping she wouldn't be noticed by any of the restaurant's visitors.

The afternoon was peaceful in this Bundist stronghold. No one was marching or ranting nonsense about the Jews, and the police and military presence was light. But by 7:30 p.m., having seen no one remotely resembling Leo Szilard enter the Café Budapest, she couldn't ignore nature's call any longer. So she entered the restaurant to get a quick bite to eat after a visit to its facilities.

After freshening up, she walked to the podium at the restaurant entrance to request a table. To her amazement, sitting at a small table and perusing a menu, was a man who could have been Leo Szilard's doppelgänger. Dressed in a well-fitting dark blue suit and white shirt, and black leather shoes, he wore a solid, robin's eggshell blue tie wrapped around his neck, held fast with a Windsor knot. Julia had the impression she was looking either at a financially comfortable accountant, or a mid- to high-level manager of a soap company.

Moisture accumulated in her palms. If this was the right man, he might think her behavior forward. Well, she thought, the hell with him and what he thinks. Sid's in trouble—and right now, nothing else is important.

"Excuse me," she said, breathing rapidly, "but are you Professor Szilard?"

The man slowly turned his head to look directly at Julia. The face was a slightly older version of the picture the City College librarian had shown her.

"Ah," he said. "If I may say so, you are much too young and too pretty to be one of our Mayor's henchmen, or henchwomen, and far too polite for a Bundist. They tend to grunt rather than speak. So yes, I admit I am Professor Szilard. And whom do I have the honor of addressing?" He rose from his chair and before Julia could react, seized her hand and kissed it, a commonplace gesture for gallant Hungarians.

"My name is Julia Falcone. I'm sorry to disturb you, but we must talk."

"Oh, of course, Madame. Please excuse my thoughtlessness. You're welcome to have a seat. Female company is a pleasant thing when dining, I've always believed."

Leo helped Julia into the chair.

"Thank you, Professor," she said.

He requested another menu from a passing waiter. "Please, I insist. Be my guest. You would be doing me a great service. One does not like to dine alone. Order whatever you like. And then, tell me what it is that's on your mind."

Julia had a strong sense Leo was not taking her seriously because of her youth, her looks, and her gender. But nothing would deflect her from her purpose as long as Sid needed her.

She made her selection from the menu—paprika in the Hungarian food shop on 86th Street, chicken paprikash at the Café Budapest.

"Oh, wonderful! You've made a fine choice," said Leo. "The chicken paprikash here is *trés magnifique!* Nothing at all like in Budapest, but for America, not bad."

The waiter took the menus away. Leo pushed back on his chair and crossed his left leg over his right.

"Now, *mein schönes Mädchen,* how can I help you this evening?"

"I believe you know my... ah, close friend. His name is Sid Peskin. A graduate student at City College."

Neither a muscle twitched nor an eyelid flickered on Leo's impassive face. "Hmmm... let me think. Ah, yes, of course; we met briefly about six months ago. I believe it was in the City College library. He and I wanted to look at the same scientific papers at the same time. Imagine that! Such a coincidence! But since then, I'm afraid we've had no further contact."

A gypsy fiddler dressed in an ill-fitting tuxedo and playing a vigorous Hungarian tune came to their table.

"Ah... a piece by the great Hungarian composer Zoltan Kodály."

Julia pushed back. "Oh, Professor Szilard, surely you recognize Brahms' Hungarian Rhapsody. It's the second of the series, I believe," she said sweetly. The fiddler gave his head a graceful nod in her direction. Julia thought she saw Leo's mouth slightly curl in a grimace.

"Did Albert Einstein ever mention Sid's name to you, Professor? He told Sid and I he would."

"Yet I'm afraid he never did. Don't be disappointed. You have to know Albert. He and I have been friends for many years. We once invented a refrigerator that used paper—oh, I'm sorry, never mind. I shouldn't bother you with these old stories. As for Albert, I can tell you, he always means well. But he's a bit absent-minded and doesn't always follow through with his commitments to people. It's an old problem with him, but he's not going to change his ways at his stage of life."

"Sid's been kidnapped. By the Mafia. Vince Mangano gave the order. He's the head of one of the largest criminal gangs in the city. I'm afraid Sid's life is in terrible danger—if he's still alive."

Leo offered Julia a cloth napkin to pat her eyes. "Here, my dear, take this. Please don't cry. It troubles me deeply to see you so distressed. But honestly, I met your friend Sid only once some time ago. I'm not sure why you believe I could be of help to you. I know nothing about his disappearance. I can only offer you my sincerest wishes for his healthy return and hope that matters will work out for the best for both of you."

But Julia was enraged by Leo's smarminess. "You're a liar, Leo Szilard," she snapped, pursing her lips. "You play the part of a central European sophisticate, but you are not convincing—because underneath, you have no heart!"

Leo uncrossed his legs. "Madame, mind your manners. We are in a public place. Please consider my reputation—and your own!"

"Well, screw both of 'em!" Julia yelled. All other conversations in the restaurant ceased, while everyone listened in on theirs. "You know better than I do that scientists from all over the country have been disappearing. First Fermi, then von Neumann, and I know of many others! And Professor Strauss shot in the head..."

Leo reddened. "Please, Miss Falcone, I insist that you keep your voice down."

Julia ignored him. "And then Sid, who was at work on an idea that even Einstein found revolutionary. I believe it concerned nuclear—"

Such talk was too much for Leo. "Damn it, shut your mouth now, Falcone." He balled his hand into a fist, extended his index finger, and pointed it threateningly at her. "You have no idea what you are talking about! And if you continue babbling, both you and your boyfriend will get yourselves killed, along with many others."

"So, you admit it! Sid is still alive!"

Leo exhaled and dropped his arm. "You think you're a very clever girl, Julia Falcone. And maybe you are. Perhaps too clever. Yes, I believe Sid Peskin is still alive. But I don't know where he is, and I wouldn't tell you anything more even if I knew it."

"Thank you anyway, Leo. You've given me a great deal to take home and think over. But I'm afraid I must run as it's getting dark. There are some very... unsavory types about."

She rose from the table. "Good evening, Professor Szilard. I hope we have a chance to talk again." She departed the Café Budapest, leaving an angry Leo glowering in her wake.

Julia was unaware that just outside the Café Budapest lurked a furtive figure dressed in a black fedora, a dark, lightweight overcoat, and blue dungarees. He had an elongated face, a high forehead, large spectacles, full lips, and a distinctive bottle-brush mustache.

As Julia had sat reading her Czech newspaper outside the Café Budapest, trying to be inconspicuous before meeting Leo Szilard, the man with the bottle-brush mustache had noticed her.

It wasn't a coincidence; the bottle-brush mustache man was responsible for Leo's security, and had also been running surveillance on the Café Budapest.

Earlier, he'd paid a visit to the Peskin family in the West Bronx as soon as he could after listening to the radio broadcast describing Sid's kidnapping. While on the fifth floor, he saw a young woman leave the apartment in an indecent hurry and dash down the stairs. At the time, he'd hidden his face with his hat and was certain he remained unidentified. Nevertheless, he got a good look at her face and figure—and there could be little doubt this was the beautiful Julia, Sid Peskin's *inamorata*.

Julius Rosenberg and his wife, Ethel, had decided to hunker down in New York and wait for better times, i.e., the Revolution. But until it came, he had to earn some money. One couldn't live off revolutionary expectations alone! His new job was serving as a member of the security service of the underground CPUSA. It wasn't the way he envisaged spending his life, but his new occupation paid the rent and food bills, though there wasn't much left over.

Rosenberg crept into the restaurant and sat at a table close enough to overhear Julia's conversation with Leo. He was horrified by what he believed he was hearing and seeing. Since he had only the briefest glimpse of Julia as she ran from the Peskin apartment at 20 Morris Avenue, Rosenberg was unsure of the identity of the woman dining with Leo. Growing more and more suspicious over the past several months, he saw an enemy of the Revolution in almost everyone he met, and threats to his meager livelihood emerging from every direction.

In Rosenberg's paranoid mind, Julia had just tricked Leo into revealing important information about the Resistance. He couldn't know what use she would make of it, but it was possible that Leo could now be compromised. Of course, he, Rosenberg, would be blamed. The thought was unendurable. He shook with fear—what would Ethel think about a man who had betrayed the Revolution? How could he ever again look her square in the face knowing what he was responsible for?

Rosenberg departed immediately after Julia, thinking she might be headed for the 86th Street station of the number 6 train, which ran underneath Lexington Avenue, one block west of Third. He observed how nervous she was on the uphill grade on 86th Street. Every few seconds, almost like clockwork, she stopped walking to gaze over to the northern side of the street and look behind to ensure she wasn't being followed. And every time she gazed across the street, and right before she looked over her shoulder, Rosenberg pushed himself into one of the many store entrances lining the popular shopping venue.

Julia was unaware she was being followed. At Lexington Avenue, she descended the staircase into the train station, found a token in her purse, and waited at the wooden entrance turnstile behind dozens of people making their way home during the New York City rush hour. The crowds were unusually heavy today, the subway platform packed with people. All except the most exhausted were jostling to get as close as possible to the train when it arrived.

As usual, the crowd was densest opposite the turnstiles, but thinned toward either end of the station. Julia allowed herself to be drawn to the right by the flow of people until she found a good waiting spot next to a painted steel pillar about two feet from the lip of the platform. Five feet below, on a pair of gleaming steel rails, ran the number 6 train. People continued to file into the station, filling in the gaps between her and the others waiting alongside.

Nervous folks looked at their watches while others merely grumbled about the slowness of train service under Mayor Trump. Most just fidgeted silently, rummaging around for something or other in their deep coat pockets or their briefcases. Julia took a step forward and peered over the edge of the platform, looking for the bright headlights of the train. She spotted them in the far distance.

The train must still have been at 96th Street. But she soon took another look and saw that the headlights were becoming larger and brighter, and moving rapidly toward her. Retreating from the edge, she awaited the rush of air that signaled the oncoming train. The platform had filled. Julia leaned over for one final look down the tunnel. The train would arrive at the station in only a few seconds.

A pair of thickset, male hands darted quickly from the crowd. Women screamed. People hid their faces in their palms as Julia was pushed from the platform into the path of the onrushing Number 6 train.

The darting hands withdrew. The crowd gasped and leaned forward, unable to take their eyes off the scene of horror. Somebody yelled, "get an ambulance!" Someone else hollered, "call the police!" Rosenberg slithered his way between the people who expected to view a stream of gore down on the tracks. No one thought to stop him because no one was certain exactly what had happened.

The hands were quicker than the eyes!

"She jumped, just like that, poor girl," cried a distraught voice. "Such a young girl—so pretty too."

"No, yer idiot, I tell ya, she was pushed. Saw it clear as day," came another.

"Well, I didn't see anybody push her, ya old drunk," said a third, a woman who looked too well-dressed to be riding the subway.

The horrified motorman brought the packed Number 6 train to an ear-piercing, screeching halt partway into the station. He cracked open the passenger doors of the first car, allowing him to squeeze his tall, thin frame through it and onto the platform.

"Everyone, please leave the station!" he yelled to the crowd while waving his hands. "Walk down to 59th Street and catch the Number 4 express train downtown."

"Awww, easy for him to say!" groused a heavily pregnant young woman carrying a large package in her arms. She immediately received three offers to share a cab. New Yorkers could be gallant when the mood struck them, which was seldom.

The police arrived and slowly dispersed the crowd, most of whom understood it would take hours to clean up the mess on the tracks and restore service. The motorman maneuvered through the crush of people to the token booth and instructed the token seller to call the dispatcher with news of the grisly accident. In less than a minute, the dispatcher shut off the power to the electrified third rail. That allowed the motorman to lower himself from the lip of the platform and walk on the tracks without fear of electrocution.

Peter Higgins never imagined he'd find himself in such a dreadful situation. The thought of such a speeding, wheeled behemoth, a packed train, slamming into human flesh and bone was unimaginable. The inevitable result horrified and disgusted him. He'd shaken and trembled in his motorman's cab as he'd watched poor Julia fall onto the tracks.

Nevertheless, the train's engineer was responsible for all that happened aboard it, and Higgins took his responsibilities seriously. He walked to the lip of the platform by the front of the train, sat down, and lowered himself onto the tracks. Making his way around the side of the train to where he thought the remains of Julia would be found, he gingerly bent over to peer at the train's undercarriage. Expecting to see dollops of flesh, pools of blood, and scattered brains, skull fragments and gore, he instead heard a woman's voice.

"Hey, get me the fuck outta here!"

Higgins was flustered, confused. Could he be hearing things? No one could survive a direct hit from a massive train. He stood, fixed in place.

"Hey, up there!" said the voice, again. "Stop dilly-dallying, man. Just get this train off me! I can barely breathe!"

Somehow, against the odds, Julia had survived. How was such a thing possible? It was only because of the genius of the designers of the tracks, and the lack of cash of the city fathers when the Number 6 train had been constructed, around the turn of the century. To save money, the wooden railway ties, which in most railroads connected one rail to the other, were cut short and mounted on elevated cement berms that ran the length of the route. The result was that a depressed space was created between the rails that a small person, if positioned correctly, could safely lie in as a train passed millimeters overhead. It was nothing short of a miracle, but Julia had fallen into the space between the rails an instant before the onrushing train crushed her.

"Oh, my sweet God!" Higgins yelled as he glimpsed her head in the gap between the rails. "You're still alive! I can't believe it! Thank you, Lord Jesus!" He crossed himself and directed his gaze heavenward.

"Yeah, and I'm scared out of my mind, too!" Julia snapped. "Y'know, you got rats down here as big as cats! An' I think one of 'em thinks I'm dinner! So, please, please, Mr. Motorman, hurry up, for Chrissakes! It's god-awful down here!"

"Ma'am, are you okay?" asked Higgins, not expecting such a feisty response. "I mean, any injuries to your head, or broken bones?"

"I'm not sure," Julia replied. "My arms are kinda wedged in here. But I can wiggle my fingers—and my toes, too, if the rats didn't get 'em. I'm not sure. But please hurry, I'm very frightened."

"We're gonna get you outta there as soon as possible, I promise," said Higgins. "You just try and keep calm, and everything's gonna be all right. So sit tight while I get all the passengers off this train. I'll be back to you soon."

"It's not like I'm going anywhere," snorted Julia.

The people stuck in the train had no idea what had just happened. They were banging on the doors with their fists and trying to pry them open. Higgins motioned for them to calm down and hoisted himself back up on the platform.

"She's alive and well!" he announced. Many people, unable to remove themselves from a scene of such horror, remained on the platform. The crowd erupted in a cheer while an ambulance, siren blaring, arrived at the station carrying a newspaper reporter in addition to a trained medical crew. The reporter penned a story that would appear the next day in one of the few newspapers still being published.

The New York Herald Tribune
May 22, 1941

LUCKY WOMAN SURVIVES SUBWAY TRACK PLUNGE

By Nicholas Pinkenson

A miracle on the rails saved the life a young woman who may have been pushed off a platform in front of a speeding Number 6 train at the 86th Street Downtown station last evening. The young woman became wedged in the small depression between the steel tracks, allowing the packed commuter train to pass harmlessly overhead.

"I saw her fall right in front of my train," said horrified motorman Peter Higgins, who claimed he averted his eyes. "And then I thought for sure she'd be dead. But she called out to me from underneath the train! I couldn't believe it! I'd say the chances against her surviving were at least a million to one."

Higgins went on to say he emptied the passengers onto the platform through the first car before being authorized to slowly back up the train so medical personnel could extricate the trapped young woman. Astonishingly, after they assisted her to the platform, she was able to stand and walk about under her own power, apparently none the worse for her ordeal. She refused any medical care or transportation to a hospital.

When questioned by police, she denied willfully jumping in front of the train, instead insisting she was pushed, corroborating the accounts of some of the witnesses. She insisted she never saw her assailant and had no idea why she might have been assaulted. The woman, who looked to be in her early 20s, gave her name as Jenny Wilson, and stated she was living at 235 E. 78th St., Apt. 2D. However, a police spokesman later stated that both the name and address were fictitious. They urge anyone who witnessed what could have been a major tragedy of the subways to come forward.

CHAPTER 19

25 Green St., Brooklyn, NY, that same evening.

It was well after dark when a bruised, aching Julia finally arrived at her home in Canarsie. Every muscle, bone, and joint in her body ached, and she was cocooned in grime from her toes to her face. The fact that her appearance was godawful was obvious from the sympathetic, and some of the not-so-sympathetic looks she received from fellow passengers when she boarded the Brooklyn-bound Number 4 train at 59th and Lexington. She instinctively reached for her purse to pull out a compact mirror she carried—until she remembered she no longer even had a purse. It had landed on a rail and been pulverized by the steel wheels of the subway car.

Because Julia hadn't driven a car to her rendezvous with Leo Szilard, she wasn't carrying her driver's license. Nothing else on her person allowed the police to positively identify her. Any contact with Trump's NYPD was bound to create even more trouble down the line—trouble no one needed. Fortunately, the cops bought the name and address she concocted. They had no reason to hold her, so she thanked everyone for their assistance, and walked out of the station into the New York evening.

Julia didn't tell the police any other lies. She didn't know who had shoved her so violently in the back, propelling her over the lip of the platform and into the path of the moving train. She felt that her spirited conversation with Leo Szilard was connected in some way, but couldn't imagine why or how. Even worse, she wasn't any closer to locating Sid, even though she'd now blown one of her last sources.

Those thoughts, added to the stress of her near-death experience, were about as much frustration as Julia could manage. Instead of tossing away her filthy clothes and scrubbing clean her begrimed face in a hot bath, Julia broke down in a helpless torrent of weeping, convinced that there was no longer anything she could do to help either Sid or herself. Head down, she sat motionless at the foot of living room sofa as her hands, fouled with the muck of the subway, blackened anything she touched.

Trapped in self-pity, she didn't notice Joey approach. He was at home this evening, and when he saw her condition, he rushed to her side.

"Hey, sis," he said with deep concern. "What's going on? Oh, my God." He recoiled after getting a better look at her. "You look like you've been run over by a truck!"

"Wasn't a truck," she said, between bouts of weeping. "It was the Number 6 train."

"Wha-a-a-at! Jesus, sis! Quit with the bullshit! You ain't makin' no sense. Whaddaya mean, the Number 6 train? That's just ridiculous! No one can survive—"

Julia looked at him angrily.

"You're serious?"

She nodded.

Joey said, "I think you better tell me about this, sis."

Julia related the events of the past several hours but edited her meeting with Leo Szilard. Her brother reddened with anger when she explained how she'd been pushed from behind onto the tracks and how she'd survived wedged between the rails as the train passed overhead.

"*Bastardo!*" he raged. "*Bastardo! Figlio di puttana!* I swear to you, sis, I'm gonna find whoever did this to you, and when I do, his mamma won't recognize him no more! I'm gonna kill the sonuvabitch. This is a fuckin' outrage! An outrage against you and an outrage against the honor of our entire family! Uncle Vince is gonna hear about this, and when he does, someone's gonna die! No one throws the niece of Vince Mangano under a train and gets away with it! No one!"

"Don't say anything to Uncle Vince," said Julia wearily. "Please. He told me 'men of honor' don't exist anymore because of Trump and Lindbergh. Please calm down before you have, I dunno, a heart attack or something. You bein' so angry isn't helpin', ya know what I mean?"

It took some time before Joey's anger morphed into lethal determination. "Don't always listen to Uncle Vince. He gets excited sometimes. And right now, he's under a lotta stress. But I know that when he hears about what happened to you, he'll blow his stack. Vince is gonna take it as a personal attack!"

"But that's not your problem, sis. Someone, we don't know who, wants to whack you. And until I can find out who, you gotta be outta the way and in a safe place. So, c'mon, get cleaned up and go 'n pack a few things. I'm takin' you outta here."

Julia was too tired say no, and at the moment, a hot shower seemed very appealing. Within the hour, all cleaned up and dressed in comfortable clothes, she sat in the front seat of the red '33 DeSoto where she fell fast asleep.

It wasn't long before the car came to a stop and a soft shake from Joey awakened her. Julia stretched out, frustrated at having her sleep disrupted.

"C'mon, Jewels," said Joey, using her childhood name. "Time to get out."

She remained bleary-eyed. "Where are we?"

"A place where you'll be safe for now."

"I think I'd rather sleep."

Joey got out of the car, walked around to the passenger side and opened the door. Julia fell out. He helped her to her feet.

"Okay, kid. Start walkin'. Just put one foot in front of another. That's right. it's all you gotta do. You can sleep all ya want soon."

Julia shook her head. "Joey, where are we goin'?"

"Right turn here. Into this store."

Joey opened the door, and was met by a stocky, tough-looking young man with a prominent chin. He wore street clothes. Two similarly-dressed young men stood behind him. One of them, who had fleshy lips and was grossly overweight, recognized Joey.

"Relax boys," he said. "It's Joey Falcone."

"What's that to me?" asked the stocky man with the chin.

"He's Vince Mangano's nephew, ya idiot!" explained the fat man.

"Okay, Vince Mangano's nephew, if that's who you are," said the chin. "Who's the dame?"

"It's my sister, Julia," said Joey. "Someone tried to bump her off today. Pushed her under a train. Thank God and all the saints she survived. She needs protection. I'm takin' her downstairs."

"No, you're not," said the third man, who drew a .357 Magnum. "Vince said no one goes downstairs without his permission."

"Oh, for Chrissakes. You think I'd do somethin' not good with Vince? C'mon, I'm his goddamned nephew! Whadda ya want me to do? Bring her home? Think what happens to you if someone whacks her at home!"

The man with the gun withdrew his piece. "Okay, go downstairs. It's on your head with Vince. And by the way, Joey," he said softly as the Falcones, sister and then brother, passed by. "Your sister is a dish. A real tomato! Can ya put in a good word for me?"

Joey smiled but ignored the suggestion.

Julia descended the staircase first, followed by Joey. "Joey, where are we going? I don't like this place." But she was too physically exhausted to resist.

"It's okay, Jewels. Ya gotta trust me. Just put one foot in front of the other, and I promise, everything's gonna be all right."

Julia had always admired her brother who, even when much younger, seemed so self-assured and confident. But when she reached the bottom of the staircase, she recoiled from the dinginess of the cellar and the absence of even the most minimal creature comforts.

"Joey. This place is a fuckin' dump. What the hell are we doing down here?"

"Ah, I see we have a visitor," said a voice she recognized. "Twice in the same day! How nice to see you again, Miss Falcone!"

Julia, stunned, spun around to see the smiling face of her dinner companion at the Café Budapest: Leo Szilard. But when she saw Sid Peskin, arms outstretched and smiling, reaching toward her, and saying her name—the stresses of the day and the tidal wave of emotions Sid evoked overcame her, and she fainted into his arms.

20 Green St., Brooklyn, NY, that same evening

On yet another warm, pleasant summer's day, Leo Szilard walked with a spring in his step down 2nd Avenue in the Yorkville section of Manhattan. Feeling pleased with his accomplishments, and with only a few loose ends to tie up, his mission in the city would soon be completed and a new one begun. Then his real troubles would start. He sighed, but that was a worry for another day; today was for feeling simply grand.

Leo paid five cents for a *Herald Tribune,* the best paper in New York after Lindbergh had forced the *New York Times* to stop printing.

America reminded him of Germany in '33. His brow furrowed. Hitler had strangled the 'lying press.' *Die Lügenpresse*, he called it. But in Germany, it was all over in little more than a day or so. At least here in this country, the battle for a free press was still being fought out in the courts, which weren't corrupted yet. But who knew how it would end?

On E. 71st Street, between Second and Third Avenues, Leo stopped before a row of stately brownstones. Each had a stairway leading up to a fine wooden doorway, the entrance. Leaning against a stone newel post at the base of one of these impressive staircases, Leo opened his *Tribune* and folded it over for easier reading. His eye caught the story of a young woman who seemed to have been pushed off a subway platform and into the path of a speeding train, but who miraculously survived. He thought of his encounter the previous day with Julia Falcone and was relieved to read that the woman had given her name as Jenny Wilson. Leo was relieved to read Jenny survived, though he couldn't recollect anyone by that name.

A man's voice interrupted him before he could read the section of the article that noted that the name was a fake.

"Dr. Szilard. A moment of your time please."

Leo dropped the paper to his side and quickly raised his head.

"Yes," he said, concerned he'd been recognized.

"Jack Kennedy, FBI, sir." Kennedy reached into his pocket, pulled out his badge, and presented it.

Leo paled. Should he make a run for it? No, Kennedy looked about half his age and could catch him easily, especially since—at the moment—this block was empty of people. His palms and brow began to sweat.

Kennedy noticed Leo's discomfort.

"Oh, don't worry, Professor." He smiled, a large, toothy grin. "I'm not going to arrest you. I'm here on more of, ah… a social visit. A way to get acquainted, I think. We need to have a chat, you and I, and this seems as good a place as any. Somewhere we won't be overheard. So please, walk with me."

Relief flooded through Leo, though he remained guarded. He recognized the name Jack Kennedy as the son of Lindbergh's crony Joseph Kennedy, former ambassador to the U.K. He knew Kennedy as a defeatist and before that, an arch-appeaser of Hitler, and currently as the Secretary of the Treasury. He had been unaware Joe Kennedy's son was working for J. Edgar Hoover and couldn't imagine how anything useful would come from this interview. But since Kennedy wasn't hauling him off to face a federal judge, Leo thought it might be best to hear him out.

The two men crossed First Avenue at a traffic light and continued along E. 71st Street in the direction of the East River. This block was distinctly shabbier than the one to its west. There were fewer single-family brownstones fronting either side of the street, and more four and five-story walkups, which increased the local population density. Still, the block was a pleasant residential neighborhood, a calm, tree-lined lacuna in the midst of Manhattan's quotidian turmoil.

"I understand, Dr. Szilard," said Kennedy, when they were about twenty yards from the motorized tumult of Second Avenue, "that you are the local head, or leader, whichever you prefer, of a group that calls itself the Resistance."

"Why, Mr. Kennedy," Leo said, his heart skipping one beat and then another. "Where did you get a silly idea like that? I'm head of nothing and leader only of myself. I'm afraid someone is making up stories about me."

"Ah, then I am sorry, Professor, for taking up your time. I have some information that would be of interest—I think great interest—to that organization. But perhaps you are not the right person after all."

Leo squinted. There was no way to know if J. Edgar Hoover was setting a trap, using Kennedy as bait. But the fresh-faced young man seemed so earnest and honest that Leo was moved to take a chance.

"And if I may ask," he said, "what kind of information? It is possible I know people who might be interested in talking with you, though I have no direct connection to the organization you are referring to."

The two stopped next to a stunted oak tree struggling to survive in the chemical ambiance of midtown Manhattan. Kennedy drew close so he wouldn't be overheard. "Information that could take down Lindbergh and the corrupt kleptocracy of fascists destroying our beloved country."

Leo stared at him. "Your father among them, Mr. Kennedy? Am I to believe you are ready to commit patricide? Do you know what the ancient Romans did to a man who killed his father?"

"Ah, something about a sack and a monkey and the Tiber, as I recall."

"You are correct, Mr. Kennedy. They tied him up in a sack with a monkey, a dog, a rooster, and a snake and tossed him in the river."

"Ah, that sounds, ah... painful, Professor." Kennedy grimaced. "But this isn't ancient Rome. Don't get me wrong; I love my father dearly, but he can take care of himself. Always has, always will. The man is indomitable. But I have to make my own way. And that's why I want to join up with the Resistance."

Leo laughed. "Mr. Kennedy, I must be honest with you, as you have been with me. The people I know—well, don't you suppose they would find your story just a bit difficult to believe? Just a bit, hmm? Not only because of who your father is, but also because you are one of Hoover's soldiers?"

Kennedy gazed off into the distance. A look of ineffable sadness registered on his face. "Leo, I swear to you that what was in the past is done with forever. I am not the man you and others believe me to be."

"Don't mind me for being incredulous. And if I may ask, Mr. Kennedy, what led to this conversion, which seems as unexpected as a similar epiphany on the road to Damascus several millennia ago?"

Again, Kennedy looked away and off into the infinite distance. "America is still a neutral state in this war, Professor Szilard. I travel widely—sometimes on official government business, sometimes not. I have been to Germany recently. I've spoken with many Germans. Most are rabidly pro-Nazi, many others are less so. I've also had the opportunity to converse with soldiers coming home on leave from the Eastern Front. Professor Szilard, I swear to you, the rumors are true. And they don't begin to capture what is really happening."

"Which rumors?"

"I'll tell you, though I expect you not to believe me. No one does. What the Germans are doing is not conceivable by normal-thinking people. They are systematically, methodically, and in cold blood, moving forward with their plans to murder the entire Jewish population of Europe. The Russian Jews were their first targets, but only the first. Thousands upon thousands are already dead, shot into giant pits by the Germans and their helpers. Men, women, and children, no distinctions made. Oh, my God, the children, Professor!"

Tears welled in Kennedy's eyes. "This is monumental evil, Professor—evil on an unimaginable scale. Evil so despicable, so malevolent, even Satan would gaze on it in thunderstruck wonder. I oppose the perpetrators of these crimes, and anyone who supports them, now and forever."

Leo stood frozen in place, almost unable to speak. "Your story is impossible to believe," he whispered after a long pause. "Impossible. I am sorry, Mr. Kennedy. But I must reject it in its entirety. Despite Hitler, Germany is a civilized country. I know the Germans—I lived with them for years. They are not barbarians."

"Correction. You knew the Germans, Professor. You do not know them now, after they have listened to the noxious, ah... spewings of Hitler and Göbbels. But I was there just weeks ago. I spoke to witnesses who saw the massacres in the east with their own eyes. Some were so distraught, they needed to speak about what they'd seen, and done, though they were told it was strictly forbidden to do so."

Szilard placed his hand across his heaving chest, as if he had pain in his heart, or trouble breathing. "Mr. Kennedy, you astound me," he said. "I-I-I am speechless. This is most troubling, most troubling, the unimaginable horror you speak of. But if it is true, what if anything can be done?"

"For the many thousands dead, nothing of course. My concern is for the living. The more than two million Jews the Nazis have ghettoized in occupied Poland. And I fear the ghetto, as bad as it is, may be the antechamber to far worse. There is no choice. To redeem our honor as human beings, we must resist. And the Resistance must begin by taking down Lindbergh—with vigor, ha!—as my old man likes to say. That's where I can help."

This Kennedy fellow was either an accomplished, brazen liar or a naïve optimist—though one who may be telling a version of a terrible truth. Leo couldn't be sure which. "Tell me, Mr. Kennedy. I'm curious. Just for my interest, how did you find me?"

"Remember who I've been working for, Professor. Mr. Hoover taught me the ABCs of investigative work—Always Blame the Communists. So that's where I started."

"I thought that by now, they'd all be underground."

"They are, but there are always a few that poke their heads up from time to time. The way I figured it, wherever there are Jews, you can always find a few Communists."

"Not all Jews are Communists, Mr. Kennedy. Most are Democrats."

"Well, of course not, Professor! I'm not a bigot—like our president and Fred Trump."

"And I sincerely regret any statement of mine that could be interpreted to the contrary, Mr. Kennedy. I hope you took no offense."

"None taken Leo, none taken, I assure you. We live in perilous times, you and I, when any comment may be misinterpreted to one's detriment.

"But to proceed—I spent some time on the Lower East Side, among the poorer and more religiously observant Jews of the city. Shaking hands, helping out, making friends, and I'll be honest—spreading some wealth—getting to know the folks, that sort of thing. Their ways are far from the ways of the Boston Irish, as I'm sure you know. But I enjoyed myself, besides meeting a few of the sharpest, most quick-tongued folks I've ever known. And some of their women are simply..."

"Mr. Kennedy, if you would be so kind, please stick to the point," Leo interrupted.

"Yes, of course. As I was saying, one day, outside a kosher butcher shop, I helped out a sweet, older lady. Rebecca Shaeffer was her name, I think. I was posing as a writer doing a piece about Communist infiltration in the labor unions and asked her if she knew any Communists personally. She said she didn't, but had a friend, Tessie Greenglass, also from the Lower East Side, who might. Mrs. Shaeffer gave me Mrs. Greenglass' address. When I knocked on her door, her daughter, Ethel Rosenberg, answered. You may have heard the name."

"I haven't," said Leo. He was lying.

"Then you're fortunate," said Kennedy. "And you're even luckier never to have met her. The woman's a harridan. At first, she was very suspicious, of course. But when I spread around a bit of the Irish blarney I carry at all times, she opened up. And then she wouldn't shut up. I must've listened to her Communist rantings for over an hour. I can't say she didn't produce accurate descriptions of the problems of society. She was often spot-on. But her solutions were badly misguided. I played along, and soon, she was inviting me to dinner with her husband Julius in their tenement apartment on Rivington Street."

Jack had charmed her just like he had charmed everyone else. Leo thought he must be J. Edgar Hoover's secret weapon. People liked to be around him and to talk with him. It must be a wonderful gift to have. "Did you go?"

"Of course. That's where I met Julius, her husband. A quiet fellow, probably by disposition—but there was something wild, even terrifying, in his eyes, as if he were sitting on a volcano about to erupt. Ethel did the talking for both of them. He's a Communist, too, and that, plus Ethel's bragging about the wonderful job her husband's doing, was all I needed to know. I put him under personal surveillance."

This young Boston Irishman is irresistibly smooth, thought Leo.

"Some people just talk too, much, don't you think, Mr. Kennedy?" he said, knowing that Communist security leaked like a sieve. "And my compliments to you, sir. You do personal surveillance very well. I had no idea I was being followed. But please, continue."

"Mr. Hoover trained me very well, Professor Szilard. In surveillance and other methods of intelligence gathering."

"Tradecraft?"

"I suppose you could call it that. But to be proficient takes great practice and never is as easy as it appears. Now, where was I? Oh, right, Julius Rosenberg. Well, I watched the man carefully for several days, but things only became interesting after he took the subway up to the West Bronx. I kept well behind Rosenberg to avoid being seen, and when he turned up on Morris Avenue and went in the door at number 20, I assumed he was visiting the Peskin household.

"That provided me with a probable link between the Communists and the Peskins. I already knew from eyewitness reports that Sid Peskin had been taken by the mob. There are extensive connections between the mob and the Communists in the labor unions in New York. But that's a story for another day, Professor. Mr. Hoover may deny the existence of organized crime networks, but based on my personal experience, I think otherwise.

"A short time later, as I was pondering the link between the Peskin family and Julius Rosenberg, I saw a young woman running out of the building. From a picture I'd located in the Bureau archives, I recognized her as the beautiful Julia Mangano, niece of mob boss Vincenzo Mangano. And I must say, Leo—the woman is an exquisite specimen of physical near-perfection. She's simply entrancing! If I ever meet her, I'm going to try my luck."

"She's spoken for, Jack. That's why she was visiting the Peskins. I think your time would be better spent pursuing unattached specimens."

"Oh. Damn, too bad. What a peach! I'm sure we could have had a very interesting relationship. Ah, what the hell, you can't screw 'em all. Anyway, sometime later, Rosenberg emerged from 20 Morris Ave, too. I released him from surveillance and took the elevator up to the fifth floor to have a chat with the Peskins. Very nice people. That Rosalie is a handful, but we had a long conversation about many things I knew and some I didn't, like Sid's visit with Einstein. From everything I heard, it seems the young man is on the cusp of a major discovery in atomic physics."

"He's a very bright fellow," said Leo. "I foresee a great career in the discipline for him."

"One, I hope, which doesn't end like that of Professor Strauss. That was a shock. Any idea who shot him?"

Leo shrugged. "How could I possibly know anything about that unfortunate incident, Mr. Kennedy? I never had any contact with the late Professor Strauss, and having been miles away at the time exculpates me completely."

"I didn't mean to imply you were the trigger man, Professor. I was just curious if you'd heard anything. You're a very well-known man in your area, with many friends and contacts."

"But only in my own field, Mr. Kennedy. I'm sure you understand."

"Of course. And oh, I forgot to mention. Julia Falcone led me directly to you, and so here we are. I was in the train station at 86th Street when she fell, or was pushed, onto the tracks. Unfortunately, I wasn't close enough to see what actually happened, but I did spot Rosenberg in the crowd. Perhaps he was trying to exit the scene of the crime, or perhaps he was just leaving the station, like many other people. I don't know. There were so many folks on the platform at the time, it was impossible to see more than an inch in any direction. Rosenberg was long gone by the time the cops dispersed the crowd."

"Mr. Kennedy, again, surely you don't believe I had anything to do with that dreadful event?"

"No, I don't Professor. And this isn't an interrogation, so please don't feel you must be on the defensive. I'm only attempting to fit the pieces of the puzzle together so I can be of the maximum assistance to your group. I hope you understand and trust my motives. What is happening in our country now is unfortunate, but what is going on in Eastern Europe is horrific beyond imagining."

Kennedy reached into his shirt pocket where he kept his badge. "Here's my business card. If you need to get in touch with me, call my number. I hope to hear from you soon—you must believe I am completely sincere."

Leo took the card. "Thank you, Mr. Kennedy. I promise nothing, but you will hear from someone, one way or the other, though I can't say when. But I'm sure any information you have on Mr. Lindbergh will be greeted with great interest."

"I suppose that's the best I can expect," said Kennedy. "Thank you very much, Professor."

Leo realized he'd not asked Kennedy an important question. "If I may, sir, just one more question."

"Yes, Professor?"

"How is it possible that you, a low-level government employee, were able to ferret out damaging information about Lindbergh? And in Nazi Germany of all places? It seems so very unlikely, wouldn't you agree?"

Kennedy paused for a moment. "The answer to your question, Professor, is that several of the wives in the Nazi hierarchy have been... ah... remarkably indiscrete."

He turned and walked off, leaving Szilard wondering if he was friend or foe. Nevertheless, Leo found something about the man impressive. Perhaps it was his sense that Kennedy was anyone's intellectual equal, and that a person with his depth of character and knowledge was unlikely to be a supporter of Trump and Lindbergh. But was he still working for Hoover, or against him? A man of Kennedy's background and expertise, if he truly decided to join the Resistance, could be an enormous asset to the cause. So, instead of disposing of Kennedy's card in the first available trash can, Leo placed it securely in his jacket pocket. The Omega, he was certain, would be interested in this development.

CHAPTER 20

J ulia slept more than eighteen hours before slowly waking up. "God, Sid," she said with eyes half opened. "It's great to see you. But where the hell am I?" She raised herself off the old mattress Sid had found in the corner of the cellar, on which Joey had deposited his sister. "Ooh, couldn't you have found someplace a little more romantic for our reunion, Sid honey? Not too many women would be impressed by a dusty old cellar."

Sid took her into his arms. "But it's our dusty old cellar, Julia. At least we're together."

"Yes, it's just me and you here in the cellar with the four goons upstairs. And you're not lookin' so good yourself lately."

Sid laughed. "You do a great Groucho Marx imitation. Humor is always helpful."

Julia was now fully awake and stretched herself out. "Jeez, this place and everything in it is god-awful. Except for you, Sid. I think I could be anywhere with you and still enjoy myself. Except maybe here. But after you kiss me, you better tell me what the hell is going on. Then I'll tell you my own tale of woe. We can have a competition for the more pathetic story. And oh—I haven't had time to brush my teeth, so please forgive my breath."

"A small detail," Sid said. "And I really don't care."

They kissed deeply and remained in an embrace long after their lips parted.

"Oh, Sid, Sid," Julia sighed. "I was so worried about you. I thought I'd lost you. No one knew what had happened, and we all thought the worst." She ran her fingers though his hair. "Thank God you're all right. I missed you so much." They kissed again.

"I can't get enough of you," she laughed as she covered his face and neck with kisses. "And if it weren't for those morons upstairs..."

"You better stop it, Julia, before I rip your clothes off," panted Sid. "You never know when they'll come galumphing down the staircase. So, I'm afraid tonight I'll have to take a raincheck."

"Raincheck," sighed Julia. "But you'd better make it up with a double-header soon."

"And maybe more," said Sid, as he gave one of her erect nipples a quick squeeze through her dress.

"Ooh, stop that," she said, pushing his hand away. "On second thought, do it again. To the other one. At least I'll be symmetrical."

Sid obliged, then slid away on the mattress to sit in a chair at the small table under the naked light bulb.

"Turn on the switch, Sid," said Julia. "I want to behold my new kingdom."

The forty watts of yellow light illuminated little more than what Julia had already seen. "Hmmm. This place needs a woman's touch. When do we leave?"

"Whenever Leo says we can, my dear. We're in this dungeon for our own good, ya know."

"Yeah, that's what Joey told me. I think he may be right, too."

Julia related the terrible events of the previous evening, when she had nearly died under the wheels of the Number 6 train.

"Good grief, that's appalling," cried Sid, hugging her tight, as if to assure her protection from any future calamity. "My poor, poor Julia! How dreadful!"

"Yes, poor, poor me! Honestly, Sid, it was horrible. Horrible! Even when I realized I'd survived, I still thought I was gonna die. I'll never forget being trapped under that train. Never! I could hardly breathe. I... I almost panicked! I don't know how I stayed calm. I remember thinking about you, and how you would want me to behave. And that I'm a Sicilian woman, as hard as a nail, who can never allow herself to panic. Then the train began to move again, so they could get me out. I must have passed out for a few minutes 'cause I don't remember much. And then I woke up, hopped up onto the platform and walked away, no muss, no fuss, no broken bones, just like that. I also gave a fake name to the cops. It's the Sicilian way, ya know."

Sid shook his head in astonishment. "You're an amazing woman, Julia. Lucky, too, thank God. I think I'm gonna keep you around for a while. Did you see who pushed you?"

"No. But it was no accident, and I didn't jump. Someone wanted to kill me, and I curse him with the Sicilian *malocchio*. May he suffer every day for the rest of his life for what he tried to do to me."

"Amen. That sonuvabitch! If I ever find him..."

"Joey will beat you to it, Sid. By the time you find out who pushed me, he'll already look like beef jerky. The Mangano family has been dishonored. They are not in a forgiving mood right now."

Julia paused. "Hey. I told you my story, Sid. You, lover boy, are now obliged to tell me yours."

"After everything you've been through, Julia, you more than deserve to know everything I know. And between the two of us, maybe we can make sense of it all."

20 Morris Avenue, Bronx
June 30, 1941

Sam Peskin arose at 6:30 in the morning. Rosalie was already awake, and had been so for about an hour. Sam found her in the kitchen, sipping her first cup of coffee of the day.

"Couldn't sleep, Rosalie?"

She shook her head.

"Me, neither."

She looked at her husband. "Tell me why, Sammy. Why would anyone want to kidnap our son? It's been three days and still no ransom note. Oh, who did our foolish boy, God love him, get mixed up with? You try to give them a good upbringing, and then they grow up and break your heart. I swear, if this has anything to do with that *shiksa*, I'll strangle her with my own hands!"

"Her name's Julia, Rosalie. Please don't make an enemy of her. Remember, she's the niece of a Mafia don and much more valuable to us as a friend."

Rosalie spat. "Sam, sometimes I think you have rocks in your head. Seriously, it's like nothing is getting through to you! Hello! Wake up, Sammy! Your son is missing! He's been kidnapped! And who's the prime suspect? Think, Sammy. Who kidnaps people off the street in broad daylight? The Mafia! And who's the only friend of Sid's who's connected to the Mafia? Huh, Sammy?"

Sam Peskin didn't answer the question.

"I see you're ignoring me again. Then I'll tell you! It's the *shiksa*, Sam! She's the one who's responsible. Can't be anyone else!"

Sam sighed. "But she came to the apartment and promised to help find Sid."

"She's a very clever girl. But she was lying. It was all designed to throw us off the scent."

"Honestly, she never struck me that way, Rosalie. Julia's strong-willed, but she seemed to me to be an honest, straightforward person—and I thought her feelings for Sid were genuine. You knew the girl for years when she was growing up. Did you ever think Julia was a monster? You always loved her like she was your own daughter. You were good friends with her mother Silvia, too. Did she ever complain about Julia's behavior? I don't know, Rosalie, but I can't square what I know of Julia with your portrayal of her now."

Rosalie thought for a moment. "Sammy, I think you're naïve. People change between the ages of fifteen and twenty-one. Maybe now, she's taking after her uncle Vince or Phil."

"So, what do you want me to do? I can't walk up to her and ask, 'Pardon me, ma'am, but did you order your uncle to kidnap your boyfriend?'"

"Oh, and why not?"

"Because it's insulting, Rosalie, and because I don't think Julia had anything to do with Sid's disappearance. She seems as concerned about it as we are. And if she believes the Mangano brothers were responsible, she'll know better than us how to deal with them. Don't forget they're her family."

"How can I forget, Sammy. That's exactly the problem. They're her family."

Four days later, Sid had not returned and there was no further communication with Julia. Rosalie slept, ate, and behaved poorly, snapping at Sam and Benny for no reason. Sam would come home exhausted from work then spend the evenings fruitlessly perusing the newspapers for any information about Sid. On occasions, he'd walk a few blocks to the nearest police precinct to see if there was anything new. But that effort was also unproductive. The police assured him the investigation was ongoing but refused to discuss leads or potential suspects. None of this was of any comfort to Rosalie, who grew more anxious as time went on, and more certain something had to be done and done fast. In desperation, when Sam was out, she picked up the receiver and dialed a phone number.

She was told she would be expected at seven o'clock that evening. Later that same afternoon, Rosalie walked out to the Grand Concourse and down the steps to the D train. She paid the fare and stepped through the turnstile. Five minutes later, the train arrived. The D was an express train and made few stops in the Bronx. In what seemed like almost no time, she was on the platform at 14th Street, where she caught the LL train bound for Canarsie and her old friend, Silvia Falcone.

Julia's mother met her at the door of 25 Greene Street, her deep concern visible in the lines on her face.

"Rosalie, I'm-a so sorry about-a what-a happened to Sid. Ah, there is-a no justice in this-a life! It is unbelievable to me how the bad-a people of this-a world use other-a people's children for their own ends."

Rosalie knew Silvia had nothing to do with Sid's kidnapping, but there was a coolness in her greeting to her old friend. Silvia tried to hug her, but Rosalie held Silvia's arms, preventing her from coming close.

"Silvia," said Rosalie. "I want to thank you again for seeing me today and for working out the... appointment. This is the life of my son, my child, that is at stake. There is nothing that I would not do to ensure his safety. I know you're not responsible for what's happened. But can you understand things from my point of view? That my son was living a quiet life before he became involved with Julia?"

"Rosalie, my friend, I swear-a to you on the grave of my holy mother, that-a my daughter is innocent of any evil intent with respect to your-a son Sid. No, it is-a not possible, and I call anyone a liar who says-a different. She cherishes him, Rosalie. And is-a not the type of-a person to do anyone harm. I tell you this because she is-a my own flesh and blood and I know her well."

"Then if not her, Silvia, I am lost."

"But that is why you are here today! To talk to the one person who may be able to help-a you. If he wants to."

Rosalie sighed. "And what are the chances of that?"

"This I truly don't-a know. It depends on the information he possesses, and how dangerous he judges it would be to say anything. You know how he can be."

Rosalie nodded her head. She'd been a resident of New York for long enough to know how the mob operated.

As the two women talked, Vince Mangano entered the house through the front door. He greeted his sister with a kiss on her cheek and Rosalie with a polite hello.

"Eh, Vincenzo," said Silvia. "If you have not met her before, this is my old-a friend from the Bronx, Rosalie Peskin. She has made the long trip here to speak to you about her son, Sid. Please, have a seat at-a the table in the kitchen. I will bring coffee and-a cake."

Silvia scurried to make her guests comfortable while her friend and her brother found seats. Mission completed, she claimed she had pressing business upstairs and left the two alone.

"Mr. Mangano," said Rosalie, who wasn't comfortable entering into a *tête-à-tête* with an individual of his reputation. "Mr. Mangano..."

"Call me Vincenzo, please."

"Vincenzo, I... I have come to talk to you about the most important thing in my life. This is my son. He was kidnapped from the street in front of our apartment building in broad daylight about ten days ago. From what we have learned from witnesses and the police..." Rosalie took a deep breath. "What we have learned, is that the kidnappers were likely Sicilians and that—"

"Stop." Mangano ordered, holding out his palm. "Stop. Mrs. Peskin, 'dere are tens o' t'ousands o' Sicilians in dis city. What makes you 'tink I know who da kidnappers are? Unless you t'ink dat I was in some way responsible... An' I sure hope you ain't sayin' dat."

Rosalie coughed nervously. "Nooo, I'm not making any accusations. But Mr. Mangano, I have heard... and perhaps it is a rumor... I have heard that it is possible to ask a man in your position for a favor."

Mangano paused for a moment. "Yes, Mrs. Peskin, it's possible."

"And I would owe you, Mr. Mangano. I would owe you if you would do me the favor of returning my son to me. But if you cannot do that, please for God's sake, let me know if you hear anything of him, and tell him that his mother and father, and of course his little brother, too, miss him terribly and want him back with us." Rosalie wept copiously, in anguish about Sid's fate.

"There, there, Mrs. Peskin," said an emotionless Mangano, who offered a tissue. "Don' worry. You can trust me. Everything is under control."

"Is that all you can do for me now, Mr. Mangano?"

Mangano didn't answer, but instead sat, sphinx-like, as Rosalie wept.

"Thank you," she said. She rose, turned toward the door, and departed the house without saying goodbye to Silvia Falcone, or giving Vince Mangano another glance.

The Berghof, Hitler's retreat on the Obersalzburg, a mountain near the town of Berchtesgaden, Grossdeutsches Reich. Earlier the same day.

"Albert, thank you for coming to tea here again," said Adolf Hitler to his Armaments Minister, Albert Speer.

"*Ja,* it is always a pleasure, *mein Führer,*" responded Speer. "The Eagle's Nest is such a wonderful, peaceful place. And the view! *Herr Gott,* it's stunning. I understand why you love it."

"It's so beautiful and peaceful, Albert, I think I may retire here someday, perhaps."

"*Ach,* but not so soon, *mein Führer*! There is still so much work you need to do. First, the Russians must be subdued."

"Their Jewish-Bolshevik state is corrupt to the core, Albert. One good shove, and the entire rotten edifice will collapse like a child's sandcastle. Mark my words. At the current rate of advance, our troops will be in Moscow by Christmas! We will then have achieved our goal of *Lebensraum* for our people!

"The Ukraine and the Russian black earth region will deliver their vast supplies of grain to us and to us only! And if millions of subhuman Slavs must starve, then that will be their fate! So be it! The German nation, on the other hand, will never starve again, as it did after the last war!

"*Und* then, after our inevitable victory in the East, it will be the turn of that mongrel nation, the Americans! Those fools sit between two vast oceans and believe themselves untouchable! But I'm about to teach them a lesson they won't forget. *Und* their president, *Herr* Lindbergh, the golden aviator, will now—more than ever—be our willing helper!"

Speer's eyebrows arched as he lifted his cup of tea to his lips. "*Mein Führer*," he said after sipping the warm, soothing liquid. "It's been my understanding that Lindbergh has always been well disposed toward us."

"*Ach,* Speer," said Hitler, waving his hand dismissively. "The man talks out of both sides of his mouth at the same time! He's worse than that Spanish idiot, Franco! *Und* he moves at the speed of an Alpine glacier! I warned him again and again that there is a Jewish-led plot in the American *Lügenpresse* to embarrass and discredit his administration! And so, what does Lindbergh do? He silences the *New York Times* but allows the Hollywood studios in Los Angeles to continue production! No, Speer, this situation is no longer tolerable!"

Hitler slammed his knee with a closed fist. "Not only that, Speer, but his declaration of martial law has also been a complete fiasco! People are laughing at him! Their army isn't large enough to enforce a girl scout troop curfew, much less control the population of a huge nation like America! I can't remember what ignoramus convinced Lindbergh to put the army on the streets, but whoever it was ought to be shot."

"*Ach,* if I correctly remember, it was the Mayor of New York City, Fred Trump. I believe his father was a German named Drumpf."

"Then this Trump, or Drumpf, whatever his name is, is a political dunce." Hitler grimaced as if his gas problem was acting up. "And I no longer will accept mealy-mouthed words and pitiful gestures from Lindbergh, in place of action!

"I also have a little surprise for the Jews of Hollywood. We have many friends in Los Angeles, Speer, probably more than in New York or Boston. Some have deep connections with supporters of ours in the local American Armed Forces, such as they are. Through these supporters, our friends in Los Angeles have obtained a large cache of military-grade weapons. They are not afraid to use them. If all goes to plan, the days of Hollywood's domination by the Jews and their minions are numbered."

Speer saluted. "Let me be the first to congratulate you, *mein Führer*, on yet another brilliant plan to confound our enemies. I remain always in awe of your concentrated genius, and I am grateful to God to be alive at the same time as the greatest German in all history!"

"Thank you, Albert. Your words mean a great deal to me, especially as I know you to be an intelligent and thoughtful man. But there's more, my friend. *Ach, ja,* much more. It seems that several months ago, our *Reichsführer*, Heinrich Himmler, uncovered information about *Herr* Lindbergh that he would probably not like to be made public."

"Astounding, *mein Führer*!"

"Yes, Albert, the word astounding is a good way to characterize this development. Lindbergh will become far more receptive to our demands since we informed him of Himmler's discovery. *Und* Albert?" said Hitler, dramatically lowering his voice.

"*Ja, mein Führer?*"

"I think it is possible to say that *Herr* Lindbergh is now, how shall I describe him, our man in the American White House."

Meanwhile, back in the cellar in Kew Gardens, Queens, NY

"I'm sorry you have to spend time in this dump of a basement, Julia. At least someone lugged a clean a mattress down here, a small table, a few folding chairs and a lamp. I hope you feel safe in your new home away from home, under mob protection. But if it were up to me, we could be, I dunno... at the theater, maybe."

"Yeah, sure. We could see *Lady in the Dark,* at the Alvin on W. 51st Street. Oh, wait a moment... that's what's playing here, wherever here is!"

"Personally, I prefer *Arsenic and Old Lace,* at the Fulton. But down here is safety, Julia. Out there is chaos. And if Leo's correct, it's only going to get worse. I know you're frustrated, but hear me out."

"I don't trust that Leo for one damn moment, Sid. How can I? I sit at his table in a restaurant, and the next thing I know, I'm under a goddamn subway train, fighting for my life! For Chrissakes, that's no way to treat a dinner guest! I still don't know how I survived, and I'm sick to my stomach just thinking about it!"

"I understand, precious, really I do. It's a terrible shock, and it's going to take time. But you'll recover."

Truth be told, Sid had no idea if or when Julia's ragged feelings would heal, but he'd heard his mother utter a similar sentiment, usually at the funerals of distant relatives. He assumed those words were always comforting.

He sighed. "It's time you knew everything I know, Julia. I can't promise what I'm going to tell you will make your life easier. But if you still want us to be together..."

"More than I can tell you, my love. I discovered how much I wanted you when I thought I'd lost you."

Sid paused, deep in thought. "It began even before Lindbergh was elected. Remember—he campaigned on a promise that he was going to teach all those slick university and finance boys from the Northeast a lesson they'd never forget. Well, the good Christians of the Midwest grabbed their Bibles and pitchforks and, with Lindbergh in the lead, vowed to throw the moneychangers out of the Temple!"

"Sid. Get a grip. Too melodramatic. Anyway, that's all old news. And just so you know, I'm usually impatient when I'm thrown in a cellar. Even when it's with you, snookums." She playfully pecked him on the nose and pinched his cheeks. "So, kindly get to the point. And make it snappy."

"But..."

"No buts, mister. I am a very distressed damsel, and as such, have certain rights and protections under the law, of which you, sir, are currently in violation. These protections include the right not to be trifled with."

"Ha! I think you're coming around, Julia. I reckon you'll be fully feisty again by tomorrow."

"Oh. Y'know. I have my moments. And you always do bring out the best in me. Please continue, absent the melodrama."

"Of course, madam. Always at your service. Now, as you know…"

"Yes, yes, go on… tell me everything you've learned. I'm fed up with having only the small pieces. I want to see the big picture."

Sid arched an eyebrow. "As you know, the Lindbergh victory was a terrible shock for many people, especially for the old progressive Roosevelt Democrats, who've seen the gains of the past eight years stripped away. The aristocrat Roosevelt was a true friend of the working man, while a Minnesota farm boy in the White House buddies up to malefactors of great wealth like Henry Ford and Wall Street financiers and tycoons."

"Hmmph!" snarled Julia. "Like Joe Kennedy! I know the type; grew up and lived with 'em for eighteen years. Men whose idol is money. More of it than they could spend in a lifetime. All of it, if they could get it, I think."

"Right. Men like that can never have enough money or power. Lindbergh's smart enough to know that, in order to retain his position, he has to energize his Midwestern base. So, he focuses their fears on groups of people who are generally disliked— blacks and Jews, of course—and on that great ethnic cesspool where many of 'the unliked' live, the City of New York. Surely, he prophesies, one day that tar pit of corruption will burst its containment and stain the lily-white American countryside a dusky brown.

"That's where the opposition to Lindbergh began: in the largely Jewish labor unions in New York—organizations like the ILGWU—"

"The International… what's the rest?" Julia asked.

"The International Ladies Garment Workers' Union. Yeah, I got it right. And the International Ladies Pocketbook Makers' Union, and other unions with New Deal-style acronyms I can't remember. A shadowy individual known as the 'Omega' seems to be the major organizer and current leader of what has become the Resistance. Leo either doesn't know or doesn't want to say much about him."

"Ooooh," said Julia, rubbing her hands together. "A shadowy organization with a mysterious leader. I like this. Omega—the Greek symbol for electrical resistance. Clever. Think this guy exists?"

"To tell you the truth, I dunno. Could be, but on the other hand…" Sid shrugged. "But every organization needs a leader, and a strong one, too, or it will crumble away.

And someone has to make the tough decisions."

"Is Leo the Omega?"

"He denies it, and I doubt it, Julia. But he could be lying."

"Leo lying? I'm shocked, Sid. Honestly, shocked."

"People do that, I'm told. But I think he's telling the truth. Though I've no idea how he and the Omega communicate."

"So, who is this sonuvabitch Leo, exactly?"

"Leo is a scientist. A very good one, a great one, even. I can verify his credentials. We've had many in-depth talks, the two of us. He spends several hours a day with me in this hole, and has been kind enough to deliver books and other reading materials for my amusement. You may peruse them in my reading room, located in the dark corner to the right."

"Does he also deliver women's magazines? What about milk in nice glass bottles in the morning? And seltzer, too?"

Julia pronounced the word *seltz-ah,* mocking a Brooklyn accent.

"I thought you didn't read women's magazines."

"I don't. But I do like milk in the morning. And seltz-ah. Mmm..."

Sid giggled. "Julia, stop being a comedian, damn it. This is serious!"

"I know it's serious, Mr. Sid Peskin. That's why I'm being a comedian. It's so serious that without humor, it might not be bearable."

"True. Now, where was I?"

"Leo Szilard is a great scientist who delivers milk and *seltz-ah,* but not women's magazines."

"Oh, right. Leo is a good friend of Albert Einstein, as you know. Leo is also the person who first proposed the idea of a chain reaction occuring as a consequence of nuclear fission. It wasn't me after all."

"I'm not surprised."

Sid ignored the comment. "However, I've added to Leo's original insight. The result of our combined work is that we believe that, in theory, it's possible to build a single bomb that could destroy an entire city."

Julia gulped. "That does sound serious."

"This knowledge must be kept out of the hands of Lindbergh and his supporters at all costs. The Resistance is very frightened about the contacts that have developed between this administration and the Nazis. It's believed by our people that information about the bomb will flow straight from Lindbergh to Berlin. Think of what this kind of bomb, an atomic bomb, would mean in the hands of the Nazi thugs."

"The entire world would be at their mercy," whispered Julia. "That can never be allowed to happen."

"Never. It would be the end of everything, Julia. Everything and everybody we value. It's unthinkable. I imagine you can now work out some of the details of what happened next."

"Yes. The Resistance needed muscle, if only for self-defense."

"Exactly. The unions were familiar with the Mangano brothers, your uncles, who'd been extorting them for years."

"And Uncle Vince and Uncle Phil loathe Lindbergh. He promised his base he'd be bad for the Mob's business interests. And he's making good on the promise. First and only time Lindbergh's been honest."

"It's not only Uncle Vince and Uncle Phil who are angry. Other wiseguys, Italians, Jews, are losin' big money, too, and they can't afford to look weak. So, the Cosa Nostra and 'Murder, Inc.' joined forces with the Resistance. I've had Lepke Buchalter, Meyer Lansky, and Bugsy Siegel over to dinner several times recently."

"Charming," said Julia.

"Forget Siegel. He's a stone-cold killer, a thug who looks like a movie star but is dumb as a stump. Lansky's no dummy but doesn't go in for the rough stuff. He controls the numbers racket and keeps the Mob's books. I think Lepke's the brightest of the bunch. I've even been instructing him in elementary physics! At his request, too! He's picking it up fast. But he's worse than Siegel, who kills for a reason. Lepke kills for the sheer joy of it. They're both psychopaths."

"But necessary psychopaths, even so. If they can keep their impulses under control. For at least a few minutes."

"Yes, very true, sad to say. The Communists became involved with the Resistance through the labor unions, which they've infiltrated over the years. Lindbergh despises them, and the feeling is mutual. But Leo says no one trusts the Communists..."

"Seems to be the universal experience," said Julia.

"...because they're devious, underhanded, and furtive. The CPUSA is by nature so conspiratorial and secretive, their leadership decided they should handle Resistance security, and somehow convinced the Omega to agree. But their incompetence almost destroyed the entire Resistance."

"How'd they manage that?"

Sid thought for a moment. "Do you remember my mention of a young CP member named Julius Rosenberg?"

Julia looked away and thought for a moment. "I... I think so. I have a vague memory of someone by that name, but I can't place him."

"That's 'cause there's nothing memorable about the man, other than he's a City College grad, class of '39. He's colorless and humorless, and usually inoffensive. Though watch out for his wife Ethel. She can crush stones in her teeth. The two of them are fanatical Stalinists. They would lie down and die for Joe Stalin and 'the cause' in a heartbeat."

"Would you mind terribly if I declined their invitation to dinner?"

"No, but you'll never get one, so no worries on that score. Their apartment on Rivington Street on the Lower East Side can't hold four people."

"Ah, a silver lining in the dark clouds."

"Maybe. Rosenberg has become the head of Resistance security. He's supposed to keep us all safe and sound, though he focuses his attentions on Leo. Leo is the local scientific head of the Resistance. But the most important Resister, without exception, is Enrico Fermi."

Julia brightened. "That's a name I know!"

"Fermi's not as famous as Einstein, but his contributions to physics have been immense. You've probably heard he's gone missing, along with several other prominent physicists and mathematicians? Fermi was on a train out of Chicago, on his way to visit J. Robert Oppenheimer, a professor and colleague at the University of California at Berkeley. Rosenberg once mentioned to me, in an off-handed way, that Fermi was taken off the train somewhere east of Denver. But he never told me why, or what happened to him."

"If I had to guess, someone was waiting for him at a train stop that wasn't J. Robert what's-his-name."

"Spot on. Hoover's men were closing in. And Fermi is the one person the Resistance cannot lose. He has a uniquely powerful mind with respect to atomic physics. After removing him from the train, Rosenberg arranged for Fermi to disappear."

"D'you know where he and the other scientists are?"

"Yes, in a general sense, though I couldn't give you a street address. But I do know where they're going, and where some of them already are."

"Can you tell me? Or will I need to be gagged for the rest of my life?"

"Both. I'll tell you, but you must never mention this place again. Not to anyone. Not to Leo, not to me. And you must never hear its name in your sleep, nor speak it when you dream."

Julia, wide-eyed, and with a dry mouth, nodded her assent.

"Oppenheimer is a difficult, arrogant man. But he's also a brilliant scientist from a very wealthy New York family. When he was growing up, he spent much of his time in the area of a ranch school located on a windswept mesa about thirty-five miles north of Santa Fe, New Mexico. The school was known as the Los Alamos Ranch School. The Resistance owns it now."

Julia swallowed hard. "So, this place that may never be named... Fermi is there?"

"No, not yet. That is my job, my mission. To ensure that Fermi, and the other scientists who have vanished, arrive safely at Los Alamos to start their work."

"Which is...?"

"Which is, at least to start, proving that Leo Szilard's theory, with my er...

modifications, is fundamentally correct. That a chain reaction occurring as a result of nuclear fission can be produced and controlled."

Sid fell silent.

"Is that it?" asked Julia.

"Almost. What do you think so far?"

"I... I don't know. Ordinarily, I'd say you were delusional. But there's ordinary, and there's Sid Peskin. And you're definitely not ordinary."

"There is one more thing I need to share with you, Julia."

"Oh, no. What could be crazier than what you just told me?"

Sid sighed. "The reason Fermi was almost trapped by Hoover was due to a breach in Resistance security."

"Rosenberg's fault?"

"No. He was not the Head of Security at that time."

"Who was?"

"Someone you knew. Someone you knew well. I. Bernard Strauss."

Julia gasped. "Bernie Strauss? Head of Resistance Security? Are you certain?"

"A detailed investigation was performed, Julia. Facts were uncovered that were very damaging to Professor Strauss. It seems he was playing both sides."

"Bernie sold out the Resistance? Oh my God, why?"

"The usual reason. Money."

"Bernie was taking money from Hoover? I don't believe it! He had everything he wanted!"

"How well did you know him, Julia?"

"I thought I knew him well. But maybe I was just fooling myself."

"Did you know he had debts? Bernie Strauss owed money to a whole lotta people, some of them very nasty people."

"I had no idea, Sid. None."

"The Resistance decided Strauss needed to be severely punished. To serve as an example of what happens to a traitor with a big mouth."

A chill settled in Julia's arms and legs. She felt her throat going tight. "Who made the call, Sid?"

"Leo."

"Sonuvabitch! *Figlio di puttana!*" she sneered, jumping up and pacing about. "Did he also pull the trigger? *Figlio di... puttana!*" Her eyes were black and fiery.

"No. Leo doesn't own a gun. Few Resistors do. Nor do they drive around town in a red 1933 DeSoto."

Julia breathed heavily and shivered. She rose and stood before Sid in the dark space where they'd been hidden. "I... I don't know what to say, Sid." A sense of doom engulfed her as the dread truth settled into her mind.

"Oh, my God! No, no, Sid, it can't be. It's impossible!" she cried, thrusting her words into the air with Sicilian passion. Then she buried her head in her hands, moistening them with her tears. "Please! At least leave me with my pleasant memories of him! He was a good man, Sid! A good... Oh, for heaven's sake, don't do this to me! Don't tell me, ever!"

Sid held her as she cried her heart out. She had asked him for the truth. Now he wished he'd said nothing. For he knew, as she now did, too, that the man who, in cold blood, had murdered her former lover, I. Bernard Strauss, with a bullet to the head, was the mob's own special enforcer for Resistance security, her beloved twin brother, Joey.

The New York Herald Tribune, July 5, 1941
[Below the crease.]

NAZIS AND SUPPORTERS RAMPAGE THRU LOWER EAST SIDE
By Richard van Hornswigge

A mob of thousands of torch-carrying Bundists bearing swastikas, German flags, and large posters depicting Adolf Hitler marched through the predominantly Jewish Lower East Side of Manhattan last evening.

The demonstration, which Bundist organizers claimed was supposed to be peaceful, quickly deteriorated into organized attacks on Jewish shops and business and on any Jewish person attempting to interfere. After smashing the glass of shop windows, looters helped themselves to the merchandise inside.

Shop owners looked on in horror as the looters destroyed their stock and their livelihoods while Bundist thugs with rubber truncheons stood by, encouraging the raiders and beating the local Jews with clubs.

"This was almost as bad as *Kristallnacht* was in Germany in 1938. I know, because I've lived through both," said Yaakov Levenstein, 53, referring to the infamous Night of Broken Glass, when the Nazis torched synagogues, destroyed Jewish businesses, and murdered hundreds of Jews.

Levenstein, a dry goods merchant, told how two Bundists had cornered him on his way home. One of them punched him in the head and threw him to the ground. The other kicked him repeatedly while cursing him as a "filthy little Jew."

Levenstein said he felt lucky to be alive and was looking for a ride to Beth Israel Hospital. Levenstein said he held out little hope of finding an ambulance after all the violence.

"Motionless bodies lay on the ground everywhere," he stated. "I personally counted a dozen, and I'm sure there are many more."

One of the reasons for the large number of casualties was the defense provided by a small group of men and women who fought under the red banner of the CPUSA.

A mere one week ago, the Communists, under orders from their red leader, Josef Stalin, would never have attacked the Bundists, as the Molotov-Ribbentrop Pact made strange friends of the two bitter ideological enemies. But with the recent German invasion of the Soviet Union, all restraints were lifted, and the CPUSA mobilized against their Nazi foes.

Though the bravery of the Communists was widely remarked on, they were few in number, poorly armed, and not as organized as their fascist enemies. Their defense of the Lower East Side, centering on Shlomo's Pickle Emporium on Essex St., may have been gallant, but it was also suicidal and largely ineffective.

Ethel Rosenberg, one of the Communist fighters, saw her husband Julius fall to the clubs of the fascists who beat him while she watched. Rosenberg, who also suffered stab wounds to the chest and abdomen, was taken by one of the few ambulances available to Beth Israel Hospital. His current condition is unknown but is believed to be critical.

"We may have lost the battle, but there is no doubt we will win the war!" said Mrs. Rosenberg with tears in her eyes. "My husband fought courageously against the fascist terrorists to defend the neighborhood he loved. I hope for his quick and complete recovery and believe in my heart that he will live on to fight again."

This massive attack by the Bundists on Jewish property and lives was, like many previous attacks, virtually ignored by the New York City Police, who arrived in strength only after most of the damage was done.

"It's a question of distance," said Patrick F. X. O'Sullivan, the NY police commissioner. "The Lower East Side is a long way from the majority of the force, which is concentrated in Midtown and in some of the more dangerous neighborhoods to the north, like Harlem." However, when asked about the looting and the fires set in stores on 125th St. in Harlem by a group of storming Bundist arsonists, he responded that he was unaware of any other disturbances instigated by that group.

A spokesman for Mayor Trump said he is appealing for calm and order, asking both sides to refrain from incendiary rhetoric, while recognizing the good intent that exists in all people.

On July 6th, an edition of a newspaper with a limited circulation was published in New York.

The *Forverts*—meaning *Forward*, in English—was founded in 1897 to cater to the needs of Yiddish-speaking immigrants to America. The paper's editorials favored socialism, but disliked Communism of the Leninist-Stalinist variety. Lindbergh ignored the *Forverts*, while Trump was unaware of its existence. There were few Yiddish speakers in the borough of Queens, and he had no intention of renting to them anyway.

The July 6th obituaries were located on page 25. If either Trump or Lindbergh had glanced at page 25 of the *Forverts*, they would have seen the following notice, printed in Yiddish:

```
Rosenberg, Julius: Fell in defense of the working people of
the Lower East Side and for the cause of justice, equality, and
the Communist world of the future. Julius was a proud graduate of
City College, Class of '39. An honest, gentle soul dismayed by the
abuse of his fellow men, he is survived by his devoted wife Ethel.
Graveside service 1 p.m., July 6 at the Mt. Hope Cemetery, Hastings-
on-Hudson, NY.
```

On the day in question, the mourners—members of the CPUSA and others—gathered in the hills of the Mount Hope Cemetery in Hastings-on-Hudson, New York, several miles north of New York, to hear their comrade Julius Rosenberg eulogized as a martyr and hero of their movement, and to lay him to rest. With somber faces, they watched as the coffin, a plain pine box, was lowered six feet down into the grave and covered over with earth, the first shovelfuls of dirt traditionally being reserved for family members.

The mourners probably didn't notice two men paying a visit to a nearby burial site. A woman was interred there whom neither had met, and to whom neither was related. The two men were Jack Kennedy and Melvin Purvis. Both were working for J. Edgar Hoover.

"The man on the far left is Leo Szilard," said Purvis who, for a brief instant, peered through a set of binoculars while trying to be inconspicuous among the gravestones.

"I suppose you're right," said Kennedy. "I can make out Ethel Rosenberg and Tessie Greenglass, her mother, but few of the others."

"Most, I'm guessing, are locals and acquaintances and the usual older folks who remember Rosenberg from before he entered grade school. They're useless to us, Kennedy. I want the real Communists—the card-carrying party members. I wanna make those bastards suffer, to feel some genuine pain. My God, I hate

Communists, every last stinkin' one of 'em." Purvis' dislike of Communists was a visceral obsession.

"They're not my favorite visitors at high tea either, Purvis. Except for Ethel, the hardliners are underground since their leader, Earl Browder, was arrested."

"But what the hell do you think Leo Szilard is doing with this bunch, Kennedy?" Purvis was puzzled. "A first-rate scientist with an international reputation at the funeral of an insignificant Communist agitator from a squalid immigrant community. Doesn't make any sense. We should pick him up now for questioning, ya know. Szilard, I mean. Hoover's allowed him to be on the loose for too long."

"Mr. Hoover's a smart man, Purvis. You gotta hand him that. If he wants Szilard to stay out of jail, I'm sure he has a reason."

Purvis didn't care much for Jack Kennedy, the rich man's son who—at a strapping six feet—towered over Hoover's "Little Mel." Purvis wasn't impressed by Kennedy's intellect, either; he amused himself with the thought that, if a bird crapped on Kennedy's head, the IQ of both would increase. The notion was a paraphrase of famed comedian Will Roger's line about the IQs in both states increasing when the Okies moved to California. Purvis found it hysterical because it was the God's honest truth.

"Seems to me, Mr. Kennedy, that our Communist friends must have formed some kind of alliance with Mr. Szilard."

"Could be, Melvin. Could be. But it could also be that Szilard is a distant cousin of the deceased and desires to renew a few old relationships."

Purvis thought for a moment. "Ya know, I don't like northeastern Harvard college boys, Mr. Kennedy. But this one time, you may have a point. C'mon, let's get outta here. I think we must have better things to do with our time."

CHAPTER 21

The Private Quarters of the White House
July 10, 1941

I'm telling you, Anne, things are not working out the way I thought they would," said President Lindbergh.

"And how should they work out, Charles?"

"Oh, the country should be uniting behind me, of course. It's a reasonable expectation. I am the president, and uniting behind the president is everyone's obligation, especially in these times."

Anne Morrow Lindbergh arched an eyebrow. "Charles, honestly. I don't think your expectations are reasonable. Why, look what happened just yesterday. People simply don't like to see other people beaten and murdered in the streets. Now don't get me wrong—it's not that I like the Jews, far from it. But—God be merciful—what's going on is just not civilized!"

"Anne, don't be naïve. Have you ever visited the Lower East Side of New York? Just look at them—those so-called people with the long side locks and scraggly beards who dress in black, broad-brimmed hats, white shirts, and black coats. Their beliefs are ridiculous and primitive to boot! I don't know why these creatures came to this country, or who allowed them in!"

"Oh. I never appreciated how many Amish people lived on the Lower East Side of New York, Charles."

"Amish? What in blazes are you talking about, Anne?"

"Except for the side locks, I think you've provided a fair description of the appearance of many of the Amish of rural Pennsylvania."

"Anne, for heaven's sake, the Jews aren't Amish."

"Yes, I'm well aware of that, Charles. But you seem to have forgotten that the American people, most of them, are fundamentally decent and compromising. They don't like to see others harmed. Not even, I dare say, black people."

Lindbergh laughed. "Now, Annie, you really are going too far. No one in this entire country gives a good goddamn about the niggers."

"Well, perhaps they should, Charles. You've been complaining that your poll numbers are going down. I have no doubt fascism of some sort is the wave of the future, but why don't you try being president of all Americans for a change?"

"That's simple, my dear. If you'd take the trouble to think about it for a moment, instead of pursuing your airy, avant-garde literary exploits. My support comes predominantly from the Midwest and the Plains states, and I'm doing better in the South than any Republican has ever done! I can't afford to alienate those folks under any circumstances! You're thinking like a wooly-headed liberal, Annie."

"Hmph! Hardly, Charles. I'm Dwight Morrow's daughter through and through! Father was a partner at J.P. Morgan, a Senator from New Jersey, and left an estate worth ten million! I've had Republicanism running through my veins since my birth! And I'm also well aware our special European blood must be protected! But I refuse to be devoid of common sense."

"So, you object to the means, but not the motive. Is that it, Annie?"

The first lady thought for a moment. "I suppose so, Charles. People are fickle. And you've worked so hard to achieve your goals. I'd hate to see you lose it all."

Lindbergh gathered her in his arms. "That won't happen. Believe me. That will never happen."

What Lindbergh didn't tell his wife was that, just the day before, he'd had a disturbing conversation with the German ambassador, *Herr* Thomsen.

"The *Führer* is seriously considering a continent-wide blockade of American imports, and an embargo on all European exports to the United States. Nothing leaves Europe for America; nothing from America enters Europe."

Lindbergh's eyes widened. "You're bluffing. You still need our grain and our oil."

"Over the last twelve months, the Greater German Reich has reached a position of true economic autarky. We now meet all our economic needs from within our own borders with the exception of iron ore, which the Swedes are most willing to sell to us. We have no need at this time for any products from your country."

"But you are involved in an enormously destructive war with the Soviet Union," Lindbergh pointed out.

"Which, I guarantee you, will be over within weeks, a few months at most. We have the *Führer's* word on it, *und* the *Führer* has never been wrong!"

Lindbergh fumed. "What does the *Führer* want now?"

"Nothing more than he has ever wanted, *Herr* Lindbergh. The *Führer* has always desired to live in peace and harmony with your country. But we must have Enrico Fermi, and you must do a much better job of suppressing Jewish influence in finance and especially in the newspaper and movie businesses. Their continued presence in high positions in these industries is an insult to the *Führer* and to everyone of Northern European stock.

"*Und*, due to changes in the global political picture over the past several years, the *Führer* believes a German naval base in Mexico, preferably on the Pacific coast, is now desirable. At or near the town of Mazatlan, perhaps. I'm sure your government could, as a gesture of good faith to us, persuade the Mexican government that it is in their best interest to lease us the land for, say, ninety-nine years?"

Lindbergh erupted. "Impossible, *Herr* Thomsen! What you're asking is politically impossible! No American president can accede to a request so damaging to our national security interests! I would be impeached!"

"It's not a request. *Und* as for your impeachment, *Herr* President; frankly, that's not our problem. Even were you to be impeached in the House and convicted in the Senate, with whom would the Democratic Party be dealing, then, as president? Your vice president, *Herr* Robert Alonso Taft of Ohio, a man who has never been reticent about his desire to eliminate all New Deal programs under the guise of preserving individual liberties. For the Democrats, impeaching you would be substituting the devil they know for the devil they don't. *Und*, no offense, for a far more politically savvy devil, too. No, Mr. Lindbergh, I do not believe you will be impeached because of our, ah... 'requests.'"

Lindbergh was about to reply when Thomsen interrupted him.

"*Und Herr* President," he said in a tone of voice that brooked no opposition, "do not forget about the special information the *Führer* possesses. We would hate to make it available..."

"You wouldn't."

"Who knows? The *Führer* may want to take his chances on Taft after all. As you are aware, *Herr* Hitler has the reputation of a being a gambler. Though unlike most gamblers, he always wins. You may obtain information about him from the French, British, Dutch, Belgians, Norwegians, Poles, Czechs, Greeks, Yugoslavs, Albanians—and, soon, the Russians."

"You guys really play hardball, don't you?"

The ambassador steepled his fingers. "I don't quite grasp the allusion, Mr. President. But to take you literally, I do admit we have the hardest balls of anyone. And we intend to use them."

"I'm certain you do, Mr. Thomsen. But this interview is now over. Please give my regards to the *Führer* and show yourself out."

The New York Herald Tribune, July 14, 1941
[Above the Crease]

NAZIS THREATEN US WITH EMBARGO AND MEXICAN BASE
By Alonzo B. Athanasius

In a radio speech to the nation last evening, President Charles Lindbergh described the German threat of a total embargo against American goods unless a list of their demands were met.

Foremost among them was that the administration was to give its blessing to the construction of a German naval facility near Mazatlan, on Mexico's west coast. Nazi sympathizers in Los Angeles rejoiced while most Californians, and other Westerners, were horrified.

"The entire United States, and the state of California—which I have the honor to represent—is in the process of being surrounded!" formerly isolationist Republican Senator Hiram Johnson announced from the well of the Senate.

Senator Rufus Holman (R—OR) also expressed similar grave concerns over Nazi activities, stating that a German embargo would cripple Oregon business, particularly the timber and mining industries. Pat McCarren of Nevada, the only Democratic Senator to reject the New Deal in its entirety, expressed his deepest forebodings about the health of the American oil industry should any such economic embargo come to pass.

President Lindbergh was uncharacteristically silent today. However, a spokesman read a prepared statement:

"The president has always maintained that the German *Führer* is an honorable man, desiring to have good relationships with the United States. The administration is working with representatives of the Third Reich in an attempt to determine German requirements for abandoning the embargo. Talks are proceeding well.

"The administration hopes to have further information, and perhaps even a resolution of the situation, in the coming days.

"With respect to the building of a German naval base in Western Mexico, we have no further information other than that the Mexican government states it has not yet been contacted."

The Department of the Treasury, Washington, D.C.
August 15, 1941

On a blazingly hot, humid day in the nation's capital, J. Edgar Hoover, the Director of the Federal Bureau of Investigation, was feeling proud of himself. Unlike his boss, the president, Mr. Hoover didn't much think about the Mafia, the Cosa Nostra, or 'Murder, Inc.' He'd convinced himself, all evidence to the contrary, that no such organizations existed. In his mind, urban crime, far from being organized, was nothing more than the product of rogue individuals glorified by news editors with overheated imaginations.

Therefore, the FBI Director felt no obligation to devote any of the Bureau's slender resources to the pursuit of phantoms. Let Mr. Lindbergh manipulate the fears of his Midwestern base with his rantings. J. Edgar Hoover was having none of it.

Personally, he had no opinion whatsoever about Italians, though he didn't care much for Jews and would never have them for FBI agents. But he doubted most Lindbergh voters had ever met either an Italian or a Jew. Nevertheless, these same voters were as sure as God made little green apples that Italians and Jews represented a grave threat to the social order and the Republic itself.

Hoover was content. At age forty-six, and with the first signs of a small pot-belly growing beneath his navel, he reflected for a moment on the true, clear, and present danger to the United States of America.

To the undoubted surprise of many of his detractors, had they known it, J. Edgar was unafraid of the threat posed by Nazi Germany. Wasn't it true, he would ask staffers, that his boys at the FBI had captured every agent landed on the East Coast of the U.S. by German submarines? In fact, Hoover allowed himself to forget that the first act of some agents, on making landfall on Long Island or New Jersey, had been to locate a phone booth and ring the nearest branch of the FBI. But that didn't matter much, as Hoover would alter the storyline to burnish the image of the Bureau— both for local consumption, and to convince the Germans that the Bureau was far more powerful than it was in reality.

Besides, some Americans seemed to have forgotten their country possessed the best military defenses of any country on the planet. Two huge moats, the Atlantic and Pacific, were sufficient barriers to invasion. Indeed, Abe Lincoln once confidently proclaimed that "no army will ever water its horses in the Ohio River unless we let 'em do it."

The true enemies of America, Hoover believed, weren't Hitler's Germans or Mussolini's Italians. Oddly, given his coming of age in the first decade of the 20th century, they weren't the Jews, either.

No, the most dangerous enemies ever to be faced by the nation were internal subversives, the men and women who flew the red banner of Communism. These card-carrying party members and their fellow travelers appeared to be loyal Americans, but took their treasonous marching orders directly from Joe Stalin in the Kremlin. If even a dime of Bureau resources was ever to be spent, it would be spent on rooting out Communists and their anti-American activities.

Hoover strolled out of his director's office and down a long hall into a small conference room. The three other participants in the conference, who had arrived earlier, stood on his entering the room.

"Glad to see you, Little Mel," Hoover said to the diminutive Purvis. "Jack, welcome back to Washington."

Purvis winced. He'd never got used to Hoover's nicknames for him, which he considered sophomoric.

"Thank you, Edgar," said Kennedy. "Always nice to be able to have a chat with the boss."

"Seems you gentlemen may have already met my deputy director, Clyde Tolson," Hoover said. "But I'd like to make formal introductions anyway. Mel Purvis and Jack Kennedy, meet Clyde Tolson."

A round of hellos and handshakes was followed by a mention from Hoover that coffee and danishes were on their way.

Tolson began the meeting as everyone sat at the conference table. "Mel, Jack— Mr. Hoover would like to know how you spent your time in New York."

"May I speak first, Mel?" asked Kennedy. "Speaking first and longest is the only genuine fault of the Irish." Kennedy's joke produced some brief laughs.

"Sure, Jack," said Purvis. "Knock yourself out."

Kennedy retrieved a folder from the leather briefcase he'd carried into the meeting. Within the folder were half a dozen enlarged photographs of the mourners at Julius Rosenberg's funeral. He placed one before Hoover.

"Who's the broad?" asked the Director of the FBI. "She a Commie?"

"Widow of the deceased," Kennedy answered. "Ethel Rosenberg. Party member since 1938. Browder knows her. Stalin doesn't, though she's a devoted admirer."

"Jesus, will ya look at that puss! What a face!" Hoover exclaimed.

"It's worse in person," ventured Purvis.

Hoover wanted to know what else they had.

"We're not sure," answered Kennedy.

"What do you mean, you're not sure, Mr. Kennedy? Hell, it's your goddamn job to be sure, ain't it? This is the security of the country we're talking about here, not a polo match, or whatever sport you Boston rich boys go in for!"

Purvis smirked.

"It's actually touch football," said Kennedy.

Hoover frowned.

"I'm sure the director knows about the tastes in physical activity of the Boston elite," said Clyde Tolson, a bored expression on his face. "Please avoid giving him unrequested information."

"Oh, lighten up, Clyde," growled Hoover. "Sounds like you got up on the wrong side of the bed this morning."

Kennedy, who'd heard the rumors about the relationship between the two, suppressed a wry smile.

"Go on, Jack," instructed Hoover. "Clyde's being difficult today. Aren't you, Clyde?"

Purvis kicked Kennedy underneath the table. "Jack, show Mr. Hoover the rest of the pictures."

Kennedy withdrew five additional enlarged photographs from his briefcase. Each contained grainy black-and-white images of multiple mourners at Rosenberg's funeral, except for one of the photographs, which featured a single man and woman. The man, of medium height, wore a dark suit, and a standard white shirt underneath his dark tie. The woman looked to be in her mid-thirties. She was dressed in a dark skirt, a white blouse with lace trim at the neck, and a well-fitting dark jacket. Jack Kennedy found her pleasingly attractive, though not beautiful.

"We were able to verify," he said with a nod to Purvis, "that almost all the people in these photos were locals—folks who had known the Rosenbergs, Julius and Ethel, since they were children."

Kennedy placed the picture in front of Hoover, who studied closely. "But we were not able to identify these two people."

"Magnifier, Clyde," grunted Hoover. The glass, about three inches in diameter, was instantly produced.

"Well, well, well," said the director, after peering through it for several minutes. "Take a good look at these characters, Clyde."

Tolson nodded his head. "Yes, Edgar. But this picture's far from optimal. Can't say as I recognize him."

Hoover beamed. "I do. I'd bet my life on it that's our old friend, Jake Golos. Now what's that godless Commie punk doing back in the Land of the Free? Thought we'd got rid of him years ago and that he'd returned to his ole' homestead, the U.S.S.R. But here he is once more, at the funeral of that young snot Rosenberg."

"Fill me in," Kennedy requested.

"Jacob Golos, born Reizen, an old Bolshevik and friend of Lenin. In the U.S., the head of World Tourists, a company obtaining visas for travel to the Soviet Union. We believe World Tourists is a front for the Soviet secret police."

"What about the woman?" asked Tolson.

Hoover shook his head. "Never seen her before."

"Should we pick up Golos, Mr. Hoover?" asked Purvis.

The director thought for a moment. "No. But put both him and the unknown woman under surveillance. I want to know who their contacts are and whom they're trying to recruit. And while you're at it, put a phone tap on that Rosenberg woman, too. Let's see what she's up to. Since the widow's a known Communist subversive like her late husband, she's probably also an associate of the organization that calls itself the Resistance. Regardless, there's a chance this ugly minnow will allow us to catch a number of great big beautiful fish."

CHAPTER 22

Get me outta before I go stark raving looney. Living in a filthy cellar never did agree with me, and it still doesn't now!"

"Julia and I want time to be alone together. It's unfair to keep us imprisoned in this dump. What would Einstein say?"

Leo wasn't impressed by either plea. "The two of you are already stark raving loonies. So, you can keep each other company for the time being," he said before storming up the stairs.

The truth was, Leo had no other safe place to put them, until he'd received a phone call from Jack Kennedy in his apartment.

"Ah, Mr. Szilard?"

"Mr. Kennedy, nice to hear from you. I recognized your Boston accent."

"Listen carefully. I won't take much of your time. I've been approached by a representative of an individual with a great deal of money who..."

"Is this individual your father, Mr. Kennedy?"

"No, of course... Oh, you were making a joke. Ha! Actually, it's rather amusing when you think about my father that way. But no, Dr. Szilard, though he may indeed have a great deal of money, my father and I actually haven't spoken in several months."

"Then I apologize, Mr. Kennedy."

"The individual of whom I speak says he is willing to devote a not inconsiderable amount of his substantial fortune to the Resistance. I must tell you, Dr. Szilard, that

I have known this individual on a personal basis for as long as I can remember. I can vouch for him as a decent, honorable, humble individual who respects his fellow men independent of their social class."

"Then how did he come into this 'substantial fortune,' Mr. Kennedy? As *Monsieur* Balzac, the French novelist, once said, 'Behind every great fortune lies a great crime, forgotten.'"

"I'm certain my friend hasn't forgotten the crimes of his great predecessor, Dr. Szilard. He would like to make several, ah... investments as a gesture of goodwill. He is willing to fund anything you need, within reason."

Szilard absorbed this thought for a moment. "Are you serious, Mr. Kennedy?"

"My contact insists he is quite serious. But his offer is time limited."

"When does he require an answer?"

"Now, Dr. Szilard. Right now."

"But that is impossible, Mr. Kennedy! While I appreciate this gentleman's good intentions, I cannot make this kind of decision on my own. Please give me twenty-four hours at a minimum."

A muffled sound indicated Kennedy had placed his hand over the receiver.

"Twenty-four hours, and not a second longer," he replied. "I will speak to you then, Dr. Szilard. Oh, and please don't forget about our last discussion, either. Your organization needs to hear the information I have about our president. Goodbye."

Minutes after the receiver went dead, Szilard walked out of his apartment and placed a call from the payphone at the corner of E. 74th Street and Third Avenue. The Resistance had provided him a number to call, instructing him to use it for emergencies only. No name had been provided. In Leo's judgment, Kennedy's requests needed to be considered by the Omega—no one else had the authority or competence to do so.

The phone rang three times. Before the fourth ring, a female voice answered. "Hello. Please state your name."

Leo used his code name. "It's Jackson."

The female voice gave him another phone number to call and requested fifteen minutes. Leo busied himself reading The New York *Herald Tribune,* which he'd picked up at a sidewalk kiosk earlier in the day. After a quarter of an hour, he dialed the number he was given.

"State your business, Jackson," said a different female voice.

Szilard relayed the gist of both conversations he'd had with Kennedy.

"The Kennedys are a clever gang and have a history of sticking together," said the voice. "Everything Jack Kennedy claimed could be a lie and a part of an elaborate trap. What's your sense of the man?"

Leo cleared his throat. "I believe Jack is naïve and idealistic but sincere. I'm sure what he heard and saw in Germany truly horrified him. For God's sake, it horrifies me to hear him speak of such things."

"Unfortunately," the female voice said, "his information confirms and adds to what we too have been learning. The fate of the Polish Jews will be tragic, and another powerful reason why this country, despite Lindbergh's rhetoric, must become involved in this war. But is Jack Kennedy truly standing up to his old man? Or is he working alongside him?"

"Forget about cratering his career, Hoover will have Kennedy castrated if he discovers he's with us. Jack's already put himself at serious risk."

The voice was silent for a moment. "Jackson," Leo was then instructed. "Go to another payphone and call the following number in thirty minutes."

He memorized the number given to him. "Understood," he said, and hung up the receiver. He walked south down Third Avenue, a major traffic artery in Manhattan, to E. 68th Street, where he knew he could find another phone booth. Security precautions had been tightened since the death of Rosenberg, though the Communists were still in charge of that department.

Leo didn't expect a female on the other end of the line. In central Europe, and especially in Hungary, where he came from, women were rarely if ever in any position even close to the top. He had known excellent female European scientists, the physicists Lise Meitner and Maria Goeppert Mayer among them. These women were exceptional people who had struggled for years against the prejudices of some of their male colleagues. Even in America, a country far freer than almost any in Europe, women's roles were often circumscribed, restricted to family and domestic roles, and to the helping occupations. But if the Omega trusted the judgment of these women, Leo would also accept them as Resistors. One day, he hoped, they could all meet to compare war stories.

At the agreed time, Leo re-dialed the phone number. Now he was inside the telephone booth at 68th and Third.

"This is Jackson. Has anything been decided?"

A prolonged silence followed. Then, a calm, soft, man's voice spoke. "You have done excellent work, Dr. Szilard."

Leo was pleased by the compliment. "Thank you. I appreciate your kind words. And I must ask—are you the Omega?"

Another long pause. "People have said so."

"Then I'm honored to be able to speak with you."

"Oh, don't be so honored. Like almost everyone else, I still put my pants on one leg at a time."

Leo laughed. "I appreciate your sense of humor, too."

"Thanks. Hitler has been accused of many things, but having a sense of humor was never one of them. Lindbergh, the same. Sometimes, I think that's what we're really fighting against—powerful men with no sense of humor. I think women understand this at some level even better than we men do."

"I haven't thought about the condition of the world in quite that way, but it makes sense," said Leo.

"Good. I'm sorry to change the subject on you, but please understand my time is limited."

"Of course, sir."

"Young Kennedy is a remarkable person."

"There's no doubt of it."

"But as you were informed, he may be malevolent."

"Yes, I admit it's possible. But I doubt it. His reaction to what he'd seen and heard about in Germany was visceral. I think only actors with years of experience can be so effective at telling bold-faced lies."

"And politicians, Dr. Szilard. And politicians—they lie with such fluency, I'm not sure they're capable of recognizing the truth at all."

"If they are, it's only when it suits their agenda," said Leo.

"And you do not believe Kennedy is such an individual?"

"I do not."

"Nevertheless, we must be cautious. Our needs are many, but at the moment, we are desperately looking for a safe house in Manhattan. Some of our people are, ah, less than happy with their current accommodations."

"I've two of those people in a cellar in Queens," said Leo. "And if I don't get them out soon, there may be a revolution."

"The opportunity presented by Kennedy cannot be ignored, Professor. Tell him that, as a gesture of goodwill, his wealthy donor should arrange to deposit a hundred thousand dollars, in unmarked hundred dollar bills, in box 3150 at the Main Post Office at 34th Street and Eighth Avenue within twenty-four hours. Inform Kennedy that the key to the post office box is held by Abe Stern, Secretary of the Pocketbook Makers Union. Kennedy should tell Abe that the Omega instructs him to relinquish the key. Kennedy must say nothing more but nothing less. Security must be maintained at all costs. We will inform Stern of Kennedy's upcoming visit.

"Kennedy must then give the key to the donor of the funds and retrieve it from him after the donor's courier makes the deposit. Then you must retrieve the key from Kennedy, open the box, and extract the cash. Handle it in the usual manner, Leo. Does that sound complicated enough?"

Leo said he understood, and that he'd relay the information to Kennedy.

"I also believe I need to have a word with that young man," said the Omega after concluding his business. "Before he gets himself and many others killed."

"Should I ask Vince Mangano and his team to bring him in?"

"Yes. Blindfolded, too, I should think. There's no reason to reveal too much to him."

"Mangano's boys should consider wearing earplugs. When Kennedy spreads the blarney, he can be very convincing. Next thing you know, he'll be kidnapping them."

"Then I'm very much looking forward to meeting this Jack Kennedy. Goodbye, Leo. I wish you the best of luck."

The click he heard indicated the conversation had ended.

The money was deposited on time at the indicated place, the key then being retrieved by Kennedy, who passed it to Leo Szilard. Within two hours, a furnished brownstone at 424 E. 71st Street, near the East River, was purchased under the name Laszlo Schlemmer, of Mt. Kisco, NY. Mr. Schlemmer, of course, didn't exist. The real estate broker who sold the town house was a trusted member of the Resistance. The seller of the upscale brownstone was the scion of the founder of Standard Oil, John D. Rockefeller, Jr. However, neither Mr. Rockefeller, Jr., nor Leo Szilard, nor the Omega, knew that the heir to the Standard Oil fortune received the sale price for the furnished house from the same funds he'd just gifted to the Resistance.

Julia and Sid sat at a table eating a small breakfast in the expansive kitchen at the back of 424 E. 71st Street.

"This house a bit stuffy for me," said Sid. "But to use a popular Yiddish expression, I'm happier than a pig in shit that we're out of that hole in the ground."

Julia wouldn't hear any criticism of it. "Hold your tongue, young man. The wooden wainscoting in the living room is the finest quality. The chandelier in the parlor beams French Versailles. And our bedroom..."

"I never noticed the décor in our bedroom, Julia. We were too busy doing more interesting things. I hope you haven't forgotten already."

She smiled slyly and gazed at Sid. "Some things can never be forgotten, *mi amore*. Be certain I will never forget what we did last night. And how hungry I am to repeat it tonight, and the night after, and on and on."

A rush of intense emotion, of pure inexpressible feeling and yearning for this woman, engulfed Sid, propelling him to rush to her side and take her there and then over the kitchen table. But while Sid fumbled with the buttons on Julia's blouse, and her hand struggled to loosen Sid's belt, they were interrupted by a broad, sunny "'ello!" from a short, middle-aged fellow who had just entered the kitchen.

This man, dressed in a light gray suit, matching vest, and blue tie had a thin, pleasant face and a wide mouth. Above it sat a bulbous nose, shining brown eyes, and a pair of ears that protruded a bit too far from his head for him to be taken seriously. But his most remarkable feature was his forehead, drawn even higher because of his receding hairline. Absent the ears, a moment's glance at him was enough to see that this was an individual of rare intellect and clarity of thought.

"Oh. I apologize. I did not appreciate there were others in this 'ouse-a. Forgive me, please. I come back later."

"Not at all, not at all," Sid said hurriedly as he re-worked the clasp on his belt and Julia buttoned up her blouse.

"Please join us for breakfast," Sid said. And then, in a moment of clarity, he recognized the unwelcome visitor.

"Professor Fermi! I didn't know who you were at first! I'm honored to meet you, though the context has been, ah, a bit unconventional."

Fermi took Sid's hand, his brown eyes beaming.

"And you must be Sid Peskin, the young man who 'as excited the world of atomic physics! Leo and Albert have spoken very 'ighly of you and your work, Sid! They tell me it is indispensable for our 'project.' And this lovely lady must be *Signorina* Julia Falcone. *Sì*, you are even-a more beautiful than Einstein described you."

"And she has quite a good a head on her shoulders, too," said Sid, concerned Fermi would view Julia merely as a trophy.

"I'm not a physicist. But I appreciate the elegance and subtlety of the discipline."

"Is no problem. My wife, Laura, who is sleeping upstairs, her degree is in general sciences. You two may want to have a chat when she wakes up."

"Thank you, Professor Fermi. It would be my pleasure."

"So," said Fermi, taking a seat at the kitchen table, formerly the love-nest. "I must be honest with you, Sid, because I am not certain. I am surprised..." Fermi was momentarily bewildered. "All right. I will come to the point. Just what are you doing 'ere?"

"I could ask you the same question, Professor Fermi."

Fermi laughed. "That's very true, Sid. Very true. So first, I'll tell you, and then you tell me."

"A good compromise, Professor."

"Call me Enrico."

"I don't think we can have secrets from each other in this house, Enrico. We're all here for pretty much the same reasons."

"I agree," said Fermi. "And possibly, between what you know, and what I think I know, we can analyze this mess we're in. So, I will start at the beginning.

"My wife, Laura Capon Fermi, is Jewish. Mussolini, that arrogant upstart, made our two sons honorary Aryans, but Laura and her family—no! And then, in 1938, came the anti-Jewish laws. It was too much to take! So we left, and I got a position at Columbia University in New York. It's a fabulous place, filled with people who think they speak with-a God, and that he speaks with-a them. How you say it? Not-a my cup of tea."

Sid had heard stories about the Columbia faculty from some of the other City College graduate students who had friends there. The place was afflicted with the usual diseases of academia: bickering and backbiting amid the perpetual quest for political power and glory; there certainly wasn't any money in being a university professor. On the other hand, despite all the background noise, Columbia was the home of remarkable advances in atomic physics in recent years.

"The last thing I heard was that you were on a train going to visit Dr. Oppenheimer at Berkeley. And a man named Julius Rosenberg, a Resistance member, and a member of the CPUSA, took you off the train somewhere west of Chicago and east of Denver. Would that be right, Professor?"

"That is only partially true, my friend. Rosenberg was on the train, that is-a true. And he convinced me I was walking into a trap. I got off the train in Chicago, and never got back on."

"Rosenberg fooled the FBI. They thought you were on that train."

"Maybe someday we can ask him how he did it."

"Afraid not, Enrico. Rosenberg's dead."

"Dead!" Fermi's face registered shock. "But 'ow? He was-a such a young man!"

"Nobly. Fighting the fascists. They invaded the Lower East Side of New York. It's a heavily Jewish area, mostly observant eastern Europeans. His territory. He fought them, heroically. And they killed him."

"I will say a prayer in his memory. Any family?"

"A wife, Ethel, also a stark-raving Stalinist Communist. No children."

"It's too bad. But in these dark days, we all must do what we must. Sadly, some will not survive."

"I presume someone put you on a train back to New York. Is that correct, Enrico?"

"Sí. I never saw Professor Oppenheimer."

"And now you have the entire world looking for you, including President Lindbergh. With all the tools at his disposal."

Fermi sighed. "Sí. This you learned from Leo?"

Sid nodded. "From Leo. And there are rumors that if, God forbid, Trump or Lindbergh get their hands on you, you'll be deported to Italy."

"From where I'll no doubt be-a turned over to the Germans, who will force me to create an atomic bomb-a, if it can be done, for them. God forbid indeed, Mr. Peskin. Do you think we are safe here in this house?"

"Leo says that as long as we keep the drapes closed, front and back, and stay out of sight, we're safe. But we're also imprisoned in this brownstone."

"It's a gilded prison, I think, Sid. Even so, much better than the terrible places Laura and I have inhabited in the past several months."

"My sense is that you and Laura, and Julia and I, are going to be on the move again soon. But I don't know when, or by what means. And I'm not certain where we're going either, though Leo believes it will be to a ranch school in New Mexico called Los Alamos. What we're supposed to do at a ranch school is a mystery to me."

"I trust Leo Szilard," said Fermi, "and I trust the Resistance. It saved my life on the train. I 'ope-a neither will let us down now."

NYC Police Headquarters, 240 Center St., Manhattan
August 18, 1941

"Well, Freddie me boy, what's the latest news in the fight for a purer America, free of niggers and kikes and everyone else you don't like?" asked Police Commissioner Patrick F. X. O'Sullivan.

"Paddy," said Mayor Fred Trump, "the problem with you is that you can never decide anything. If there were two toilets in front of you, you'd pee your pants. At least I know what, and who, I don't like."

"Now that you think of it, Freddy, I'm not going to deny it. It's the one true talent I have. I'm terminally indecisive. Me mother told me I'd never amount to much, but all me life, I've been true to me talent. And now I'm the commish—I wonder what me mother would say!"

The mayor and his police commissioner were a touch tipsy after paying a visit to the commish's stash of Jim Beam, a frequent event these days. And when they were a touch tipsy, they tended toward sentimentality.

"Yeah, well, my father would wallop the living bejesus outta me if he knew the trouble I was in," moaned Trump.

"Aye. I heard you was down on yer luck, Freddy boy. Somethin' about that martial law business, eh? Wasn't it yer idea to have a soldier at every corner in New York? Ya know, me boys weren't happy bein' watched over by folks who weren't members of the Ancient Order of Hibernians. If you know what I mean."

Trump was indignant. "Wasn't my idea. It was Lindbergh's, start to finish!"

"And yer just coincidentally takin' the blame, ain't that right, Freddy? So yer in the shitter now."

Trump wanted to explode with the unfairness of it all. In his view, the declaration of martial law was appropriate and necessary. The problem was that Lindbergh had limited the American Army to only 150,000 men, far too small to control a country the size of the United States. And no one had counted on the strength of the Resistance. After the brutal bloodshed of late June, when Rosenberg had died,

Jews, Italians, blacks, and other minority groups armed themselves to the teeth in preparation for the next assault. They found no shortage of armaments dealers happy to sell. No sooner would a disturbance in one city be quelled, then violence would break out in another. The American Army was unsuited to the task of policing, the police were resentful of army interference in their job, and everyone was angry and unhappy.

Trump didn't care a fig if large numbers of people were angry, but he did care if certain very special people were unhappy. These were members of the small number of very wealthy families with annual incomes larger than the budgets of some small American States. Much of this wealth was inherited. Few of these individuals had ever done a day's honest labor in their lives. However, they understood that, if people were on the barricades rather than purchasing their products, the nation could be hurled back into a depression so deep that a social revolution would be inevitable. That would put a substantial kink into all their lifestyles.

This was the same Wall Street crowd Lindbergh and Trump ran against, the Mellons, the Astors, the Rockefellers, cursing them then as predators who devoured the labors of the working man. But now, the predators were making their opinions known to Lindbergh, who in turn made his opinion known to Trump in a series of angry phone calls.

"Trump!" Lindbergh yelled. "Some of the biggest donors to the Republican Party have been marching through my office for the past few days! And they're mad as hatters!"

Trump winced. The metaphor was misplaced, but he caught Lindbergh's drift. "Mr. President, I understand you're upset. But please, try to calm them down. Your declaration of martial law was the correct policy. I'm sure it only needs a little more time to be effective."

Lindbergh exploded. "Calm them down? What am I supposed to tell them, Trump? That our great American Army is too small and too unprepared to take on a job it was never meant to do? That the Mayor of New York, the strongest proponent of martial law, and of 'law and order' incites Bundist carnage on the streets? Sometimes, Mr. Trump, I wonder whose side you're really on!"

The president needn't have wondered; Mr. Trump was on no one's side except his own. "Mr. President! Any insinuation that I have encouraged anti-Semitic or Bundist activity in New York is categorically untrue! It is a smear by my political enemies, who you may recall are the same as your own.

"Now you've asked me how to address the concerns of our donors. You might consider the following points, sir. You, Mr. President, our donors, and I share common enemies. They are Democrats entrenched at all levels of government and society that still cannot accept that Roosevelt is dead and buried and that you are the president. Our foes will never cease to undermine your administration and delegitimize your election. But the people have spoken, decisively. You, Charles A. Lindbergh, have been democratically elected president. That verdict cannot be undone. And, Mr. President, you also cannot undo the declaration of martial law because that would make you appear weak—and you, as president, must never appear weak. So my advice, sir, is to stay the course, and you'll piss on their graves in the end."

Lindbergh paused. "I'll consider the points you've raised the next time Mr. Rockefeller threatens to withhold his donations. It might get us a few weeks' leeway, but not much more. In the meantime, I'll be kissing his behind, and all of his friends' behinds, to keep them happy. Freddy, you've made a career out of underestimating the intelligence of the average voter, but don't make the same mistake with our donors. Unlike the electorate, they're not imbeciles."

CHAPTER 23

FBI Headquarters, The Department of the Treasury, Washington, D.C.

At 11:00 in the morning of August 20, Melvin "Little Mel" Purvis yawned deeply. "Kennedy," he demanded, "run and get me a cup o' coffee, will ya?"

"Aw, go fuck off, Mel," answered Kennedy, with a huge grin on his Irish face.

Despite Purvis' early proletarian dislike of the patrician Kennedy, his feelings soon mellowed with exposure to his charm.

"He's a good man," Purvis had told Hoover. "And I trust him. Still a bit green about the ears, but he's only twenty-four. He has the makings of a first-rate agent, Edgar. But I'm pretty sure he's thinking about politics."

"Republican? Or will he throw in with those other ineffectual idiots and disappoint Kennedy Senior?"

"Not sure. Sometimes I think he can go one way and sometimes the other. I don't think he knows his own mind."

Hoover relaxed in his chair. "Okay, so he's not politically biased. That's good news, Mel. Gives me confidence in him and in our work together. Tell Kennedy I want to see the both of you in my office tomorrow, two o'clock sharp. There's some new intelligence coming in that we need to discuss. From its looks, we may have a source that knows what happened to Fermi. This may be the first good lead in this case since the bastard disappeared."

"Yes, sir. We'll be back tomorrow, two o'clock."

"Gentlemen," said J. Edgar Hoover to Melvin Purvis and John F. Kennedy, at two o'clock sharp the next day. "Remember the wiretap that we placed on phone of the Communist Ethel Rosenberg, widow of the late Communist Julius Rosenberg?"

Hoover employed the word 'Communist' in much the same way as the Hitler regime required any Jew remaining in Germany to include 'Isaac' or 'Sarah' as part of their name.

"Yes, sir. Remember it well. Smart move, Mr. Hoover."

"Thank you, young man. Here's the text of the tap." Hoover handed Purvis and Kennedy copies of Ethel's chats from the past few weeks.

"Most of what you'll read is not significant for our purposes. But several times in conversations with her mother—a Mrs. Tessie Greenglass—she refers to her late husband and to another individual who seems to be have been his boss or supervisor. As Julius Rosenberg had no known occupation at the time of his demise, it's unclear what the nature of the relationship with this man was. Regardless, his name is Leo. After consideration of this and other information, we believe Leo is in reality Leo Szilard, a noted Hungarian scientist whose KAs include Albert Einstein and J. Robert Oppenheimer, a professor at Cal Berkeley. All these individuals have research interests in atomic physics."

Sweat began to drip from the top of Kennedy's forehead. This information, in the hands of Hoover and the FBI, could imperil the entire Resistance. "Yup, top o' the line, these fellows."

"Yeah, and no one from Haaavahd." Purvis mimicked Kennedy's Boston accent.

"That's fine, Mel. But we don't know who Leo's boss is, do we, huh? So don't count the Crimson out yet!"

Hoover continued. "It's all connected. Leo, Oppenheimer, Einstein, Fermi, and that kid from City College, Peskin. Find this guy Szilard, and we can roll up the entire operation. And bag Fermi, too. Talk about burnishing the image of the Bureau!"

"We're on it yesterday, chief," said Kennedy.

Purvis vigorously nodded in agreement.

One hour after the meeting with Kennedy and Hoover, "Little Mel" Purvis sat at his desk in his office.

The resources of the FBI were limited, and a significant amount of information of use to the Bureau came from newspaper articles. Purvis had requested copies of the major New York papers to be shipped to him daily. He now had several recent issues of the staunchly Republican *Herald Tribune* and older issues of the *Times*— printed before it had been shut down—on his desk. However, instead of the first page of the paper above the crease, today he studied the first page below the crease. The paper had been turned upside-down.

That's when Purvis noticed something he'd previously overlooked. In the far left-hand corner at the bottom of the first page sat a series of small numbers printed in boldface. To the extent he'd ever thought about it, Purvis assumed those numbers related to the distribution and sales of the paper.

He grabbed several other issues of the *Herald Tribune*. The small numbers at the bottom left corner of the first page were also present. Every day, the identical number of integers, thirty-five, were printed in boldface. The first and last five of these integers were always identical. But those in the middle of the series of thirty-five were highly variable, though Purvis could discern no particular pattern to them.

He picked up the receiver of his phone.

"Operator, this is Melvin Purvis. Call information in New York City. I need to speak with Ogden Reid, the publisher of the *New York Herald Tribune*. Yes, operator, it's urgent, and I'll wait."

One hour after the meeting with Hoover, John F. Kennedy could be found in a taxi on the way to Union Station, D.C., waiting for the train to New York.

He had dashed out of the Treasury building, caught a cab to his apartment at Dupont Circle, and packed a bag. Moments before hailing a hack for the ride to the train station, he remembered to ring Leo Szilard from a nearby phone booth.

"America first," Kennedy said grimly on hearing Leo's friendly "hello." It was a pre-arranged code phrase indicating that Hoover or Lindbergh was in possession of information damaging to the interests of the Resistance. It meant a high-level meeting was imperative. Kennedy knew that by now, Leo's phone was tapped, and that his own voice would be recognizable on the tap. But matters were spinning dangerously out of control. Kennedy no longer felt he had any choice.

"The lion and her cubs sit at the campfire," he said, and repeated it so there could be no doubt of the message in Leo's mind.

Kennedy's message was met with silence. Only a faint crackle came over the line. Leo hung up the phone.

Five hours later, at approximately 8:30 p.m., after an anxious train ride with stops at Baltimore, Wilmington, and Philadelphia, Kennedy arrived at New York's Penn Station. The first thing he did after emerging from the cavernous arrivals hall was to hail a cab and tell the driver to hurry him down to Little Italy in lower Manhattan. He departed the cab at Frankie's Trattoria on Mulberry Street.

The restaurant was busy, but the maître d' sat him at a table after Kennedy gave him a five-dollar note. He asked for water and a menu, ordered a plate of spaghetti and meatballs, and drank two glasses of ice water. Refreshed, he stood, climbed on his chair and then onto the cloth-covered table, and began to speak.

"Thank you, my friends, thank you for coming here this evening. Please excuse my interrupting your dinner."

The low-level chatter in the restaurant ceased.

"I have come here tonight not to criticize our president, Charles Lindbergh, but to praise him," he announced. "The true Americans of this great country, I say, suffering too long from the oppression of the Jewish-dominated Democratic Party, have finally been freed from government overreach and over-regulation. That's right, folks. Gone are the bureaucrats that strangled business and destroyed old-fashioned American self-reliance!"

The other diners murmured. Kennedy wasn't finished. "And I say to you, my fellow Americans," he continued, "that I welcome— yes, I welcome—the resurgence of the good ole' Protestant religion in our politics, because it was good for my father and it's good enough for me!"

Bowls of ravioli remained uneaten at empty tables as people headed for the exits, front and back.

"And, ah, ahem... And finally, summing up my argument," Kennedy continued, running out of things to say, "I want to leave you with a final word: I, ah, mean three final words, spoken by your ancient Roman ancestor—*veni,* and *vidi,* and *vici.* I think that should about do it."

Kennedy climbed down from the table, sat at his chair, and slowly worked his way through a large bowl of spaghetti and meatballs. He needed the protein to put meat on his bones; at six feet tall and weighing just one hundred forty pounds, he was painfully scrawny.

After three-quarters of an hour, satiated and still on guard, Kennedy asked for the check and deposited $1.50 with the waiter. He picked up his bag from the coat check girl, emerged into the steaming heat of a New York summer's evening, and parked himself under a lamppost where Mulberry Street bent south into Columbus Park. Twenty minutes later, a black, four-door Chevrolet drove up and braked sharply in front of him. Tires screeched. Doors flung open. Three sweating, burly men dressed in black overcoats climbed out. The largest and sweatiest waved a .357 Smith and Wesson at him. "Get inta da car," he ordered Kennedy. "An' don' try nuttin' funny."

Kennedy sighed. "Christ! I didn't know what it would take, but you guys are finally here!" He gathered up his overnight bag and wiped the sweat off his brow. "Thank God and all the saints! I've been expecting you."

Within thirty minutes, Kennedy and his mob bodyguard crossed the Williamsburg Bridge and bee-lined toward the same candy store in Queens where Leo had imprisoned Sid and Julia. Kennedy had no idea where he was—he'd been blindfolded when he was tossed into the back seat between two fleshy, perspiring Sicilian foot soldiers.

Kennedy tried to strike up a conversation with his captors. "Say, thanks very much for coming for me this evening. And so quickly, too. I'm sorry if I've disturbed anyone. Especially anyone with a young family."

The foot soldier on Kennedy's right chuckled. "Hey, what's wid dis mick? T'inks he's a comedian," he said to the mob soldier on Kennedy's left.

"Oh, I'm no comedian. Not at all. Just an average Joe, tryin' to get by."

"Some 'average Joe,'" said the capo holding the Smith and Wesson in the front seat. The man spoke with a heavy Brooklyn accent. "You boys know who dis sonovabitch is? Dis is John Fitzgerald Kennedy, son o' dat lump o' human crap, Joe Kennedy. Lindbergh's consigliere, if you know what I mean. Know what, Kennedy? Vince Mangano don' like Lindboigh... or your ole' man, neider. An' neider do I. Jus' lettin' you know."

"Well, that's, ah... terrific!" Kennedy answered. "Because I have issues with the both of them, too. So, we're both on the same side, and now we can all be friends. I also have information useful to Vince and to his associates. That's why you fellows are here. To hook me up with Vince and his friends."

The capo waving the Smith and Wesson lowered his weapon.

"Vince did tell us to go easy on dis one," said the driver. "No rough stuff."

The capo thought for a moment. "Okay. Seems harmless enough. We can talk wid him. So, uh, talk to me Kennedy. What's goin' on in your life? Huh?"

That was the opening Kennedy needed. For the next half hour, he entertained Mangano's foot soldiers with ribald tales of the women he'd bedded, sparing none of the more intimate details. As Leo Szilard had predicted, it wasn't long before the soldiers of the mob were prepared to march under Kennedy's orders.

The four, the capo and his crew with a blindfolded Kennedy in tow, entered the Queens candy store laughing and clapping him on the back, insisting they wanted to meet him again for drinks under easier circumstances. Down the stairs into the dim cellar they went, still in stitches. Then, they sat Kennedy in a chair under the naked light bulb as ordered, and tied his wrists together behind him.

"Bye, fellas," Kennedy called out. "Thanks for a great trip and a wonderful evening! Looking forward to having drinks with you when I get outta here."

"Great guy," said one of the foot soldiers to another member of his crew. "But I t'ink he's a little.... How do the micks say it... *meshuga*."

Kennedy had a poor idea of how long he'd sat in that cellar, but he knew his wrists hurt. It could have been twenty minutes or two hours before he heard the tramping of feet descending the staircase.

"Welcome to my castle, gentlemen. Or ladies and gentlemen. Please step in. The butler will take your hats and coats. Aperitifs will be served by the blue-coated wait staff. Dinner will be served in the great hall at the unfashionable hour of ten p.m.

Otherwise, if there is anything I can do to convince you to remove my blindfold, please let me know—at your convenience, of course."

A man's voice answered. "I don't believe that would be possible, Mr. Kennedy. It's a security precaution, and we take security seriously. However, I certainly can offer you a glass of wine after your ordeal. Red or white? Which would you prefer?"

"White, please. A good *Chardonnay*, if you have it."

"Of course we do, Mr. Kennedy. We've been anticipating your arrival and have had plenty of time to prepare."

Kennedy heard the liquid being poured and smelled the wine's aroma. A half-full glass appeared at his lips. "Are you the Omega?" he asked, before drinking deeply.

"I serve that function in the Resistance. You made quite a scene back in Frankie's this evening, Mr. Kennedy. I'd like to ask—to what purpose?"

"That's easily answered. To the purpose of Vince Mangano's crew finding me and taking me to see you ASAP. I couldn't call Leo on this telephone—it's tapped. So, I made sure word got around there was a crazy Irishman jumping on a table in a restaurant in Little Italy, praising Lindbergh.

"Sir, there's a great deal we need to discuss. And I prefer my discussions face-to-face, not face-to-blindfold."

"Too risky," said the other man in the room. The accent was Sicilian. Kennedy presumed the voice was Vince Mangano's.

"You'll have to trust me. You have bigger problems than me. Hoover knows about Leo Szilard. That means it won't be long before either his agents or Trump's cops pick him up. Then your entire operation is in danger."

"How d'you know dis?" asked Vince, suspiciously.

"Because at two p.m. this afternoon, I was sitting at a meeting with J. Edgar Hoover, who told me himself. Now here's more bad news, Mr., ah... Mangano, I presume. Hoover put another agent on this case: name's Mel Purvis, one of the finest in the history of the Bureau. Name familiar to you? Don't ever underestimate him. He's loyal to Hoover, and once he gets his teeth into something, Purvis is more tenacious than a bulldog. So, if you're planning anything for the near future, act soon, before Purvis catches your scent."

"Your information's distressing, Mr. Kennedy. But it sounds like it has the ring of truth to it."

"Could still be a trap," hissed Mangano.

"As could everything these days, Vince. But Mr. Kennedy has already given us valuable information demonstrating his bona fides. I think we should honor his wishes."

"You won't regret it," said Kennedy, who felt his hands being untied. The blindfold was removed, leaving him face-to-face with two men, one with Sicilian features, the other more nondescript, possibly Jewish.

"Mr. Mangano, I presume," he said to the man with the Sicilian features, who nodded in return.

"That means that you, sir, are the Omega. Honored to meet you. I want you to know I'm with the Resistance heart and soul."

"Your fadder—" interrupted Mangano.

"My father's values are not my values. What Lindbergh, Trump, and their cronies are doing to this great country is a monumental disgrace. And not only to this country, but also to the entire world, which needs American leadership now more than ever. And we are failing them miserably."

"Mr. Kennedy," said the Omega, "you are very young and enthusiastic, and I believe you to be truthful. We are in complete agreement with your arguments. You said there is information about Mr. Lindbergh you wish to share with us. Now is the time—if you remain confident in your sources."

Kennedy paused for a moment before replying. "In this cloth bag at my feet is a series of folders. In them, you will find photographs of checks that our president, Charles Lindbergh, paid to a German woman. Her name is Hilda von Treitzler. Hilda, despite her aristocratic last name, has fallen on hard times since the death of her husband."

"Hush money," said the Omega. "Buying Hilda's silence about their affair. This could be useful."

"Hilda and Lindbergh had far more than an affair, sir. They now have three children. The checks demonstrate that the cash contributions of Lindbergh to von Treizler increased immediately after the birth of each child. It appears our president has a second family, and they are citizens of the Third Reich."

"Mr. Kennedy, if what you are saying is true, this is political dynamite. Mr. Lindbergh's Midwestern base will tolerate a great deal of misbehavior, even rank stupidity, but this crosses a line, even for them. Who else knows about this?"

"Oh, the Nazis, I'm sure. What a gift Lindbergh's given them! The Germans have probably been blackmailing him for years."

"It accounts for how closely he toes their line. Sometimes, it seems Hitler thinks the words and they spew forth from Lindbergh's mouth.

"Mr. Kennedy, you've given us a hammer, but we'll need to use it like a scalpel. This matter must be handled correctly. I anticipate the blowback from the White House will be vicious."

Vince Mangano remained skeptical. "I... I dunno 'bout all dis. You weren't in da bedroom. Dis could all be a lotta hot air."

"Not likely. The ages of the children? They exactly match the dates Lindbergh visited Germany, minus nine months. There wasn't any need for me to be in the bedroom. And von Treizler has told her friends Lindbergh is the father of all her kids."

"Then our president is screwed," said the Omega. "Sorry; a bad pun."

"How you get all dis good stuff?" asked Vince.

"Simple. I was in the bedroom. Well, a different bedroom, but you know how gabby some women can be."

"And dat's good enough for me," laughed the Mafioso, producing three of his finest *Romeo y Julietta* Cuban cigars, passing them around, and striking a match.

Meanwhile, at 424 E. 71st Street
3 a.m.

"Jesus Christ!" exploded Julia as she bolted upright in bed. "Sounds like the entire American Expeditionary Force is marching over our heads. Wake up, Sid, wake up!"

She shook Sid's left shoulder. "Wha...?" He was reluctant to open his eyes.

"Oh, I think you would have stayed asleep during the sinking of the Titanic! Don't you hear that?"

"Hear what?" Sid asked, still half asleep, before a loud bang roused him, too. "Oh, that. Sure, I heard it. That's just Leo moving more people in. He told me earlier today there could be trouble, and to be prepared for some new arrivals. But he never said they would arrive at three in the morning."

In the room above their bedroom, feet tramped, furniture moved, and suitcases were dropped on the floor.

"I wish they could be a little quieter. It's very annoying. Hmm... maybe I should bang on their door and say I'm the FBI. How's that for irritating?"

"Wait till you find out if any of these physics geniuses have a sense of humor before you go doing something like that. Or you won't make any new friends."

"Damn you, Julia. You're always sensible, and I just wanna have some fun. Sometimes, I think you're as bad as my mother."

At three in the morning, Julia was uninterested in Sid's idea of fun—or in his issues with his mother. She nestled against him. "Sleep now, sweetie. Fun later. And save your strength. I've a feeling we're about to get very busy soon."

Leo called all the inhabitants of the brownstone together in the parlor at sunrise and confirmed Julia's instincts. Assembled together were some of the greatest scientific minds in the world, a bonanza of talent and determination that would have been the pride of any nation on the planet, had they the wit to appreciate it.

Sid was astonished to be greeting Albert Einstein as an old friend on the basis of their one meeting. Einstein was pleasant and proper, but a priority of his seemed to be getting to know Julia better. Sid flashed her several dark looks, ensuring that the great man's flattery hadn't turned her head. But he needn't have worried. Julia had eyes for him only. Besides, Einstein was too cerebral and self-centered for most women, traits the perceptive Julia could easily detect.

Fermi and his wife, Laura, had risen early and were making conversation with the great Hungarian mathematician, John von Neumann, and his wife, Marietta Kovesi. Marietta was not a happy lady—she'd had to leave behind her young daughter Marina with relatives. The parting had been wrenching, with neither mother nor daughter certain when they would see each other again. Julia tried her best to befriend the woman.

Von Neumann and Fermi, meanwhile, eventually got into it around the kitchen table.

"Jonny, I'm telling you, it can be done. And I'm gonna do it! Me and *Signor* Peskin. We're a team. Come 'ere, Sid, my friend. And tell dis, 'ow you say, 'knucklehead,' about your work."

"Oh, c'mon Enrico," replied von Neumann. "You're a bonehead. As usual, you don't know what you're talking about. I admit that you may be able to demonstrate a chain reaction, but nothing more beyond that, despite Peskin's most excellent work. To make a functioning device, an actual atomic bomb, would require calculations so extensive they couldn't be completed in a hundred years."

"So, Jonny? You're-a the mathematical genius! We have a few hours yet. Why don't you get to work? I expect solutions by later this afternoon."

Von Neumann wasn't backing down. "Challenge accepted, Enrico! I guarantee that whatever your problem is, I've already solved it. And if I haven't, I'll invent a machine to help me. It will compute thousands, maybe millions of calculations a second. And I think I'll call it a computer. What do you think about that, Enrico?"

Fermi and von Neumann continued their bantering while other diners listened in and dropped out, and then came back for more. After a while, the discussion between the two was at such a high level no one, including Edward Teller—another young genius who'd been moved in overnight—was able to keep up. The two soon took to scribbling vigorously on sheets of paper supplied by Einstein.

"Sid, come 'ere. I don't think dis knucklehead is right, but I wanna hear what you t'ink."

Fermi handed Sid one of the papers on which he'd sketched some of the criteria for building an atomic weapon. Von Neumann countered with his own work.

There was silence in the room until Hans Bethe, a young physicist from Cornell, began to create a betting pool.

"Twenty-five cents on von Neumann," wagered Einstein.

"Von Neumann's a has-been," said Teller. "One dollar on Enrico, the man of the future."

"I've been telling him he's a has-been for years," said Marietta Kovesi, von Neumann's wife. "Two dollars on the Italian."

That prompted an equal counter-bet by Laura Fermi against her husband. Robert Sorber, from Columbia, diplomatically bet on both men, while the diminutive Lepke Buchalter, a late-night arrival, watched in utter confusion, having no idea who any of these people were or what they did.

After Hans Bethe collected all the bets, he made an announcement. "The house is giving six to five odds on von Neumann and will be accepting additional bets in the kitchen for the next fifteen minutes."

"Wait a second!" said Sid. "You're only giving me another fifteen minutes to figure out this mess?"

"That's right. You're moving with a fast crowd, Sid. You need to keep up."

Sid returned to examining the papers, while Bethe retired to the kitchen to collect additional wagers. The bettors were charitable and left Sid alone for the next ten minutes. But when they returned, they took turns sitting next to him, looking over his shoulder, and making a general nuisance of themselves.

Sid was about three-quarters of the way through Fermi's mathematical argument when he saw the Italian genius had made a slight error in the calculation of an integral. Even though the mistake was small, its effect ramified through the remainder of Fermi's reasoning. His end result was thrown off in a big way.

With a minute left to go, and everyone in the house surrounding him, Sid theatrically placed the paper down on the table, looked about, and proclaimed, "Ladies and gentlemen, I have given this weighty matter a great deal of study. Only one of these two gentlemen are correct. The other needs to start over again in high school trigonometry."

"Time for another round of betting!" Bethe announced. "The house is giving eight to five odds on the Hungarian! That's eight to five, ladies and gentlemen, and I promise you can't get better odds anywhere. Come one, come all and place your wagers; only one minute remaining!"

Dollar bills and silver coins emerged from purses and pockets as Bethe scooped up the cash. At thirty seconds, he called a halt to the betting. With a pile of dollars and coins in front of him, he motioned to Sid for the verdict.

"Folks," said Sid. "You have asked me to determine who will be the winner in this contest of brainpower. Who will receive the approbation of his peers, and who will retreat, tail between his legs, forevermore to be known as a loser?"

The seconds ticked down.

"And I can now reveal that the winner is... Jonny von Neumann!"

The room erupted with a mixture of applause and curses as Bethe started handing out cash to the winning bettors.

"It's not possible!" roared Fermi, who wasn't mollified until Sid demonstrated his calculation of an integral was incorrect.

Fermi had to admit defeat. "You won this one, Jonny, but it will never happen again."

Von Neumann collected his winnings. "I hope not. Or we may blow up the entire planet."

An hour later, Julia caught Sid alone for a private moment. Leo Szilard had arrived and was about to address the group. Before he did, Julia wanted a word with her man.

"What was that about? I thought these were serious people."

"They are. But as I said a few days ago in a different context, the subject about which they are serious is so serious, it is too much for anyone to bear."

"A chain reaction? I guess I don't understand..."

"I think you may not remember, my dear. That chain reaction may lead to the production of the most horrifying weapon in the history of humanity: an atomic bomb. Fermi was skeptical. He thought the amount of fissile material, an isotope of uranium, necessary to create a bomb must be impractically large, as big as a house. Based on his own mathematical modeling, von Neumann insisted the mass needed to be no larger than a baseball. Jonny won the argument."

"So that means if Leo Szilard is correct, and a chain reaction can be produced, the development of this... this, horrible atomic bomb is possible?"

"All I can say, Julia, is that mathematically, John von Neumann, as always, is correct."

Meanwhile, at 424 E. 71st Street
3 a.m.

Within the hour, the inhabitants of 424 W. 71st Street were busy complaining about almost everything to anyone who would listen, or engaging in vigorous disputes with each other about subjects as esoteric as Mozart's later violin quartets. Or, like Jonny von Neumann, trying to organize a poker game.

"You are always trying to zucker us in, aren't you, Jonny? Because you never lose, *und* I don't zink you'd admit it even if you did."

"*Natürlich,* Albert. Of course I wouldn't. But even I cannot account for lady luck. Care to try your own fortune? You always had a way with the ladies."

"*Ach,* I know I'll lose my money, but I can't resist an invitation from ze great von Neumann—especially if I have Julia Falcone at my side. Julia, *Liebchen,* pull up a chair and be my good luck talisman."

She good-naturedly did as Einstein bid her. "For a short time, Albert, darling. But when you cash out, I'm taking your place."

"*Ja,* whatever you choose, my dear. I'm afraid zat like God, I'm not much of a gambler." He turned and whispered in her ear. "Careful with von Neumann. He cheats, you know."

Julia had seen her share of cheating at poker while growing up in the Falcone-Mangano household and was sure she knew all the tricks. But three-quarters of an hour later, admitting the poker gods were against him, Einstein pushed away from the table.

"*Ach*, I'm kaputt. Not one hand, not one good betting hand!" he whined. "I zink it's a conspirazy. Julia, *Liebchen*, the seat is yours. Enjoy it if you can. As I told you, von Neumann is invincible. Between his math *und* his poker game, he's ruined my life. Enrico," he said to Fermi, whose cards had been better and who was breaking even, "take good care of zis young woman. Don't let Jonny do to her what he's done to me."

Einstein stepped into the kitchen, where he engaged in an intense discussion with Edward Teller. The subject was another of Einstein's attempts to produce a Grand Unified Theory, an amalgamation of all the basic forces in the universe into one mathematical equation—a "theory of everything." But Teller was having none of it and turned on Einstein with a rudeness typical for Teller.

Einstein was giving as good as he got when the booming voice of Leo Szilard called everyone to attention and commanded their presence in the parlor.

Seats were brought in from the kitchen, and within moments, everyone was assembled. Sid found his Julia. The two sat holding hands in adjacent folding chairs. Einstein sat in a beautiful chair worked in an old French style. A Rockefeller buyer on the lookout for antiques for his boss had plundered it from an ancient nobleman's chateau.

"Ladies and gentlemen," Leo said. "I hope you all had a good night's sleep and are all well rested from your nocturnal adventures."

A chorus of booing and thumbs pointed downward met his greeting. Of course, Leo was undismayed—the assembled group comprised his colleagues and many of his dear friends, except for Edward Teller, who found it difficult to be friends with anyone.

"Thank you, thank you, my dear friends. I expected nothing less from this crowd. But I am afraid the time for fun and for poker has drawn to an end—yes, Hans, I'm afraid you must shut down your illegal betting parlor."

Bethe smiled and shrugged.

"The time for holiday is over. We all must get down to business."

Another chorus of boos rippled through the parlor.

"Listen, everyone. Zis is a serious matter." No one, no matter what their opinion, could ignore this voice. The room fell silent.

"Thank you, Albert," said Leo. "You all know why you are here, along with your wives. We are in agreement that our first goal must be to defeat the Nazis, who represent a threat to the civilization of the West, to the values of the Enlightenment, and to the progress of liberal democracy. Those of us who are Jewish or who have had to flee Europe with little more than the clothes on our backs know personally the horrors the Nazis can inflict. But to achieve this goal, the enormous resources of the United States must be brought to bear against the Nazi menace.

"Our president, Mr. Lindbergh, either fails to see this, or is so ideologically blinkered, he does not realize our country is now in mortal peril. But we believe recent advances in atomic physics, and the talent assembled in this room and in other rooms across the U.S., can provide the nation with a weapon that will render it defensively invulnerable. It may, if the need arises, be employed in an offensive capacity, too. You all know to what I'm referring.

"In order to prove the concept that a chain reaction—and thus a nuclear weapon—is possible, Professor Fermi has agreed to design what he refers to as an 'atomic pile.' In his creation, a controlled chain reaction can be achieved by the insertion of large pellets of uranium oxide into graphite blocks. Rods of cadmium metal will moderate the neutron flux. These rods can also be inserted into the blocks. The creation of the pile has already begun at Los Alamos."

"I looked carefully at a map of the U.S.," cried Robert Sorber, of Columbia. "With a magnifying glass! There's no such place as Los Alamos!"

"I don't see any problem with that," answered Fermi. "It's a secret place, you numbskull!"

"Los Alamos is in the middle of nowhere," said Leo. "In the mountains of New Mexico, north of Santa Fe. Beautiful place; I've been there. Fresh mountain air, lots of privacy. No cops, no Feds, and to all intents and purposes, no locals."

"Sounds boring," Julia whispered to Sid.

"Who is making the fuel rods?" asked Hans Bethe calmly. Even in the most difficult situations, Bethe was imperturbable. In that way, he was unlike some of his more emotional colleagues.

"I was about to address your question, Hans, so please bear with me for a moment. As you all are aware, Mr. Lindbergh's popularity rests mainly with that section of the population, mostly poor, mostly uneducated, mostly white—people that have an internal need for an image of a strong man as president."

"He's a fascist!" yelled Edward Teller, who'd emerged from the kitchen in Leo's wake. "That's all you have to know about Lindbergh."

A louder chorus of booing rocked the parlor and continued for long after Leo's pleas for quiet.

"Lindbergh's an evil man," he said as the parlor stopped rocking. "The mystery is why people support him regardless of what he does or how he behaves, even when his policies contravene their own interests."

"Because they're fascists, too, Leo!" replied Teller. "Isn't it obvious?"

"I'm not going argue with you, Edward. I wouldn't win no matter what I said. But hear me out! Lindbergh has a certain charm, an aura about him preventing anything or anyone from damaging him."

"Then what we need is a kilo of kryptonite!" blurted out Sorber.

"Wouldn't work. Lindbergh's no Superman. He's a rube from the provinces who did one grand thing in his life and now feels entitled to be president. But I've brought a young man with me today who will be genuine kryptonite for Lindbergh. I'd like to introduce him. Don't be shocked by his name. He has an amazing story to tell. Ladies and gentlemen, please meet John Fitzgerald Kennedy!"

Kennedy appeared in the parlor from the kitchen at the back entrance of the house, in the courtyard formed by all the other houses on E. 71st and E. 72nd St., between First and York Avenue to the east. The jaws of every person in the room, except for those in on the secret, dropped a few centimeters.

"Leo!" Edward Teller was distressed. "How did this man get through security? For God's sake, how dare you bring this son of a bandit in here! For anyone who doesn't know, Professor Szilard's friend is the son of Joseph P. Kennedy, a co-conspirator in Lindbergh's attempts to bring fascism to the U.S. And now every one of us is compromised! And the entire Resistance, too!"

Leo was exasperated. "Edward! For once in your life, sit down, shut up, and listen! This is the son, not the father. They are different people, Edward! Listen to what John Kennedy the son has to say! And if you don't like him or his message, you can form up a lynch mob afterwards and hang us both! But until you've listened, sit down and open your ears."

The parlor erupted in a torrent of vigorous comments.

"Ah... you're not serious, I hope," whispered a nervous Kennedy.

"Oh, don't take me literally," said Leo. "Or Edward, either. He has strong opinions, but he's really not the hanging type. The tongue's the problem. He'll just smear you to death."

"That's a relief. All right, let's have a go at it, then."

With the help of Einstein, Leo brought the room to order.

Kennedy spoke of his father, and of how he had turned away from the values of the elder Kennedy, especially in the face of the ongoing cataclysm in Eastern Europe, which he warned would only worsen. It was long past time, he concluded, that the U.S. should rearm and take on the Nazis. That could only be done by removing, or at least severely weakening, Lindbergh.

The reaction in the parlor was almost identical to Leo's when Kennedy had described to him the Nazi atrocities in Eastern Europe. The consensus was that Germany was a civilized nation, and such actions as Kennedy described were incompatible with the German character and German honor.

Enrico Fermi disagreed. "I have heard what this man has to say. And frankly, I don't see much of a choice. Either he is wrong, or he is right. But if he is right and we do nothing, then we are—what is the word? Ah, complicit. I would prefer not to be complicit, rather than to live with the shame of my complicity for the rest of my life."

"Another reason to hate Nazis," said Teller. "As if we need one."

"Thank you, Enrico, Edward," said Leo, nodding his head to each in turn. "I also want everyone here to know that Jack Kennedy has uncovered information about Mr. Lindbergh that will damage that golden aura that clings to him."

"Oh, I know what it is!" laughed Robert Sorber. "He plays the ponies!"

Kennedy shook his head. "Good try! But not nearly salacious enough. His Midwestern fans love the ponies."

"He trades equities on the New York Stock Exchange on the basis of inside information," said Hans Bethe.

"Doesn't everyone?" asked Kennedy. "Who would know better than me?"

"Only your old man," said Einstein.

"He deals heroin up in Harlem," cracked Lepke Buchalter, in the spirit of the moment.

"I've no data to support any of your hypotheses. But I can prove our president, Charles Lindbergh, has a second family. Three children with a German woman, all citizens of the Third Reich."

The audience greeted the bombshell with an audible gasp.

"How do you know all this?" asked Teller. He was always the skeptic.

"I've traveled through Germany," replied Kennedy, who repeated what he'd originally told Leo Szilard. "I've brought copies of photographs of several of the atrocities I was informed about by horrified Wehrmacht soldiers. But I warn you... don't look at them if you don't have a strong stomach.

"Now with respect to Lindbergh's child support payments to Fräulein von Treitzler, I have photocopies of his checks, too. And how, you may ask, did I get them? Let me just say that, ah, remnants of the Social Democratic Party still exist in Nazi Germany. But I'm not at liberty to divulge anything more about my sources for fear of reprisals."

Teller was satisfied. "Okay, I'm sold. I hope that bastard Lindbergh gets what's comin' to 'im."

"Lindbergh wants to take us back as a nation," said Hans Bethe. "And I for one hope he does. In the town that I came from, the penalty for adultery in the 15th century was castration."

"That despicable bastard," was Laura Fermi's opinion. "I feel so sorry for the first lady."

Einstein, as befit his dignity in the physics community, was given the final word. "On ze basis of ze testimony of Lieutenant Kennedy, I am now convinced zat our president will zuffer ze greatest of all possible indignities. In ze world of ze future, men will either speak of him mit utter contempt, or zey will not speak of him at all."

"From his lips to God's ears," said Julia to Sid.

"Amen," he whispered.

"Whatever happens to Lindbergh in the short term," said Kennedy, "is beyond the control of anyone in this room. But of this I am... ah, certain. You must be gone from here as soon as possible. By tonight at the latest. Your safety and your very lives are at risk. Don't ever underestimate the forces arrayed against you!"

CHAPTER 24

Gracie Mansion, E. 88th St. and East End Ave, Manhattan
The Next Morning, 7:30 a.m.

The phone rang on Fred Trump's desk. In recent days, things had not gone well for the mayor of America's largest city. Far from being an organization Fred Trump could manipulate to do his bidding, the Bundists, under their leader Fritz Kuhn, had become an ungovernable force terrorizing Aryan and non-Aryan alike. Even New York's Finest were forced to battle rogue mobs of American Nazis, who rampaged at will and made New York after dark—and during daylight hours, too—a city where people were assaulted with impunity. Synagogues were wrecked, black churches firebombed, Catholic priests beaten, and ministers preaching tolerance and racial harmony threatened at gunpoint. The Democratic Party was rapidly in the ascendant in the polls, and Trump's personal popularity, in a recent Gallup survey, had declined to an almost invisible 6.5%.

To make matters worse for His Honor, the business and Wall Street leaders of New York had abandoned Trump, and Mr. Lindbergh no longer considered Fred Trump politically useful—truly a spectacular slide for someone so recently at the apogee of the greasy political pole!

But it wasn't his fault. He had never made a single, incorrect move. Malign forces, far beyond human control, had engineered his takedown. And at the core of the infernal, Satanic machinations that had done him wrong were the usual spawn of hell: the Jews.

Trump wasn't an unintelligent man. He'd built a substantial real estate business in the outer boroughs of the City of New York. His business was a reflection of his enormous abilities. But when he, Fred Trump, took time to think things over, he grudgingly realized those Jew sons-of-bitches deserved some credit.

Oh, he'd warned people about them for years. But had they ever listened? Jesus H. Christ, he'd gone after them in every way he could. He'd even marshaled their worst enemies, the German-American Bundists, to do them some real damage. And what happened? They came back stronger than ever in a conspiracy larger and far more complex than anything he'd imagined. Clever, clever folks, those Hebes. Just maybe, Trump reasoned, he should re-consider whose side he should be on during the next war.

But that thought was for another day. At the moment, his staff was receiving *Herr* Thomsen, the German ambassador, at the front door of Gracie Mansion.

"*Guten Tag, Herr* Ambassador," said Trump brightly, as Thomsen stepped into his office.

"Trump! Today deserves no *guten tag*! It is a terrible day! *Und* your German is just as execrable. From wherever did you get that horrible accent?"

Trump thought Thomsen must have woken up on the wrong side of the bed. "I'm sorry to hear that, *Herr* Thomsen. Anything I can do to help?"

"Of course, there is, Trump, and you know it! You can return the money we invested in your idiotic building scheme."

Trump didn't need to remind *Herr* Thomsen that the Third Reich had loaned him one hundred twenty million Reichsmarks to build Trump Tower. The monument to Trump and the Nazi regime was to be erected in the middle of midtown Manhattan, one of the most exclusive real estate locations in the entire country.

"What's the hurry, Mr. Ambassador? The project is coming along exactly as planned. It will be the biggest—"

"What are you babbling about, *mann?* There isn't even a hole in the ground at the proposed address! It's still a vacant lot with boards surrounding it stating, 'Post No Bills.'"

"But... but... that's the way large building projects work in America. It takes time to pull together all the investors. It's all very intricate."

Thomsen was having none of it. "Let me make it clear, *Herr* Mayor. We are no longer interested. Intricate or not. Please return our money. We have decided to invest our capital in other ventures."

Like attempting to defeat a Russian army stubbornly refusing to be beaten, Trump thought. The resources of the entire European continent wouldn't be sufficient for the Third Reich to accomplish that goal. "I suggest you be patient, Mr. Ambassador. This project will generate far more revenue in the future than what you invest today."

"That may be, *Herr* Trump. But our capital needs are for today. The future will have to take care of itself."

He felt that frisson of anxiety again. The last thing Trump wanted was to admit to the ambassador how he'd purloined the Nazi money. It wasn't like playing fast and loose with investors' cash was anything out of the ordinary for him or for anyone in the New York real estate business. He'd just done it on a far larger scale than he ever had before.

Fred Trump knew his plan had been brilliant. How could it possibly have turned out so badly? This is what he'd done: Fred and his partners had formed a Joint Partnership Trust. The money for Trump Tower gathered from investors was placed in the trust. Everything was straight, legal, and by the books. He had convinced the Germans to provide the funds in the form of bearer bonds. That was legal, too. The Germans liked bearer bonds, because the bonds bore no one's name—meaning the money couldn't be traced back to any particular individual. Trump liked bearer bonds, too. That was because the lawyer for the trust—who was a partner in an upper crust New York law practice—had gambling debts. He was involved with one too many women for the health of his own finances.

The bottom line was that Fred Trump, through this corrupt attorney whom he'd subsidized, had gained effective control of thirty million dollars of untraceable bearer bonds. He then used the bonds as collateral to fund additional real estate deals and to speculate in equities that some people were saying simply couldn't miss.

Trump bought tens of thousands of shares of various stocks, many of them on margin. And that's when he, and many of his wealthy friends, took one of the biggest financial hits of their lives. The turmoil in the large cities in the U.S. had caused a noticeable slowing of overall economic activity. Instead of a general stock market advance as he'd anticipated, the share price of equities declined—and along with them, the value of Fred Trump's portfolio.

This wasn't an insoluble problem, at least not until he'd received a demand for immediate repayment from the Germans. The war against the Soviets was costing far more than anticipated. It was impossible for Trump, without taking a financial bath, to sell enough properties or equities fast enough to refund their money. Combined with the margin calls on his reckless stock market speculations, Trump was now in significant financial trouble. His desperate solution was to try to restructure his loan from the Germans, offering to repay over the next fifteen years. But this offer was summarily rejected, as were all the others he made.

Nothing Trump said or did would shake the German resolve. They wanted cash—cold, hard U.S. government notes—and they wanted it now. But those dollars were gone. Fred Trump knew he had no one to blame. Not the Jews, not the blacks, not any far-fetched conspiracy theories—but himself, alone. And the specter would follow him everywhere and every day, and would cling to him like a bad case of influenza. It would be the most gnawing fear of his life—the specter of corporate, and then personal, bankruptcy and the collapse of his dreams not only for himself, but for his wife Mary and for countless generations of Trumps yet unborn.

CHAPTER 25

The White House, Washington, D.C.
The Next Morning, 7:30 a.m.

Charles!" shouted Anne Morrow Lindbergh the instant after she saw the three-inch headlines and read the article in the morning edition of her favorite newspaper, *The Chicago Tribune.* The paper was customarily provided for her on the same tray as her breakfast.

"Oh, my God! Charles!" she shouted again.

A sheepish President Lindbergh appeared in her bedroom.

"Oh, Charles, how could you? How could you?" she moaned, bewailing her fate as she held up the newspaper so he, too, could observe the florid accusation of his adultery—and the claim that he paid support to his second, German family.

"Think of what you have done to the family, Charles! Think of how you have shamed me in front of the entire country—the entire world! You have disgraced us, Charles. And in the process, you have disgraced yourself!"

"I don't suppose you'll accept my denial and forget about all this, Anne?" asked Lindbergh.

"It would ring hollow with me because I know you too well, Charles. And right now, I am so appalled by your behavior, I'd prefer not to see or talk to you."

"But Anne, what about your fling with Jack Kennedy?"

Anne Lindbergh's eyes blazed. "That pretty boy—for that's all he is. Charles, you disgust me utterly!" The first lady grabbed a china cup full of hot tea and flung it at the president. The liquid splattered his shirt, while the cup missed him and crashed against the wall, breaking in pieces. One after another, a saucer, a glass emptied of its orange juice, and a plate holding an omelet and two strips of crispy back bacon were also discharged in his direction.

The Secret Service, alerted by the clatter of smashing china, burst into the first lady's bedroom, guns drawn, their bodies ready to take a bullet for their commander-in-chief.

"Do be sweet and put the guns away," said Anne with upper crust insouciance. "There's nothing to see here but an early middle-aged couple having a private, marital spat and tossing a few condiments."

The Secret Service men looked—eyebrows arched—at the president. With a glance and a motion of his hand, he gave them permission to withdraw.

"Are you certain you're safe, sir?" asked the Secret Service captain.

"Ask her," said Lindbergh.

"Ma'am?"

"He was never in any danger," said the first lady. "Unfortunately. My throwing aim, as you can all see, is remarkably poor. The nearest hit was the boiled egg, there atop the door frame. It missed his head by two feet. But anyway, I promise—no more violence."

"Call if you need us," said the captain. He and his men departed.

"Well, Anne," said Lindbergh, "you've certainly made a fool of yourself."

"Nonsense, Charles. The Secret Service is sworn to secrecy. Hence its name. It's you who's made a fool of himself, and in front of the entire world! I am Senator Dwight Morrow's daughter, Charles! I will not be shamed in this way! I now see only one course of action compatible with my dignity. I shall leave the White House, effective three days hence, and return to New Jersey."

Lindbergh looked stricken. "Anne, for God's sake, how can you do this to us? And to me? Please, before you do anything rash, I beg you to consider the consequences!"

"You should have thought about the consequences before you debauched yourself with that whore, Fräulein von Treizler, Charles."

"Anne, I—"

"Oh, don't, Charles. And don't come near me, either. I don't understand what that German woman gave you that I couldn't, but I will withdraw gracefully. I don't want to be a millstone around the neck of your happiness.

"And by the way, don't send Hoover or Kennedy to me, or any of those other FBI types you love to talk with. I think you've picked up some of their bad habits with women."

"Anne, that's unfair and you know it. I met von Treitzler long before I met Kennedy."

"Oh, so you admit you've been cheating on me for quite a while, Charles! It's not that I'm so blind I didn't know it. I can't imagine how many times I waited up late for you, and all the while, you were in some other woman's bed. Oh, what a fool I was.

But no longer! You and I are finished. And get out of my bedroom before the Secret Service detail has to return."

"You're making a big mistake, Anne. Think about it! You won't be first lady any longer! You'll be the first first lady to... to... have abandoned her position!"

"Get out of here, Charles!" Anne hollered. She tossed a half-full pitcher of water in his general direction. It missed him by about ten feet but soaked the carpet.

Lindbergh reddened with anger. "You will regret this every day of your life. And if you leave, don't ever try to come back! The doors of the White House will be locked and bolted against you!" Lindbergh disappeared through the door of his wife's bedroom.

He could threaten her for a month of Sundays and then some, if he liked, thought Anne. She was done with him. And about being first lady, that was a job she never wanted and didn't care for anyway. She didn't like greeting corrupt foreign dignitaries and despised pompous, long-winded ceremonies. And she disliked jealous Washington society matrons who fawned on her but watched her every move like vipers, ready to puncture her neck with their fangs. They knew the average first lady hung around for only four years or so while they reigned in Washington forever! This house, this city—she wouldn't miss either of them. She'd rather be in New Jersey doing her gardening, or working on her writing.

Anne reached for the phone near her bed and dialed the White House operator. Connection made, she gave the operator a phone number in New York. He had said she'd be able to reach him there. After four rings, he picked up the receiver.

"Hello?"

"Oh, Jack, Jack darling. I'd hoped you would answer. Jack, it was terrible!"

"He knows?"

"Yes. He saw the newspaper. Everyone's seen it!"

"What did he say?"

"I didn't give him much of a chance to say anything. He was too busy dodging the china I threw at him."

"You threw china at the president of the United States?"

"Yes."

"I think that's felony assault, Anne. It'll get you one-to-three in Leavenworth."

"Oh, never mind, Jack. I missed. Badly. And I told him I was moving out of the White House. That I'm finished with him! That I'm free."

"How do you feel, Anne?"

"How do I feel? I ache all over, Jack. All over. I can't tell you how much this hurts. I loved him once, and I'm sure he loved me. And now it's finished. Oh, that bastard humiliated me in front of the entire world. I don't know how I can ever show my face in public again! I love him and hate him so!"

Jack Kennedy heard her sobbing at the other end of the line. Anne was doubled over at the side of her bed in misery.

"Anne, you can forgive him, pretend nothing happened and take him back, ya know."

"Impossible, Jack. He'll say all the right words, but he won't mean a single one of them. That's because my husband, the president of the United States, is a lying, cheating, son of a bitch."

"Is there anything I can do to help you, Anne?"

"Yes. I want to see you. As soon as you can make it back to Washington. But it doesn't matter. I'm leaving the White House in three days, and nothing can stop me. I want to hold you in my arms, Jack. To be with a real man for a change, a man who knows how to treat a woman right. A man who's not a shameless, deceitful creep with two families!"

Kennedy placed his hand on the phone receiver and let out a low whistle. Three days—not much time, he thought. This would create some real commotion in the newspapers. Anne Lindbergh could be a great asset to the Resistance, if she could be used correctly. But he was going to disappoint this confused, unlucky lady because he, too, needed to disappear.

The Chicago Tribune, August 22, 1941
[Above the crease]

LINDBERGH HAS GERMAN SECOND FAMILY

By Siegfried Hunkapiller

President Charles A. Lindbergh has been publicly accused of *de facto* bigamy. The accusation was made by a Miss Henriette von Treizler of Berlin, Germany, an attractive, blonde, twenty-eight-year-old secretary who stated she had a longstanding romantic relationship with the president.

In a written document, Miss von Treizler also claimed he is the father of each of her three children, two boys and a girl, ages eight, six, and two.

Based on information obtained by this newspaper, Mr. Lindbergh made excursions to Germany approximately nine months prior to her delivery of each of these children. Photographs of checks bearing Lindbergh's signature and purporting to provide financial support to Miss von Treizler are also in the possession of the *Tribune*.

The White House, when asked for a comment, refused to respond. There has also been no comment from the first lady, Anne Morrow Lindbergh, the president's wife of twelve years and the mother of three of his children. These include Charles A. Lindbergh, Jr., who was kidnapped and murdered in 1932. An itinerant carpenter, Bruno Richard Hauptmann was convicted of the crime and eventually executed.

However, reaction was swift from many erstwhile Lindbergh supporters. This was especially true from among the Evangelical community, who voted in overwhelming numbers for the president over his Democratic opponent.

Minister Otis Bunkrump, of the Baptist Little Church of Bethany, angrily opined:

"We have been betrayed! We had never doubted the president was an honorable individual, a true man of God who walked in the footsteps of Jesus Christ. We believed he was sent to save this nation from the sinful behavior afflicting it, for which it is in dire need of repentance! But alas! He, too, has departed the path of righteousness and succumbed to the devil's most vile temptations."

Other clerics, however, were more forgiving. Pastor Ezekiel Entwhistle of the Church of Christ the King, felt Lindbergh's transgressions were relatively minor compared to the great issues of the day.

"Didn't King David commit adultery with Bathsheba? And wasn't their child Solomon the wisest of men as an adult? If we condemn the president, must we also condemn the great Israelite king, too?"

However, most men in the street, and all of the women this reporter spoke to, were highly critical of the president's behavior.

"Shame, shame, shame on him," said Mrs. Anne O'Malley, of Lakeshore Drive, in the City of Chicago. "I have no sympathy for a man who violates his wedding vows in such a callous way!"

"Think of how the first lady must feel, poor woman," commented Mrs. Gussie Kupersmith, of Cicero. "If that were my husband, I'd give him more than a piece of my mind! And I'd hire a fast-talking lawyer to do it, too! Lindbergh is living proof men evolved from apes!"

Several calls for Lindberg's resignation have already arrived from Capitol Hill. In a statement, Senator Robert Wagner (D-NY) condemned the president's "complete loss of all moral compass," and noted his "behavior is not worthy of a man fit to hold the Presidency. If he can't be trusted in his marriage, how can he be trusted to run the country?"

However, it is not clear if members of the president's own Republican Party will pressure him to step down in favor of Vice President Robert A. Taft of Ohio. People close to the situation have unofficially stated this is the gravest crisis of the Lindbergh administration. Its resolution may depend on the interactions between the president and first lady over the next several days to weeks.

424 E. 71st Street
Later That Same Morning...

"You didn't answer my question, Leo. And I'm not sure why."

Leo, Hans Bethe, and Sid Peskin were huddled together in a small office on the first floor of the townhouse, where Leo was providing them with last-minute instructions.

"What question was that, Hans?"

"One that's a matter of some importance to me, Leo. Who machined the cadmium rods for the atomic pile?"

"Hans, I assure you no offense was intended. There is no longer any reason for you not to know. Have you ever heard of Henry Kaiser?"

"The West Coast industrialist? I didn't realize he was interested in uranium or cadmium. I thought he built boats."

"He does, Hans. And he employs a fair number of metallurgists to build those boats."

"Ah. He is putting his resources to good use, I see."

"Yes. Kaiser is a patriot. He loathes the Nazis and anyone who supports them. It seems he and that old fascist Henry Ford, as the American say it, have 'had words.' Ugly words, according to those who heard them."

"I'm jealous of the fly that was on the wall during that conversation," said Sid. "But since you're answering questions, Professor Szilard, I have several. One," Sid held up his right index finger, "what exactly am I doing here? And, two," Sid held up his adjacent finger, "how will all these people travel to Los Alamos, in New Mexico, without being detected?"

Bethe nodded his head; these were questions he also wanted answered. Especially the latter.

"You've both understood our need for secrecy, gentlemen. And in general, everyone has behaved with great, even superhuman, discretion. But now it's appropriate for you to know everything.

"It's no longer possible for the Resistance to transport the physicists and their wives living in this brownstone out of New York either by rail, truck, or auto, and flying is not practical. Between them, Trump and Hoover have this city almost locked down. But there is one way out of New York that neither the local cops nor the FBI can control."

Sid and Hans Bethe looked at each other, mystified.

"Our plan, gentlemen, hinges on the fact the mob has retained its control of the

New York docks. Nothing moves in or out of this city by boat unless blessed by the mob, and no attempt by Lindbergh or Trump has been able to shake that control. Sometimes, corrupt local cops and officials can be of use to the cause.

"Tonight, you will all be taken to the Fish Market, at the foot of Fulton Street and the East River. Tied up near this emporium is a Mexican freighter, the *Cinco de Mayo*. The stevedores will handle you and your baggage. No one will see or hear anything. Capish?"

"Sounds promising," said Sid. "And then what?"

"And then, you will embark on an all-expense paid cruise south, around the tip of Florida, and into the sunny, humid Gulf of Mexico. The Cinco de Mayo will deposit you at the port of Veracruz. From there, it's a five-hour train ride to Mexico City. Then it will be north to the Rio Grande by train, car, or pack animal, if necessary. Trusted guides will be with you at all times—if they know what's good for them. You'll be smuggled back into the U.S. near El Paso, Texas. From there, it's a relatively short auto ride north, past Albuquerque, to Santa Fe and Los Alamos."

"I never thought I'd be an illegal alien in my own country," said Sid.

"And how are the accommodations on this... adventure?" asked Bethe.

"On the whole, rather miserable," said Leo. "But don't be overly concerned about these things, Hans. We all must sacrifice for the sake of the Resistance."

"Tell that to my wife," said Bethe glumly.

"I'll be happy to. I've scouted out the entire route, you know."

"I'd no idea," said Sid.

"Me, neither," Bethe admitted.

"That's right. The five days on the boat to Veracruz weren't pleasant. But one can always lie on the deck, take in a good book, and work on one's suntan. After that, I had a wonderful few days touring Mexico. The people were delightful, the guides efficient, and the Federales corrupt. We pay them well for their silence. The sole difficult part of the trip was the mile hike through the desert from Mexico to the U.S. border. It was hot. Very hot. But I survived, my friend, and so will you."

"Why not an alternate route? North to the St. Lawrence, down to Montreal, then take the Canadian National Railroad west, to Calgary?"

"We thought of that, Sid," said Leo, "but ruled it out. The Mounties can't be trusted. Too damned honest. Also, we know Hoover has his men in Canada, and there are official agreements between their government and ours. Winston Churchill may reside in Canada, but he has no political power there. And also, Los Alamos is far closer to our southern border than our northern. We don't anticipate anyone searching for us in southern New Mexico. Our calculation is that no one will be on the lookout for atomic scientists invading the U.S. from the south."

Sid sighed. "I've come along this far, Dr. Szilard, so I suppose I'm good for the rest of it. But why ever did you get me involved in this madness? I liked my old life in the West Bronx."

Leo paused for a moment. "Excuse us, Hans, if you'd be so kind. Young Peskin and I need some time together."

Bethe gave Leo a slight Germanic bow. "Of course. It's long past time when my wife Rose should be up and about. What a wonderful way to greet a new day—with the news Lindbergh is a bigamist! Who knows how many families the man has sired?" With a spring in his step, Bethe left the small office, leaving Leo and Sid alone.

"I think you owe me some answers, Professor Szilard."

"I agree, Sid."

"Do you remember the first time we met, in the library at City College?"

"Of course. You and I were interested in the same research papers. About nuclear fission, I remember."

"I don't believe that meeting was a coincidence, Professor."

"No, it wasn't."

"I presume the late Dr. Strauss put you up to it."

Leo paused. "No, in point of fact, he didn't, Sid. I had contact with Strauss, but he didn't initiate the meeting in the library with you."

What Leo was saying didn't make sense. If Strauss didn't initiate the meeting, then who did? There was no one else in the Department of Physics at City College who had any knowledge of his, Sid's, research interests. Those who did know had become acquainted with him only after he'd first met Leo Szilard in the library!

"I find that difficult to believe!" he blurted out at the news.

"Sid, I can only tell you what I know to be the truth. Whether you accept it or not is up to you."

"Then who did it, Leo? Who on God's great green earth got me into this gargantuan mess?"

"Sid, the person who first gave me your name was Vince Mangano. I don't know the details, but the mob has had an eye on you for some time. It seems they selected you for a very important job—as someone young, energetic, resourceful, and above all, loyal—an all-American kid who would assist Mangano and his associates as they fled New York with us."

Sid remembered his early doubts about Julia—whether or not she was doing a favor for her uncle by dating him. But whatever her initial motivation, Sid was confident in her love now, which he knew was genuine. He was certain that long ago, she'd ceased being beholden to Vince Mangano.

"And what about you, Leo? What was your cut of this arrangement?"

"Oh, I needed someone with the same characteristics Vince Mangano did, but with a few additions. The young person—man or woman, I was indifferent—was required to have a deep understanding of science, preferably atomic physics, because he or she would be spending most of his or her time in the company of people that often spoke of little or nothing else. Knowledge of the German language was critical because many of our scientists were either born or educated in Germany and are still more comfortable in their native language than in English.

"And finally, Sid, I needed a person whom I could trust and one that could handle some of the more, er, difficult people on this trip, like Edward Teller, yet who could also earn the respect of someone as august and inscrutable as Albert Einstein. I'm not sure there is any person in the City of New York who fulfills these requirements as well as you do. Especially when coupled with your recent advances in theoretical atomic physics."

Sid absorbed Leo Szilard's words and sat deep in thought. It took some time for him to admit Leo had thought things through.

"All right. I get the logic. You know how passionately Julia and I feel about the Resistance—but for taking such liberties with my life, I ought to punch you in the snoot. And, oh, about Julia! God, how could I almost forget! Who pushed her under the train, Leo? And what bastard gave the order to do it, and why?"

Leo lowered his head and shook it from side to side. The thought of what could have happened to Julia was too dreadful to ponder. "That was a terrible thing, Sid. Terrible. Not only because poor Julia was almost killed, though that was the worst of it. The event almost caused a complete rupture in the relationship between the Mangano family and the Resistance. That would have been a disaster, as without Mangano assistance, we'd have no way to leave New York. Believe it or not, Lepke Buchalter, Chairman of the Board of Murder, Inc., patched things up between the Manganos and us. But of course, there was a price.

"Who did it? I'm certain it was Julius Rosenberg. Why? The man was emotionally unstable—paranoid, perhaps. I would be, too, if I were I married to that termagant Ethel. Rosenberg must have overheard the conversation that passed between Julia and me at the Café Budapest. I'll admit our words were heated, and our meeting almost ended in violence before Julia fled the restaurant. I've thought about that meeting every day since it happened. My conclusion is that, in his unstable, paranoid mind, she represented a threat to me, and thus, to the entire Resistance. Thank God he didn't get away with what he tried to do."

"He was killed a short time later fighting the Bundists."

"Ha! Is that the party line these days? Well, I suppose it's not all that bad he's a Resistance martyr now. Though a close look at the lethal knife would reveal a blade forged in Sicily."

"Men of honor have a strict code, and a long reach," said Sid.
"And they never forget a thing," replied Leo.

The Reich's Chancellery, Berlin, Grossdeutsches Reich
September 12, 1941

Albert Speer, his documents held in a leather case clutched securely in his grasp, had been summoned to Berlin to advise his *Führer*, and Supreme Commander, on the state of armaments production. He was also to render an opinion on whether the Wehrmacht was adequately supplied for the war against the Soviets.

As he approached the *Führer's* desk, he stopped sharply, rendered a crisp *Heil Hitler*, and received the Nazi salute in return.

"Sit, Speer, sit. Please," requested Hitler, who motioned to a comfortable chair to Speer's left.

"It is always a great pleasure to see you. *Ach,* I have so few pleasures these days, even though the war is going well."

Speer wondered if Eva Braun hadn't yet arrived in Berlin from Berchtesgaden, the *Führer's* Alpine retreat. "I trust you are in good health," he said as he settled into the chair.

"Bah, no more than the usual. The same digestive troubles as always. Nothing I eat agrees with me. I can't seem to get any sleep. And I also have no energy—except when Dr. Morell injects me with his latest *schweinerei*. And now I have a new problem—a slight tremor in my left hand. Sometimes, I can't control the shaking, especially when I try to drink tea. Then I spill it on my pants. Speer, let me tell you, the *Führer* of the *Grossdeutsches Reich* cannot appear in public with a stain on the front of his pants! Morell says the tremor is due to the injections and that it will disappear soon. *Ach,* sometimes I feel like an old man, Speer. A few more years, and perhaps I'll retire and eke out my last few days writing my memoirs as I did with *Mein Kampf,* back in the '20s."

"It would make a fascinating read, *mein Führer*, but please stay on the job at least until the war is won. We all need your guidance and leadership."

"*Ja,* Speer, *vielen dank.* I know I can always count on you. Now, what information do you have for me today?"

Despite Hitler's breezy optimism, all was not proceeding according to plan on the Eastern Front. It was Speer's duty to report to Hitler the actual military situation on the ground. This was rarely a pleasant job.

"*Mein Führer*, your troops have made excellent progress on all fronts. But the going has not been quite as easy as we had hoped. It seems the conquest of Great Britain finally convinced Stalin we were not involved in a capitalist plot with the

British against him. Because he became concerned about our military strength in Eastern Europe, Stalin finally listened to the voices of his generals instead of murdering them.

"The most prominent voice among them now is Marshal Grigory Zhukov, an intelligent but brutal commander. Zhukov advocated a defense-in-depth strategy rather than positioning the majority of the Red Army at the Soviet Union's western border. When we attacked last June, the Soviets retreated in good order, lengthening our supply lines and shortening theirs. The Russians also constructed innumerable tank traps and other defenses that blunted the edges of our Blitzkrieg strategy and produced large numbers of German casualties—"

Hitler rolled his eyes and slumped in his chair. "Speer! I've heard much the same from everyone who has been in this office for the past week! Have you absolutely nothing else to report, goddamn it, man? Listening to you is like listening to an old woman jabbering on and on. The same things, over and over."

As his mind whirred, Speer considered how to phrase his words with delicacy, with diplomacy, providing Hitler mostly with what he wanted to hear. "We suspect this will be a lengthy struggle, *mein Führer*. Of course, we will ultimately be victorious with your help and our great God's love for the Reich. But right now, the production of armaments for the Wehrmacht and planes for the Luftwaffe is less than optimal. The labor shortage in the German economy is also becoming a problem."

Hitler pounded his fist on his desk. "*Ja,* Speer, I agree, I agree. We must determine the correct priorities for the use of our resources, which are large but not infinite. I admit I did not expect the Jewish-Bolshevik state to the east to be so militarily competent or resilient. Nevertheless, in consequence, all unnecessary civilian spending must be curtailed immediately in favor of military investment and procurement. This is why I've ordered the withdrawal of all German funds from overseas. This includes investments in that nation of Jews and mongrels, the United States. Are you aware, *Herr* Speer, that some idiot wanted to lend the Mayor of New York one hundred twenty million Reichsmarks to build a skyscraper in the middle of Manhattan? Utter foolishness! I put a quick end to such nonsense."

Speer wondered which idiot Hitler referred to. There were so many to choose from. But only Hermann Göring, Head of the Luftwaffe and long-term morphine addict, was capable of approving idiocy on such a gargantuan scale. He, Speer, would file this information away in a corner of his mind. It might prove useful at a later date, when the currents of bureaucratic infighting shifted, as they did with rapid regularity in the Hitler government. But Albert Speer was a survivor—and he survived because he knew his *Führer's* mind.

"My understanding, *mein Führer*, is that the mayor, a *Herr* Frederick Trump, is a close political friend of *Herr* Lindbergh. Calling in the German loans may have interesting consequences for the American political scene, don't you think?"

The *Führer's* eyes twinkled as they frequently did when he was creating difficulties for someone else, or for someone else's country. "Good for you, Albert, good for you! Complementing your technocratic expertise, you are beginning to develop a political mind. But, of course, I'm several steps ahead of you."

"Of course, *mein Führer.*" The obsequious Speer smiled. "I will never be anywhere near you in political knowledge or skill. But I'm very interested in learning from your experience. You are perhaps the greatest master of the art in all human history."

"Then I will give you a political lesson, Speer. Listen closely. The first thing you must understand is that people love to conform and to be a member of a crowd. Even better, of an entire movement. Do you understand, Speer?"

"Completely, *mein Führer.*"

"Good. The second thing to know is that, if you tell people something often and long enough, regardless of whether it is true or not, they will believe it. This is true even if it contradicts their own experiences and interests.

"But there is always ten percent of the populace who will believe nothing at all of what you say, regardless of how often you say it. Fortunately, most of these free thinkers immigrated to America years ago, where they interbred with Jews and negroes. The products of this miscegenation now inhabit North America and are less malleable and controllable than the average European. They have a different history than we do and therefore must be handled differently. This is precisely where *Herr* Lindbergh has failed us."

Speer's eyes widened. "You astonish me, *mein Führer.* I had always believed *Herr* Lindbergh to be a great asset of the Third Reich."

"*Ja,* it was something we hoped and prayed for, too, Speer. But we discovered Lindbergh was a novice, an amateur, a man with no practical experience in politics and no basic understanding of the American people and what they want. He speaks only to his close band of followers, who are a small fraction of the electorate. He is erratic, reckless, and a bigamist. Not that any of these traits are intrinsically problematic, Speer. They are not. *Nein,* Lindbergh's greatest failure has been his inability to control the racialist elements in his country."

Speer was perplexed. Weren't the racialist elements, as he had heard for years, the healthiest elements?

"You look confused, *Herr* Speer. But paradoxically, the racial violence that lifted us to power here in Germany has not been to the liking of the Americans. They prefer a gentler approach rather than a rough wooing. Americans are like women. Some need the back of your hand, while others insist on flowers and chocolate. The Americans need flowers and chocolate.

"Sadly, the extreme violence of the Bundists backfired on our friend Lindbergh. The Democratic Party is in the ascendant in the polls again, and members of Lindbergh's own party are questioning his fitness for office. America is far away, but we need stability on our western front, especially if the struggle against the Jewish-Bolsheviks in Russia will be a long one."

"Ah," said Speer, believing his *Führer* could see three moves ahead in any global game of chess. "I now grasp the reason *Herr* Heydrich provided the information about Fräulein von Treitzler's affair with Lindbergh to that young, naïve American, Kennedy."

"Of course. Kennedy believed the information proving Lindbergh's adultery was turned over to him by stay-behind Social Democrats. He never suspected that anyone who provided him with information was Gestapo. Nothing of the story of von Treitzler and Lindbergh, and their children, or the checks Lindbergh wrote ever could have left Germany if we'd not let it out. Kennedy is too inexperienced to understand these matters and believes his sexual charm and the women he bedded were critical. But his lovers were all Gestapo, too!

"Kennedy, despite his father's influence, is a foolish man. Our people were also not impressed with either his intelligence or his personality. I suppose he'll disappear in the vastness of America, and no one will ever hear from him again."

"So, *mein Führer*. It is clear from our discussion that you desire Lindbergh gone. Do you believe *Herr* Taft, the vice president, will be any more useful?"

"That is a good question, Speer, a very good question. Taft is older, calmer, and more thoughtful than Lindbergh. He is also the scion of a dynasty of politicians and has significant political experience himself. Did you know his father was at one time president, and later in his life, the chief justice of the U.S. Supreme Court?"

"A most accomplished individual," commented Speer.

"*Ja,* but the greatest accomplishment of the senior Taft was that he ate enough food to weigh well over three hundred English pounds. The current, smaller, Taft is not indisposed to us but also will not encourage the violence Americans seem to abhor. And we need him to keep the peace until the Russian war has been successfully completed, *und* we are victorious. After that, we'll dispose of him, if necessary, in much the same way as we disposed of Lindbergh!"

"*Mein Führer*," said Speer, gushing. "Your plan is the work of a genius! Without anyone knowing, we will control who is president of the United States! It is nothing less than fantastic! You are, without a scintilla of doubt, the greatest German of all time!"

That day, in the ghettos scattered about occupied Poland, and in the green killing fields and forests of Belarus and Ukraine, over two thousand Jews, regardless of age or gender, were either starved or shot to death by actions initiated by Adolf Hitler and organized by Reinhard Heydrich. Over four thousand Soviet soldiers and civilians were also slaughtered. It was a slow day on the Eastern Front.

CHAPTER 26

424 E. 71st Street, New York
Later That Same Day.

The meeting between Sid, Hans Bethe, and Leo Szilard had just broken up when a group of men armed with tommy guns emerged from the back of the house.

Leo had arranged the living accommodations in the brownstone so little traffic could be observed entering its front door at 424 E. 71st Street. Food and supplies came from the other side of the courtyard at 402 E. 72nd Street, a large apartment building also controlled by Rockefeller interests. All materiel designated for the brownstone would simply pass through the apartment building into the courtyard, and then through the back door of the brownstone, which led into the kitchen. The brownstones and apartment buildings surrounding the central courtyard were the homes of some of the city's wealthiest elite. Their dwellings were rarely occupied in the middle of the day, when Leo had arranged for the deliveries of most of the needed supplies.

For added protection, a detachment of Mangano's foot soldiers guarded the back door of the brownstone night and day. To everyone's surprise, the two wiseguys were unobtrusive except for bumming the occasional cigarette off of passing physicists when they ran out. They instantly deferred to Vince and Phil Mangano when the brothers, accompanied by a troop of half a dozen other high-profile hoodlums, stepped into the brownstone.

Sid, standing nearby, recognized several of the gangsters—they'd been named in the newspapers as members of Murder, Inc. First through the door was nattily dressed, movie star-handsome Bugsy Siegel, smiling at everyone and flashing a long wink at Julia. Then came the dour Italian Albert Anastasia, a.k.a. the Lord High Executioner, an assassin of spectacular proficiency. He was followed by Phil Kovalick, Lepke Buchalter's close associate and mob enforcer in the needle trade unions in New York. Several steps behind them were lesser lights in the murder business. These included Louis Capone, brother of Al, then Mendy Weiss and Allie "Tick Tock" Tannenbaum. Last man into the kitchen was Joe Adonis, famous for his impeccable hair, grooming, and preening vanity. Each of these gentlemen was a brutish, stone-cold killer with an impressive *curriculum vitae* and a lit cigarette in his mouth.

"We're here to see Buchalter," said Siegel in a tone commanding immediate respect and obedience.

"You're seeing 'im," said Lepke. He'd just emerged from the first-floor toilet with a look of surprise on his face.

"Is dis all o' youse guys? What happened to Frankie Carbo, Gurrah Shapiro, Max the Jerk, Jack Parisi, and all the other wiseguys?"

"They couldn't make it," said Siegel.

"Benny, I t'ink we need to have a chat. Everyone!" he ordered, waving his arm at the physicists and their spouses. "Outta da room. All o' youse! Go on, up to the second floor. I'll let ya know when we're done."

With Leo leading the way, the physicists, their spouses, and active FBI agent Jack Kennedy (who stared in disbelief at what he was witnessing) tramped up the long staircase to the second floor of the brownstone, closed the doors to their rooms, and stayed well out of sight.

The hoods of Murder, Inc. lowered their weapons and nestled into the chairs just vacated. Bugsy Siegel waited several moments before speaking.

"Lepke," he said. "We have a problem."

"I t'ink dat's obvious," Buchalter replied. "We got, what, twenty, twenty-five guys dat gotta get outta town! And how many you got here today? Half a dozen, maybe?"

"Some of 'em's dead, Lepke, and some of 'em's in jail. Trump or the feds got 'em," Albert Anastasia declared. "Da rest, in hidin'. An' da talk is, Lepke, if anyone leaves town now, he betta not show 'is face in Noo Yawk again! I'm tellin' ya, it's true! Dat's what people are sayin'. You leave, you can never come back. Your territory's gonna get redistributed."

Lepke leaned back in his chair, removed a cigar from his shirt pocket, and lit up.

"Dis come down from da Commission?" he asked, referring to the mob 'Board of Directors' consisting of the heads of the five largest crime families in New York, plus the Chicago Outfit and the Buffalo family crime syndicate.

"Nothin' personal against you, Lepke," said Siegel. "Not like they want you to get caught, or nothin'. But the Commission is composed of practical men. But dey, and we, got a problem. Dere's a new gang outta Hell's Kitchen in the West 40's. Call demselves the Westies, bunch o' fuckin' crazy micks. Small stuff right now, but dey got big ambitions. Da Commission t'inks dey're plannin' an attack on some of our made men, and dey want all our manpower to remain in Noo Yawk. So the Commission says—no one leaves until further notice."

Buchalter thought for a moment. "All youse guys agree wid dis?"

Seven gangster heads nodded in unison.

"The Westies, sick bunch o' bastards," said Bugsy Siegel.

"All right," said Lepke, disappointed at the news. But he didn't have the power to defy the Commission.

"So, I ain't goin'. I'll tell Leo Szilard. And dat's the way it is." Ash from Lepke's cigar fell onto the expensive carpet.

"Smart move, Lepke," said Albert Anastasia. "Now the Commission don' have to issue a contract, and I don' have to whack ya."

"T'anks, Albert. I'll remember dat when yer hour comes."

Siegel said it was time to leave. The mobsters scattered, some through the front door, others through the back.

Vince and Phil Mangano asked to remain. "Our nephew, Joey Falcone, is coming over. Wants ta say g'bye to his sister," Vince said. Lepke granted permission and said he would also remain to cover the departure of the scientists. He explained it was part of an arrangement he'd made with Leo Szilard.

Lepke yelled from the foot of the staircase, "Hey Leo, you can come downstairs now."

Leo and the physicists slowly opened their creaking doors and assembled at the top of the stairs.

"Who's going to be brave enough to be the first person down to the parlor?" asked Edward Teller.

"Certainly not you," answered Hans Bethe.

"Not von Neumann, either," said Einstein. "He has a child. Nor Enrico... wait, where is Enrico?"

"Oh, no, don't look at me," said Robert Sorber. "I have a wife."

"So do I," said Leo. "Sid, I'm afraid we all nominate you. You have no child, no wife, and no choice but to accept."

Sid sighed. "C'mon, Julia. Let's shame our elders and betters." Grabbing her hand, they gingerly walked down the stairs and into the parlor where Lepke Buchalter was inhaling a last puff from a stogie.

"Well, where's Szilard?" he asked, irritated.

"Leo, get down here!" Sid called out, loud enough to be heard at the top of the stairs. "Lepke wants to speak with you! I don't think he's killing anyone today!"

The remark earned Sid a sour look from Lepke and a poke in the ribs from Julia.

Leo came down the stairs. He and Lepke walked into the small office off the parlor.

"No one comes in here," Lepke warned Sid. "Or I might change my mind about today. Geddit, kid?"

"Understood, Mr. Buchalter." Sid closed the door and stood watch.

"Siddown," said Lepke.

"Is there a problem?" asked Leo anxiously.

"Yeah. I ain't comin wid ya. None o' my boys, eider."

Leo pondered the implications of Buchalter's comment. "Anything I can do to help, Lepke?"

"No. And if I was you, I wouldn' ask no more questions. An' if anybody asks you, tell 'em no one can understand a word youse guys are talkin' about. It's like another fuckin' language, and we ain't interested in nothin' dat ain't Inglish. Geddit? You don' need to know nothin' more."

"What about your commitment to protecting us? We'll be vulnerable from the time we leave here until we're well out to sea."

"Most o' dat is up to Vince Mangano. But fur me, a deal's a deal. No one ever said Lepke Buchalter welshed on a deal. You helped me out when I was in a tough spot. Okay, so now I help you out. That's called reciprocity. I like dat woid. Don't know where I hoid it, but I like it. I'll make a phone call, 'n my men'll be here in five minutes. You can set yer watch on it."

Lepke preferred to take his chances with Trump's cops and Hoover's men than risk pissing off the Commission. He knew he could avoid the law indefinitely. The Commission was another story.

Leo relaxed. The loss of mob protection would have doomed the entire enterprise. He was still confident in the Mangano brothers—they had a niece who would be departing with the physicists, and they wouldn't want her to fall into the wrong hands. And not having to travel thousands of miles with a group of armed, touchy, psychopathic killers could only be viewed as a net gain.

"Okay, Lepke," said Leo. "I'm not going to argue with you. We'd have liked to have you accompany us. Your presence would have added a little, ah, spice to the mix."

"I appreciate da thought, Leo. Ya know, yer all right. My kinda guy. And good wid numbers, too. If dis t'ing yer doin' don' work out, my friend Meyer Lansky, he's lookin' for a guy like you. Meyer runs our bookmaking and numbers operations. Maybe I could introduce ya to 'im."

Leo shivered. "Thanks, Lepke. If I ever return to New York and need a job, I'll contact you."

"You do dat, Leo. Jus' call any o' the union bosses in the needle trades and say Leo Szilard wants ta' speak wid Lepke Buchalter."

The two men smiled and shook hands. Leo opened the door of the office, motioned to Sid to get moving, and left Lepke to his own dark, felonious thoughts.

Washington, D.C., the Treasury Building
September 12, 1941, 5:30 p.m.

Little Mel Purvis paced nervously in his office. He'd spoken earlier in the day to Ogden Reid, publisher of the *Herald Tribune,* but the conversation wasn't satisfactory. After federal agents had muzzled the *New York Times*, Reid, like most newspaper publishers, was suspicious of anyone associated with the Lindbergh government. But after Purvis had explained the matter was in the national interest, Reid said he was willing to look into who had purchased space at the bottom of the front page of the *Tribune.*

Two hours later, Purvis received a phone call from Reid. He was very sorry, but the space in the *Tribune* had been purchased in cash and no records had been kept. Cursing under his breath, Purvis hung up the phone. The thought of speaking with Hoover crossed his mind, but he just as quickly suppressed it. Purvis knew from bitter past experience that J. Edgar would stop at nothing to take the credit for his work. Yet if things went south, all the blame would fall on Little Mel.

Anxious, he called his friend Len Parsons in cryptography, located in the basement of the Department of the Treasury building.

"Lennie, whaddaya have for me?" asked Purvis, tapping on his desk with a pencil.

Len was exasperated. "Oh, for Pete's sake! It's only been an hour, Mel. Gimme more time! Listen, I know it's a code of some kind, but it all depends on how complicated this baby is, and whether we've seen anything like it before. So keep your shirt on!"

"Call me the minute you have something. This is damned important! I'll be here at my desk all night if necessary!"

"When I know, you'll know. My boys love a challenge. They'll break this thing or fall asleep in the attempt!"

"Thanks, Len. I'm counting on you."

Purvis also counted on his smokes, one after the other, to calm a bad case of impatience. Over the next several hours, he was often tempted to run down to Len Parsons' office in the basement and demand an answer. But he knew the effort would be counterproductive. The oddballs and eggheads—the Brits called them 'boffins'—that worked on cracking codes were best left to do their work in peace.

In the meantime, Purvis called Jack Kennedy, who didn't answer the phone and never returned the call. Two hours later, he called again. The result was the same.

Where the hell is that effin' mick? he thought. *He was supposed to check in with me hours ago.* All Purvis' instincts as a G-man told him something wasn't right—that something big with the physicists was happening soon, perhaps tonight, perhaps even in the next few hours. And whether or not the Bureau could prevent it depended on if the boys in Len Parson's shop in the basement could figure out the coded messages in the *Tribune*.

It was at 11:50 p.m. when Purvis, hungry, tired, and on his last pack of Camel cigarettes, heard the phone ring. He ripped the receiver from its cradle.

"Whaddaya got, Len?"

"I dunno, Mel, and the boys are pretty well tired out. They don't think so well when they're like that. I can tell you this is a complicated code, my friend. Whoever put this thing together is no dummy."

The name John von Neumann floated through Mel's head. If he was the person who encrypted the messages, Len and his boffins could work till the crack o' doom and still not decipher them.

"Listen, Len. Gimme what you got. Anything is better than nothing."

"Okay, Mel, but what I got may not be much more than that."

"Then I'll take whatever it is."

"We really scratched our heads over these messages, Mel. Honest! Maybe if we had more time—"

"Forget it, Lennie. I ain't got no more time."

"Okay. From all these messages you handed us, we think we pulled out two important numerical sequences. We know how Mr. Lindbergh feels about the *Times*, but we got nothin' from it. Whatever's encoded in that paper is locked up tight as a bank vault after business hours. On the other hand, it looks like whoever encoded the messages from the more recent issues of the *Tribune* may have slipped up."

"Whaddaya mean 'slipped up', Lennie?"

"What I mean is that the encoder, probably by mistake, repeated two different sequences on different days. That's gotta be important, but we're still not sure what it means. Are you taking all this down?"

"Yes, go on, Lennie, go on," said Purvis, on the edge of his chair.

"The first sequence is 424671. You got that?"

"Yeah. 424671."

"And we're not too sure about the six. Could be standing in for somethin' else. Like a letter."

"What about the second sequence."

"That's 402672. Got it?"

"Yeah. You have the same problem with the number six?"

"Same problem. Both sixes probably represent the same letter, but we're not sure what letter it is. Well, there's only twenty-six or so to choose from, I guess."

Purvis thought, this was New York City they were talking about. The number six could stand for either east or west, E or W. That substitution would convert the sets of numbers into addresses.

"Lennie, you and your boys are fuckin' geniuses!" he shouted. "I'm gonna take you all out for a steak dinner when this is over. I promise!"

"Glad we could help, Mel. Put in a good word for us to the boss, okay?"

"You got it, Len. Thanks again."

Purvis hung up the phone, and just as quickly picked it up.

"Operator! Get me Fred Trump, the Mayor of New York. And hurry!"

Fred Trump was sound asleep when the telephone operator at the Gracie Mansion switchboard picked up the phone and explained that His Honor had left strict instructions not to be disturbed.

"I don't give a damn about his instructions! Wake the sonuvabitch or he'll have to answer to the president!"

Moments later, a groggy Fred Trump was on the other end of the line.

"Purvis, if this isn't the most important thing since the hole in the toilet seat, I'll have your ass for waking me up in the middle of the night!"

"Aw, crap, listen to someone for a change, Mr. Mayor. I got a hunch the scientists are moving tonight."

"Who?"

"The scientists! You know, the physicists. Fermi, Einstein, von Neumann, all those geniuses who disappeared. I think I know where they are! You and me, we can bag the whole lot of 'em! And when we do, you'll be Lindbergh's golden boy again."

Trump bolted upright in bed. Lindbergh was a wounded president, but being on the inside with a proven winner was better than the political wilderness where he himself was heading.

"Gimme the story, Purvis. I'm listening."

Trump climbed out of bed and began to dress himself.

"The Resistance has been planting coded messages at the bottom left of the first page of the *Times*, and then after you shut that rag down, the *Herald Tribune*. The screwballs in the cryptography section of the Bureau cracked a small but critical piece of the code. The scientists are at either 424 E. or W. 71st Street, or at 402 E. or W. 72nd Street. So get your police commissioner on the phone, and tell him to get his ass out of bed!"

"Thanks, Mel!" he crowed. "Sweet, holy Jesus! I'm all over it. I owe you a big one for this. Lindbergh's gonna crow when we get these guys. This'll be all over the papers! Maybe the public will forget about the fight with his wife—that ungrateful bitch!"

Moments later, with Police Commissioner Patrick F. X. O'Sullivan in the lead car, the New York City police, with sirens blaring, made a beeline through the dark, deserted streets. Everyone headed for the addresses Purvis had provided.

At 424 E. 71st Street, four of Lepke Buchalter's fully armed associates had arrived. Two young thugs sat in the parlor enjoying the brownstone's stock of scotch and bourbon. The drinks had been provided for the scientists, but none of them had touched the stuff. The other two hoodlums stood outside the brownstone guarding the ramshackle bus Leo had hired to transport the group downtown to the Fulton Fish Market and the *Cinco de Mayo*.

Joey Falcone also arrived after making the long trip in from Canarsie to say farewell to Julia. They parted with mutual hopes of seeing each other again soon.

"Don' worry about Guido and Silvia, Jewels. They're all right. They know where you're going and they understand your decision. Mamma and Papa also know how to keep a secret."

"All right, everyone!" called out Leo. "We're all going down to the bus, and we're gonna do it in absolute silence! And no lit cigarettes, either, so put 'em out now! We want to draw as little attention as possible. Set your watches! It's 3... 2... 1... one o'clock in the morning! Teller, you take the lead and go straight to the back of the bus. You'll be less trouble that way. Professor Einstein, please bring up the rear. Everyone else, grab your bags and form a line! Up the stairs if necessary!"

The physicists grumbled but did as Leo directed. Out of the brownstone and down the front stairs they marched in silence, and on into the bus.

Sid and Julia were in the middle of the line. Joey Falcone embraced his sister one last time while Vince Mangano and his niece, now reconciled, hugged each other. Then Sid and Julia, the scientists behind them, stepped out into the warm New York summer night, onto E. 71st St., and up the stairs into the bus.

The driver revved up the engine and closed the door. The engine coughed and gurgled as the bus juddered west along 71st Street, caught a green light at 1st Avenue, and hung a left at 2nd Avenue for the trip downtown. As far as anyone on that bus was concerned, their departure was uneventful.

Back on E. 71st Street, both of Lepke's soldiers had retreated into the brownstone after the scientists had departed.

"Okay, boys!" said Lepke. "You can put away the heat. They're off ta da Fish Market! Jeez, I woulda' liked ta' go wid 'em!"

"Don' press it, Lepke!" warned Vince Mangano. "The Westies are bad actors. Remember, dey whacked Tony Ficcini a few mont's ago."

"Ahh, Ficcini was a jerk. He deserved to get whacked. Anyway, fuggedaboudit! Let's all have a drink to da memory of Tony Ficcini, a real jerk!"

Lepke filled everyone's snifter with Courvoisier cognac.

"To Tony!" he proclaimed.

"To Tony," replied the hoodlums in unison.

But no one in that room ever got to enjoy a sip of that cognac.

With a battering ram that splintered the wood, the police broke down the outside door of 424 E. 71st and came pouring into the brownstone before anyone inside could react. Lepke, the Mangano brothers, and Joey Falcone were quickly surrounded, rifles and pistols pointing at their heads. There was only one thing to do.

"We surrender!" shouted Lepke, putting down his drink and raising his hands. With a show of hands, the other mob soldiers also meekly gave up.

Commissioner O'Sullivan stomped into the room, like a T-Rex catching the odor of a new meal.

"Well, boys, what bad bastards do we have here?" he asked.

"Hey! We was havin' a party," said Lepke. "Me 'n' some o' my friends. Anyt'ing illegal 'bout dat?"

O'Sullivan grabbed Lepke's cognac snifter and slowly poured the contents over the mobster's shoes.

"Party's over, Jew boy. Where in fuck are they?"

"Where are who?"

"Don't waste my time. The scientists, Lepke! You know where they are, and now you're gonna tell me!"

"Honest, officer, I ain't got no idea who ya talkin' about. Dere ain't no scientists around here. Most o' dese guys never graduated the sixt' grade!"

O'Sullivan issued orders. "Ryan, Matthews, check the rest of the house, and then go back to your precinct. Grady, Flanagan, Joyce, and Boyle, take a squad car and go looking for 'em. They can't be far. Finn, Gorman, and Shaughnessey—you stay here with me. Lepke and the rest of you gobshites, form a line from left to right, face to the door! And keep your fuckin' hands up!"

The mobsters and Joey Falcone did as they were told. The three cops formed a parallel line in the parlor, behind them.

O'Sullivan nodded his head.

No one knew precisely what happened next. But later that morning, the bodies of seven dead Mafiosi, all shot in the back of the head, execution style, were found on the floor of the parlor in the brownstone at 424 E. 71st Street.

In the face of falling popularity that dropped precipitously after the departure of Ann Morrow Lindbergh from the White House, the Lindbergh administration, under intense political and legal pressure, relented and allowed the *New York Times* to resume publishing.

Mayor Fred Trump wasn't pleased by the decision.

"It makes you look weak," he told the president in a phone conversation the next morning. "It will be viewed as an apology by your enemies. I think you are receiving very poor advice, Mr. President."

"No poorer than yours has been," answered Lindbergh, who abruptly hung up.

Later that afternoon, the *Times* issued an abbreviated edition, its first in months.

The New York Times, September 13, 1941
[Above the crease]

MASSACRE ON E. 71ST STREET

By C. Rex Perry

In the wee hours of the morning, gunmen invaded a mob gathering at 424 E. 71st Street on Manhattan's chic Upper East Side, slaughtering seven men in cold blood. All of the slain were believed to be associated with one or more of the great crime families of New York.

Among the dead were Louis "Lepke" Buchalter, mob overlord of the needle trades of New York, and reputed Chairman of the Board of Murder, Inc. This organization is the murder-for-hire enforcement arm of the sinister New York Cosa Nostra. Along with Buchalter, the dead included the brothers Vincenzo and Philip Mangano, prominent narcotics traffickers working out of Canarsie, Brooklyn, and four soldiers who may have belonged to their gang.

The Upper East Side property at 424 E. 71st is registered under the name John D. Rockefeller, Jr. When asked for a comment, a spokesman for Mr. Rockefeller said that "he owns many properties in New York and has no idea whatsoever how these hoodlums gained access to this vacant brownstone, nor why men of such unsavory character would be using it for their drunken carousals."

When questioned, neighborhood residents recall seeing armed men guarding the rear door of the brownstone, which opens into a courtyard between E. 71st Street and the back entrances of the apartment buildings on E. 72nd Street Otherwise, they report no suspicious activity, with the exception of a large number of deliveries to the adjoining house over the past several weeks.

Police Commissioner Patrick F. X. O'Sullivan explained, "It was a horrible thing to see, truly horrible. Yes, they were Mafiosi, and hardened criminals, too. But I swear to you, my men were almost in tears. Seven people gunned down in such a hideous way. Words can hardly describe the scene, and I've seen many of them."

When asked who could have committed such a heinous act, O'Sullivan commented, "At this time, it's still early in the investigation, so we're not certain. But from the way these men were killed—assassinated, I'd prefer to say—our lead suspects are the Westies."

He went on to identify the Westies as a gang of Irish criminals from the Hell's Kitchen area of West Manhattan, who are known to be most active in the West 40s between 8th and 12th Avenues, not far from the Theater District. "I shouldn't want to insult my own Irish brothers," said O'Sullivan, "but the Westies are some of the most violent men in New York. The New York City Police have information they're trying to break out of Hell's Kitchen and muscle into areas controlled by the Italian Mob. The assassination of mob leaders may provoke an upswing in gang violence as the mob seeks revenge for their fallen members."

According to O'Sullivan, the investigation is progressing well, with indictments expected soon. In the meantime, extra patrols have been extended into Hell's Kitchen to protect residents in case gang gunfights break out.

CHAPTER 27

St. Louis, Missouri
October 1, 1941

T wo men were sitting at a bar at St. Louis' Union Station, located just off the Great Hall. Both were in their early twenties. One had an almost empty bottle of whiskey and a shot glass in front of him. The other was a reporter for the local newspaper, the *St. Louis Post-Dispatch*. The man with the whiskey bottle was a traveler. He wore rumpled clothes, hadn't shaved in three days, and was about to polish off the bottle. He'd also become thoroughly blottoed.

The reporter, twenty minutes away from meeting a colleague coming in from Chicago on the train, was perusing the day's edition of his newspaper. The traveler was also interested in the latest news. Rudely, he began to read over the reporter's shoulder.

"Hello, friend," said the reporter with typical Midwestern friendliness. "Where ya off to?"

The traveler was inebriated and slurring his speech. "Out West. Far out West."

"Oh, that's nice. And where ya comin' from?"

"New York. Had to get outta' town."

The reporter sensed a story. "Sounds interesting. Who are ya running from? The mob? A jealous husband?"

"Jealous husband? Say, stranger, that's a good one! I wish. No, I'm runnin' from the cops. Now don' get the wrong idea or nothin'. Didn't commit a crime, or step on someone's toes. Nothin' like that. Nope, not me."

The reporter managed not to roll his eyes. "Remember a few days ago?" asked the traveler. "A headline in the *New York Times* about a massacre on E. 71st Street?"

"Yeah. As a matter of fact, I do. It was the lead story in the first issue of the *Times* in months. The *Post-Dispatch* carried the entire piece."

"Well, I'm gonna tell you a lil' secret, bud. I... me... I survived that massacre. That's why the cops are after me."

The reporter's interest was aroused. "Mind if I take some notes?" He pulled out a small pad and pencil from his shirt pocket. "What's your name, if I may ask?"

"You may not. That's my secret."

"The cops are after you because you're a witness?"

"Yup."

"Then why not give yourself up and tell your story?"

"Did you read that the cops blamed the massacre on an Irish gang called the Westies? Eh?"

"Of course..."

"Wasn't them at all. It was the cops who did it. Shot everyone down in cold blood. But not me. I survived."

"And how did you do that?" asked the reporter skeptically.

"I was standing next to Vince Mangano. Before I got shot, he fell on top of me. Saved my life. The police commissioner, what's his name...?"

"O'Sullivan, I think."

"Yeah, that's right. O'Sullivan. He stood over the bodies, still bleedin' and everythin', and said: 'Just like Capone on St. Valentine's Day back in '29. Piece o' cake, boys. Ha! That ole' bastard Trump can't accuse me of being indecisive! Now let's get outta' here. You all know what to say.'"

"And you were lying on the floor, under Vince Mangano," said the reporter as he took penciled notes on the drunken traveler's story.

"That's right. Scared shitless. But I didn't make a move, 'cause if I did, I would've been next. Even when I got kicked in the head. See?" The traveler pulled back the hair on his upper right temple to reveal an angry-looking gash.

"Jeez, you better get medical attention for that, my friend. It may be infected!"

"Can't! Don't wanna miss my train!" The traveler rose, deposited money on the table, and grabbed his bag.

"Wait! Before you go. What's your name? Your story has the ring of truth to it, my friend, but it'll sell better with a name attached."

The traveler paused and thought for a moment. In a short time, he'd be far across the Mississippi and in a place the New York City cops would never find him.

"It's Joey. Joey Falcone. The cops killed my uncles, Vince and Phil Mangano, and all the others. Vince and Phil and Lepke Buchalter weren't... weren't good men. But they didn't deserve to be shot in the head by a gang of angry cops acting for a batshit crazy mayor. So, publish that. I dare you!" He wiped his hand across his mouth and then stumbled away.

Los Alamos, New Mexico
October 12, 1941

The morning on the mesa, the site of the Los Alamos Ranching School, dawned cool and crisp. A mild breeze crept down from the mountains to the north, causing the leaves of hundreds of cottonwood trees, for which the site was originally named in Spanish, to rustle slightly in the wind.

In the past forty-eight hours, the Los Alamos Ranching School had become a beehive of human activity. For after a journey of a month, and one delay after another, the gaggle of scientists and their wives who had departed the New York docks on the Cinco de Mayo had finally arrived.

"Like a latter-day Moses leading the Israelites to the Promised Land," said Hans Bethe to Leo Szilard, clapping him on the back.

"This is the place! Ugh!" said Edward Teller sarcastically, mocking Brigham Young's proclamation to the migrating Mormons as—after much hardship—they reached the valley of the Great Salt Lake.

Accommodations had been hastily constructed for the influx of people. In addition to the scientists from the eastern half of the country, others, such as J. Robert Oppenheimer, were expected within the next few days from the universities of the West. And as Sid soon discovered, Western industrialists such as Henry Kaiser, others representing mining interests, agents of the Rockefellers, and even the occasional Texas oilman—all committed members of the Resistance—had gathered together at Los Alamos.

This was not a site one simply dropped in on and abandoned after a day or two. If you landed at Los Alamos, you were there for as long as it took. Sid was both pleased and astonished that Eleanor Roosevelt had also made the long trip. Lindbergh and Trump feared and hated her more than any other woman alive. Others considered her the mother of the nation, a beacon of hope and human decency in evil times.

Enrico Fermi and Sid bumped into each other in the men's dormitory. "So, is time to get to work, no?" said Fermi.

"Do we have sufficient graphite to construct the pile?"

"More than enough. I'm impressed-a with the work so far. I wouldn't have believed there was so much-a graphite in the entire world! I tell you, Sid. The more I see of your country, the more astonishing it is! Such great wealth! So many resources! If used properly against them, the Nazis don't have a chance!"

"From your lips to God's ears Enrico, as they say where Julia and I come from. You're right. What we lack now in America is the political will. Too many people don't have the insight to understand how Lindbergh is damaging the nation. They express their anger by voting for despots like our president who feed them what they want to hear! Truth, falsehood, the fact that others might be hurt... none of it makes any difference to them."

"You put your finger on it precisely, Sid. From a scientific viewpoint, their logic is flawed. The truth is—there are no 'others.' There is only one common 'umanity.'"

"Except for Nazis."

"True. Because they have chosen to remove themselves from our common 'umanity. And so, we have a right to defend ourselves against them. But enough philosophy for today, Sid. It's time to get to work."

At approximately the same time Sid and Enrico were chatting, a bedraggled Joey Falcone, who'd made the two thousand-mile trip from New York, showed up at the gate of the chain link fence surrounding the Los Alamos community, clutching his bag.

Mickey Cohen, a young Los Angeles mobster on the rise, and a protégé of Bugsy Siegel, had sent two armed hoodlums at Siegel's request. They were standing guard at the Los Alamos gate as Joey approached them.

"Well, would ya look what da' wind just blew in," said one of the thugs, who finished his cigarette and flicked the still lit butt at Joey.

"Shaddup, shithead. I'm Joe Falcone, the new don of the Mangano family, nephew of Vince and Phil Mangano. Hello? Remember? The wiseguys who got shot in the head with Lepke Buchalter on E. 71st Street? I'm part of this whole Resistance operation. I've been running from New York for the past four weeks! So, let me in!"

"Sorry, Joe Falcone, if dat is your real name. No can do," said the other hoodlum. "No one comes in here widdout da' express permission of da' boss."

"Who is?" asked Joey.

"Oppenheimer. J. Robert Oppenheimer, to be precise."

"My sister, Julia Falcone, is on the inside. Bring her to the gate. With Oppenheimer, or better yet, Leo Szilard. You heard o' him?"

Cohen's men conferred. The hood who flicked the cigarette butt at Joey retreated to the interior of the site.

"Yeah, we heard o' dem all, so we believed what you was sayin'," said the hood who remained at the gate. "Anyway, ya sound like ya come from Noo Yawk. I know Vince Mangano and Phil Mangano, God rest deir souls, had a nephew. So, I am very sorry for your loss."

"Thanks," said Joey, who shared the details of how he'd escaped the massacre by the grace of God.

"Jeez. Yer one lucky sonuvabitch!"

"Yeah, unless the New York City cops ever get their hands on me."

By this time, Leo Szilard had appeared at the gate, with Julia behind him. "Joey!" she yelled, clapping her hands and jumping into the air. She had long since accepted her brother's role in the liquidation of her lover, I. Bernard Strauss, a traitor to the Resistance.

"Joey, oh my God, it's so great to see you! How did you ever get here? Oh, I was so worried about you after I heard about the massacre and about what had happened to Uncle Vince and Uncle Phil—but thank God, your name was never mentioned as one of the dead. I can't imagine how you escaped those awful Westies! C'mon, hurry, let him in! You gotta tell me everything! But first, some food, Joey. You must be starving!"

Leo gave the nod, and the gate was opened. With a pat on the back from Mickey Cohen's thugs and further expressions of condolence, Joey was admitted into Los Alamos. Julia fed him from canteen leftovers and led him to the dormitory. He slept for sixteen straight hours.

Under the direction of Enrico Fermi and Sid, the atomic pile grew taller by the day. In essence, the ten-foot-in-diameter pile was little more than blocks of graphite, about nine inches long and three inches wide, through which holes had been drilled in order to accommodate uranium oxide. The yellow, neutron-emitting powder had been packed into tin cans and soldered shut. Each layer of graphite containing the uranium oxide was completely surrounded by a layer of graphite containing no uranium. Wooden timbers surrounded the pile, now six feet in height, so the workers could move easily from one level to another.

Every man and woman on site, even Albert Einstein and the cranky Edward Teller, participated in the human chain delivering the blocks from the floor to the highest level of the pile.

"I'm doing my bit, like everyone else, to defeat ze Nazis," groaned Einstein, who labored for hours without a break.

"Aw, crap, not another graphite block," whined Teller, who worked at the top level fitting the blocks into the pile.

A complex set of equipment, including boron trifluoride neutron detectors designed by Leona Wood, a Resistance scientist, measured whether a sustained chain reaction of the type envisaged by Leo Szilard years ago on the streets of London was occurring. Twenty thousand graphite blocks and tons of uranium oxide had already been used in the pile's construction, but the detectors remained silent. No neutron flux meant no sustained chain reaction.

"So, Sid," asked Fermi, "what is it we do now?"

"*Lasciate ogni speranza, voi ch'intrate,* I guess, Enrico. Abandon all hope, ye who enter here."

"'Ey, forget about it, wiseguy. I know my Dante much-a better than you."

"Okay, let me do some calculations. How much more graphite we have?"

"Oh, I think about enough for a few more levels."

"How many bricks is that?"

"About twenty-five-a thousand, depending on the final-a pile geometry."

"And uranium?"

"Sufficient to fill all of the graphite-a blocks."

Sid scribbled on a handy scrap of paper. "I think we can just about make it with what we have on hand and achieve a critical mass. But I propose we take a break. It's been a long day for everyone."

Fermi agreed and called it quits for the day. Teller was the last one off the pile.

"Slave drivers. You're a bunch of slave drivers," he groused as he emerged from off the timbers, his hands and face black from graphite dust. "I'll never forgive you for this as long as I live, Enrico. Never."

"And I expect nothing less, Edward."

"Don't worry about Teller," said Leo, who was standing nearby. "He'll clean up well."

At thirty-five thousand blocks of graphite, the pile was more than ten feet in height. However, Leona Wood's neutron detectors remained silent. Even Albert Einstein and Hans Bethe were beginning to have doubts. But John von Neumann looked over Sid Peskin's calculations and agreed that, given the limitations of the detection system, the only option was to keep on building.

Several mornings later, when the pile was twelve feet tall and contained forty thousand graphite blocks, the word made its way around the community that a big-shot politician from somewhere in the Midwest was paying a visit to the site. No one was certain of his name. Few of the serious scientists cared what it was. Leo was tight-lipped, but reassured everyone that security would remain tight and that the politician, whoever he might be, was a strong Lindbergh opponent and would reveal none of the Resistance's secrets.

"I do not zink it advisable to trust ze word of a politician," warned Einstein.

"But we need politicians on our side," replied Leo. "Think about it, Albert. Lindbergh is deeply wounded by scandal and no longer has the moral authority to govern. The entire western half of the country, economically dependent on exports, is up in arms because of his appeasement of the Nazis. And the German naval base near Mazatlan is making our military leaders and many others believe the country is being surrounded. All this, and the violence in the streets, has been laid at Lindbergh's feet."

"*Ja, ja,* I agree with everyzing you zay, Leo. But can zis man, zis politician, truly be trusted? We don't even know where he's from or what his name is."

Leo shrugged. "Neither do I, Albert. We'll have to trust Robert Oppenheimer and the Omega, who I understand will also be arriving tomorrow."

"Hmm. I'd like to meet zis Omega fellow. Probably quite ze specimen. I zink he must be a genuine Zuper-*mensch*—not one of zose wretched Nazi imitators—mit X-ray vision to zee through walls, *und* zuper hearing *und* zuper strength—a hero who can also fly like a bird. The children read about him in *Action Comics,* you know."

Sid looked silently at Leo. They both had the same thought: It looks like old Albert has been taking a nip on the side outta the ole' *Action Comics* bottle.

"I wouldn't know, Albert," said Sid. "Never met the man."

"Me, neither," Leo chimed in. "And I only spoke to him once. He sounded human."

"*Ach,* I'm so disappointed. *Und* here I was still hoping for zome magic in zis terribly grim, ugly world."

By the next day, forty-four thousand graphite blocks had been layered on the pile, but the needles on the large, round neutron detectors still recorded no neutron flux.

"David," Enrico hollered to a graphite-covered worker. "Please, drill some more holes for us."

"Enrico, who is that man?" asked Sid. "I've seen him around, but I don't recognize him underneath all that graphite."

"'Oo? David? That's David Greenglass. He's a machinist here. Drills holes in graphite for the cause. David, he does-a good work. I think we'll keep him."

Greenglass. Sid had heard the name before but at that moment, couldn't place it. Unfortunately, by the time he remembered that Greenglass was Ethel Rosenberg's maiden name, and that David was her brother, it was far too late to create a fuss. But like his sister, David Greenglass was a dedicated, fanatic Communist and was also on Joe Stalin's payroll. The Resistance didn't know it, but it had embraced a viper whose poison was later to bring much grief to many.

"How much graphite we have left, Enrico?"

"Twenty-two 'undred-an' fifty. And not one-a more."

"Jeez, it would be embarrassing if the Omega and this big-shot politician turned up and the pile wasn't producing anything."

"Having doubts about your-a calculations, Sid?"

"Who, me? Enrico, this is a very confident El Sid you're talkin' to about now. Doubt is not a word in my vocabulary."

Fermi ignored him while focusing on the dials of the instruments attached to Leona Wood's boron trifluoride neutron detectors. The needle twitched for a second and jumped four millimeters from dead zero but just as quickly fell back to zero again, immobile.

"Sid! Did you see that? Detector number one! Neutrons Sid! Neutrons!"

Sid looked up at detector number one, but it was still registering nothing. "Hmm... I think you're hallucinating again, Enrico. All I see is a motionless detector."

"No! I know what I saw! That-a needle moved! Of that, I'm certain."

Together, the two watched the needle for the next ten minutes. Not even a twitch.

Fermi called out to Teller, who was at the top of the pile. "Edward! Throw another layer of graphite and uranium oxide on-a the pile, eh?" He turned to Sid. "We'll see who's hallucinating."

Teller's blackened face appeared at the top of the pile. "Throw on another level, goddamit, Fermi? How's about I throw one on your head!"

Sid pleaded with him. "Just do it, Edward. I mean on the pile! We think something's happening!"

Teller moaned. "Oh, so now I have to take orders from a child without even a Ph.D. to his name. Yet another insult to bear in humiliating silence!"

With each graphite-uranium oxide brick added by a reluctant Teller to the pile, the needle on the detector began to rise, first two and then four millimeters. Then, it increased spectacularly from four to eight and then from eight to sixteen millimeters above zero.

The neutron flux was becoming dangerous. "Edward, stop adding bricks!" shouted Fermi. "And get down from there fast!"

The pile had gone critical. More neutrons were being produced than were consumed. The control rods made out of cadmium, a rare, poisonous metal, were dropped by a pulley system into a different set of holes in the graphite blocks to stop the neutron flux. About a half a watt of power had been generated.

Leo Szilard's vision of the chain reaction, as demonstrated by the atomic pile designed by Fermi and Sid Peskin, was proven correct. Enrico and Sid embraced, laughing and smiling, each clapping the other on the back. They were joined by a filthy but happy Edward Teller, who made sure he blackened Fermi's clothes.

"I told you I'd never forgive you, Fermi. And now I bet you don't even care."

"Not a bit, Edward. The only thing-a that matters is the chain reaction—and we have achieved it 'ere at Los Alamos."

"And let's hope to God the Germans haven't, anywhere," said Sid.

"I think we can all say amen to that," answered Teller.

The pile produced power via spontaneous fission of the uranium atoms embedded in the graphite. Each time a uranium atom spontaneously cracked itself roughly in half, it emitted neutrons, subatomic particles with the mass of a proton but no charge. These emitted neutrons bombarded other uranium atoms, inducing them to undergo fission, and on and on, until one-half watt of power was produced by the pile. At that point, Fermi shut it down. The pile was not a weapon; it was not the atomic bomb that many in the Resistance felt would be America's answer to the Nazi menace. The bomb would come later, but as everyone knew, it would take a massive financial investment to build it. Some, including Fermi, had scientific doubts it could be done at all. But if the administration changed, then anything might be possible.

Word that the pile had gone critical raced around the site at the speed of light, which Einstein had once declared was impossible. Within moments, the room was filled with happy men and women. Some of them hadn't smiled in months, if not years. Someone found a bottle of champagne and a metal device to remove the cork. But it was Leo Szilard, the great visionary, who poured out the liquid into Dixie cups for the milling scientists.

"Your baby has been born, alive and well and kicking!" said a congratulatory Fermi.

"I'll have to contact Robert Oppenheimer as soon as I can," said Leo, who deflected most of the acclaim and credit onto others. "But he's entertaining politicos at the moment. We'll have something exciting to show them all tomorrow."

"Now you've tweaked my curiosity," said Sid, who'd been joined by Julia. "Do you know anything more about this great and powerful person who will be visiting us?"

"Do you mean the esteemed member of the Senate? No, nothing more. But that's more than you knew yesterday. And I have a strong suspicion you'll know even more tomorrow."

At eleven o'clock the next morning, Sid and Julia were tinkering with some of the graphite blocks hanging off the pile at jaunty angles, probably the result of having been knocked about by other blocks.

The two inspected the cadmium rods, looked for any additional damage to the pile, and walked down the floors of timbers to the bottom, which was slippery from graphite dust. There, with a broad smile on his face, was Jack Kennedy.

"Good morning, my friends," he said, holding a current Santa Fe newspaper. How he'd gotten hold of it was a mystery.

"There's good news today. First, the international story: The Russkies are making an orderly retreat into their enormous country. Hitler's Blitzkrieg tactics have failed to break their lines.

"And in the national news, I noticed it says here on page, ah... let me see... yes, here on page twenty-five, underneath the item about Miss Durman's prize-winning pig, that a team at the Los Alamos Ranch School has produced the world's first self-sustaining nuclear reaction!"

"Oh, cut it out," said Julia.

Kennedy folded back the paper to the first page. "But there's more. Anne Lindbergh has formally filed for divorce, citing adultery as the grounds."

"That lady has balls, I have to give her credit," said Julia.

Sid took a few steps backward to view the pile. The monster was quiet, but soon enough, the cadmium rods would be removed, and the neutron flux would commence again. He almost backed into a man in late middle age who wore a broad-brimmed fedora and a gray suit.

"Excuse me," said Sid, who didn't recognize him.

"No, excuse me! I'm sorry. Harry S. Truman, Democrat, Senator from the great state of Missouri. Pleased to meet you! Are you one of the folks that built this behemoth? If you are, then I wanna shake your hand! My God, this is a marvelous invention! Just don't ask me how it works or what it's supposed to do."

Sid shook the meaty hand Truman offered.

"Oh. You must be the big-shot… er, I mean, the politician who's here for a visit."

"Well, I am a politician, and I am visiting, so I suppose that's me." Truman took several steps forward and introduced himself to Julia and Jack Kennedy. "Say, you're Joe Kennedy's son, aren't you? I know your old man. Don't mean to cause offense, but I think he's got his head stuck so far up his ass, he's coming out his own mouth. When I'm president, he'll be out of a government job. You can count on it."

"Well, I uh… have the same opinion of my father much of the time, Mr. Truman. But I'd no idea you'll be our next president."

"Oh, you can count on it, Mr. Kennedy. The incumbent, Mr. Lindbergh, is a lame duck. No one in Missouri is gonna' vote for a philandering bastard with a second family, and I suppose most folks from other states feel the same. Forty-four is gonna' be a Democrat year, and I'm gonna' ride the wave right into the White House and clean up the mess Lindbergh's made. And at the same time, beat the livin' bejesus outta' those goddamned Germans!"

Sid, Julia and Jack Kennedy applauded.

"I wish you the very best, Mr. President-to-be. And when you get to Washington, remember J. Edgar Hoover isn't your friend."

"I already know that. But he's got impeccable anti-Communist credentials. We'll need experienced folks like that when we win the coming war against the Germans. Then it's gonna be the Russians who'll be giving us trouble."

Out of the corner of his eye, Sid caught a glimpse of David Greenglass. "Oh, Mr. Truman," he asked, seeing the Missouri Senator begin to pull away. "Do you have just one more moment?"

"For a young man who's done as much for his country as you, I have all the time you want. What's on your mind, my friend?"

"I... I understand you've recently spent time with the person we know as the Omega."

Jack Kennedy and Julia gathered around Sid and Truman. Any information that could be gleaned about the Omega provided great fodder for gossip.

"I certainly did, young man. Rode in from Santa Fe and spent all day yesterday with him and Oppenheimer."

"So he's here? At Los Alamos?"

"Sure is. I saw him a half hour ago, right here, looking at this great big beautiful atomic pile you folks built for us."

"Do you know where he is now? I'd like to meet him."

Truman pondered the question. "Well, the last I saw of him, he was walking with Oppenheimer over to the men's room. I'd say that's where most of us do our clearest thinking. After that, they ducked into one of those offices on the long corridor down thatta' way."

Truman pointed to the far corner of the room, where a hall led to the only facilities in the building, one toilet for each gender. For the women, the wait time could be excruciating.

"Thank you, Mr. Truman. I'm gonna' take a look. I've wanted to meet the Omega for a long time—and to give him a piece of my mind."

"Be, ah... careful, Sid," warned Jack Kennedy. "The Omega is a special person. He might have X-ray vision or some other superhero power."

"Thanks for reminding me, Jack, but don't worry. I think I can take 'im."

Kennedy shook his head. "Okay, Sid. But it's your funeral."

Sid walked across the room and into the corridor, flanked by rooms repurposed as meeting spaces containing desks, chairs, and blackboards. All the newly painted doors to these whitewashed rooms were wide open, except for an office door close to the men's room, which was tightly closed. Sid listened at the door but couldn't pick up the traces of any conversations.

Summoning up his courage, he rapped softly three times on the door. No one answered. His next three knocks were sharper and louder.

"Come in!" said a voice Sid didn't recognize.

He entered the room. Facing him and sitting at a wood-and-chrome steel desk was the new chief of Los Alamos, Professor J. Robert Oppenheimer of the University of California at Berkeley.

"Sid!" said Oppenheimer. "Good morning and congratulations to you and Enrico and the rest of the team! I understand the pile has produced a self-sustaining chain reaction! Marvelous! Please, come in and take a seat!" Oppenheimer pointed to a chair next to his desk.

Sitting on the other side of the desk from Oppenheimer, with his back toward Sid, was a man of average height who was wearing a black fedora and a gray overcoat on this cool morning. Peskin detected something familiar in this man's posture, the way he positioned his body and how he held his head. But he doubted he'd ever made his acquaintance.

It was when he came around the desk to Oppenheimer's side that he received the greatest shock of his life.

"Dad!" he yelled, wide-eyed and hyperventilating. "What...?" he gasped, collapsing into a chair. "What in God's name are you doing here? Oh, my God, this can't be real! But... but, it's the only damn explanation possible! Why didn't I see it earlier? Jesus Christ, now it makes sense! My father, the soft, weak, and always ineffectual Sam Peskin is the Omega, the *capo di tutti capi*, the leader of the Resistance! No wonder you were always looking at the goddamn newspaper—messages were printed on the first page in code! And you had to maintain an open phone line as much of the time as possible in case of emergency! How you ever kept this from Mom, I just can't imagine... Does Mom know?"

Sam Peskin removed his fedora and laid it on Oppenheimer's desk. "She does now," said Sam, who turned to face Sid. "You should have seen her. I'm surprised I survived. But if it makes you feel any better, Sid my son, no one else ever figured out it was me, either. Now c'mon and give your tired old father a hug. We've been apart for too long."

But Sid was having none of it. Instead of affection, a wave of anger overcame him. "You tricked me, Sam Peskin! You placed me in terrible danger without my knowledge, without my consent, without ever saying a word to me. I've been living in the same apartment side by side with you for over twenty years, and you couldn't trust me enough to even ask my opinion. That's painful to me, Dad, very painful—God, I feel like someone just punched me in the chest. I never would have deceived you like you deceived me!"

Sam shook his head. "Think about it for a moment, Sid. You were never really in any danger. Everyone you met on your journey here was working for the Resistance—to all intents and purposes, for me. In fact, I'd say you were never in any danger at all. Think about what our people are suffering in Germany and Eastern Europe before you say how much you've suffered."

"But what you did was wrong, Dad. Don't you see that? You used me for your own purposes, and you now expect me to forget about it as if it never happened! Damn right, I'm pissed off, and I don't think I want to deal with any more bullshit right now!"

Sid stomped out of the room, almost knocking over Leo Szilard, who was arriving for his meeting with the Omega.

"Whoa, young man," he said, grabbing Sid by the arm. "Slow down. I've never seen you this angry. For God's sakes, what the hell's set your hair on fire?"

Still beside himself, Sid told Leo about his father's betrayal.

Leo sympathized. But he needed Sid to remain calm, especially in front of Truman and the other Los Alamos staff. "Technically, my friend," he said, "perhaps you're right. But I guarantee everything he did was to protect you; to get you out of town ahead of Lindbergh's goons. Your father and others, including your mother, God bless her, could envisage a situation in which physicists were rounded up and forced to work for our government. The atomic secrets would then have been passed on to the Nazis. That could not be allowed to happen. I'm sure you'll agree."

Even through his rage, Sid remained rational enough to grasp Leo's point. His anger slowly began to dissipate.

"My father, the Omega?" he said as he shook his head in disbelief. "It seems impossible. But so many impossible things have happened in this country over the last six months... why not one more?"

As upset as he was, it was difficult for Sid to remain white hot with anger for long with his beloved father. But only time, a great deal of it, would diminish his astonishment that Sam Peskin had led a double life under everyone's noses. It seemed so completely out of character for the man—at least for the character Sid thought he knew, but perhaps really didn't.

After more frank discussion with Leo, Sid felt ready to see his father again.

"Sid," said Sam. "I'm glad you decided to return. I want you to know I understand how you feel, and to explain I did it for you."

"I know, Dad. Leo explained everything to me. It's going to take me some time, maybe a lot of time, but I'll be okay. So now I know the why and I have to ask you— how the hell did you do it?"

"Oh, it was easier than it appears now. I approached several union activists who had similar thoughts. Unfortunately, they were Communists. Too interested in theory and useless for much in the way of practical work. Julius Rosenberg was an exception, as you know. But it was through Communist contacts I eventually hooked up with Leo Szilard. And the rest, as they say, is history—and the dogged work of Leo and many others.

"But we can talk more about all these things later, Sid. I just want to tell you how proud I am of the work you've done. Leo here thinks the world of you. As do Enrico Fermi, and Hans Bethe. And Albert Einstein, too. They all tell me you've done important work in atomic physics—and also demonstrated true leadership in dealing with the very difficult personalities here, like Edward Teller. I'm so proud of you, son."

"Sid's discoveries, combined with those of Fermi, Bethe, Teller, and everyone else at Los Alamos will help save Western civilization from the most dangerous menace in its history," said Oppenheimer. "These contributions will put us years ahead of the Germans in the race for the 'A-bomb,' a race they must never win.

"But we haven't won the race yet, not by a long shot. It will take a massive effort, scientific, political, and financial, to build a working weapon, in addition to great insight as to the best way to use it against the Germans."

"I suppose we can hope," said Sid, "that a weapon as terrible as an atomic bomb will never have to be used at all. That other ways will be found to defeat the Nazis."

"I think you've hit the dilemma on the head squarely, Sid," said Oppenheimer. "We must have the device, if it can be built, before the Germans. But hopefully, we will never have to use it."

"How have Mom and Benny been, Dad? God, I miss them both. It must almost be time for Benny to start playing in the World Series of West Bronx stickball. I hope he has a fresh, new broom handle."

"Benny wants you back home more than anything. And your mother even more than Benny. But she understands you're playing a historical role and in a theater much greater than the Loew's Paradise on the Grand Concourse and 187th St. But I had a devil of a time convincing her, Sid. You're still her little boy, of course, and that counts for something."

Julia, followed by Harry Truman and Jack Kennedy, entered the room.

"Sid?" Julia asked in wide-eyed stupefaction. "Is this who it looks like? Christ, I'm either dreaming or hallucinating. Sam Peskin? Really? Maybe it was the mushrooms at last night's dinner. Sid, your father is he... is he...?"

Sid nodded. Julia, stunned, sat in a chair near Sam.

"Well, I'm... ah, very pleased to meet you again, Mr. Peskin," said Jack Kennedy. The two chuckled and shook hands.

"This is a wonderful family reunion," interrupted an irritated Oppenheimer, "but I'm afraid there's work to do today. Sid, we're all looking forward to a demonstration of the activity of the pile."

"It's a finicky creature. Like some women I know."

"Sid!" said Julia.

"I was thinking of my mother, sweetheart. They both can be difficult, but they get the job done."

"Before the demonstration, a moment with both of you gentlemen, please," said Kennedy to Sam and Oppenheimer. "No need for anyone to leave. We've been through so much together.

"Gentlemen, we discussed the threat to the Resistance still posed by J. Edgar Hoover and my former colleague Melvin Purvis. Purvis will still be out there until Hoover calls him off. My concern is that there are so many people privy to our secrets, leakage is unavoidable. It's almost certain Purvis will find Los Alamos in another month or two at most. What, ah... happens then?"

"It's my job to worry about that," said Truman. "New Mexico Senators Dennis

Chavez and Carl Hatch are both good friends of mine. As is Governor Miles. They're all Democrats and detest Lindbergh and his Nazi supporters. The New Mexico National Guard will protect you."

"But what if Lindbergh federalizes the Guard?"

"That's a good question, Jack, but I doubt he'll do it—or much of anything in the near future, if ever. He's a badly wounded president—not that I feel sorry for the bastard, he brought it on himself—but a divorcing bigamist occupying the highest office in the land is no one's idea of how a president ought to behave. George Marshall, Douglas McArthur, Ike Eisenhower, other military men, they're ready to put him up against the wall. He's a danger to national security, they tell me. He may also be a traitor, selling us out to the Germans. Hell, even my Republican colleagues can't look away, though God knows, they try. Lindbergh no longer has the moral authority to govern. And he's not likely to pick a fight with a Congress growing daily more personally antipathetic to him and frightened by his policies."

"You're telling us we should feel perfectly safe sleeping in our beds at night?" asked Kennedy.

"At the moment, Los Alamos may be the safest and most secure place in the world."

Julia and Sid hung around at the canteen until eleven p.m., when it closed.

"This business of not being able to sleep in the same bed has become tiresome," Julia complained. "I'm not sure how much more of it I can take."

"How do you think I'm feeling about now? I have anatomical considerations. Besides, I want to tear off your clothes."

"We'll have to find a way, Sid... I know! We'll lead a revolt against the Resistance. We'll be the Resistance Resistors!"

Sid laughed. "At least wait until I get over my shock at discovering my own father was the head of the entire organization."

"You really had no idea?"

"Julia, I'd swear to you on a stack of Bibles I had no idea. The thought never occurred to me. Don't get me wrong—I love my father. But he never seemed the slightest bit ambitious. To me, he always appeared content with the world as it was—it might not have been to his liking, but he accepted things as they came. I still find it difficult to believe he was the great mastermind. But now I know why he was always looking at his newspapers.

"And by the way, Julia; I don't think I ever gave you my formal condolences on the loss of your uncles. In their own perverse ways, they also contributed to the Resistance."

"I'm not sure we could have succeeded without them, bless their little hearts—in hell. Terrible men used for a terrible purpose. The world is better off without them, even though they were my flesh and blood. Ditto for Lepke Buchalter, a beast that sat like a giant octopus over New York's working men, squeezing their blood out. I hope his fate is to end up in Dante's first circle, or whatever pit Jewish people reserve for their monsters."

They kissed, first lightly, tenderly, and then with the passion of youth as she opened her lips to admit his tongue. But she pushed him back quickly because, as they both knew, there could be no more fun tonight.

"Good night, my Sid," said Julia as they parted. "And may none of your dreams be about nuclear chain reactions and atomic piles."

"And good night to you, too, my princess. Sleep knowing you are in the safest and most secure place in the world!"

They parted, each walking to his or her gender-appropriate dormitory.

But in a dark shadow of the canteen, David Greenglass the Communist machinist, sat unseen by Sid and Julia. And while the two were canoodling, Greenglass was listening, looking and waiting, and planning for the future. The next morning, he would write a letter to his sister, Ethel, with coded details about the atomic pile. That letter would be passed to Jacob Golos, the KGB's man in New York.

CHAPTER 28

One month after the atomic pile became operational, a consortium of Democratic and Republican leaders of the House and Senate, and military leaders represented by George Marshall, Army Chief of Staff, descended on the Oval Office. President Charles A. Lindbergh was told he had lost all credibility with the public because of his bigamy. His only option was to resign in favor of his vice president, Robert A. Taft.

For all the threatening talk and bluster he employed effectively on campaign, Lindbergh went quietly. He protested to the end that it was a conspiracy of Jews that had done him in and vowed to spend the remainder of his life playing golf at a resort in Florida.

Fred Trump didn't fare well, either. A special recall election was held in New York City in early 1942 as a referendum on his time in office. He lost badly. Deep in debt due to his unwise speculations, and unable to rely on graft to supplement his income, he was forced to take any employment he could find to support his wife's expensive tastes. At the time, most jobs were war-related, but Fred was so notorious, no one was interested in hiring him. An old contact procured him employment in the kitchen of the Brooklyn Navy Yard.

His co-workers were predominately African-Americans and Hispanics, and every other day he, Fred Trump, was required to vigorously sweep and then mop the floor of the spacious dining room.

Patrick F. X. O'Sullivan remained New York Commissioner of Police. The story he concocted about the Westies went unchallenged, except by the Westies, who passionately argued their innocence. There was also a small article in the St. Louis *Post-Dispatch* claiming cops were the killers. That article also went largely unnoticed.

But curiously, the Italian mob undertook no act of revenge against the Irish mob for their crime. Three Westies were eventually indicted by a grand jury for the murders, but were later released for lack of evidence. No one was ever convicted, and within a few years, the country had moved on, and the case went cold.

The Germans were uninterested in Lindbergh and Trump and soon found they had misjudged Taft. It was true he had formerly been an isolationist and an appeaser, but Taft was a professional politician of long duration with many good friends on both sides of the aisle. More importantly, he understood governance and how to work the system, which he knew was through compromise rather than confrontation. Taft was also acutely aware the mood in the country had changed because of its experience with Lindbergh's blinkered ideology. He changed with it.

One of the first measures of Taft's administration was to reinstate the draft.

"We'll have a million-man army within six months!" he announced. "And a two million-man army within the year!"

The government's procurement services were instructed to let contracts for weapons of war as the American economy was forced from a consumer to a war footing. Tanks rolled off assembly lines that formerly produced luxury cars, and aircraft factories produced fighters and bombers rather than passenger craft. Food, drugs, and trucks were dispatched to the totalitarian Soviet Union, the great new American ally.

"The puissance of our great southern neighbor, the United States, has gratefully and at long last awakened from its lengthy slumber," proclaimed Winston Churchill, who was invited to speak to a joint session of Congress. "The people of this mighty nation and the products of its farms and factories will give the Nazi Empire a blow from which it will never recover! Together we, the free peoples of the world, will march to victory over hatred, over bigotry, and with abiding respect for each and every member of the human family!"

The New York Times, January 10, 1942
[Above the crease.]

NAZIS EVACUATE BRITAIN

By W. Laird McDermott

In an action that has stunned the world, the Germans appear to be evacuating one of their most recent conquests: the Kingdom of Great Britain. Using any method of transport available, including their own battleships and destroyers, and purloining whatever remained of the British pleasure sailing fleet, German troops of the occupation have been embarking from all the Channel ports and heading for France.

This unprecedented move by the Nazis comes at a time when they are increasingly bogged down in their titanic struggle with the Soviet Union. At the moment, the Soviets have held the Germans outside Moscow and are beginning to push them back. Unlike the Russians, the Germans are not prepared for a winter war, and as the weather cooled this autumn, they began to suffer severely.

Accepted military strategy dictated that the Germans retreat to shorten their lines, but the *Führer* refused to consider it. Casualties have been immense on both sides, but the Russians have far greater reserves of manpower, hence the need for the Germans to withdraw from Britain to focus on the Eastern Front. The Royal Navy, which will carry the Royal Family and Prime Minister Winston Churchill, is laying plans for a joyous homecoming to the newly liberated island.

"It's a great day for freedom," said President Taft. "The British people have been through hell. They have felt the sharp teeth of tyranny and oppression and have prevailed. The struggle before us is still long and arduous, but it is certain that they, and we Americans, too, will prevail over hatred and intolerance, and restore human dignity to this blighted earth, and to all its oppressed peoples!"

And the others...

Albert Speer lived through the war to later be convicted of crimes against humanity at Nuremberg and serve twenty years in Spandau prison. He never killed anyone but was complicit in the deaths of millions.

Hans Bethe and Enrico Fermi went on to win Nobel Prizes after the war. Edward Teller became the father of the American hydrogen bomb and gave testimony against J. Robert Oppenheimer during the latter's post-war security clearance hearing. He remained a controversial figure until the end of his long life in 2003.

After failing to find the scientists before they escaped from Manhattan, Melvin Purvis retired for the second time from the FBI before—so rumor had it—J. Edgar Hoover could fire him.

Joey Falcone and John F. Kennedy were declared non-essential workers at Los Alamos. Joey was drafted, sent with his army unit to what remained of England after the Germans departed, and was in the first attack wave on Omaha Beach on D-Day. It was the second massacre he attended, but he survived them both. After the war, Joey gained control of a car dealership in Vegas and spent the rest of his life smoking Cubans and paling around with West Coast mobsters and their celebrity friends.

John Kennedy became a war hero because of his well-publicized exploits in PT-109, a U.S. Senator, and then president. Harry Truman, as he himself predicted, also became a U.S. president in 1944, and served two full terms. He wasn't well-loved as president, but as he aged and a new generation grew up, so did his popularity.

Anne Lindbergh became a novelist and resuscitated her reputation.

Fred Trump became even more miserable and embittered, qualities he passed on to at least one of his children.

And Charles Lindbergh was either forgotten about, or when remembered, reviled as the worst president in the history of the nation, a caricature of what a holder of such a high office should be all about.

Sid and Julia never called off their romance. After long, hard hours of work, they enjoyed walking on the mesa, breathing the clean, crisp air of Los Alamos, so unlike the tainted ambiance they'd experienced in New York City. Julia proved to be a talented, creative physicist in her own right. When given a chance, she was accepted as a scientific associate by some of the most brilliant physics minds of the time.

She and Sid got 'hitched,' as she liked to say, in the autumn of 1943. Silvia and Guido Falcone made the long train trip out to Los Alamos. They would have preferred the ceremony be held among friends and family in Canarsie, but wartime exigencies prevented it. Sid had asked Albert Einstein to be the best man. He accepted, saying it was as great an honor for him as his Nobel Prize and far more comfortable, too, as he didn't need to wear a tuxedo. Leo Szilard was given the role of gentleman usher, as Sid and Julia thought he was such an excellent usher of scientists to Los Alamos. He accepted the role graciously.

The Omega, now Sam Peskin once again, traveled back to New York after Lindbergh's resignation. Rosalie peppered him with hundreds of questions, and he was days in answering them. Both Peskins, along with Benny, accompanied the parents of the bride on the long ride to New Mexico. It was a wonderful experience for the two families, none of whose members had ever been far from the big city.

In time, Sid and Julia left government service. Both were eventually awarded their Ph.D. degrees and became professors of physics at Columbia University. They settled into a comfortable domesticity with their children in suburban Westchester Country, not far from the Bronx. Their home was a long trip from Canarsie, though Silvia and Guido, the happy grandparents, were always pleased to be invited and never complained about the distance.

In later years, they often spoke of their time in the Resistance, and at Los Alamos.

"Folks now don't always realize the choices we had to make then," Sid would say.

"They don't understand what things were like in this country with Lindbergh in the White House, and Nazis roaming the globe unchecked."

"At least," said Julia, sitting in the garden of their favorite summer vacation site in New York's Finger Lakes region, "nothing like that will ever happen again. Will it Sid?"

"You mean another Lindbergh? Nope. He was unique. A fluke. A one off. A product of a bad time in the country's history. Fascism's dead in America. It will never dare raise its ugly head again, so don't worry yourself about it."

Perhaps when he offered those words, he believed the American people had been inoculated against racism and bigotry by the Lindbergh experience. Perhaps, he thought, they'd taken to heart the aphorism the Spanish artist Francisco Goya had transformed into a work of art: When reason sleeps, monsters emerge. Perhaps they were all truly living at the dawning of the Age of Aquarius.

Well, perhaps.

ABOUT THE AUTHOR

Cy Stein's love of history began in his earliest childhood, spent in the New York City area. Over a lifetime of reading, he developed a special fascination with Roman history. His first book, *The Medicus Codex,* was initially published in 2016, and will be soon be reissued.

Rocket's Red Glare grew out of an intense interest in the history of the 20th century, focused particularly on the events of 1914-1945, and from his consideration of some of the events of the 21st, especially the threat of renewed authoritarianism.

Dr. Stein is a graduate of both Brown and Stanford University. He is currently a senior physician and Ph.D. scientist. He and his wife divide their time between New York and Southern California, and they like nothing more than spending time with their two daughters and adorable grandchildren.

www.cysteinbooks.com